Praise for *Time of the Child*

"I am such a fan of Niall Williams." —Ann Patchett, *New York Times* bestselling author of *Tom Lake*

"On the surface, *Time of the Child* by Niall Williams is an elegiac portrait of life in an Irish village in the Christmas season of 1962. But it is so much more than that. My own life feels so much richer for having read it. I was deeply moved by this novel." —Mary Beth Keane, *New York Times* bestselling author of *Ask Again, Yes* and *The Half Moon*

"A powerful pleasure to find myself back in Faha where the prose is luminous, the people irresistible, the stories mesmerizing, and it never stops raining." —Karen Joy Fowler, *New York Times* bestselling author of *We Are All Completely Beside Ourselves* and *Booth*

"Oh, the utter goosebumpy pleasure of reading this book! The experience will fill you up, even if you didn't know there was an emptiness there to begin with. Niall Williams reminds us again and again that the small and the ordinary are married to amazement, that dailiness and miracles walk hand in hand, and that other people are a mystery: Approach with curiosity! Approach with grace." —Catherine Newman, *New York Times* bestselling author of *We All Want Impossible Things* and *Sandwich*

"There is so much to admire in Niall Williams's new novel—the lyrical language, how landscape and destiny intertwine, the complex bonds of community—but what impresses most is how vividly he enters the innermost thoughts of his characters, thus revealing their seemingly quiet existences brim with the profoundest questionings of how we should live our lives. *Time of the Child* is a triumph." —Ron Rash, author of *Serena* and *The Caretaker*

"Another glorious and touching novel from Niall Williams, one of the world's greatest storytellers." —Anne Griffin, internationally bestselling author of *When All Is Said*

"Niall Williams is one of Ireland's greatest storytellers, and *Time of the Child* is his finest and most compelling work to date." —Simon Van Booy, author of *Sipsworth*

Praise for *This Is Happiness*

"Escaping into the pages of *This Is Happiness* feels as much like time travel as enlightenment. Halfway through, I realized that if I didn't stop underlining passages, the whole book would be underlined . . . Williams is engaged in the careful labor of teaching us to hear the subtler melodies drowned out by the din of modern life . . . This is a story about the beginnings of love and the persistence of affection, about the loss of faith and the recovering of belief. If you're a reader of a certain frame of mind, craving a novel of delicate wit laced with rare wisdom, this, truly, is happiness." —*The Washington Post*

"Comic and poignant in equal measure." —*The New Yorker*

"This big-hearted story is an intimate study of a small place on the brink of change." —*The New York Times*

TIME OF THE CHILD

Four Letters of Love
As It Is In Heaven
The Fall of Light
Only Say the Word
The Unrequited
Boy in the World
Boy and Man
John
History of the Rain
This is Happiness

TIME OF THE CHILD

NIALL WILLIAMS

BLOOMSBURY PUBLISHING

NEW YORK · LONDON · OXFORD · NEW DELHI · SYDNEY

BLOOMSBURY PUBLISHING
Bloomsbury Publishing Inc.
1385 Broadway, New York, NY 10018, USA

BLOOMSBURY, BLOOMSBURY PUBLISHING, and the Diana logo
are trademarks of Bloomsbury Publishing Plc

First published in Great Britain in 2024
First published in the United States 2024

ISBN: HB: 978-1-63973-420-7; PARNASSUS SIGNED HB: 978-1-63973-630-0;
EBOOK: 978-1-63973-421-4

Library of Congress Cataloging-in-Publication Data is available.

2 4 6 8 10 9 7 5 3 1

Typeset by Integra Software Services Pvt. Ltd.
Printed and bound in the U.S.A.

To find out more about our authors and books visit www.bloomsbury.com
and sign up for our newsletters.

Bloomsbury books may be purchased for business or promotional use.
For information on bulk purchases please contact Macmillan Corporate and
Premium Sales Department at specialmarkets@macmillan.com.

For Esme Willow

'Beidh Aonach Amarach i gContae an Chláir.'
There will be a fair tomorrow in County Clare.

TRADITIONAL IRISH SONG

I felt like a soul being prayed for.

SEAMUS HEANEY,
'THE LITTLE CANTICLES OF ASTURIAS'

This is what happened in Faha over the Christmas of 1962, in what became known in the parish as the time of the child.

To those who lived there, Faha was perhaps the last place on earth to expect a miracle. It had neither the history nor the geography for it. The history was remarkable for the one fact upon which all commentators agreed: *nothing happened here.* The geography was without notable feature but for being on the furthermost edge of a fabled country, where Faha had not so much sprung up as seeped out when the ice retreated, and the Atlantic met the western coast of an island with a native weakness for the heroic.

Resolve was the first requisite of life here. It was the hares that discovered it. They came from the fringes of the forests, drawn like all after them to the mesmerism of the River Shannon. They stood on their hind legs and in the sublime stillness of their surveillance were persuaded they had found paradise.

The first floods drove them back.

The first storms put salt in their ears.

Still, what began as a hare-track along the riverbank soon enough became a road, the watering hole a stopping post, camps and earthworks a settlement that took a name to become a village, opened a public house, a second one for those who would not darken the door of the first, five more for customers with complaints and grudges too various to catalogue, two general grocers, a blacksmith's forge, a butcher's, and soon enough a church and graveyard, all of which had the Fahaean character of sinking, but so slowly as to defeat reality.

***

Those who were wedged into the pews for second Mass on the first Sunday of Advent in 1962 were a congregation of silent fortitude. They had lived through revolution, seen the poet-revolutionaries replaced by bank managers, and discovered the thorned truth that independence had left them as poor as before. Recently, they had lived past the last evenings of the world, when the Russian ships were on their way to Cuba, and the end of time was near. Grown used to walking in an eroding world, they had the tidal eyes of estuary people and the translucent flesh that came from living in an absolute humidity. There might have been an invisible force pressing down on each day, but rain and religion had left the people a twinned philosophy of offering it up and getting on with it.

That first Sunday of Advent, it was as though, by virtue of living in a margin on the edge of Europe, the people had made actual the story of legend and escaped time, the entirety of the past become one unending day in which their fathers and mothers, and theirs, and theirs back along, were all the one family, tramping around in the same place, coexisting like memorial cards inside a missal.

On many of the men, life had perfected an unapproachable look, their age unguessable because they already looked this way at forty. If this week was no different to last, what of it, the comfort of reliving the same Sunday gave the illusion of defeating the terminus of life. Only in the look of some of the younger women was there a glimpse of the new world coming.

But real change is often only seen in hindsight. If you took a wrong turn and came into Faha that Sunday morning you would see a village like many others in that country, paused for Mass, a mournful rain coming a small ways inside the open doors of Bourke's and Clohessy's, but no customers until the bell for Communion, when the tongues of the registers would be out once more. Down the uneven fall of Church Street was a handful of cars in approximate align to the footpath; in Bourke's yard old horses and older carts; shouldering the wall of McCarthy's Hardware twenty or so iron bicycles; outside Ryan's Ryan's dog; further along, Harry, a black-and-white sheepdog who, in protest against living in a parish without sheep, always lay in the middle of the street, rising with the affronted dignity of a deposed monarch when a car wouldn't go round him, returning after to the same spot in the restored illusion of dog's dominion over the King of Sundays.

In the village then, an emptiness populated only by a holy ghost.

For the most part, Mass that morning in Faha was without incident. One of the comforts of ritual is immutability, and any parishioner could have set the congregation into the pews like the pieces in a board game. From Mary Falsey at the front of the Women's Aisle to her husband Pat, sniffling next to Sonny Cooney at the back of the Men's. From Matthew Leary, head bowed in the front of the Long Aisle, down past Mrs Prendergast, the post-mistress, with various Prendergasts, past the Cotters, Clearys, Penders, Murrihys, McInerneys and all the Morrisseys, past Gertie and Philo, the Mohill sisters, Pilkington the poet, Mai Toal, Betsy Breen, Micho Dolan and family, Haulie Tubridy and family, any number of Crowleys, Carmodys, Fennells and Keanes, until you got to the two Talty brothers, two benches in from the back.

That morning, in the midways pew that had become his by custom, was Doctor Troy, and Ronnie, the one daughter who was living with him always.

The doctor attended Mass, but without devotion. After his wife Regina was taken by a cancer he hadn't seen coming, he had lost the relic of faith he once had. To mask despair against God, he chose an old tactic: retain a semblance of order, and in this way meet the greatest challenge of life, which is always nothing more nor less than how to get through another day. For the sake of his three daughters, the doctor had adhered to the chronic custom of Sundays. He always came in the church door as the priest appeared from the sacristy, left mid-blessing in the last Sign of the Cross, before *Could I ask you just one question, Doctor?*

Seven days of the week the doctor was never seen out of an ironed white shirt, navy tie and charcoal suit that, though corrugated at the knees and elbows, still retained an air of the formal, or what passed for that in the parish. On top of this, in winter he wore what Faha called his German coat, gunmetal grey to the shins, broad wings of lapels, and the strip of dark fur on the inside of the collar. A compact man, it lent him a commander's air, which, in the packed church, gave licence to the black felt hat that took up its own berth on the pew alongside him.

He was not yet sixty but felt like a hundred. Silver-haired, grey-eyed, he still had the same handsomeness that compensated for the shortness of all the black-and-white film stars, but he awoke each morning inside a cloud of melancholy, and now believed that nothing in this life could burst it.

Melancholy was an occupational hazard of the General Practitioner who, in rural places, ran a solo operation that came with the guarantee of spirit-exhaustion for three reasons. It had no operating hours, everyone in the parish was your patient and the human being was a creation in which human life kept finding flaws. But to these Jack Troy had long ago grown accustomed. They were in the small print of his vocation. On the first morning he had unbolted the door of the surgery in Avalon House, there were ten patients standing in the rain at the bottom of the steps. Though for most the surgery then was the place of last resort, somewhere after appeals to the saints and martyrs, after holy wells and penitential rites, after the cures of Mrs Casey, whose hot bran in a stocking defeated pneumonia, no morning since had had a smaller number. So as not to be overwhelmed, early on the doctor had learned to combine his natural aloofness with an arm's-length philosophy, whereby he kept largely to himself. But he left the door to the waiting room unlocked.

Over time, the lessons of the Royal College had been replaced by life experience, and he had developed a diagnosis style informed by years of treating a marginal people of quiet dignity who had learned how to live in a place that was mostly water. There was no one in Faha he did not know. He had been there long enough to have treated most of their fathers and mothers, many grand-fathers and grandmothers too, and recognise ailments that were like artefacts passed down the family, inarguable proofs of the theory that since human beings first stood upright, nothing was ever really cured.

In the parish, the doctor had the standing that close acquaintance with suffering bestowed. Beneath his waved grid of silver hair, his sunken eyes said that acquaintance came at a cost. He had a worn air, his complexion tending now to ashen, his top lip covered with a shoebrush moustache he had grown to put a small distance between himself and the hurt of the world. Although he lived in the magnificent dilapidation of Avalon House, and carried himself in a manner that Faha might have summarised as *Not like us,* he was vouchsafed a place of honour in the parish by the twin virtues of not leaving and being indispensable.

Every doctor was in the business of trying to delay the inevitable, and in every day there was failure. *Some good was done,* had been his summary when he finally collapsed into the absolving hollows of the bed and his wife Regina woke to ask what had happened that day. *Some good was done.* It was for him a kind of creed, but the air went out of it when she died, and he was left with the ashes in his mouth. Still, three days after his wife's funeral, nine abashed patients were back in the waiting room, and *Sickness goes on* replaced the motto. Caring, if not curing, carried him forward, as well as the imperative of raising the three Troy sisters, a business something like herding butterflies.

In all churches, the time between settling into the pew and the starting of Mass is its own interlude, and in Faha was the only certified moment of stillness. You sat, and if you didn't join the rosary, or sideways survey the congregation, you went to that inner place where the pages of your life lay open. For Jack Troy those pages contained the same defeats and regrets familiar to all whose years lived outnumbered years left, but added to these was the realisation he had come to that morning in the shaving mirror: four years after the death of the amateur chemist, Annie Mooney, he was still in love with her.

It had not been a storybook love. After the death of her husband, Annie had taken over the running of the chemist shop in the village. It was to have been an interim measure, but in a place where everything was on the way and never arrived, that was a nonsense term. Under the exigency of ailments too many and various to be numbered, nobody looked for her diploma on the wall. Together she and the doctor formed a two-person confederacy, which was a marriage without the blessing. A widower, he was in her house above the chemist shop at all times of the day and night, the whiff of scandal aromatised away by the licence of his profession.

Soon enough, for emergencies she gave him his own back-door key.

Approaching seventy then, Annie Mooney had the repose of old grief and aged beauty, and at the other end of life had achieved the most seductive quality in human beings: absolute self-possession. She looked at life with such a direct gaze that God Himself would be shy, Sonny Cooney said. Caring nothing for the safeguards of convention, there were times when she attended the doctor in her nightdress, the warm smell of the bedclothes still on her and the long fall of her grey hair working its own chemistry. But, recognising in himself the dangerous innocence of the old, who are always secretly hoping for a chance to love properly, Jack Troy put up a shield of indifference. And though later he would return to those nights with a clinician's obsession, to try and identify the moment the shield had been penetrated, as with all things of the heart, it was impossible to tell.

What Annie Mooney felt for the doctor, he could not say, other than what he could read in the language of looks and nearness, the touch of her hand on his shirtsleeve, the stirring of his tea in the blue-ringed mug, or the way she smoothed his suit jacket over the hoop of the chair. He may have been at the point of declaring himself, but was muted when, like a page out of a storybook, in the last year of Annie's life her first lover, Christy, had appeared in Faha. She was already gravely ill but told the doctor she was glad for the visit of the memory of love. '*This way I can say goodbye to it forever.*'

In the four years since she died, Doctor Troy had had to find a way to live with the acidic knowledge that with Annie Mooney he had missed the last chance of a lifetime. In his practice he had found time a greater medicine than pharmaceuticals, only slower, and so bound himself to a course of carrying on, hearing his own phlegmatic advice, this time to himself: *It will go away.* To which he added one of the most useless commands of mankind: *Stop thinking about her.*

But still the acid ate away. And now, waiting for Mass on that first Sunday of Advent, he was aware his condition had worsened. He realised not only had he the macabre virus of being lovesick for the dead, but he had the more fatal one too: he had lost his love of the world.

It was a desperate diagnosis for a father, and the thought of it tightened the lines at the corners of his eyes. He glanced across to Ronnie alongside him. Her head was bowed, beneath a leaf-patterned headscarf, the coil of her auburn hair clipped in place. What was open in the pages of her life then, her father could not have said. In a green gaberdine over grey cardigan, cream blouse, grey wool skirt and prudent shoes, Ronnie Troy had the composed look that came after her mother died, and at twenty-nine made it seem she had put girlhood far behind her. Her two sisters gone now, one to marriage, and one to England, she had the natural reserve, not of one who had been left behind, but of one privy to the secrets of a household and surgery, who admitted the patients, watched the levels in her father's brandy bottle, and guarded all behind green eyes that were the same as her mother's, only without the anxiety. Added to this reserve was not only the screened lives of all the women in the parish at the time, but the marginal nature of all writers, for Ronnie Troy's closest companion was her notebook, and it alone knew what she was feeling.

Doctor Troy's glance told him nothing, and at ten past eleven one of the Kellys rang the bell and the Canon came to the altar. Rosary beads were holstered, and the congregation shouldered into position. For the Latin Mass, little outward participation was required other than kneeling and standing and striking your breast, which took place by rote behind the priest's back, until, in his purple chasuble, the Canon came up the corkscrew stair of the pulpit and faced the people.

Having heard enough confessions to lose the illusion that words mattered, Father Tom had ceased writing out his sermons. He was a large man, soft of body now, with a lumpish hairless crown that alone recalled the fire-and-brimstone of his curacy when the short-hand in Faha was that he went at sinners bald-headed. Now that fire was gone, the brimstone antidoted by a daily pint of Grogan's goat's milk, and with two strips of white feather over each ear, he resembled nothing so much as Alastair Sim in the Sunday matinees of the Mars picture house. The early phrases of his sermon he delivered in his corroded baritone and, though amplified by the new electrical system, these vanished in the parish memory on the instant they were spoken. Of that Mass, nothing in fact would be recalled until the moment the Canon paused.

Father Tom looked out into the middle distance, and then he faltered.

At first it may only have been a feather in the brain, one of those flicker moments that, in recognition of the weight of life, is both expected and pardoned in the aged. Since the electricity had come, all of Faha now had an amateur understanding of circuitry, and to the workings of human beings applied it willy-nilly, expecting the internal repairmen were on the way and service would resume shortly.

Only it didn't. The priest looked up and to his left, as though the next sentence was up there. And when it wasn't, when it wasn't above the Men's Aisle or the Women's, he looked out over the congregation and smiled. He smiled benignly, the way you do when the doom you knew was coming has become actual, and your knowledge is confirmed with the click of an inner bolt sliding into place. To the smile he added a nod, then another, smiling and nodding, as though to a story only he could hear.

The uncrossable chasm between priest and people kept the congregation dumb, and they sat in a tightening knot of embarrassment, doing the two things habitual at moments of catastrophe: looking the other way, and thanking God it wasn't you.

Father Tom blinked. Softly, two-handed, he tapped an amplified tap on the invisible keyboard of the lectern, waiting for the words of his Christmas message to come. Though his heart must have been going crossways, he showed no outward sign, but retained his doughy look, with the placidity that follows the realisation some inner part of you is no more.

From his position midways back, Doctor Troy studied the priest with a physician's dispassion, from that distance interrogating the brightness of the Canon's eyes and the musculature of his face, but to all appearances doing nothing.

In the meantime, the church was held in mute suspension from which it may never have emerged. In the silence that descended, the rain that fell so persistently in the parish that it had lost the right to be named was suddenly heard tattooing against the stained-glass windows and played the part of clock, showing time was continuing. The front door of the church, which was at the back, was, as always, open. A small crew of chronic latecomers and those men who knelt on their caps and attended Mass by ear only, were gathered in the part-shelter, and when it was clear there was a breakdown of some class there was a general lean. Martin Considine supposed it was him and turned the good ear towards the doorway, and when that one heard nothing, he said 'What?' out loud to make sure he still had the one working. Seanie Devitt, who had only come back to the church when the Bishop of Cork stopped preaching against dancing, as commentary on a Mass that grew longer each week, muttered, 'Jesus Christ.'

Ronnie Troy looked to her father. The doctor's eyes hadn't left the priest. He didn't move a muscle, not from a reluctance to intrude with science into the place of religion, but for the humane reason that he didn't want to embarrass Tom, who, in the cause of privacy, he treated not in the surgery but in the wine-carpeted parlour of the Parochial House. He knew the priest's deepest need, which was to pretend he didn't have a body, with failings and desires, and that the stomach pains that dogged him for years were not revealed to the parish. It was misguided, but at this stage mankind had too many foibles to be fixed, and the doctor had ceded to the request, wrote the prescriptions that were filled in a chemist in town and left Father Tom to pretend nothing corporeal was ever wrong with him.

For a while now, the old priest had let vanity turn a blind eye to the popularity of his confession box, ignoring the simple signpost that with the Canon all knew their sins would be forgotten before the telling of them was over. Age was not the only culprit.

A lifetime's curacy in a sinking parish had also worked its own erosion, for although Our Lord forgave wave after wave of sins before noon on Saturday, by the following Friday the scummed tide of them washed in again.

The moment defied its own definition by prolonging, lending weight to Sonny Cooney's theory that time is not clockwork. The congregation found it needed to assert its actuality by cough, sniffle and throat-clearing. Children escaped the containing looks of their parents, some finding the bars and kneelers of the pews the perfect climbing frame, others turning back to stare at the motionless circus that was grown-ups at devotion. In the adults, a tension that found home in necks and shoulders was released by a general stir and shift of no more than inches, the interior of the church momentarily a human sea of small motion, the waves meeting the walls with the Stations of the Cross and coming back again, but without improvement in the predicament.

Among the wisdoms of General Practice was the axiom that in the nature of stroke, time was everything. There was a mathematics of damage, a measure correlating blood and seconds, brain and flow, and so, while looking up over the row of Morrisseys in front of him and the pew-climbing Penders, Doctor Troy was in the instant of the calculation, watching the priest for tell-tale signs, and readying to get to his feet.

Father Tom gazed out from that place above the people with a boyish expression. It was as though he was only just discovering he had climbed into the top of a very large tree, had no idea how he got there, or how to ever again land back on the ground.

Ronnie, weighted as ever with the burdens of the eldest, looked to her father. 'You should go to him,' she whispered.

The doctor's gaze didn't move from Tom's face. Like all in the congregation, he was still trying to answer the common question of everyday, whether this was something or nothing. In Faha, the line between comedy and tragedy was drawn in pencil, and oftentimes rubbed out.

'... the birth, you know, of...' said the Canon, but no more. If he had offered a blessing, and gone back down the corkscrew stair, all would have looked the other way at a Mass with a blip in it. But because he stayed where he was, lost in the fog of a message he could not remember, the inevitable happened. Because the language that contained it had fallen apart, the fabric of the religion frayed. The longer the wait the more the idea of the birth of any lord and saviour came to seem first doubtful, then unlikely, then outlandish. And in time to come there would be some who would recall the story of that Sunday in Faha when, for one interminable moment, it was uncertain that Christianity had been invented.

Jack Troy looked away from the priest, as though that way he could break the moment. Below him, his fingers were clasped in the loose bind that in adults passed for prayer-hands, the thumbs a cross. He looked down at them as if they were a mystery, lifted his head, and to his right across the Long Aisle saw the young boy of the Quinlans watching him. Jude Quinlan was twelve years, thin and winter-pale, a loop of brown hair falling forward. He had a look older than himself, that depth of expression that some say is the wisdom of suffering, and others the need not to see more of it. Either way, he looked to the doctor with some urging, but his lips pressed closed, as though he was a messenger unaware of what message he bore.

The doctor registered it but looked away without enlightenment. It would not be until the night of the Christmas Fair that he would remember it. Then Jude Quinlan would be standing at the front door, with the child in his arms.

The doctor looked away. He reached for the top bar of the pew in the reflex that comes before rising. But he did not rise.

All of which happened in the paused time in which story stretches to allow for the four dimensions of human nature.

Up in the pulpit, Father Tom moved his hand from his mouth and tapped the lectern lightly, and again. To the emergency, his flesh was pumping out a dewy response, lending his forehead a semblance of lambency. He looked back across the altar-rails to the alabaster figure on the cross, but the figure with the introverted eyes retained his customary impassivity. Softly then, under his breath, Father Tom began to hum. It was tuneless – or a tune unknown – but in the silence of the stone church travelled out from the pulpit like a broadcast in bass whale, setting up a sound-shield between the Canon and the sea of faces turned to him.

What the people wanted him to deliver he could not, and it was unbearable.

Lips pursed, in the pulpit he hummed, louder now.

Whether he was aware that everyone could hear or not was unclear. If they did, by an instinctive grace in country people, they wouldn't mention it, but consign it under the general heading *The poor man*.

How long the priest might have continued is unknown. Keeping reality at bay is its own discipline. There is no primer but practice.

In the church, coughs and throat-clearances made the music of the living and confirmed that all were still in the human dimension.

Those in the Long Aisle looked to Doctor Troy. Ronnie felt the pinch of their looks and nudged her father, but the doctor retained his independence by an inflection of his elbow and tightening of his moustache. *Come on, Tom. Come on* was in his eyes but not on his lips. He had practised long enough to have witnessed every kind of suffering, enough wretchedness and pain to doubt the doctrine that men and women were creatures loved by their Maker, but the humiliation of the old priest was a cruelty he couldn't bear. At last, he stood.

Then, in a moment that would become part of parish legend, take the road of all story, existing in that place somewhere between the *This happened* and *Did this really happen?* of all human endeavour, the entire congregation saw the Canon see the doctor stand, realise the crisis had come, and, smiling now the smile of the implausibly saved, raise the forefinger of his right hand to pause the doctor, and everyone else.

Then, in a voice that passed below the compass of baritone, came in a register uncaught by one half of the penitents and unbelieved by the other, Father Tom said, or seemed to say:

'... to celebrate the birth of ... Jack...' And then a small laugh, because of course that was it, how had he forgotten? '... Christmas. Amen.'

For the priest, it was a stunning moment of triumph. Father Tom blessed himself in a sweep, his right hand encircling his breast in a blithe anticlockwise that returned time to where he had left it, then he spun round and went down the corkscrew out of the pulpit. When he got back to the altar, he had the spirit-lightness of reprieve, and though the one of the Kellys that was his altar-boy grinned the buck teeth, the Canon ignored him, and when he got to the *Credo in unum Deum* of the Nicene Creed he was back inside the handrails of the rite, and the remainder passed without remark.

***

The doctor and his daughter left the church briskly, but could not outrun illness, and there were three parishioners between them and the car. It was customary; the human telegraph that had no inventor meant that neighbours knew what was wrong with each other without being told. When the wrong wasn't coming right, a word to the doctor was wise. In Faha, there were sick people who would never appear in the surgery, and whose preferred first encounter with a medical man would come when he thumbed their eyelids closed. It was a way that pre-dated General Practice and the Gladstone bag, its foundations a combination of faith and fear, the prayer of *Please God*, and an inveterate reluctance to bother a learned man over the likes of you. Doctor Troy took no offence, nor did he question the fact that in Faha many considered the surgery the station of last resort, adhering to a contradictory wisdom: you only called the doctor when at death's door.

We are not in the business of counting patients, his father had told him. The old doctor, stooped and broken, but with the beard of Bernard Shaw and wrinkles of a sage, had retained to the last a crossed manner of Old Testament-Victorian. He had been a lover of the declarative sentence. Among these: *The sick are not a currency*, and *Doctors should only* look *like they are wealthy*. It was a philosophy that bankrupted the family, but slowly, which he believed was how life was meant to be. The balding roof, the whistling windows, the staircase that was always trying to get away from the wall, these were all on the long finger, whose length was Michaelangelo'd beyond the horizon. The declarations were a keep-back stratagem, a shield against the personal and a check on the possibility of intimacy. Young Jack Troy had not been aware of any loss: this was what a father was. He did not look for the old man when he came home on holidays from boarding school, nor did his father look for him. When the old doctor discovered him, three nights into his stay, passing in pyjamas on the upper landing, it was always with a mild surprise, *You're home?*, a momentary look of appraisal followed by a short nod, *Good.* That was the extent of it. When Jack was too young his father had given him *The Meditations of Marcus Aurelius* and three of the novels of Graham Greene; he had also taught him the moves in chess, which were each forgotten until they became indispensable. The old man could be curt, dismissive, judgemental. He had a warped view of politics and a special tone he reserved for talking to women, but in his last years, in Faha, he had achieved the sainthood of those who had devoted their lives to care and never sent out an invoice. The old doctor had relied on the not-yet-vanquished belief that, however long it takes, people want to make good. It was an attitude already out of date before he died, but was repaid in part the week before Christmas each year, when, a beast sold and cash in pocket, or with a homemade currency of potatoes, cabbages or turf, in a steady trickle the cured would come to the back door of Avalon, each with the same declaration: *I'm here to settle up, Doctor.*

Despite setting out to do all things in the opposite way to his father, by the time he was fifty Doctor Troy realised he had become him. It was perhaps inevitable in a place where the tide came in and out like memory and the rain made all the seasons one. Jack Troy's bills were unsent, his care of the house non-existent, and, except for holding on to his hair, he was, as Faha said, *the very head of his father.*

Circumvention was a preferred way in Faha, so, between the doctor's car and the church gate, those parishioners who wanted a word did not gather, but stood sentry in by the wall or on the fringe of conversations in which they played a non-speaking part. These were always women. Although invisible to Church and State, it was women who knitted the country together, and in Faha, on Sunday morning after Mass, you could see the needles.

The rain came through the sky like it was a thing of nothing, but it made no difference. Need was not only for the fine day, and the women were not put off. Mrs Mac got to him first. A doughty woman of low stature in a big coat, she landed in the path before the doctor, her enormous bag held up two-handed in front of her, as though someone might want to take it away.

It is an inescapable truth that doctors cannot meet a man, woman or child who has onetime been their patient without an instinctual flick back through the records. Patients who got well did not return to say so. So, although, by a one-sided accord, Doctor Troy would never bring it up when you met, he had a professional interest, wanted to remember what it was you suffered and see for himself if you were cured. Some patients of course could at any moment come out with the latest on their ulcers, polyps, piles or gallstones, and suppose the doctor would not only remember, but be on a first-name basis and awaiting the update. Outside the surgery and without the notes he wrote in a spider's shorthand, it was a strained situation. The convention would not allow him to ask, *What was wrong with you again?* and in Faha only Tommy O tackled the human condition head first by the barbarous greeting of, *The bowels, Doctor. The bowels.*

Standing in front of him, Mrs Mac was *earwax, imbalance, chilblains.* She had reached an age when she had a fear of falling, 'unsteady on the pins' her summary, and always looked up and down the path, as though expecting the bowling ball at any moment.

To make her request smaller, she shot to the point: 'You wouldn't drop in to Doady, Mrs Crowe, would you, Doctor?' To show the pain of asking, she pulled her whole face tight. When the doctor said he would, the scrunch dissolved, and she lowered the bag slightly. 'God bless you, Doctor. You're a saint,' she said, and then confused that designation by adding, 'I'll say a prayer for you.'

Doctor Troy made a small noise through his nose. The rain was dipping off the brim of his hat, drops starring the fur on the collar of the German coat. By way of acknowledging her, Mrs Mac passed Ronnie a pursed smile, looked up the path and down, and then was off.

Like the triangle that has one leg longer than the other, Ronnie had an asymmetrical relation with Faha. She was and was not part of the community, known by everyone, but kept at that distance that had too many causes but was condensed into the phrase *the doctor's eldest*. And, because she was the one who opened the door to patients in the morning, the one who wrote their names in the book, helped those who needed help getting to chairs in the waiting room, help rising from them and getting down the creaking hall into the riverward room of the surgery, she shared the perspective of those statues prayed to across the penny candles: she knew the parish through its illnesses. She was also the only person in the parish you could tell your complaint and not hear that she had that too or was suffering from worse. Like many roles in life, Ronnie had fallen into it, and then come to see it as inevitable. She neither resisted nor regretted it. For the role met her need to feel useful, service and community both still retaining their sense of agency, and it answered the prompting that there was something larger than yourself. What that was she could not have said, but as her sisters left and she stayed, she had come to think of Faha first as a place as good as any other, and then better because here the people were, in a phrase she had read in a Russian novel, *great-souled*.

Mary Mulvey, *pleurisy*, was one of those who wished the tide of emigration had taken her out with it. The entire parish knew that for ten years Mikey Corry didn't ask her to marry him. Though she lived in a country with the lowest percentage of married women in the known world, in a twist she hadn't seen coming, it came to seem that it must have been her fault. She had some lack, she thought, not to be able to get him to propose and take her into the house with his mother. She was not beautiful enough, she decided. It was a corrosive conclusion, the acid kept inside her by the cork of the unpopped question. It ate her youth and flattened her curls, leaving her with a let-down, stranded air and the tight mouth of the unchosen. In a sensible wool coat, and headscarf not too showy, she stood with head low, like the mute swans of the Shannon.

'Mikey Corry on the back road, Doctor,' she said in a low voice. From things unsaid, the mouth found a way to tighten a little more. In the deeps of her eyes, any could see her ardent heart. 'Since the mother died, I don't believe he's come out the door,' she said.

And last, the low, round bundle of Bridey Eyres, *chronic catarrh, cataracts.* A scuttler, she came last. She didn't consider herself important enough to have more than a few words with a learned man, so abbreviated her request to: 'May Nolan's boy, Ciaran, Doctor. You'd hear the cough crossing the field. Thanks very much now, thanks,' didn't wait to see if it was so or no, but began to scuttle away, the tiny black shoes beneath her like winders wound up and let off.

As always, between the church and his car, Doctor Troy confirmed nothing, but gave some of his father's nods. Under the only umbrella that acknowledged the rain, Ronnie took mental notes and would remind him later before taking out her notebook.

While listening to the petitions, St Cecelia's had been emptying around them, the congregation pouring out into Church Street. No car or tractor could move, the Communioned taking over the thoroughfare and making their way in quiet or conversation without regard for rain. No one was hurrying away. Many from out the townlands were in the village only once a week and would make the best of it. For the most part, the men and women lived in separate worlds, out the land and in the house, but were brought together for an hour on Sunday morning. Coming from the church with slow step and a good look about, they had a sense of witness and participation in these after-Mass moments, one.

From under the rim of his hat, the doctor's eyes watched them, his melancholy deepened by the defeat of those who found it hard to believe in God when presented with evidence against Him every day, and by a simple envy for those who did. He knew there was contradiction in it.

The Canon shot out the sacristy door in his black biretta and coat. There were always some whose spiritual needs were not satisfied by Mass alone, who stayed behind for private intentions that had no bounds, so Father Tom left the locking up to Tom Joyce, the sacristan, and hurried out down the slope of the churchyard. He came at a pace that signalled he wouldn't pause for questions.

Crossing the street, he and the doctor exchanged a look of fish and hook. Father Tom was caught until he remembered he hadn't blessed himself, and did a duck's foot version, a flap at his chest, and went in the front door of Prendergast's that had the key hanging in the lock.

When Jerome Prendergast was the postmaster, it had become customary to have the priests come across for tea and buttered biscuits after Mass. A large man with a flat face of few expressions, Jerome had a bishop's rigour and a deliberate step. The parting of his hair was an articulation. His brown suit had the material for two; a great wall of cloth, it dissolved his human lineaments and gave him an ex-officio look. By a secretly negotiated treaty with the shopkeepers, the post office sold the daily papers from the counter, and by a confrontation less secret Jerome had seen off Conlon, the newspaperman from town who had tried to establish a trade at the church gates selling petrol-smelling Sundays out of the back of his van.

Jerome Prendergast had invented the Summit out of a want he couldn't voice but which had to do with the tumult of family life he had seeded but couldn't stomach. Once the *Closed* was slid across on the post office, the last thing he wanted was to go through the adjoining door that separated postmaster from husband and father. And so, in keeping with the various committees and sub-committees that absolved him in the evenings, he had first suggested the Sunday mornings as a way of evading family and preserving eminence.

To the summit the priests were not the only ones invited, but they were the star attraction. The doctor, the Master, the temporary chemist, the almost-solicitor, the auctioneer and the creamery manager were at one time or another all told: *You should come across after Mass.* Where they gathered was in Prendergast's front parlour, the one with the dark and heavy furniture, crocheted doilies on the armchairs, a nest of inlaid side tables that had come from the continent, on the wall the framed picture of the Pope of two Popes ago, one of the Sacred Heart that all year wore a branch of the desiccated pine which passed for palm on Palm Sunday, and across on the mantel, so he could smile his dazzling smile back at both of them, the new American President. In here, in the smoke and aftershave that were the savours of government, there formed the informal Sunday council which was a cross of after-the-match and state-of-the-nation, the men kicking topics back and forth under the referee's eye of Jerome Prendergast, and the sideline one of Mrs P, as he called her when she lingered on after bringing in the tea and buttered Mariettas. The timekeeper was a thickening aroma of roast meat from the kitchen, where the eldest Prendergast girl was made lieutenant, deputised the second eldest to look after the third, the third the fourth, and so on down to the youngest over the cat. That the council was Men Only was a subject that shared a distinction with everything from corporal punishment to Protestants: it never came up for discussion.

Once Jerome died, Mrs Prendergast got a budgie that, with the indecipherable depths of a wife's commentary, she called Mr P. For catching bird-do she lined the floor of the cage with her husband's adored *Irish Press*, put the cage on a side table and reopened the summit with an inarguable widow's behest, *You'll come across after Mass, Canon.* The change was notable not only for the budgie, who had a teacloth put over him whenever he tried to interrupt, but because it was discovered Mrs Prendergast had opinions.

Mrs Prendergast was short and stout, easier to jump her than go round her, was Sonny Cooney's assessment. She had nine children. As memorials, each of them left her the original eight pounds of their birthweight, so that after the eighth she was a round of bosom, belly and buttock, which parts were only nominal. She retained a doll's face with a miniature mouth, and hair so tight to her skull it seemed not to have grown but been placed and, like a puppy, commanded: Stay! From a leaning towards both gentry and Irishry, she only ever wore suits of tweed, greenish or brownish, which gave her the appearance of a small bolt of the cloth, with, at halfway, the one heroic button. Through marriage to a secular bishop, some rigidity may have rubbed off on her, for when crossed she had a quelling look, but for the most part Faha considered her firm but fair.

The after-Mass custom was one Doctor Troy had all but fallen out of. But he still took a Sunday newspaper, and wanted to be sure the Canon was recovered. While Ronnie waited in the car, he went across to the post office with the intention of being moments only.

The papers were laid out in an immaculate display the length of the counter. The one of the Prendergasts whose job it was to carry them in, cut and ball the twine, count the copies, check them against the invoice, whichever Prendergast that was, had done so with a regimental discipline and the papers lay in low columns along the counter, crisp and grave and formal, as befitted emissaries from the greater world. Adhering to the tone set by Jerome, the racier of the English Sundays still met the upraised hand of an impassable censor, and from the lurid headlines and the scantily clad, the parish was spared.

In a holdover from earlier times, in Faha, all goods were looked at before they were bought. When the doctor entered, Sean, the pimpled eldest of the Prendergasts, was standing by while some with craned necks were lined along the counter, in a Sunday ritual reading all the news fit to print above the fold. Beneath the readers, the chequered linoleum the floods lifted got its own weekly press. That there were those like big Phil Lillis, bent low, squinting through the found glasses of three prescriptions ago, mouthing each word with the studied care of High Babies in school, shuffling along at his own pace, reading from five or six newspapers but purchasing only the one, was not cause for concern. Looking without touching was harmless, and unhandled knowledge free. As custom was the first requirement for customers, all the shopkeepers knew that coming back was more important than coming in, and in the parish it was understood that reliving the same Sunday again and again lent the illusion that things were just grand.

The moment the doctor crossed the threshold, he was acknowledged by a parting of the readers and low-voiced greetings of 'Doctor'. It went without saying that he should go to the front of every queue, and Sean Prendergast was already getting his paper from the short stack of those who, by the hierarchic virtue of a standing order, had their name pencilled above the masthead.

If there was talk before he got there, it went out the door he came in. For a moment there was only breathing and snuffles, the camouflage of symptoms that was universal when in the company of the medical. A throttled buzz came from behind the partition where Connie Prendergast operated the switchboard, built for the futuristic number of a hundred telephones, of which Faha had nineteen. 'He's not at home,' she said to the caller, 'I've just seen him in the street.'

'There you go, Doctor.' The boy had only recently graduated to Sunday counter duty, but in a claret tie of his father's made a passing mimic of authority, abashment only betrayed by the flare of his pimples.

Behind him, the door was opened into Prendergast's parlour, and the doctor could see in to the cloud of cigarette smoke that was an after-Mass exigency. The shone black shoes and white shins of Father Tom protruded from where he sat in the wingback armchair, but the doctor could see no more of him.

He stepped into the summit but did not remove his hat. The Canon's eyes came to him with a sheepish look learned from a lifetime in the confessional. The look made clear he had not forgotten what had happened in church but was grasping the uncharitable hope that doom was visiting elsewhere. In face and manner, he had all the appearance of being himself, and, having already dealt with the matter of His Holiness's illness, had just been asked his opinion on last night's programme.

One month earlier, in a genius move that had consolidated her eminence, Mrs Prendergast had gone for a television.

It was the first one in Faha.

For a decade, under the jurisdiction of the Department of Posts and Telegraphs, a plan had been established to consider the value of a national television station. Like all aspirational, unbudgeted policies, progress was indeterminate, but, following anecdotal evidence of Christmas dinners in Dublin paused for the BBC broadcast of the young Queen's speech, and fearing the country they had won back getting away from them out through the television, the government bit the bullet, and the national station was born.

Teilifís Éireann had begun broadcasting the previous New Year's Eve. The first months' programmes were unseen in Faha but reviewed by a general hearsay: it was no radio. But when, in July, *The Late Late Show* went behind the curtains of the country, by accident of budget discovering that what Irish people most wanted to watch was Irish people talking, and westerns, Mrs Prendergast had sent word to town that she wanted a set.

It was delivered by the bandy-legged Danny Crowley, who was called Cowboy, smoked hands-free and in the soft rain threw up the ladders like they were playthings. Misguided by a technician's priority for the best picture, Cowboy had placed the set with its large backside to the window that looked across to the church gates. With a keener sense of what counted, Mrs Prendergast had him turn the sofa and place the set on the table on the far wall.

It was the first time in the history of the parish that a room was not aimed at the fireplace.

The result was that all Faha could see it. Mrs Prendergast didn't care. She adhered to the unwritten code that a postmistress should lead by example and secretly liked the prestige of being, as Sonny Cooney said, Faha's first televisionist.

Discussion of television programmes had become a standard of all after-Mass summits.

Being asked his opinion on anything was the Canon's least favourite moment. But, after sixty years in a collar in a parish without a straight line, he had developed an expertise for circular thinking, tactical evasion his main characteristic. Master Quinn was his deputy without a badge, made all the actual decisions but wanted none of the attention. Short and wiry, in a black suit whose cuffs were permanently greyed with chalk dust, he was sitting to the right of him, eyes averted with a look of disinterest but ready to cut in. Father Tom fired off a quick flurry of blinks.

'Well,' he said, 'well now.'

All in the summit knew his gift for inconclusiveness, expected no declaration, but his cloth and age meant he always had to field the first question.

'What I would say is this.'

For a blink it seemed he may have thought that sufficient. Doctor Troy did not move from the doorway or divert his gaze. Those in the seats took advantage of a new behaviour and looked at the television that wasn't turned on. Just when it appeared catastrophe had followed across from the church, the priest lifted his teacup, and said, 'The world didn't end, did it?' The answer in the form of a question resolved nothing, unclear whether it was rhetorical or not, if the Canon was asking if he was in the next life, until he blinked once more, swallowed his tea and delivered the coda, 'No. God is good.'

It was a passing response. Matty Riordan, who played the parrot, repeated, 'God is good.'

Father Tom added a single nod to lend a guise of wisdom, beamed at the benignity of being spared again and tapped the fingers of both hands on the balls of his knees to signal it was someone else's turn.

'You're joining us, Doctor?' Mrs Prendergast had a manner that blurred the line between questions and commands.

'I won't, Sheila. Thank you. I have Ronnie in the car. I only came in for the paper.'

Mrs Prendergast didn't press. A foot and a half shorter than the doctor, she looked up at him with a postmistress's scrutiny. On the doll's face the arched eyebrows never moved, but in the small brown eyes was a keen discernment. Word of the morning's events had reached her before Father Tom was out the church gates, but she had employed the diplomat's manoeuvre and made like it never happened. Her eyes held Doctor Troy long enough to understand his true purpose, and to let him know she knew. As farewell he tipped his hat a touch, turned, and heard Mrs Prendergast switch the summit back on with an 'Amen to that, Father.'

***

The moments only that Doctor Troy had intended had elasticated. But in Faha this was customary, richness of life the alibi that everything took longer than supposed. He returned to the car with a look of apology, but without the words. Headscarf off, notebook closed on her lap, Ronnie was sitting in the seraphic patience that with each year had become more her character. Knowing he had abused it, the doctor turned the ignition sharply. The men standing in front of the Morris stepped aside with the chastened look of ones who had briefly forgotten there was a reality beyond their talk. Doctor Troy pulled out without looking or indicating. Neither were required, his car with the fluted bonnet was well-known and had the primacy of always being on important business. Harry lay in the middle of the street in a pretend sleep. The doctor drove to three feet of him, stopped, waited. In the holy drowse of a drizzling Sunday, he didn't tap the horn. The dog rose in dog-time and with untellable weariness made his twentieth journey of six feet back to the footpath, to lie down, lower his head, in a moment get up, and come back to the centre of the street, lie down, king of Faha once more.

The Morris drove on past the shops. In an undeclared fight to the death, Clohessy's and Bourke's were taking the congregation prisoner, each shop selling the same things, but the customers, like the enlisted, loyal to one or the other. Both shops had the design of bottlenecks and the doorways were thronged, those trying to get in meeting those trying to get out, making for a swarm look, and the pronouncement from both Clohessy and Bourke that, despite the fact that the Christmas Fair was only days away, they were fierce busy, *just fierce now.*

Outside Bourke's yard was Talty's tractor, the twin brothers loading onto it their week's messages. Tim and Tom, both bachelors, both in the same suit in the same size, medium, were to the parish eye indistinguishable. It was a conundrum solved years ago by a reverse Solomon, whereby on the parish tongue the two became re-joined into the one, Tim-Tom. Whichever one you were speaking to, they were Tim-Tom, so there was no fear of insult or mistake. The brothers didn't mind, had long ago stopped saying which one they were, and, ever since The Treaty, knew the native pathos for the worm the spade halved. Now in their seventies, supple, sinewy, with the same soft eyes and florid complexions, they were a pair of gents, small farmers, nice and tidy, fierce honest, by an old-world regimen of humility and decency keeping themselves to themselves. They travelled by the Zetor, which though antique was younger than themselves, one Tim-Tom driving, one standing in the box at the back like a jouncing general surveying.

By the regularity with which the brothers lived their lives, they went mostly unremarked, but that Sunday, as the doctor passed, he noted them. He couldn't have said why. He had no foresight of what was to come, premonition a nonsense to a medical man, no reason to suppose two brothers that in Faha were the definition of the commonplace would be part of the story that would change his life. Still, four nights later, when they would be standing at his door with Jude Quinlan and the child, he would recall this moment: the Talty brothers, loading their tractor with the same imperturbable quiet and compose the world employs when it pretends its plot is not turning.

It was a moment only. Doctor Troy looked away as the two brothers turned to him, but he had a sense that, like ones with their finger in the book, they were holding their place in a story just starting.

'Crowe's?' Ronnie asked.

'I'll drop you home first.'

'There's no need. I'll wait.'

She had already waited for him three times that day, for breakfast, for Mass, and after. He was aware of it, regretted it, passed no comment.

They drove out of the village, past Craven's and the forge, past McInerney's and Considine's and the last lookout of Clancy's dog, who, tongue out, tore alongside the car in a passing mimic of Rin-Tin-Tin, as always daring himself to go under the wheel, see what that was like, until they passed Duggan's and he stopped short, stood panting, but with the puffed crest of a victor.

Since the days of Bianconi, who, at twenty-four stone with size-four shoes, had had a man with a red flag walk ahead of his motor car, in Faha all traffic commandeered the centre of the road, until just before collision. The national driving test was still only a rumour; driving licences came in the post to anyone who could write the letter asking. It stood to reason: handwriting was a badge of intelligence and keeping the letters between the lines visible proof of an ability to steer.

Down the centre of the road went the Morris. After the holy hectic of Sunday morning, the country had settled back into its natural hush: backsides to the rain, in an attitude of absolute unconcern, the herd of Crowley's cattle, composed, complete. In Sheehan's five-acre, along the western bounds, Sheehan, *pneumonia*, standing; in Hayes's, a half-dozen horses, running. Walking at a good clip was Sam Cregg. He was a man in a suit of many yesterdays who liked to carry today's newspaper. A gentleman in spirit, if not in circumstance or standing, he carried himself as though these were secondary. To offer him a lift would break the illusion. He cut the doctor a sharp salute as the car passed, in the mirror growing small until dissolved back into the rain.

The road ran along by the river, left it, and came back to it, as if neither could stay apart. From a love affair without end, fields were some part-submerged, and would stay that way until spring when, if a fine spell came, for a time the love would go the other way. They were fields with the soil washed away, and then washed away some more, in a timeless surrender or slow return to when the world was water. The ground was mud, thin-skinned with a shallow benevolence of grass that acted as glue. Animals out on it all months of the year, it was pocked in all the places that were not stone. The low parts were bearded with rushes, and this morning even the best of it wore the silver puddles of fallen sky. In a December light, weak and watered, was a palpable sense of the year thinning out.

It was not only himself that was exhausted, Doctor Troy thought, and not for the first or last time wished that Annie Mooney was alive. The wish was its own doorway and lent proof to the adage that the loved are never dead. No sooner did her name pass across his mind than she was the same as there. There had been an evening in April once, he had let himself in the back door of the chemist shop, passed the shelves of remedies, and at the stairs to her rooms called her name. He had called it first by way of announcement, not wanting to come up the stairs without invite. But the instant he heard it, her name coming out of his mouth, he had a swift sensation of revelation. It was this: he wanted to say her name again. In the same instant, he knew that this was absurd, and that he would never allow himself to succumb to the role of senescent schoolboy. As though for the pleasure of the sound they might betray him, he had pursed his lips. He had raised his chin, lowered his shoulders, and waited for Annie Mooney to come or call down. When she did neither, when he could neither go up the stairs nor leave, in the trapped scents of soap and springtime, he had stood sentry against his own desire. Right up to the moment he was overwhelmed. Then, alone in the April twilight, in a whisper that was in the same register as the one heard on silk pillows and into the exquisite shells of adored ears, Jack Troy had sounded the softest *Annie*.

At Commodore's Cross, the Morris turned left for Crowe's, and came through a string of the loose cattle of Quinlan, which, like the man himself, could not be contained.

Doctor Troy was aware he had not spoken to his daughter since they left the village, but the truth was he had lost the knowledge of how to do it. In the years since his two younger daughters had left, without either of them purposing it, between him and Ronnie there had formed a way of being that, though smooth and companionable, did not include any but the most perfunctory dialogue. It had the mutuality of a pact but shared the lot of the emotionally blind, because, as each saw it, they were doing the other a favour. Ronnie had the beauty of all the Troy sisters, a less obvious kind than Charlotte's, less tender than Sophie's. Her face was perfectly formed, features deepened by living and loss. Her hair was auburn waves, tied forever up or clipped back, showing a high forehead that revealed a truth known to portraitists by seeming eloquent. Ronnie was intelligent, serious, solitary, had, according to the solicitor in town, O Sullivan, the badge of genius because she was capable of keeping several thoughts at the same time, possessed a natural flair for organisation and the foresight to know what tomorrow's problem would be. O Sullivan was fulsome in his praise. To divert from any subterranean motive, he had concentrated his comments only on her mind. By the end he might have been describing a future prime minister, but Taoiseach was a noun only known in the masculine and he drew his conclusion by leaning forward across his stomachs to say *Do you know what? She'd make me just the perfect secretary.*

The doctor had had the sense his daughter's bottom had just been patted. He had made a movement of his moustache but said nothing. The offer was made in person two days later when, from the open surgery window, he saw a black Austin rise a cloud of dust up the avenue, and soon after O Sullivan panting up the steps of Avalon. At his breast was a red silk pocket square with a three-peak fold, signalling the game was on. Balanced on his right palm was a white cakebox tied with string. The doctor had not gone out to meet him. It was a summer's early evening. He had no patients, but making diagnoses was an infallible excuse and he had sat at his desk with his fist holding up his chin. He heard Ronnie's footsteps in the hall, her professional greeting, the clank when she shut the front door, and the toffee in the tone O Sullivan used when he told her he was not here to see her father.

The doctor heard them go into the front room, then heard no more. He didn't rise from the desk. He didn't look at the correspondence awaiting him or have a go at the books to figure out what exactly was wrong with Mina Corry. He stayed where he was, transfixed by a sick feeling of the heart and the agony of trying to know what it was a father should do.

When he saw the Austin drive away, he thought Ronnie would come to tell him her decision, and when instead she went upstairs, he found himself trying to interpret the sound of her footsteps across the floorboards above. A central principle of his fathering was not to stand in the way; it was a policy that resulted in an excess of silence. Because he knew his word carried such weight, it was as wrong to suggest a way as it was to oppose one, which left him to say only *I see* or *Good* when Charlie told him she was engaged or Sophie that she was going nursing in England, and after to Africa. That long afternoon he sat in small agony in the surgery until Ronnie called him for teatime.

There was a hard tomato, two leaves of lettuce, the half of a boiled egg and two slices of ham with a squirt of mustard on the side.

It was not until she was pouring the second cup that Ronnie had told him of the offer.

'I see,' he had said, and reached for the milk. He poured with perfect evenness, watching the tea cloud, replacing the jug alongside the matching sugar bowl. He took his teaspoon and stirred a single C. He knew she was waiting for him to ask her what she had decided but he could not trust himself to find a neutral tone.

'Mr O Sullivan brought cake,' she said, going to the sideboard and bringing it on a plate.

'Not for me, thank you.'

The uncut cake sat in sunlight on the table between them, the knife alongside. The sash of the window was up, and the birds of summer evening sang. In the hall the pendulum in the wooden throat of the grandfather clock pulsed dully. The doctor noticed that one side of the cake had been partly flattened in transit. It had lost its round, the sugar icing pressed up in a little creased wave. It wanted someone to press it back into place.

He drank his tea. He had tried to daydream himself out of the scene, but his eyes kept coming back to the cake. He could not have said why but he wanted Ronnie to take the knife and repair the icing. Repair the cake, or throw it away. She did neither, nor did she cut herself a slice, and the cake sat forlorn, a shaft of the late sun catching it, glistening the sugar, and soon enough bringing the bees, one of which became affixed. The bee did not realise at first and for a time gorged on what was suffocating it. Only when it tried to take off did it start to buzz. Its wings were weighted with sugar, and it sank a little in the pool of its print. It buzzed with the fury of the duped.

'I said no thank you,' Ronnie had said at last, taking her knife and laying it flat in under the bee, freeing it. In a drowse, belly-heavy and sated, the bee took off, and by dip and rise made its way out the window.

'I see,' said the doctor, folding his napkin and standing. He did not say the 'Good' this time, lest it reveal preference. He was aware he and she were in a trapped place. He wanted her to marry, but not to anyone she was likely to meet in Faha. It was a situation without remedy, but, when he came across the cake in the bin two days later, he was stricken with an indigestible guilt. In a vain attempt to dissolve it, he had suggested she might move to Dublin for the opportunities there. It was a suggestion made with the fingers of both hands crossed against her saying yes, but it was made.

'I'll stay here and help,' Ronnie had replied. 'If you like.'

His heart had lifted instantly, a weight he wasn't fully conscious of gone, but all he managed was 'Whatever you like,' and left the room with the pressed lips and footstep of his father.

Driving in silence, their separate thoughts fogged the windscreen. Ronnie wound down the glass two inches and the freshness of the air returned them to the business at hand. The road found the river again, a reacquaintance that took some portion of Quinlan's field each year so only the top strand of thorny wire hung loose along fenceposts in water, as if in memory of comrades drowned. The sky came down in heavy drops, and soon enough, in a mirroring love, the road did its best impression of a river. The world was swollen with rain it could not take, and still more fell.

Crowe's was not a call-out: the doctor was not expected but was attending out of an unwritten contract somewhere between service and courtesy. As with the priest, in some cases, Doctor Troy's unannounced appearance at the back door would bring that blood-drained look that had a contrary effect, making all instantly sicker and the actual patient a grave case until advised otherwise. That advice didn't carry the same weight as his appearance though and in Faha the whispered news *Clancy's had the doctor* was the starter's pistol to get the funeral suit ready.

Doctor Troy knew he was not always welcome. Houses were not prepared the way they were when it was known he was coming; sometimes he would be held at the door while an emergency tidy-up went on inside. It didn't matter. When he eventually entered, it was always with a sense of finding the world in its underpants. He could not step inside the houses of the parish without a feeling of intrusion. He had had to train himself to look straight ahead on the way to a back bedroom, or a chair with blankets doing duty as sickbed next to the fire.

Sometimes, he was refused outright. The reasons were not always straightforward. When he was in his first years in practice, O Dea had barred the door to him, though his mother was dying. Fearing that cost might be an obstacle, the young doctor negotiated against himself on the doorstep and said there was no fee for a courtesy call. O Dea considered it an insult in translation, and the sentence was not out of the doctor's mouth when the thump in his chest sent him backwards. From those first days, the doctor soon learned the lesson that in all places far from the centre there is no standard way of being. People make it up as they go and prove their individuality by being unpredictable. In a parish of one-offs, each house was its own story.

Out beyond O Neill's, they followed the ribbon of grass in the centre of the road until they pulled in past the dungheap to Crowe's yard. There was a line of stone cabins, one stabling a venerable mare, dark ribs of hay about the door, another that was a sour-smelling milking parlour, a pig's shed, the door holed at snout-height but patched with the lid of a biscuit tin, and a squat earthen-floored henhouse, all with the whitewash faded and the recalcitrant look of stones that wanted to sink back to where they came from. The hens were out and under the shelter of a height of mixed fuchsia, bramble, box and rose. It was a hedge of its own forming, let off, and it leaned over and east, all its life trying to get away from the western wind.

'I'll stay in the car,' Ronnie said.

But what will you do? he didn't ask, for he saw her hand bring up her writing notebook and knew that it was her truest companion. 'I won't be long.'

'Say hello from me, to Ganga and Doady,' she added, remembering their pet names from the summer their grandson had visited.

The house was a long low farmhouse of the traditional kind. It was thatched, but the thatch had the air of the earth's overcoat, ancient and sombre, here and there patches like black flags of surrender to inevitable defeat by a lifetime's pressing skies. At the western end the roof ridge had sunk some. There were colonies of green moss on the dark reeds, elsewhere what looked like fungi and at the base of the chimney a frilled lichen, the whole a mass of the living and dead laid over the limewash walls. In the cold rain it had an air of desolation. Only the turfsmoke, that seemed reluctant to leave the scene, coming out the chimney and down over the garden, sent the signal of life going on. From the reeds a second rain dripped harder than the first and the brim of the doctor's hat released it as a third. When he went to knock, the back door was opened to him.

'Doctor,' said Mossie Crowe, loudly. A man of medium height and more than medium girth, he was a round of trouser and shirt, seventy-eight years living. His eyes were bright and his face welcoming with a genial smile that had become habitual despite circumstance. In the past year his wife, Aine, had had two strokes, the first bad, the second worse. She had lost her sight, her speech and her walk, and lived now on the far side of that, at a remove where she could not be reached. Mossie was still in his Sunday clothes from first Mass when a girl of the Keoghs had come in to watch over Mrs Crowe but had taken out the teeth that were a torment he only bore for Christ. His dog, Joe, came forward to smell the doctor and his leather bag as he stepped down the two steps into the kitchen.

'God bless.'

A down-puff of turfsmoke came out as greeting, ascended slow and regal into the rafters. Having lived so long in a way that had proved endurable, the Crowes had not taken the electricity when it came to Faha four years earlier, and in the dim interior of the house you were in the nineteenth century, but with a wireless. Its battery on the floor, the wireless was up loud, but in gesture more than effect. In the stone house reception only came in the kitchen window, which as a result was never closed, a loose wire snaking out and across to the roof of a cabin to catch what it could of a Radio Éireann that pulsed from Dublin to Athlone strong enough but from mast to mast thereafter thinned, wavered, crackled, dropped, gave up the ghost, came back louder, only to fade out again into a whistling rising falling buzz that was somewhere between a national tinnitus and a broadcast undersea. Because it could come back at any time, in Faha nobody rose to turn the wireless off when the signal dropped, and instead let it be, carrying on with the requisite unperturb and patience of all followers of an intermittent God. Mossie had the wireless on for his wife in the far bedroom, in the hope that the sound could reach her. For himself it didn't matter, the dong of the Angelus Bell the only thing that now penetrated his deafness.

Doctor Troy had been there several times, but not recently, and realised at once he should have been. The house had the feeling of the life gone out of it. The front door was open and the air inside barely heated damp. The flagstones sloped to a fire on the floor, but the turf was mostly ash and smouldering only. The black crane hooked a cauldron of antique origin. It may have been the same one that had been there in the famine, what was in it cooking by an un-clocked method of done when it was done. In a cluster by the grate three simple trivets of Tommy the blacksmith's making, on one of them a tin teapot with only the lid unblackened, and in alongside a banking of turf ash a Batchelors pea-can that had a second life as a slow-cooker for eggs. Above the fire a cord was hung, pegged on it three pairs of socks and some cloths, once white, sucking what drying there was. Facing this, two matching chairs of unknown vintage. The one for the patient had a tartan blanket, a flattened cushion for sitting on, and two more for supports, all with handknit coverings in bright green and red. The one for Mossie had surrendered its crocheted cushion to the floor for the dog, the hard seat bolstered by old issues of *Old Moore's Almanac* that were no less prized for predicting a future that never came.

The doctor took off his hat and put it on the kitchen table. 'How is she doing, Mossie?'

'O now,' said the older man, and smiled, the sunken pink of his gums contradicting the smile by making it look that life had put its fist in his face. It was a combination that confused because Mossie Crowe eschewed all pity with a toss of the head and an undefeatable demeanour of *Ah well*. He nodded towards the open door where two hens sat squat on the threshold, flat-eyeing the weather, and said, 'Rain be off shortly, Doctor.'

There was a moment filled with what the world calls nothing. Mossie rocked some in his Sunday shoes, both chewed by Joe but made passable for Mass by a resurrecting polish.

'I'll just go down to see her,' Doctor Troy said, thought to say it louder, didn't, pointed, and carried his bag down into the bedroom.

Under a low hill of blankets, in the thin light admitted by the deep window, Aine Crowe was lying prone on her side of the bed. A small woman who had grown smaller in age, her eyes were open and magnified by the glasses that each morning her husband placed on her nose. His thumbprints were in the lenses. It was small matter, for all that Aine Crowe was seeing. Ruby rosary beads were tied on to her hands. She did not move when the doctor entered, but remained in a stillness that had escaped definition because it had no ending. By instinct he looked to switch on a lamp to see the patient better, and then recalled where he was.

He washed his hands from the jug and basin, drying them in the cloth that was cooler than the air. He sat then on the outermost edge of the bed. He knew at once that his presence there was gestural more than medical, but he was not so far gone as to believe that was worth nothing. *The sick are ourselves*, was a thing his father had said. *When you stop understanding that, take your name off the wall and throw your bag in the river*. It was advice he had only sometimes forgotten.

The bedroom had a miniature fireplace, a grate that took only three sods of turf standing, the fire mostly ash-coloured smoke, slowly rising. On the floor was a thin green carpet bought from the back of a van when it was passing. Underlay or felt were extra and that cost was spared. The carpet hadn't the dimensions of the room and along one wall was a gap where a beaten earth showed. The walls were three feet thick, and the window had a deep sill on which were unlit candle-stubs, saints' cards and holy pictures, some preserved from soiling in a wrinkled cellophane. They were the same tokens that had already been in several houses of the sick, loaned out, taken back, and loaned out again by neighbours whose belief was undimmed by the frequency with which the lending was followed by the funeral. They were well-intentioned and had the dual purpose of being a reminder of community both in this life and the next. Aine Crowe could not see them, but that didn't matter. The saints could see her, the inference. The same was true for the portrait of Jesus. The doctor gave it only a glance, not for the last time wondering what comfort lay in that look, near and impossibly distant.

From time to time the patient would be visited by callers, mostly women, inside whose compass came the sick, by the curate, who was better on the bicycle than Father Tom, and by the buffalo-armed, no-nonsense figure of Nora Eyres, the district nurse. In the evenings, two women might come together, appearing at the back door without invite or announce, licensed by the unwritten code of community. Within the pungent glow of the paraffin lamp, they'd tell their bits of news, whether heard or not no matter, then rise a protective rosary over the patient, afterwards leaving a sweet loaf or *Just the few buns* they'd brought in a teacloth, before crossing up home under the stars.

This, the doctor knew. He knew the custom of the country and what, if only by virtue of remoteness, yet remained. Unlike his counterparts in town, he did not dismiss it, for in it was the solace of invisible allies and the understanding that for the ails of the human condition medicine came not only in tablet form.

'Hello Aine. Doady, it's Doctor Troy.'

Doady's eyes were open, but her face did not change.

He undid the beads and took her hand. For a long time now, he had considered the hand one of the marvels of the human form, as individual and expressive as a face. Its twenty-seven bones were not only a feat of engineering, but, once fleshed, were in articulation sublime, the individual communication those bones capable of attested to by the fact that no two handshakes were the same. In Faha, the hands of men and women had their world in them. They were hands swollen, sored, scarred, hands formed by weather and work, hands crooked, curved, with the one finger that couldn't be straightened or the one that couldn't be bent, the finger that was part-tobacco, the one with the thorn embedded or nail turned amber, purple or black, from a puck or a blow unrecalled but memorialised, hands with fingers clubbed, contracted, with joints that cracked loud like sundered timber, yellow knobs for knuckles, hands that wore assorted lumps and ganglia, ones with skin roughened, toughened, from contact with earth and animals, from the rubbing scrubbing and scouring that all the world needed, hands that wore history and geography, which was nothing more or less than the signature of place and your time in it. His own were pale and soft, developing from the ten thousand soapings of General Practice the paradoxical look of wrinkled innocence. Inside the doctor's, Aine Crowe's hand was light as a bird's construct of twigs. It was cold as a corpse's, but in the blue riverwork of veins at her wrist was yet a pulse. The doctor did not so much hold it as lay it across his palm, like a bridgeway, to where he could not have said.

When he came back to the kitchen, the wireless was turned down, and Ronnie was sitting, leaning down to rub the head of the dog.

'Didn't Joe know she was in the car?' Mossie said with the gum-smile. 'Didn't he know?' he asked Ronnie.

'He did, Ganga.'

'Would you sit down, Mossie?'

'Do. Sit down Doctor, sit down let you.'

They sat by the window, and the doctor took his hat from the table and held it.

'You'll have the cup of tea, Doctor?'

'I won't, thank you.' He shook his head to make clear his meaning.

The table was covered in an oilcloth, a pattern of apples, but scored by a knife in three places, each repaired with tape whose edges were seamed dark. On it was the child's blackboard that served as telegraph when the old man needed a message sent or received. The blackboard was better than the jotter by being everlasting, and from an aeon of chalk and rag had an opaque look that made it appear you wrote on a cloud. The doctor was familiar with it, took no notice, until he did. For, in a condensed dialogue that stopped his breath, in the unmistakable loops of Ronnie's convent handwriting was chalked a single word: *NOE?*

Beneath it, in oversized blocks of white, was built: AMERICA, a line underneath it.

On the board, it had the look of a scholar's sum. Instinctively, the doctor turned his head away the moment he saw it, but unseeing is not in the gift of mankind and for the rest of the day he would return to the fact that, constrained under the limits of time and the child's blackboard to abbreviate the entirety of her feelings into a single word, Ronnie had chosen just this boy's name.

Noe, he knew, was Noel Crowe, the old man's grandson who four years earlier had spent a summer in Faha, one time or another calling on each of the three Troy sisters. At the time the doctor had first considered him like those mindless midges that rose each May, in minuscule tracing a line old as creation by finding human heat and moisture irresistible. He was a nuisance but would pass. The doctor had given him no encouragement. While adhering, only just, to the unwritten code of fathers not to publicly adjudicate on their daughter's choices, he had narrowed his eyes and hedgehogged the moustache to let his look tell the boy the Troy girls were not for him. By the end of summer, the two younger sisters had lost what interest they had in him and then they were gone away. But like an illness that comes into a house and won't leave though all the windows are open, Noel Crowe had persisted. He came to talk with Ronnie, the two of them strolling down the avenue under the archway of falling leaves at the slow pace of serious discourse, back up again just as slow and as serious, into the front parlour where Ronnie poked the fire back to life and brought tea and two cuts of Mary Keane's boiled cake. Between them, there was no end to the talk it seemed. It leaked out under the parlour door when the doctor paused in the front hall. It came in when, of a September evening, he went to draw down the sash of the window in the surgery and, above the small gravelling of footsteps outside, there rose their met voices. What the talk was, he could not quite discern, and for reasons known to all fathers, could not ask his daughter directly. Once, with his back to her in the kitchen, he had shown his hand with the question: 'He was to be a priest, wasn't he?'

Whether intended or not, the implication was of a failure of character, and had drawn in a silence behind it. The doctor had busied himself with the tea things in the basin, waiting to see if a bridge was lowered.

'Do you mean Noe?' Ronnie had asked. Her head was in a book.

The diminutive of the boy's name, the one his grandparents used, seemed to the doctor the frontier of intimacy, and all he had managed was, 'Yes.'

'He has chosen a different life,' was what Ronnie answered.

And there the conversation had ended.

But on the following Sunday afternoon, when the tentative fall of the brass knocker signalled the boy on the doorstep once more, the doctor had stridden to answer it. Chest and chin out, he had stood on the threshold with a prize-fighter's look and with raised eyebrow said a single interrogative *Yes?* that had condensed into it the scene of a nineteenth-century novel, *What exactly are your intentions towards my daughter?* a judge's verdict, *You have no employment, no prospects*, and something of the cloudy fungicide his father used to pump out to protect his beloved roses.

'I was wondering if Ronnie, Veronica, was home?'

'She's poorly today.' It was not exactly a lie.

'Would you give her this, please?' Noel Crowe held out a novel. It was his copy of *The Lake* by George Moore.

The doctor had not taken it at once. The book, he understood, was a love letter in translation and he had kept his eyes fixed on the boy, for a few seconds saying some more of what he hoped did not require language.

'I told her she could have it.'

And still, Jack Troy had not taken it, trapped in the perplex of what a father was supposed to say when he disagreed with what he understood to be his daughter's likely choice.

Into his moustache, he sighed audibly.

But he did not tell the boy he should leave Ronnie alone. He had not said a single word more. Not one. That is what he assured himself one week later when, noticing that Noel Crowe had not called to the house for some days, he chanced, 'The boy of the Crowes', he hasn't...?'

And Ronnie, lost in *The Lake*, said only, 'He's gone to the States.'

***

Jack Troy had thought no more about him, and until this moment, had presumed his eldest daughter had not either. The knowledge that this was not the case disturbed him, not only because it came around the shield with which he tried to keep vicissitude at bay, but also because it meant that, like himself with Annie, Ronnie was harbouring feelings for a ghost.

Though each morning transatlantic aeroplanes followed the route of the flying boats by coming in over the estuary, some in Faha still waving up at them, the passengers who emerged at the top of the steps had a New World look, and by the bestowed glamour of travelling the sky were considered millionaires. None of those who had left the parish for the asphalt dream of Queens had yet returned. The land of the free proved pricey enough, Mick Kirwin wrote his mother, he and all the others on the slippery slope of trying to get ahead, losing ground, growing older, but in the stew of sentiment on Saturday nights renewing a pledge with the salmon's toast, *Death in Ireland*. In the meantime, all that came back of them was Christmas parcels.

So, in the dim of that Sunday kitchen with the front door open to the river beyond, and the rain running off the thatch like an inconsolable weeping, all three knew that the chalked AMERICA on the child's blackboard was a door closed; Noel Crowe was unlikely to be seen in Faha again.

They sat some moments in a triangular quiet. The spiral staircase of golden flypaper was hanging from the rafter overhead, on that echelon to nowhere the corpses of last summer. In a gentle draught, it spun.

Doctor Troy didn't meet his daughter's eyes but ran his finger along the brim of his hat, standing raindrops out of the felt. He did not want to think what he was thinking, that he had been an impassable barrier to love, and gave three curt strokes to the drops, banishing them.

'How are you managing, Mossie?'

The old man's face didn't change. He blinked, and the doctor repeated himself, louder. Mossie looked down to Joe alongside him, as though the dog were his ears. And by whatever means Mossie got whatever message, he nodded and said, 'O now.'

The situation was hopeless, but to the doctor not unfamiliar. With their children gone into the world to find the work that was not in Faha, all the old people lived on the countdown of last days. They were *grand*, their appraisal, until one of them took ill. The policy of the state was to provide care homes in each county for the elderly ill. But in Faha the concept was flawed by being unimaginable. There was only one home, and you didn't need to attach the word care to it.

The paint wasn't dry on the County Home before in the parish it became the byword for doom. Reports, second-, third- and fourth-hand, described a cold place without a fireplace at all, the patients a hodgepodge of the desperate in a patrolled limbo with the windows nailed shut. For those who had lived on land with animals, with neighbours they had known since birth, the confines of the quarters had an anonymous cruelty and a displacement worse than the coffin. In the next life, at least you'd be with your own people, Sonny Cooney said. For many the institution was their first encounter with the State since the bell was rung in the schoolyard, had the same intolerance of the individual, but added to this by defying definitions of care because even the crows wouldn't eat the food when it was thrown out the back. No, the County, as it became known, was never mentioned without a grimace and the inference it was the waiting room of death.

In other circumstances, Aine Crowe would have gone from the hospital to the County, but when asked if her husband was fit to provide for her care Doctor Troy had lied and said yes. His own visits to the institution had buckled his spirit. He came away each time with the sense that God must have exhausted his love for people. Jack Troy had let Aine Crowe come back home. He knew that anything else would break the old man. He had written out prescriptions and instructed Mossie to call the surgery day or night if he saw a change in his wife. But in the months since, no call ever came.

'You won't have the tea, Doctor?'

'We have to be going, Mossie.'

He shook his head, but he didn't rise straight away. He had the familiar feeling of wanting to offer something more, and the same dilemma of not knowing what that could be.

'You're good to call, Doctor.'

'We were passing,' he said, then, realising he hadn't been heard, smiled his tight smile.

It was Ronnie who stood first. If she hadn't, they might have remained for the rest of that Sunday in the impasse of a plot that could not move forward. She put back her chair with the vanquished cushion, said 'Thank you, Ganga' and the doctor delivered the instruction of all in his profession by telling Mossie to call him if he noticed a change. He said he would call again soon. What the old man understood impossible to judge, but he nodded and smiled, his big open face brightened by the oldest medicine.

The doctor and his daughter went back out into the blown rain. From under the hedge, hens darted towards them, realised it was not feeding time, darted off again. In the house the volume on the wireless had been turned up again, a thumping ceili music competing with the wind. They got into the car without talking, and the doctor turned the key. Holidaying in the heat under the engine, a cat came from beneath the car, dashed to the haybarn.

Doctor Troy did not drive away. The noise of the engine was all that attended them until Ronnie turned to him and said, 'What is it?'

He could not look at her. He kept his gaze straight ahead, his eyes fixed on what he had only now understood.

'Stay here.' He snapped open the door before Ronnie could query him further. Leaving the car running, he went at a pace of purpose, in the greatcoat his shoulders tight and his head forward, crossing the yard and going in the back door.

This time he was gone minutes only. He came back and sat into the seat with the throwaway explanation, 'I forgot something', and pressed the accelerator to close the door on questions.

He did not say that the moment he saw the blackboard he had realised he had made a catastrophic mistake. He did not tell his eldest daughter that the misjudgement had come from a father's burden of wanting to guide the three Troy sisters to a happiness impossible, did not say that he knew that guidance had been an abuse of privilege because based on his own verdicts, or that his heart had hurt and his throat dried with the thought that because of him Ronnie had missed her best chance for love.

When he got back into the car, he said none of this. Doctor Troy roared the engine as though under starter's orders, drove out the front street past the dungheap. In his breast pocket, on a page torn from his prescription pad, in that Royal College handwriting decipherable only to himself and the dead Annie Mooney, was written the address of Noel Crowe in America.

***

The middle of that Sunday was remarkable only for the rigour with which it matched its fellows. The doctor and his daughter drove into town. They took their Sunday dinner at the Old Ground Hotel. Seamus, the head porter, greeted them by name at the front door, and Higgins, who had the operatic manner and morning jacket of a maître d', showed them to the table by the front window that was theirs by the fact that on Sundays they went nowhere else. Doctor took the beef, daughter the chicken. 'Excellent choices,' agreed Higgins, as though it was a unique combination or they ever chose anything else, snapping shut the leather covers of the menu and heading to the kitchen with head back, as though reprising his part in the Operatic Society's *Pagliacci*.

By turn, father and daughter made the small comments that constitute the standard of company without demands. The hotel had been newly dressed for Christmas. There was a tall tree in the lobby, the sharp clean scent doing the business of festive promotion by going everywhere. Beneath it, for imaginary children, was a little stack of parcels of air that had been in service since, in thrall to *Miracle on 34th Street*, the wrapping had been brought from Macy's in New York. From the same source, on the mantel above the fireplace, was a plump Father Christmas made of papier-mâché, alongside him a small wicker sled with bulging sack. Green or red paper bells that, folded in on themselves, were flat nothings, but unsnapped, opened in frilled intricacy, hung from wall-lamps by woven strings of scarlet. None of the decorations were Irish, the figures as unalike anyone in any parish, but that was part of the point, the dressings of the season combining to dissolve reality and say ordinary time was suspended. Although only ten miles distant, the hotel was a world from the house the doctor and his daughter had visited that morning. The only concession towards the native the branches of berried holly that had been placed over each of the gilt-framed paintings.

'They have the holly, I see,' said the doctor drily.

It was a comment with a backstory. At the top of the avenue at Avalon was the best holly tree in Faha. It had the notable character of being venerable yet berry-full. The local wisdom was that the estuary gulls frightened the small birds whose voracious hunger took the berries off all the other hollies in the parish. Having driven off the birds, the gulls remembered they did not care for berries, and by this imperial twist, each year the Troys' tree was spared. It was a known part of the natural clockwork of the parish that, come the first weeks of December, the old tree would be showing the ruby fruit that had the crossed character of being beautiful and toxic. And because holly had its place in custom and lore – from the Druids' Holly King to Christ himself – berried branches had to be got for each house in the parish. Other adages, that the tree was the favourite of the fairies, that when brought inside if the leaves were thorny, the man was in charge, if smooth, the woman, were told in the same manner as all pishogues, with a dismissive grin and a furtive look over the shoulder.

Each December then, so routine as to constitute tradition, the Troys' holly tree was ravaged. Up the avenue at all hours of the day, with mixed shyness and licence, carrying slashers, handsaws, or in the case of Senan Hosey, two kindling axes in the belt like toma-hawks, came the holly-men. Under the ordinance of a custom older than memory, the imperatives of Christmas, and the persis-tent ask of the woman of the house, *Did you get the sprig of holly?* they came singly, on foot or bicycle, going at the tree their fathers had gone at before them, so that by now the entire lower limbs of Troy's great holly were no more, much of the sheltered eastern side too, the tree grown literally lopsided by a hand more butcher than surgeon. In recent years, as the berries only appeared now on the upper branches, men came with their sons, hoisting them on their shoulders so they could climb up into the blind scratch-world of the tree, finding the saws blunter and the wood harder than last year, but not stopping until they had a berried branch to bring home. There were many Christmas Eves the doctor would drive up the avenue home and a troop of last-minute holly-men would be coming down against him with the thorny trophies and the bashful look of ones caught between religion and rite.

'Yes,' said Ronnie, looking at the branches tucked behind the ancestral portraits. 'I like it.'

'I might put a fence around our holly this year.'

'No. Why?'

'The tree won't survive.'

The waiter arrived with the food, Higgins in his wake, superin-tending at a small distance until the plates landed. When he had stepped away, Ronnie concluded the discussion with the inargua-ble: 'It has survived this long.'

The beef was thinly sliced and fanned on the plate, the pota-toes mashed and domed like cupolas, carrots, parsnips and peas a sideshow, and like a flourished paint-stroke, slathered gravy. The doctor's head was lowered, but he was not looking at the food. He no longer said the words of Grace Before Meals, but he paused as if, so the ghost of the grace was present, then he lifted the napkin and shook out its folds.

Across the street the cathedral bells rang the hour. The light was going out of the day. They ate in the manner of their family, the hot food overruling the need for conversation. When the time came for dessert, the doctor did what he always did and had a cigarette but urged Ronnie to have something. She gave her customary answer: she'd have tea at home. 'Very good,' said Higgins, taking back the menus with a smile that denoted nothing because he'd used it every day of his adult life.

They drove back home. The doctor and his daughter separated to their quarters, like ones reprieved. On wet Sunday afternoons in December the old house took on the air of a ghost ship, adrift. It had a miscellany of creaks, whistles, cracks and noisings general without human source. The wind's marriage to the rain gave birth to a third weather that could quench the candles of whatever it was that kept you living and required countering. For the doctor, this was achieved by withdrawing to the upstairs bedroom and escaping into an afternoon nap that on Sundays was constitutional. Until four o'clock he was to be undisturbed. Once the four dongs sounded on the grandfather clock in the front hall, the world could be switched back on.

This afternoon, it came back with Chopin. He opened his eyes after his ears to the sound of Ronnie playing her mother's piano in the front room. The chords of the Chopin rose through the floorboards and came to him imbued with a melancholy that was not there yesterday, each like bruises on the air. She played carefully, with the trained hands of hours of practice. The fact of those hours was apparent, the mistakes few, but faultlessness was not the first requirement of music. Still, by a three-part alchemy of instrument, music and musician, in the notes were the constraints and sorrows of his daughter's life. The doctor sat on the bed pressing into his shoes, breaking down the heels because when he fell on the bed the quibble of undoing laces had defeated him. Not for the first time did it occur to him that music was the most potent of the arts, in

44

it too a ghost magic, for Ronnie played exactly like Regina. The tenderness in the nocturne gave the impression of a naked human heart, and as he put on his jacket with Noel Crowe's address in the breast pocket, he knew he could not stay in the house while the music continued.

He did not disturb the playing but took his hat from the crooked coat-stand in the hall, roughed the car's engine, and raced down the ruts of the avenue under the sanction of making house calls.

In the fallen dark, the parish vanished. Those houses that had taken the electricity kept it inside behind the impenetrable curtains Marion Boylan sold from her drapery at the end of Church Street. Marion had turned down Smalls & Hosiery somewhere in England to come back to Faha, and she wasn't shy about letting you know. It was a certification without the paper. For all items of clothing, her sales pitch was *Washes like a hanky* but for curtain material she had an addendum, *Nothing comes through it*. And she was not wrong, the houses invisible against the lumpen land and only detectable when you could smell the turfsmoke. The doctor drove by the river, the regulation of the motor doing the work of mechanical mesmerism and making it seem it was not important where he was going, only that he was. Unseen, the estuary along-side him had the air of an unhealed wound. But, melted into the black sky, you knew it was there.

He made house calls to Breaffy's and Nolan's. Breaffy was a man in combat with the world, over which he was resolved to be boss. Doctor Troy disliked everything about him. His children were many but stood in by the walls when their father was in the room. His wife, a wan figure called Terese, called him 'Daddy.' Breaffy had a grunt for welcome, as though he was only ill because the doctor was there. From a rearing in a boghole, he had a calloused look, from illness no softening. Hair that grew in dark twirls out of his ears without purpose lent him a look halfway to beast, an impression furthered by the solid wodge of his neck that was pocked like hide. Above the course hair that climbed his cheeks his eyes were watchful slits. The doctor took Breaffy's arm, feeling for the pulse. The man had no wrists, the muscles of his forearms had eaten them. His children were listening at the door to hear if he would be living still.

45

'Here to make more money out of me?' he said, when the doctor turned him on his side.

'I want no money.'

'He wants no money. He wants no money! You'll get your money all right, no fear of it.' The cry brought Breaffy to coughs, which brought him to wheezes and from there to gasps, the eyes of him widening and watering, Terese standing by, holding her hands in a tight clasp, not quite prayerful.

After the examination, a rasped call: 'Make him tea.'

'No tea, thank you.'

'You'll have tea! The doctor'll have tea. Terese, tea!'

At Nolan's there was a child, Ciaran, with whooping cough. In her own childhood May Nolan had been in the tuberculosis hospital in town and retained a terror of what could take over your chest. Her son was ten years, thin as a rail, the coughs larger than him.

In both houses, the doctor unsnibbed the bag to leave analgesics and bottles that came without charge, in both houses delivering different versions of his classic diagnosis, *It will get better, get worse, or stay the same*. He had learned it from his father when the old man had pronounced it over his son's bursting appendix, making no apology when, to young Jack's screams later that evening, his father pressed his abdomen, nodded, and with perfect sangfroid said, 'Worse.' From doctors, patients want certainty, which was not in the human realm. But the old doctor's dictum was genius in disguise, for it had the twin advantages of voiding debate and always being right.

The third call was to Nora Haugh. She was a woman who looked like the springs were being taken out of her through her skull, her hair a wizard circuitry of white wire rising, but she retained the wit that was her hallmark, was resolute and would make ninety. 'Topping altogether,' she said when the doctor asked how she was. Among a range of ailments, she suffered from chronic infections of the urinary tract, a fact she blamed on a life lived beside a river and a house built on the way to the fairies' toilet. There was no rejoinder. While he examined her, Nora told a story she had told before. It had the quality of all stories in Faha, the ending: 'He wanted jam on it. Well, he wasn't getting jam from me.' She chuckled like she was hearing it for the first time. Her husband Mick chuckled too. He had a hop in his walk, one leg carrying the other that got a kick from a beast in the otherwise forgotten time known as *fado*. He didn't draw notice on it, neither did anyone else. He and Nora were married too long to count. In that time each had taken over some of the other's character. When she got the flu, he got the flu. 'We're the one mucus, doctor,' Mick said, with a pirate's gaiety, the time Jack Troy visited the both of them snuffling in the narrow bed.

'She'll do, Doctor?' Mick's ask when the consult was done.

'She'll do, Mick.'

Mick had the tea poured. 'Cup in the hand, Doctor?'

'I will so, thank you.'

They sat in the small kitchen in the company of all of Nora's clothes, which were displayed on the horse before the open fire, all of them steaming nicely with an air of abandon and what-have-you worthy of the saints and them going marching in. The table was plain, the setting simple, from damp the sugar thinly crusted. But the tea was strong and fulsome with flavour and the cut of sweet loaf a small sensation.

Jack Troy got back in the car with a lighter step. Medicine was not nothing, from the anguish of spiritual meaninglessness there was reprieve in aiding another, though there remained the mystery why caring for the sick was easier than for the well, and for the stranger than your own blood. They were mysteries he couldn't solve, and under the grace of Nora Haugh's good humour and sweet loaf he could let them be, sitting behind the steering wheel and not for the first or last time recalling his father's adage that the central challenge of life was to accept that the world is a place of pain, *And yet live. Yet live, Jack.*

The rain came hard out of the dark. The wipers were unequal to it, between the judders the windscreen awash. But if he was to wait for the rain to end, he'd be there still. He drove slowly away and along the boreen that was sunk on both sides, the tuft of grass in the centre marking it as not-river. Mimicking life, the Morris's headlights showed just the bit of road directly in front of it, leaving it back into the dark after.

In this way, the herd of Quinlan's cattle appeared with the suddenness found in dreams.

The doctor stopped just in time. The beasts were spread across the road in the dark. They had overcome the first excitement of being outside bounds and stood now in the meditative trance of those neither here nor there. To the taps on the car horn the cattle paid no attention. In the flare of the headlights, the scene stopped where it was. Jack Troy did not get out. The cattle did not clear the road. The motor and the river ran, but the sense the doctor had was of a hand on his shoulder. With thin curiosity, the cattle came around the car, nosed the glass, found nothing remarkable. Still, Jack Troy sat there.

Then he saw the figure by the river.

In the otherwise dark the headlights captured the gleam of a human face. It was momentary only. The figure had turned away, not towards the light, dissolving as though within a drawn cloak. Jack Troy rolled down the window. The rain spat in.

'Dammit.'

He stood out of the car and called, 'Hello?'

The Quinlan cattle took it as a translated *hup!* and went through the wire into Talty's place. Under the brim of his hat, Jack narrowed his eyes but could make out no figure. Between rescue and doom are only moments, and he was getting back into the car when he saw the three peaks of the biretta with the trampled tuft lying in the road. *Jesus*, he didn't say but had the look of it. He turned and called again, this time a louder 'Tom!' And again, 'Tom!' as he went to the bank of gorse and bramble, scanning the dark for the priest.

On the third 'Tom', midway across the muck and suck of the river-field, he saw him. He saw him as darkness on darkness, an impress of black against the movement of the estuary: that was Father Tom at the eroded edge of the Shannon where always, day and night, Faha was falling away, and where in moments the Canon would be in the current.

The old priest didn't turn until the doctor's hand was on his arm. 'Tom?'

The doctor came around to face him. Immediately Jack Troy had the relief of disaster averted, but also the guilt when a patient worsened, and he had not done more.

'You all right, Tom?'

It was clear at once that the priest had been astray for hours, his clothes little more than a congruence of rain, one of his shoes gone. On his big open face the drops were running, but what was absent in it was upset. Father Tom blinked the water and then he smiled. It was a smile of recognition, although perhaps not of Jack Troy, because what he said was 'You?' He said it as if it was the unexpected answer to a puzzle he had been working on for some time and had the look of one who gets to the end of a book and realises they must read it again from the beginning.

'Jack Troy,' the doctor said.

The priest nodded softly, with the same benign smile he had used for half a century after First Communions, confirmations and weddings. In the parish it was known that the Canon had reached an age when he forgot new names the moment he was told them. He had his lapses, but these were natural, and none took offence from a failing that only proved his mind was full. But this, it was clear, was more than that. This was not age but illness, and though it could have been seen coming, only at that moment did the priest's manner confirm he had reached the second part of the Troy medical axiom: it had got worse.

The doctor could not tell if Father Tom recognised him. Though with the look of disarray in a December night with the rain blowing sideways, nothing in the old priest's manner showed awareness of urgency.

'It's Doctor Troy,' Jack prompted again.

'Yes. That's right,' the Canon said, with the same gratified tone he used when he got the correct answer to the questions in the catechism as he went through the Master's room, the quarter pound of Satin Cushions in his cassock lightening as he left the sweets on the desks after him. He nodded once more, 'That's right.' But he did not move, and in a moment the doctor saw some puzzlement cross his face. It was light, a small thing really, it came out as: 'And I'm...?'

'You're Father Tom.'

'*Father* Tom?' It seemed unlikely and then hilarious, and he put his hand across the traffic of laughs coming.

'Yes, Father Tom.'

The older man's eyes came to the doctor and held him in a look not so much lost as baffled, and in it a kind of fierce beseeching. Doctor Troy would remember it for the rest of his life. He drew the priest by the arm.

'Come on, Tom. We'll go back to my car now. All right?'

'Yes,' the priest said, unclear if he was answering the doctor or an inner other, but he let himself be led back across the field towards the headlights, the one unshod foot dipping his step, the doctor each time making the move to catch him though each time the priest did not fall.

Doctor Troy sat him in the passenger seat, put his biretta on the dashboard. When he got in the car, he did what he always did in the first company of a patient, asking a question to which he did not need an answer, but which gave the excuse to study the face. 'You got caught in the rain, Tom?'

The priest may have thought the water dripping from his face passed for reply, he did not say anything, only tapped his two hands on his knees in the gesture that was his signal for *onward*. But for the drowned look, his demeanour was without distress, and the doctor drove him back into the village with no further questions.

With no resolution but the one of getting the priest into a bed, Doctor Troy passed through the village, around the back of the Parochial House and killed the headlamps. Father Tom said a soft 'ah' at the sight of home, as if he may have been brought elsewhere. With no grounds in science, the familiarity of the place acted as an analgesic for whatever was awry in his mind, and he blinked the three blinks of recovery, showing some realisation of the situation by turning to the doctor and with a supplicatory look asking, 'You won't tell?'

It was a question with the air of a pact. In it the doctor saw the desperation of the old priest not to be taken from what he loved most, saying Mass, and his horror at the thought of the cleric's retirement home, which Sonny Cooney said was crows in a box.

But in truth, there was no need, Jack Troy had not yet betrayed a patient's confidence, and adhered to the adage that the inner health of each of us is the last privacy this side of death.

'I'll see you in, Tom.'

The doctor was out the door before the priest could object. Alongside, but with the aim of being invisible, he shepherded the older man to the back door where, lying against a weatherboard swollen from drinking too much rain, Tossie Brogan's Sibby was watching the drops dancing off the saucer and waiting on Christian charity. Father Tom greeted the cat with the universal *whis-whis-whish* that was love in translation, and the cat rose and arched her back for the scratch she had learned was the prelude to milk.

'You'd like a drop?' asked the Canon of the cat. 'You would of course.'

The moment undid gloom, for in it was the substance of every-day, the small and ordinary which, against catastrophe, is discovered marvellous. In the blown rain Father Tom bent, gave the knuckle of his forefinger to the neck of the sibby in an exchange that made a nothing of the fact that an hour earlier he had been about to go walking in a river. With helpless curiosity, the cat sniffed the mud soak of the priest's black sock, found it thin of interest, came back for the knuckle once more.

The plan was to get the Canon to his room without drawing the attention of the curate, but it foundered on the tightly wound character of Father Coffey who, for a little time now, had had his suspicions that the walls of the old priest's mind were thinning quickly. When he heard the report of the breakdown in service at Mass that morning, those suspicions started nodding. And when Father Tom had not answered the call to tea, when he was not in his room, not in the church, nor in Prendergast's parlour, they had started pointing at him, saying *See?* The curate had gone up to high doh, and in his agitation to the postmistress blurted a confession mired in metaphor but which amounted to a shortfall in the matter of Father Tom's marbles.

The assembly of the search party was complicated by the native custom of keeping all things clerical private, and illness of the mind an absolute no-no. While Mrs Prendergast was working

out the ranked order of who should be told, Connie commandeered the switchboard, one by one calling the outlying houses and
adopting a wouldn't-melt-in-her-mouth tone to ask, 'You haven't
seen Father Tom out that way at all?'

In all of this, Father Coffey had been like an overwound toy. He
could picture any number of appalling outcomes, and was part-
nered in this by the postmistress's sister, Mona, out for her routine
visit to a parish where tedium was chronic but animated by the
whiff of disaster and the thrill of tomorrow's headlines. A tightly
tucked woman with thick glasses but an unerring eye for drama,
when Father Coffey said 'The river,' she chorused 'Drowned,' when
he, 'The dark roads,' she, 'Run over,' making actual the bump of
the car going over the body by an involuntary lift of her buttocks
on the edge of the settee. She turned off the television and cracked
open the rosary soon after, and the first stages of the Canon's
funeral were underway before the body had finished breathing. At
last, Master Quinn arrived and took charge with the professional
command of one who had trained the Kellys to sit in their desks
and thirty-six children to fall silent when he raised his face from the
newspaper. A bachelor of fifty, the Master had a mathematician's
mind and a manner imperturbable. He asked what was known,
subtracted all surmise, and made the decision it was too early to tell
Greavy the guard. Instead, he performed an audit of battery lamps,
delegated search parties to the three cars available, two more on
bicycles, and told Father Coffey to go back to the Parochial House
in case the Canon was undead and came back when the ache in his
gums told him it was time to take out his teeth.

But the doctor knew none of this. At the back door of the
Parochial House, he shooed the cat with a foot feint and brought
the older man in with the hope of being undiscovered.

'Softly now,' he said to the priest, who put his finger to his lips
and turned to him the face he had as a boy, boxing apples from the
orchard at O Meara's.

The electric light was off, the passageway blind. They went with
soft step in the exaggerated mimic of housebreakers, until they
bumped into the mahogany furniture that was without purpose
but lived along the corridor to the stairs and were given up by the

moment Father Tom stubbed his toe. The cry wasn't out of his mouth when Father Coffey was upon them. Having been praying for the Canon's soul, it took the curate a minute when faced with the body. As an aid to reality, he flicked down the pip on the wall and the front hall came to illumined life.

It looked better in the dark. Though the house had been built with dimensions of grandeur in landlord times, ceilings high and windows tall, its upkeep was beyond the little largesse of church dues and the house was each day further along the road to ruin. Of the twelve chimney pots only two ever sent out smoke. Trapped in the air of every room was a scent of candlewax, sausage and cigarettes. In the front hall the walls wept. Beneath a Persian-look carpet the wide floorboards of pitch pine had a small seesaw in them, along the skirting the tell-tale signs of a subterranean traffic that had grown daring on the knowledge that the priests' cat preferred its food to come to it.

Here then was Father Coffey, agape, taking in the drowned look of the one-shoed Canon with exclamations of muck on his cuffs. He put his hand across his mouth to keep the *O God* from coming out. With an incendiary zeal, both evangelic and revolutionary, the curate was of an age to believe he could and would change the world, from the inside, each day undoing a little more of the cold absolutism of an institutional Church that had terrified his boyhood, and of which the Canon was in fact the flesh-and-blood epitome. Still, in the angular concern of his look to Father Tom it was clear that, although theirs was a made marriage, of unequal parts, old and young, no day inside the rattling windows of that parochial house that one of them wasn't visited by some new frustration in the other, it was one nonetheless.

The doctor held Father Tom by the arm. 'I'll bring him up to his room.'

'No,' said Father Coffey, 'I will,' coming forward with the courage of ministry, taking Father Tom by the elbow, touching him for the first time since the handshake of his introduction five years before. The two of them advanced on to the creak of the stairs with a couple's singularity, a togetherness that had the effect of closing the curtain behind them.

Doctor Troy went back through the house and out to the car. He had the engine running when the headlights caught the cat still waiting by the back door. The wipers jagged and pushed the rain, but the sibby remained, her eyes a reflecting yellow not of this world. He said his second 'Dammit' of that Sunday then, and was out of the car before his suit had settled into sitting creases, crossing the puddles of the yard in the lit arrows of slanted downpour that was the same as made no difference, for his clothes were already a tailored rain and the inside band of his hat a clinging crown.

In the scullery was the tiled fireplace of a chimney that was never lit. With an irony that undid the name *fireplace*, the tiles kept the cold all day and did amateur duty as the priests' refrigerator. There, alongside the pat of butter with cicatrice of strawberry jam, he found the enamel jug with the cows' milk that Marty Hehir provided even in December. Inclining towards souring, the milk had a come-together substance of clots, plops in the pour but fresh enough for the cat when he placed the saucer in front of her.

Doctor Troy drove past the post office and back to Avalon. When he got in the door, Ronnie was there to tell him that Father Tom was missing.

'He's found.'

He went to the phone, lifted the receiver to get Connie on the switch and told her the business was resolved, to call off the search. He played the doctor's card of privilege and explained nothing.

'Change your clothes,' Ronnie said, when he hung up. 'I'll make tea.'

'I can drink no more tea.'

He had not meant to be curt. Living every day on the point of exhaustion had shorted courtesy, the only saving grace that he knew it, and he added 'thank you' before it was too late. He put his hat on the stand with a sense of relieved burden, as though the hat itself did the doctoring, or was the milliner's version of the axiom of Faha's visionary, Martin Meagher, who said our souls were only waiting for us to put our bodies on the hanger.

Ronnie was standing watching, both hands pressed in the pockets of a house cardigan that had lost its line from that habit, rose at the back and made it seem she carried stones.

'I'll see you in the morning,' her father said, and raised a palm a few inches in a compendium gesture of *Goodnight farewell thank you I'm sorry and I love you*. He lifted his eyes to look at Ronnie in the hope that in their grey depths she would see he could not say another word to any human being.

'Goodnight,' she said, and, with hands still in pockets, came forward and kissed his damp forehead in the same way she did every night. Then she turned the iron key in the lock in the front door, went up the stairs without word or look.

***

The doctor went into the surgery to find the Napoleon. Through the afternoon Ronnie had kept the fire in the grate going, and the heat though small made clammy his suit in the places where the rain had found home. He took off his jacket impatiently, the silk lining of the sleeves turning inside out, and he was of a mind to ball and fire it in a corner when he saw the tip of the prescription paper in the breast pocket, and remembered.

Although worth more than the paper they were written on, prescriptions had a life expectancy of hours only, hours at most between the lifting of the doctor's fountain pen and the handing over in the chemist's, where, after a moment's consult, its life ended on an upright skewer that had the look of the butcher's but was the coded inventory of all that had gone wrong in the parish. For this reason, the paper was featherweight. This, and the fact that in Faha weatherproof was a nonsense term, meant that when Jack Troy took the page from his jacket pocket it had the consistency of a butterfly's wing in water. A thumbsworth came away at his touch, and he went more carefully then, withdrawing the sheet with calipered fingers, bringing it to his desk and laying it flat inside the arc of the lamplight.

There, in the crabwork of a handwriting that had become more cryptic as he had, he read the boy's address in America. He had not written the name *Noel Crowe*, for he knew it, remembering him again now, remembering their first meeting, when Noel was brought into the surgery the time he had tried to catch a falling electricity pole, remembering his thin figure and ardent eyes when he came calling, that look he had the day he stood on the front steps and handed over the book.

It was not love that was between them, or Jack Troy would have recognised it, he had been certain.

Right up until that afternoon in Crowe's.

The moment he saw the name on the blackboard in Ronnie's hand, he knew he was mistaken, knew in the way she had not met his eyes but had looked away, as though from the memory of love, knew not only that his eldest daughter had not forgotten Noel Crowe, which was in the make-up of her nature, but more, that she had cared deeply for him.

And cared still.

What was also certain was that if her father said to her *Here is that boy's address*, Ronnie's look would say *What?*, her face a frown, a hand pushing away a straying hair as she turned to some urgent chore, shutting down discussion by an intractable industry, need to be elsewhere, or any one of those checking behaviours we use to shield ourselves from the life we haven't lived.

At the thought of that, the doctor pushed back in the chair. His right hand came across his mouth, and he held it there, as though to stop himself letting out the emotion that brimmed in him. For he could not think of failed love without thinking of Annie Mooney, and the many times he might have declared himself to her. His fingers moved slowly back and forth across his lips. Then he reached for the cigarettes. The struck match was its own solace, a small, flamed release and he looked at it a moment before bending to it.

Since her death, Jack Troy had worked diligently to keep each of his memories of Annie separate. He did not want them to blur into one indistinction, the general and everyday more fading impression that was the fate of so many of his dead. For Annie, he wanted to retain the scenes exactly as they had been, the place, time of day or night, what she had been wearing, what she said. He had no photograph of her. He had nothing of hers, but the knowledge that she wore the Guerlain perfume she said was the favourite of Katherine Hepburn. When she said it, he had passed no comment.

It was a Saturday in May. They were in his car. The night before she had told him she needed to go to town for supplies, and he had lied that he was going in himself and could bring her. He had collected her at one o'clock. She slid the plastic *Closed* across and stepped out in a spring coat of strawberry-red to where he held the car door open for her. She chose the front seat and thanked him again for the treat of the lift. They went without talk, she tilted forward a little, looking ahead at everything, he at her only when they turned left. The countryside had thrown itself open to blossom, a burst yellow in the furze. Which at first was what he thought he was smelling, and thought the surprises of life are without end, for it was never as wonderful as this. His head must have angled back, the more to take it in, or he made the small involuntary sound that signals pleasure, for Annie Mooney had turned to him then and said, *Guerlain*. He had a caught look, but pretended it was confusion, so she said, *My perfume. I have a heavy finger on the spray. I know I am too old for it.* To which he had been, stupidly, eternally regretfully, unable to offer a gallant reply, only crinkling the wrinkles at the corners of his eyes. *I can roll down the window?* Annie had asked. *No. No, it's fine,* is what he had said, shortly, and said nothing more, nor looked across at her again, even when she had added, *It's Katherine Hepburn's favourite,* and turned to see what he made of that.

All of which was as clear to him this evening as if it had happened an hour ago. He could recall all of it, could recall her pushing back her hair to expose the whorl of her ear and the flesh of her neck where the scent had kissed, could recall the risen hem of the strawberry-coloured coat on the seat and the fingers of her right hand coming down in repose on it, but no matter how he tried, he could not make himself turn in the car seat and tell her that, though at his age he thought it ridiculous, it was nonetheless certain: he was falling in love with her.

***

Changing your mind is one of the most difficult feats of the living. Easier to change your nose. In the case of Jack Troy, it took considerable time, and as much brandy for him to return from thinking of Annie Mooney and decide he had been hopelessly wrong about Noel Crowe and Ronnie.

Napoleon had the same block build as Jack Troy, unknown how many snifters clarified his thought on the eve of Waterloo, but for the doctor the brandy bottle had more air than liquid by the time he uncapped the fountain pen, and on the bonded paper with the address on top prepared to write the least likely letter of his life.

Untutored in the art of playing Cupid, what came to him was the time Brother Leo cast him as Portia, when, in a full-length amber eiderdown that was the closest the college had to heiress-wear, he had stood on a wooden dais to receive the affections of McGrath, Miller and Brady, in the Best Actor eyes of Brady having a terrifying first flash of what it might mean to love. The memory had the effect of a hand on his shoulder, and the letter nearly stopped before it began.

He started it in the safe harbour of *Dear Noel*, but then failed to push off, going back only to add the comma. He held the pen at the ready. It was not that the words weren't there, it was that too many of them were. As a pretence to his brain that he was still in process, he put down the pen, took the blotting paper and pressed it against the name. Above him, as if under the tread of a wooden angel, the floorboards made the crossing sounds of Ronnie getting ready for bed. It gave him further pause. Regret is a fruit of age. The longer you live the more you know its sour taste. And he was caught between the vision of his eldest daughter standing at her forward slant in the long cardigan with a look that said *How dare you?* and the conviction that he had stood in the way of her happiness.

He got up and went to the window, drawing back one of the long curtains to face the dark that at first made one of river, land and sky. It was only gradually that each of the trinity separated, only by slow looking did he see. Once, it had come to him that the whole history of mankind had failed the Sermon on the Mount, the bitterness of that only resolved by the understanding he came to that maybe the aspiration was more important than the realisation, and maybe Christ knew that. As he stood by the window, what filled Jack Troy then was the fantastical idea of grace as an actual thing. That it was something real, and at that moment the thing he suddenly longed for the most: for one last time, to make an act of grace, even if he was not sure he believed in it, or in the daylight could have explained why. Only that he wanted to feel a sense of grace, which, by what calculus of cause and effect too mysterious and human to say, he knew was bound up with freeing his daughter from him and pushing her gently, but surely, towards love.

God wants us to love, was a saying of his father's, *despite the way he made us.*

The wedge of cardboard that did duty between the sashes was sodden, and he drew it out. Liberated, the window rattled at once and let in the scent of salted rain. The sharpness of it had the effect of rousing him from an undignified surrender, head on the desk and passed out on a primary-school composition that went no further than salutation and swollen comma. He went back to the desk to get the thing done.

As a bargain against himself, he would hold off on the final mouthful of brandy until the letter was in the envelope. He tapped out and smoked another cigarette. He balled the page of the first draft, began again, lowering himself over the new sheet and applying the nib with a stenographer's speed, as though the letter was being dictated from elsewhere, or he could take the words by surprise, have them on the page before his brain could say stop. He wrote the *Dear Noel,* dashed the comma and had *I am writing to you this evening* out of the nib when the chill of his shirt across his back tightened his shoulders, and he was suddenly aware he was very cold. The fire had died. His feet were inside his shoes, but he could not feel them. He had a sense of stumps and stamped two steps of going nowhere without improvement. The brandy would warm him. The twist his brain took was that if he put down the fountain pen, he would not take it up again and the moment would be lost. Reneging on a deal that had been made under duress, pen still poised between thumb and forefinger, he took the brandy bowl left-handed and drank the last, under the twin guises of tidying up and a medical aid to keep his blood moving. Above him, the floorboards made their ache-music once more, Ronnie un-bedded, crossing to the window or the dresser, crossing back again with a restlessness that her father translated theatrically as stirred by their visit to the boy's grandparents.

By a learned blindness, suffering in another can be borne; in your daughter not, and his pen was back on the paper before he had put down the glass. He did not write *I wronged you*, nor *I myself missed a last chance at love*, nor *If I stood in your way, I regret that now*. He was not a schoolboy, he was not certain that Noel Crowe was his eldest daughter's true love, but the exemplar of others who may have wished to come calling, against which he had been a bulwark, and the only one he had an address for. He did not write the question that had first lodged in his heart, *Why does no one love my daughter?*, for that afternoon he feared he had found the answer. Instead, on the mixed fuel of the brandy, the missed chance of Annie Mooney, a parent's fear of the unmade world after them, and the longing for an act of grace, in the inscrutable hand of a disguised Cupid he wrote: *Your grandmother is dying. I do not believe she will make Christmas.*

He told Noel Crowe that if he wanted to see her again in this world, he should immediately plan to come home. He thought to say that his daughter Ronnie had been with him when they visited Doady and Ganga today, thought to say that it was she who suggested he write, but thought the better of both, taking recourse in his signature brevity, adding only *My daughter, Veronica, sends her greetings.*

He put the page inside the envelope, pressed it on the tip of his tongue, the sour of the gum unequal to the coating of brandy. The address was care of a Patrick Clancy on 12th Street, New York, and when writing it he paused, for a moment seeing Noel Crowe in the company of those musical musketeers, the Clancy Brothers. He put the letter not in *Outgoing* where Ronnie would find it, but inside his Gladstone bag among the bottles and vials of remedies for all that went wrong with people and had the first small easement of the stricture that had entered his heart that afternoon.

He sat back in the studded chair and let the tide of all that had happened since he opened his eyes that morning come over him. *Was this only one Sunday?* It seemed impossible, his thinking something along the lines of Martin Meagher, who, crinkled face to the sky, had said, 'Don't people put God in His place by calling this "ordinary life"?'

Going up the stairs to fall on the bed was beyond him. He made it as far as the divan with the tartan blanket. Laying his head, what was coming to him was the idea that if a body could exhaust itself in living, so could a heart. Could a human heart be filled to capacity, like any other vessel? Could you reach the point of being unable to take on more care? With the primacy of an emergency exhaustion, these were questions that had to be postponed, along with *I pray the Lord my soul to keep*, the last of Jack Troy that night a snuffled breath through the bristles of a silver moustache, arms crossed in an embrace of one, and a shut-down look that said *Let tomorrow take care of itself.*

2

Before the dawn on the day Jude Quinlan would find the child, a rough hand shook him awake.

'Come on now.'

In the narrow bedroom his father was a congruence of dark, a hunched shadow that smelled of damp, dead cigarettes and old stout. In boots, cap and overcoat, his father was already at the starting gate for a day that had been ring-marked on the calendar since it came from the butcher's. It was the last fair of the year in Faha. Pat Quinlan paused only long enough to see the boy stir, then he was gone, thumping down the garret stair with a quick step that signalled he was already overwound.

Jude was twelve years old. He was thin, an assemblage of bone and spirit that was all angles but had sprung into a new tallness that endowed him with authority. He dressed quickly, as though to catch up with where he should have been, and when he arrived in the kitchen he took the griddle-bread from the plate, eating it hands-free as he pulled on his boots, taking another wedge with him in a walking breakfast that was not to feed a hunger that was still sleeping but the one that would come in the long day ahead.

'Jude, take your time,' Mamie Quinlan said, without effect, duffel-coating his three standing sisters, eight, nine and ten, and under the burning of the hanging bulb rubbing the sleep from the face of the youngest. She was a soft and kind woman, with blue

eyes of long hurt, and the anxious look of one married to an insta-
bility. 'There's tea,' she said.

He drank it in one go, 'Put on your jacket' ignored under
the licence of being the eldest, and a boy, and at the dawn of a
Christmas fair.

His father was already pacing in the yard. There was no rain,
under the backstreet lamp only a fine mizzle dandling. 'Are they
right?' he said, when Jude came out alone. Pat Quinlan was fifty-
three, but his body was ten years ahead of him. There was an
invisible sack on his back, pressing his head down into his shoulders. His face was a fist, tight, eyes sunken, the line of his lips
betraying that he was a man for whom the world might never come
right. Dogged at every step, he'd say, on the stool in Craven's, not
expanding nor being asked, only with the air of one who, if he
knew the address, would send this life back to its maker.

'They're coming.'

At the side of the cowhouse, they kept the droving sticks. Jude
had a favourite, a sally, supple, one end hand-smooth, the other
acute from whipping nettles and briars. For moving cattle, he no
longer needed it, but he had not let go of the boy-soldier feeling of
it tucked under his arm, and he took it now imagining the same
alliance as between a cowboy and his horse. As his sisters bundled
out the door, he handed their sticks to them, one, two and three.
Their mother held the only hand-lamp. In the henhouse, the cock
crowed.

'Jude and Mary'll go up and hunt 'em down,' Pat said. 'Teresa
at Considine's gap turn 'em over, Mammy at Kelly's turn 'em back
to me and I'll hold 'em until Jude catches up.' He made moving
animals in the dark seem mere mechanics.

Not being named, Una, the youngest, looked to her mother who
squeezed her hand.

''Tisn't right light yet,' Mamie said, but without conviction, as
though day and night were in her husband's authority, and she was
only wondering. Pat was already tramping ahead out the yard, Jude
swiftly following, and Mary him.

They were not alone in this. In that between-time, neither
night nor day, the parish was already moving with small armies of

drovers, men and women, old and young alike conscripted into stick-in-hand troops whose mission was clear and who had primacy over school-time because the fair was a parish fundament since before the school was built.

Jude and Mary went without words. He was faster, but she was even. Their mother was right, it was not yet dawn; the dark, at first absolute as they left the yard, was layered, like cloths, thinning here, thickening there. Clouds came and went from attending their moon. When she showed, the waters of the river peaked with small lights, the stars like scales in a fisherman's net. Then the clouds came again, and river and land alike were folded back into the dark, as if without light they did not exist, or in the night had been taken elsewhere, and only now, in the coming dawn, would they be forced to return.

Next to Talty's, Quinlan's farm was poor land. All of it in need of care, the long battle to stop it turning back into mud and rushes lost and the estuary licking its lips at the prospect of victory. The way up to it was not a public road but a rutted cart-way of rough gravel, pocked with puddles.

Jude didn't wait for his sister. He ran, in boots trampy but still swift. Ahead of her on his own, he clicked his tongue, making the sound of a picture-house horse as well as riding it, in a boy's way burnishing the chore to adventure. He was of an age to think it childish, and an age to still want to do it. He could have gathered the cattle without Mary, he did not look back or wait for her, unaware that she idolised him.

When she caught up with him, he was untying the gate into the field they still called the Bog Meadow. It was an iron gate made by Tommy-the-smith's father's father at the forge in the village and would outlive them all. By a hairy rope it was tied, not hinged, to the gatepost, had to be lifted to be opened. He took it two-handed, Mary further back furrowing her brow with an effort Jude didn't notice. Inside was the apron of muck where, in the daylight, the cattle would stand waiting for erratic deliveries of hay. If Jude called out, the older animals would start to come. But, for the fair, only the yearlings were to be brought down.

In other farms these would have been separated the day before, but the day before Pat Quinlan had gone to the village for a message and not returned before bedtime, Jude writing the Norman invasion into his copybook and all the while waiting for his mother's *Will you go for your father?* She wouldn't say *To Craven's.* He had done it often enough to know. He could not remember being placed on the bar counter as an infant but had been told. He could not remember the Michaelmas fair when the drink undressed Pat Quinlan's reason and he had crowed he could throw his son as high as Ryan's house. *Bet you I can catch him. What do you bet? What do you bet I can?* Not the flight from his father's arms up through the blue air, not the crocheted coverlet falling away, the inbreath of the crowd, the apex of ascent when, for a single instant, he must have known the aerial ecstasy of souls, not that, not the escape from being earthbound, nor the engagement of gravity, then the retraction, the heavens pulling away, and the plummet, the fall faster than the rise, and faster still, a lance of sunlight, bad luck to it, blinding Pat Quinlan's catch, and the baby landing not in his arms, but crash, against his shoulder, and bang, down on to the pavement, not the gasp, the reflex signs of the cross, nor his father's *He's grand, he's grand* as he quickly gathered the infant up, could Jude Quinlan recall. He could not recall being brought by jostling horse and car at speed up the gravel avenue to Avalon House, from the cracked shell of his skull the blood outlining his father's fingers, not the hammer on the brass knocker, the anguished cry, *For the love of God, open the door!,* the white-shirted figure of Doctor Troy taking tempered stock of catastrophe, not even his eyes asking what happened but cradling the infant against that white shirt and walking away from a stout-sunk Pat Quinlan down the cool of the hallway to the surgery, not the days after when the balance of his life was the lead story in Faha, when he was prayed for in the church and in homes throughout, offerings made in penny candles and all the saints called upon for intercession. None of this could Jude Quinlan remember, but he had been told.

He was the boy the saints had saved.

He was also a boy who knew the full dimension of his father's nature. He had been with him when Pat Quinlan wept over a new calf that died in his arms, as well as the time he thrashed the backside of an old Friesian that wouldn't come up out of a boghole, strafing the black hide at close range until the blood rose crimson in parallel lines and the cow moaned a last time and dropped her head into the water. He had witnessed him, fired-up, flush-faced and expounding on the Thursday nights in Dan Carey's, an informal out-the-country convention for those who failed to make the cut for Prendergast's parlour, a free-for-all of contrary opinion and independent thought that had no women members, the wives both giving their husbands standing and taking the trousers off them, by calling it 'The Dail'. *Oh, he's above in the Dail* a Faha shorthand for useless. At the keen, heady, smoke-filled gambles of Forty-Five, Jude Quinlan had seen his father lit with wild gaiety when for once the cards came right, heard him sing 'Spancilhill' to an entranced crowd, watched for the tipping-point that could come at any moment, had secretly finished his pint for him so his father might come home at last, *You little thief you*, the big hand tousling his hair with a buckled pride. *Two more pints for the men so!* He had known the darkness that descended without warning, the snuffed candle of his father with not a glimmer of life, no word to say but a bad one, the growl of his disappointment and the cuff of his hand if a thing was done wrong. Jude knew all, and though he had not the words to say so and would only realise it eight years and six thousand miles away, the large, twisted response inside him when he thought of his father was in fact love without condition.

The evening before the fair, in lined copybooks, the Norman invasion was contained, an *aiste* on *Daidí na Nollaig* written, by hard labour six sums of long division solved, and still Pat Quinlan had not come home. His mother put his sisters to bed, and when she came out and took up the needles of the next jumper to be knitted against the clock of Christmas, she did not tell Jude to go get him. She told him to read his book, blinking as if under blows, and then looking only at the row of purl and surrendering to the lot of the hopeless, knowing that until the doors were closed Pat would be drinking the money he hadn't made yet from the Christmas Fair.

So, Quinlan's herd had remained undivided until the dawn.

The gate opened; the children separated. By a lieutenant's look, Mary let her brother know he did not need to tell her what to do and went along the western bounds below-side the stand of blackthorns where the cattle nightly sheltered. With the aim of getting above-side them, Jude took the eastern way, both brother and sister going with the intent of being invisibles, and next to the animals before the animals knew they were there. Both ways were rushways, the wet spires painting their legs with cold. Where the rushes gave up, the brambles took over, what the cattle ate or why God let thorns thrive unknown.

With each moment, the sky changed. In one, as Jude ran, the stars were bumping off a black-blue screen. In the next, the stars had been taken in, the whole of the east towards Limerick a commotion of charcoal, taupe and grey that swirled in mingle, as though a liquid light had been poured into a darker substance and you could not say if night or day would emerge. All lending substance to those who since before Christ had watched the December sky for portents.

As the dawn rose, the estuary established the coastline of Kerry, but not yet the mountains beyond. Seabirds, crying the coming rain, made the first sounds of day.

In the Bog Meadow the cattle appeared first as horned darknesses, standing in their made muck under the thorn bushes, as if modelling for figurines to attend with Magi. With the silence of a spirit, Jude had come above them without notice and he could make out the younger animals from the old. He could not see Mary, but he knew she was there. The yearlings were wild, and the surprise could stampede them. Everything in Jude tightened. He was not like those boys, some no more than six, who cavaliered among cattle. He had history and was careful. He came forward with fierce stealth, one step and then another, squelch of boot and haw of breath both reveals.

He was slow until swift, at the last moment coming in between the yearlings and the older animals with a raised shout and an air of command. To force the division, the sally in the air and his other arm out to make himself larger than a human boy.

Out of their dreaming, the animals started. The young took off in haunch-kicks and leaps, flying muck and puddle in a bucking charge without aim or direction other than to get away down the dark. The cows trotted, their elders' quickstep slowed by the swaying burden of slack udders, and Jude was able to run ahead to turn them back up the land with accomplished ease. They had no further part in the day.

He ran then after the beasts that were gone into the dark. He could hear Mary's *hups!* and tracked them across the hoof-holed river-ground, his step sucking and splashing.

In the middle of the field the ground sank, as though the land was surrendering by seepage to the sea underneath. It was the bog of the Bog Meadow. Here was the last place they wanted the cattle to be, but here they were, shifting, snorting, turning about their options in a mire softening more by the minute. They knew Jude and Mary were there now, knew too that they were being herded down the slope that led to the gate, but because for the wild there were no imperatives, no leading, nor gates, there they would not go.

The cattle could as easily turn and charge back up the land as go forward, could as easily charge either of the children for no reason other than outraged dignity.

'Easy now,' Jude said, coming closer. He was saying it to himself as much as to his sister, who was on the far side, and echoed, 'Easy now.'

They had moments only. Their father's dictum was if you gave a beast its head you were lost.

Light was leaking into the sky, the country an emerging paling of greens and greys, and in that dawn tableau two children, above and below a shifting stand of frisky young cattle.

Jude looked across to his sister. Her eyes hadn't left him since he appeared out of the dark. How well she had done to get the cattle this far and hold them until he came, he forgot to acknowledge, and she didn't ask, her face grave and focused under the distinction of being his deputy. With a nod, he signalled they would move in together, one step at a time, arms outstretched, and they did, walking two sides of a triangle towards the cattle in the hope that if they went slow and easy enough the animals would take their lead and maybe walk on out the gate. 'Easy now,' Jude said, by way of prompt and direction.

And the cattle took both.

For a good five seconds.

For a good five seconds they moved towards the open gate.

Then Mary raised her stick just slightly, just into the eyeline of a thickset and horned bullock, and at once he jostled against another, threw a kick, and took off, setting off the others, all of them stirred and wild and charging now down the field.

They raced down to the gate, not because they ceded defeat or understood intention, they raced down to it because the land went that way, and as well that way as another. They raced right down to the open gate, at the last minute passing not out but right by it, and back up the land in a hot-blood mix of bucking terror and glee, the hunt party heading back up after them.

'They're as wild,' Jude said, by way of letting Mary know he did not blame her.

'They're as wild,' she said.

At the next pass, one of the cattle tried to leave the field not through the gate but through the wire, breasting between the fenceposts that were footed in ground mostly river and which came away without protest, one two three, like that, as the animal charged onward, wearing now a necklace of barbed wire and posts, getting a good fifteen yards in a dressing of bloody boundary without appearing to notice.

With each minute, the delay was costing time at the fair. Jude and Mary knew it. They went back up the land three times, each time starting again, and postponing the dispute of all children as to whose fault it was that time.

At last, the baulking of the cattle was defeated not so much by droving as by their own curiosity of life on the road, and on the fourth try they herded out the gate in a hurry to a literal who-knows-where, Jude and Mary running behind with a mixed air of both victory and train.

Once out the gate, the cattle could not be slowed, were a force funnelled by ditches and stone walls, running free until they came to Mamie Quinlan in headscarf and farm coat with Una at her side and waving a stick to turn them over the road, towards the living signpost of Pat at the next cross.

Once the cattle passed, Mamie and the girls could go back and close the gate, school and the day to be got on with. Only Jude would go to the fair with his father.

'Now,' his mother said. She looked at him for the last time in the grey light, the red Aran jumper she had knitted too small in the sleeves now, the whole of him stretching out of the child he had been. It was both a blessing and a loss to her. She reached over and gave a tug to one sleeve with small effect, then the other. 'Did you comb your hair?' required no answer.

'I could go with them,' Mary said.

'You'll go to school.'

'They might need me.'

'You'll go to school.'

'You're too bright for cattle,' said Jude, by way of acknowledging a sister who read everything that came into the house. His smile dissolved her objection. 'Thanks though.'

Mamie hadn't taken her eyes from him. There, in the narrow road with the morning coming over it, she held him in a look that needed no translation. It was *Mind yourself*, it was *God bless*, but above both of these it was *Bring your father home*, and Jude heard each, and more. He knew the same as she that at every fair Pat Quinlan went with sworn vows to return directly and with a ball of money, that he always went with high hopes and always came back with the bad news of a mean crowd, low prices and a base world out to best him. The evening of a fair, to repair his losses he would be drawn into gambles, the cards not coming right either, one time losing a legacy of his uncle's and not returning for three nights, when he gave his word, next time would be better. Jude knew, and Mamie knew, and no words were needed.

When, in a helpless reflex, his mother brought her fingertips to her tongue and pushed across the limp hair that curved across his forehead, Jude pulled back with a 'Mammy!' that sounded appalled but wasn't.

'Go on so,' she said, adding a 'Be good' as he was already running off down the road the cattle had gone. He did not look back, and at the turning was gone from them.

***

Alone, Jude ran. He ran with the pleasure of his own propulsion. In the Master's school there were already nine Ronnie Delaneys, boys who since the heroics of the Melbourne Olympics had fallen in thrall to the simplicity and beauty of natural speed, and the idea that an Irishman could beat the world. They were athletes fuelled by imagination, some with vocational devotion counting laps and seconds, others who did their own radio commentary, but all overtaking invisible competitors from many countries as they took the tape. They were boys who ran to school and back again, who ran in the schoolyard for the duration of the Small *Sos* and Big *Sos*, who ran up to touch the wall and back again, and back again, inside that confine unstopping until the ringing of the handbell. With a kind of breathless fidelity to excellence, there were boys fleet and eternal, who ran barefoot, ran without strategy, know-how or training, ran for gold medals unsmelted and imaginary, but more, because when they ran they were free. Jude Quinlan was one of these.

That morning he ran at breakneck and caught up with his father in the time they call no-time.

The old man was following the cattle at a marching pace. He was all business. He showed no sign of waiting for his son or that without him the enterprise would fail.

'Did ye have trouble?'

'No.'

That was all their talk, and for a time they went on in the wake of the beasts, silent and solemn, the sky all the time evidencing the existence of time and the mercy of creation by a thin but constant lightening, the day that was coming still young but in the old year a pale kind.

Clouds the colour of new welding appeared, heavily made, apprentice-work, in shapes unshapen like vapour. Father and son were travelling along by the river on a road mostly bends and without mark of change but for the electricity poles that to western gales had surrendered the perpendicular, some tilting to ten o'clock, one in the swamp of Skelly's near enough nine, so they had an air of the temporary and were the first cause of the blackouts that in Faha were now the custom of winter.

***

In the elbows of the road, they lost sight of their cattle, walking on the trail of tramped ditch grass and broken bramble, the spasmed dropping of fluid dungs that were the signature of an animals' day out. But they showed no panic. For close on two miles of road there was no cross.

Father and son marched on. They marched the same way Pat Quinlan had marched to the same fair with his father, and his with his, and his too, back along into the rain that was falling on that road two hundred and more years ago. From time to time they heard the noising of a tractor, or the distant cries of children and men at the business of herding. They passed Hayes's place where, stirred by the travelling cattle, the horses ran as one, like something feathered in wind. They passed Mick Heaney standing in a gap, and Sorley, the grandfather of the Fennells, who had lost his walk but in cap and tartan blanket was set astride a donkey with a switch to play his part in turning their cattle towards Faha. From both, they got greetings and good lucks, and Pat gave them back, taking from both, who knows how, the inference that today was going to be his lucky day.

His son could see it land on him, the same as a white dove. He could feel the fluttering come into him, and when his father clapped his hands together with an 'All right by God', he feared the night's porter still in him and the day's footing already awry. He looked sidelong at him and looked quickly away again. Pat Quinlan's eyes were glitters, his mouth mobile with a smile that was coming and being held off, as though the joke hadn't rightly landed yet.

'We'll do, today. We'll do, today, Jude boy. We'll do for Santy.'

73

When he turned to his son, his face surrendered to a smile. It came through all defences, a helpless happy, curving his closed mouth and playing with his eyebrows.

'Am I right? I'm right!' he asked and answered. Alongside him, his son was touched by the nearness of rapture, for that moment ceding that even the unlikely had limits and maybe it was true, today would be the lucky day.

All of which would return to Jude later that night when the child was in his arms.

An uplift to his chin was Pat Quinlan's signal to let Jude know it was time to get ahead of the herd.

It was a job for light bodies, crossing into a field and cutting across ground to come out over a wall ahead of the cattle, where the objective was to control the stampede, be the embodiment of *whoa!* and, once done, came with the privilege of marching ahead of the herd into Faha with a proprietary air and a captain's cool.

Jude went over Naughton's gate into the Fort Field. In the upper ground was a ringfort that was the place of the fairies, a huge wild thorn tree growing blackly aslant out of a low mounding of grassy stones. In the parish such places retained their lore, stories about them still told, always by the old, and always late into the evening when, cards laid aside and Radio Éireann gone to bed, the *cuaird* was rounding the corner into the next day. The stories were always of place, '*I'll tell you now about the fort above in Griffin's*', and always of people a step or two away, '*This was Mick Honan's mother's second cousin Packie, and he coming home that night from Donnellan's.*' They were told in a tone both wry and real, the tellers landing the tale on the thin line between humour and caution, bringing both a smile and a shiver, a thing not to be thought of, until it was. Jude had heard some from his grandmother, of a fiddler who had disappeared for three days and nights to play for the fairies, a woman who had a child stolen, or a boy led to a bag of silver coins by a music in the air. They were told with consummate craft, the pace and pause of artful delivery, and to the hush that signalled the still honoured place of stories. *Did that really happen?* was never asked.

So now, coming from his father's forecast of good luck, as he ran across the field towards Naughton's fort, Jude had an urge to seek help there. It was nonsense, a *seafoid* he would not have admitted or said aloud, but because he was on the rope-bridge between man and boy, the world had a sway in it and the answer to if he believed in spirits was both no and maybe.

He ran, a flash of red jumper crossing the wet grey grass. His way was a wide arc, clear of the cattle's peripherals and only to come back towards the road when he was well ahead and could see their heads above the brambles at Breen's. That arc now he broke, his eyes on the thorn tree and his feet taking him towards it in a way that appeared decisive without the known making of a decision.

None but the birds could see him, and he ran towards the fairy fort like a dawn messenger, attesting to nothing as much as the desperation of hope. What good luck consisted of he had no formulation, no catalogue or listing for what exactly their family needed, but in the clear reasoning of a corkscrew logic, if the fairies existed, then the fairies knew.

He ran towards the fort as though it were a destination and on arrival all depended. He ran quicker than his mind could ask *Why?*, the fairy tree that burst white in Maytime looming against the heavens in the charcoal of a demented line-drawing, all thorns and quarrels, and, beyond, the grey floor of the river sweeping time away.

In thrall to the thrill of his own speed, he approached the bounds of the fort with his heart racing and the ghost of his breath short-living on air not cold enough for snow.

He would run up to the mounded bounds, step inside the fort and say his father's name. That was all. He would say *Pat Quinlan* to send the luck that way, neither believing nor disbelieving but taking the best side of a wager that risked nothing, and be gone before the fairies looked up from their breakfast.

That was as near intention as he got. It formulated between the course of his blood and the pump of his legs. It was what he planned as he came through the gaps of the gorse, from night-traffic each bush wearing the intricacies of webs, pearled or translucent, and together acting as portcullis to faery-world. He would ask the fairies for good luck at the fair today, neither specifying nor demanding what that would be, for it was his understanding that fairies often answered on their own frequency, the same way God did prayers.

Jude ran through the gaps and up to the very lip of the fort.

Then, without breaking stride, he ran straight past. He did not say his father's name, nor ask for the luck to come their way, at the last moment reneging on a plan that now seemed child-ish nonsense, fortune and fairies nothing, and which Jude would forget, until later that night when he would be back there to beg the supernaturals to look his way.

***

In Faha, the fair was without fairground. By a decree neither writ-ten nor judicial, the village itself became the open-air marketplace, and once a month each fair day, from early morning until past midnight, the animals took over Church and Main streets, stand-ing in corrals without bounds with the air of ones looking to see what you had done with the place. The set-up operated on a first-come basis and the best spots were always taken before the daylight broke. Some, their animals still on round-up, sent their children ahead as stand-ins, a tactic that smelled of cheating and gave rise to various skirmishes and fallings-out, some out-living the individual parties for years and leaving the sour taste that in the parish came under the general judgement: *Pure ignorant*.

With their splayed look of welcome in the centre of the village, the church gates had long proved the prime locus for trade. In the Parochial House this was a longstanding cause for chagrin, and in his first year Father Coffey had been delegated to ask the farmers not to set up there. He was unaware it was a perennial question, or that when Father Tom looked up from the spreading of his marma-lade and said, 'Do, you ask them,' he was partaking of an innocent mischief, a kind familiar to all backwater parishes where the chal-lenge of everyday is how to put down the time. 'You ask them not to stand their cattle there.'

As it happened, the curate's appeal fell on deaf ears, but he took some satisfaction when he was able to negotiate a treaty whereby Mick Lynch promised a rope corridor to let the daily Mass-goers through. As a goodwill gesture, Lynch said, the farmers would take their dung with them when they left, which Father Coffey reported back to the Canon, unaware it was a joke until the older priest put the hand across his laugh to stop his teeth flying.

Before the following month's fair, the curate went back to try again. This time he had a firmer standing and the secret advantage of knowing one day Lynch would be kneeling in front of him.

Mick Lynch had the walk of a man who owned his own bull. Short and broad, he carried a blackthorn, wore a frieze coat and low hat with red feather in the band. That hat never came off his head outside of church. He wore it at the counter in Ryan's, in the spartan confines of his iron bed, and when he went to wring the necks of geese. From victories in cards or trade, Lynch took a deal of pleasure. With a contrary nature, his cheeks were where the most of his hair grew, furred sideburns made key-shaped by the shaving of his chin which gave him a jailor's look. Lynch had the reputation of being what Faha called *a right cool man*, a designation that pre-dated refrigeration, meant he could not be hurried or ruffled, and once, when asked by a dealer, 'What are you looking for in a horse, boss?' had delivered the incontestable answer, 'Leg in each corner.' He had not married. For women he hadn't the handbook, he said, and children nothing but hosts to headlice and worms.

In a routine rain that didn't merit mention, the cattle spread down the village in a horned and heaving mass, the line between one farmer's animals and the next indistinguishable but for the fact that each knew their own by sight. When Jude walked into Faha ahead of the small Quinlan herd, the sought spots were taken. After Lynch's, down the eastern side were the jostling cattle of Crowley, Carmody, Murray and Fennell. Heading to the cross, in lesser groupings, were the sometimes three, maybe four beasts that constituted the offering of what were designated small farmers.

That Christmas Fair of 1962, there was only one female farmer. She was a Morrissey, Delia May, the kind of earthy woman irresistible to airy men. She had married a dosey called Donal, who had the name of being useless in all departments but one: Delia May had twelve children. She was fine-looking, which was Faha for beautiful, had married into thirty-two acres of scrub, but by the time Morrissey Four was in Three's boots the place was already like a new pin. With a husband who had a strong antipathy to getting wet, *You'd catch your death*, Delia May was the one who hunted the cattle, pulled the calves, delivered the doses, repaired the stone walls and strung the fences, often with one infant tied on to her, another in handed-down brother's or sister's clothes clinging alongside. It was a life that in the parish eventually won respect because, even after Death caught Donal, Delia Morrissey never complained. Her cows had the name of mighty milkers, she could curse as good as any man, and was awarded Faha's highest accolade, *A Trojan worker*. As Sonny Cooney said of her, 'You could learn more from women than just putting down the toilet seat.'

Here, in a narrow spot next to her in front of Mohill's shop, Jude landed the animals. His father came in behind.

The four miles of walking were in Pat's face, a florid purpling at the nose and eyes wet. Coming through the village, he had greeted many already in place by nod or name, actions of a camaraderie that didn't exist, but confirming his character, *That's Pat Quinlan*. Passing Lynch, he had given no wave, but called out to the cattle, commanding where none was needed but making the show all the same. When Jude turned the animals in alongside Morrissey's they were stirred and lively and when his father came next to them, he saw he was the same. It was inevitable. In a life where each day masqueraded as ordinary, fair days had the feel of theatre, but without the safety net of being make-believe. The breaths of men and beasts pluming in the street in the first of the morning, the greetings and small talk, a sharp command to cattle over here, a shushing over there, the dogs that barked and those that tracked by nose to the windows of Ryan's butchers, the shift and jostle, studied closeness and edged anticipation, all constituted the custom of the fair day and in Faha had the translated air of an orchestra tuning up.

In Jude's father this took the form of a look and manner. The look was gleamy, the manner exaggerated congeniality and the helpless animation that came from being in the company of trousered banknotes. This morning it included the sudden snapping of his fingers without purpose and the taking off and putting back on of his cap to relieve the bursting of his head. All of it, Jude dreaded.

'Delia May,' Pat said, eyes flashing and grin breaking, as though he was raptured in the happenstance of neighbour, and she too was a sign today was the day.

'Shite morning,' Delia said.

As though of a sudden his head larger, Pat lifted the cap and looked into it, put it back on again. He clicked his fingers. 'You know Jude of course?'

'I do. Jude.'

Jude nodded at his name, but he was watching the guard coming past McCarthy's.

Each month, Mrs Prendergast, with the eminence of a state office and vocation to preserve civilisation, insisted Guard Greavy make the pass to inspect that the footpaths were kept clear. All knew it was window-dressing for a directive that wouldn't be followed, the cattle back up on the footpaths before Greavy had adjourned to the barracks.

There was no fair day in Faha that did not leave the village in disarray, a littered debris the human handprint, and smears of dung three feet high along the walls. It made no odds. In a place whose history began the day after The Deluge, the fair came with the confidence of its own primacy. For it, even death had to be postponed. There could be no funerals on fair days.

Greavy had gone into the guards for the common reason: the pension at the end of service. Mostly jowl, he gave living substance to the weight of the law, with polished boots that could sing and silver buttons under a pressure not measured in pascals. Slowly, he came up the centre of Church Street in a routine patrol that established the existence of order and said the same thing to every third farmer.

'You'll keep them off the footpath.'

'I don't know, will we Jude?' Pat Quinlan said when his turn came, an attitude without substance, but enjoying the extra inch of the posture. He turned from the guard to his son, as though the decision was his, and Jude saw the wild look, something hectic inside trying to find a way out. Jude hadn't the lines for his part; he gave no answer but moved in alongside the animals that had only just settled.

'Now, Pat.' The jowls lifted and lowered, but the guard said nothing more. Greavy had known Pat Quinlan for fifteen years, drank along the counter from him in Craven's, played cards with him, had seen him in both polarities of his person, morose and lit, but for a finish adjudged him something like Dunne's dog without the licence, harmless enough.

'Would you ever go and shite?' Delia May said.

She was a woman Greavy was afraid of; he just could not look at her. He said nothing, turning away with that measure of forbearance required of authority, living proof that laying down the law was a heavy business. He went three places along, calling out 'Animals off the footpath!' in basso profundo as he passed the post office, with temporary effect on the fair but with the aim of securing once more the Christmas box Mrs P always dropped at the barracks.

'Isn't he one prize-winning bollocks?' Delia said to Jude. Her hair was a waterfall of brown waves, her hands large. From a life whose blessings came in disguise, her brown eyes had a chary look, but at Jude she smiled.

'Get 'em back up,' his father said. He clicked his fingers quickly, on a beat, like Joe Diddle, who had a ceili band playing inside his head.

From a confusion of contrary commands, the animals shifted; one bullock broke and spun, pushing past Pat like he was a figment, and heading for the open ground of Church Street until Tim-Tom stepped out in front of it, arms cruciform, making a living boundary that turned the bullock back and restored order.

Before the morning was rightly made, in open stalls without wall or roof the whole of the upper end of the village was filled with animals. Latecomers, from baulky cattle or clocks unwound, arrived with a look of dragged-through-bushes-backwards, and fitted their animals into gaps where none existed. Life its own excuse, there were no apologies or explanations. Soon enough Faha settled into the shifting stirring look of a fair no different from those before, only with the turkey- and geese-sellers further down, their horseboxes and carts packed tight, feathers escaping, and an imprisoned gobble and honk making the music of Christmas.

***

At all markets, for the seller, the action of anticipation is a tensing one, and Pat Quinlan showed it from his fingertips to his eyes. Here, he was a different version of himself. Although they lived only three miles distant, when he came into company and had concrete underfoot, he rose a little. Jude had seen it happen. His father pushed his shoulders back, gave a straightening tug to the front of his coat, held his chin at a cocked angle that refuted the crushing of circumstance. Though in the same creased clothes and toe-scuffed boots in which he had walked from home, sweat uncooled and the drink of last night still travelling inside his skin, he took from the fair air a cue of occasion and soon enough had something of the bearing of a king in a kingdom of one. It was a stellar performance, and one which grew by the minute. Throughout the day it would elaborate, starting with the small rise, the cock of his chin, soon enough growing a deigning manner, a mask of disinterest, that he was not there to sell anything, money a thing of nothing to him, was there only to fondly regard poor misfortunes at the squalid business of turning animal flesh into coin. It was a performance of dignity where none was felt, and, when he had the drop taken, so good it convinced himself. To any who would pause to consider his cattle, Pat Quinlan would give them no encouragement, might walk away down the street at the very moment another would step forward, in a wild gambit that was all the time daring God to show Himself.

Jude had seen it before, and though he feared his father falling off the stage, he was not a little awed by it.

'Today's our day,' Pat said, his eyes flicking up the way towards Lynch, and away again, fingers clicking.

'That right?' said Delia May, taking the cigarette from her lips and looking up to see if there were pigs flying.

'You don't believe me, but you'll see. You'll see. By God you will.'

As though the godsend had already arrived, Pat pushed back the flap of his coat, two-fingered his trouser pocket, and took out a sixpence. He had never paid his son for droving cattle or otherwise acknowledged that he was part of the enterprise. There was no call for it, Pat would have said, weren't they family? So, the silver coin with the wolfhound was a startling thing, held out between two fingers not so much a wage as a ratification of standing, and Jude was touched by it.

Knowing they were a family without finances, Jude shook his head, and with a force not intended, said, 'I don't need it.'

It was a momentary stand-off. One-eyed under a cloud of an ambrosial Sweet Afton, Delia May was watching. Pat Quinlan twisted a crooked smile, the lip lifting some, as though by an ugliness hooked.

And in that moment, in the look of his father's eyes, part-sheep part-lion, Jude understood his father wanted him out of the way, that though up to then he was critical, now he was a reminder of desperate circumstance, a hindrance to performance, the sixpence a bribe, and a translated *Get lost.*

Pat Quinlan gave the coin a coaxing jerk, the way you might a carrot to a horse refusing, and, making his meaning clearer, said, 'Get a haircut.'

***

That December morning, Church Street was heaving with animals by the time the lid had been lifted on the day. To get first dibs, dealers and jobbers from Limerick and Tipperary had arrived the night before. A clientele without a happence of couth, they stayed in various places in and about the village, private dwelling houses that once a month became amateur hotels. In Faha, hospitality was a female attribute, as was the knowledge of what it cost to live, and so Mrs Brogan, Mai Toal, Bid Healy, Mrs O Grady and Betsy Breen all did bed-and-board. As too did the Mohill sisters.

Two tiny women of redoubtable character, Philo and Gertie Mohill ran the cheapest establishment, sandwiched in what was once an alley between Ryan's and McCarthy's. It said 'Mohill' above it, after Mick Mohill, deceased, and recalled his character by looking like it had been thrown up overnight. The whole of the interior was without a straight line, each wall only meeting by the obligation for a ceiling. Under the sisters' jurisdiction, it was decorous and compact, with a tangible air of fierce endeavour. In here Philo and Gertie sold stuck-together sweets, shards of toffee, dusty chocolates, cream, pink and yellow bars, and geometric shards of bright-coloured stickiness without name or wrapper, dips from a jar of fizz, single cigarettes, half-cigarettes and damp matches that would strike if you kept them a day beside the fire. They took in sewing, darning and what have you, offering a compendium of services that expanded by necessity, and by stratagems wily and many devolving a way for single women to support themselves.

When the cattle dealers came the night before the fair day, the sisters converted every possible space to sleeping quarters, then rented out their own bed and slept in the front room in two armchairs under horsehair blankets, stoppered jars of hot water for company.

There were eight residents in Mohill's the night before the fair. They were all called Mister.

None of them, it would be recalled later, either came with, sought out or otherwise referenced any two-legged female, nor did any make mention of a newborn.

Once the barons had sleeved the breakfast from their chins (only remembering the napkins when upon standing they fell to the floor) and had gone outside to take a first gander, Philo and Gertie commandeered the room inside the back door and set it up as the fair day barbershop for the visiting scissors of The O Siochru.

Faha had a barber, Jack, but the shilling he charged for the short-back-and-sides was undercut on fair days by The O Siochru, who knew that in matters of commerce footfall beat margins. A North Kerryman without Christian name or known age, The O Siochru had been cutting hair for the most of the century. His first custom-ers were the dead. During the War of Independence there was a

83

share of shot martyrs, and, laying out on trestles and tables in the glamouring candles, an imperative that they should look their best going out the door of this life. Not everyone can barber a corpse, but The O Siochru had no squeam. He travelled from fair to fair by horse and car, with pipe and perspicacious dog, going about the western places in the manner of one who hadn't been told modern times had come.

After a negotiation that concluded along the lines of a penny from each head cut, Philo found the chair that would sit inside the back door and give birth to one of the looks of fair day, men's locks brown, black and silver swept into the air from Mohill's and transiting towards the river like the shed feathers of passing cherubim.

At the time, in all boys, getting your hair cut was a dreaded thing.

Jude's hair was brown and straight. In a lank loop across his forehead a lock fell. It was the one his mother always pushed aside, in a gesture he wouldn't admit to liking until long after, when, in Fort Polk, Louisiana, a buzzcut would make uniform his look, and Faha would take on the unreality of all made-up places.

Jude Quinlan wanted no haircut. But in the run-up to Christmas all the male heads of the parish would be shorn. There was no escaping. Though the lessening of hair when the days were at their coldest would defy common sense, logic always took a backstep for the birthday of Jesus.

When Jude came around to the back door of Mohill's there was already a line of men smoking by the wall. Heard but not seen, the soft clicking of The O Siochru's scissors was a pianissimo that made clear the instrument was in the hands of a maestro. In Faha, the universal review was always *Scalped, by God.* But to men used to slashing briars, the shorn look had local standing. The O Siochru didn't ask for opinions or listen to critics. He had only the one question: *Rum?* To which the answer was never no, for he was already reaching for the bottle of the clouded amber that had the name of that Jamaican liquor and may have had a passing acquaintance, for when The O Siochru smacked it on his palms in preparation for application the backroom of Mohill's had the eye-widening pungency of a nectarial Caribbean.

There now, Gertie would say, coming forward with the oval mirror with the porcelain handle. And with the sweetness of her smile, and the truth that men believe they are better-looking once women tell them they are, even those with the bald lumpish heads of last year's potatoes had a handsome moment.

All of which added to the wound-up sense of the day, and the focused completeness with which it entered Jude Quinlan's memory.

He stood at the back of the line of men, holding the sixpence. On the river two pilot boats were leading larger vessels, a wake of seabirds crying. These too he would remember, because although he was aware it was a kind of madness to believe it, he would come to think that in that day maybe every ordinary thing was a sign.

Gertie Mohill came out the back door and considered the numbers. She was wearing a yellow dress of her sister's making and a cardigan of pale cable knit that pocketed her hands. She came down the line with an apologetic look, as though the popularity of custom was her fault, and when she stopped alongside Jude, he looked at her eyes and had a sensation he couldn't explain but was to do with being in the company of a sadness without end.

'You might come back later?' Gertie said. 'If you wouldn't mind?'

'No. I will.'

He turned on his heel and walked away, her 'Thank you' behind him, but something of her coming with him too, the way a prayer might.

He could not return to his father, went instead past the rear of shops and houses and out into the lower part of Church Street.

He was a boy, unremarked; if called upon he'd help any, and be glad of it, but mostly he was on his own, silent, standing, walking on a bit, standing again. Over his imagination the Christmas Fair had a mesmeric hold. He watched all, not only for the ticketless performances of buyer and seller, but also because the thing his father had said he had said with such conviction that some element of it had stuck to his son. *Today's the day.*

And why not? Why was it not possible? Surely one day it could be true, and if so, why not today?

Jude moved on.

At the crossroads, the fair changed its clothes and character. In the wide street that nobody called Main, the hawkers set up a separate kingdom. Landed like a circus, it wore the splash of colour and didn't smell like cattle. There were no animals down this street, the telephone box the divider, before the sundry of set-ups – some with awnings, with riggings, tarps, roped-off parallelograms, tables of saw-horses, clothes-horses, washing lines with goods pegged, benches and forms of all kinds – announced the terrain of the travelling traders and a display of wares too various to be numbered. This was a kingdom of criers, pitchers, suitors of sales, self-contained theatres of one, mongers and merchants who made up for the absence of a premises by a magic of language, for they were those who, in the shorthand for making actual the impossible, could talk the hind legs off a donkey.

In the rain that could be counted on, sheets of milky plastic sheathed many of the goods, but if you only inclined your head the sheet would be lifted pronto. Taffe had two children to do it. Like pale birds, they rose the covering in unison at the very moment curiosity peaked, raindrops rivering sideways as their father began with, *Mighty bargains today, missus*, while trying to follow where her eye had landed.

Down this street, the fair was slower to start, the customers a slow parade of women who came after the jobs were done and the children in school. They came in their good coats and headscarves and handbags large enough to carry a small child, came neither wide-eyed nor eager, following the original directive: there was no harm in looking.

The hawkers were a composite collection of the miscellaneous, or what could be found in the bottom of life's pockets. The judgement of the parish was that they were a tribe of melted rogues, but from a history of harmlessness and longstanding they had become part of the furniture of the fair. The same ones came year after year. Living a life without borders, on the road that never ended, they had a worn-out glamour and achieved an ageless air by already looking old when they were young. There were men and women both. On the principle that all business was show-business, some men wore hats of character, feathered or banded, suits of hues and cuts not on the hangers in town. Some wore an earring, bandana or the baggy and striped pants of Persians, were of a complexion Faha adjudged Spanish, had eyelashes of exquisite fineness or the one flashing gold tooth. Many had the godlike gift of remembering the names of their customers in each village. Some could go further and recall the children, what illnesses attended the family, would ask after an aged grandmother and by a show of care open the leather lips of a woman's purse. There was Noone the knife-sharpener, who looked like Douglas Fairbanks in *The Corsican Brothers*; McGreal, the pots-and-pans man, wire wool extra; a Dodd from the north who sold brushes, and his own version of Chimno, Soot-Go he called it; Mrs Peggy who sold men's underpants three-in-the-pack, and socks, five-in-the pack, all grey, *Good enough to wear to your own funeral,* neither of which were bought by men, whose socks and underpants never surrendered, but by wives and mammies who had seen the toenail and blast damage. There was a trader who sold nothing but turps until the electricity came, when he branched out to fuses; a man with suits of clothes, *I got them for next to nothing, selling them for half that;* a woman with wool; another with outfits on hangers and shoes without shoeboxes; as well as Madame Majella, whose years had not diminished her fecund look: she'd tell fortunes if she had to, but the future was passé now, perfumes and lipsticks a better line, *Christian Door and Channel!*

That December morning, to the ordinary fair was added the spice of Christmas. The pressures of the season had been building since the clocks went backwards. Throughout the parish the puddings were already made, cakes baked and secured under both a marzipan and royal icing that not even the mice could crack. The goose that had the name of Christmas dinner on his head was enjoying an extra fist of meal, uncrowded quarters, and the terminal privileges of those whose days were counted.

That morning the festive imperatives were signalled by, On Special, tall beeswax candles of a shade too yellow for bees. ('The monks feed the bees butter,' MacEvilly's clarification.) The long candles were a must-have, the one in the window on Christmas Eve understood to be the signature of Christian faith, a sign of Not-being-a-Bethlehem and welcoming Joseph and Mary should

87

they be passing. This year, one of the traders had brass-like candle holders that were a step-up from turnips. For the table the same one had a Christmas log made out of plastic, *You'll always have it*, with a lifelike dusting of snow, miniature figurines and three detachable sprigs of holly.

As Jude watched he saw no money change hands. The haggle, at which some women were supreme, had not yet started, a game of looking the character of the early market. If you didn't know better, you'd think it a poor day. In response the marketeers raised their voices a notch, expanded their repertoire of gesticulation and beckoning, confident they had the tripart winning formula of merchandise on your doorstep, things that couldn't be got anywhere else, and which would be gone tomorrow.

In recent times, this last was a feature of weakened standing. The shopkeepers frowned on the merchandise, *You buy cheap, you get cheap* the aspersion Daddy Bourke cast, when the earlier tactic of claiming that none of the wares were legitimate failed to slow the trade. Cheap also failed to be the denigration he thought, and he continued to suffer the shopkeeper's vexation at seeing money and goods changing hands outside his own doors. That, at the clearing-up at the end of the day, some of the traders were seen carrying merchandise in the back door of the shop, that some of the goods would appear soon after in Bourke's, with what seemed a small increase in price, proved the precept that principles are no match for the ringing of the register. In his everyday uniform of pinstripe suit and waistcoat, with white runners for his sore feet, Bourke enjoyed a shrewd month-long smirk, but had the look of his fallen arches when, at the next fair, the hawker they called King Henry cried out, 'Two shillings in Bourke's, get it here for one and six!'

Without the means to make a purchase, but with a boy's yearn to see everything, Jude did not browse. He found places behind stalls or along by the walls and with pretend detachment watched.

He watched the latecomer, Moriarty from Cork, tumble from his red van, opening the back to set up a ramshackle emporium of toys, trinkets and assorted knick-knacks. Moriarty had a winking eye and a reputation for paramours in every place he parked. With tousled curls and a white shirt that wouldn't stay tucked, he had the look of an unmade bed, which Sonny Cooney said accounted for his conquests. Seeing Jude standing, Moriarty summoned him with 'Give me a hand, boy,' kicking out the folding legs on a display table and pointing into the van for what needed carrying.

Jude Quinlan had an accommodating nature but an inveterate shyness. He wanted to help but not step forward, and in this crux was often caught. But Moriarty had a swashbuckling charm and commanding charisma and there was no way to say no to him. Despite being a late-starter, that day he would outsell all, and though he had previously been the prime suspect when Patrick Leary found the lady's knickers in his haybarn, bringing them to Father Tom for what the Canon might glean from them, Moriarty had an unreachable quality that was catnip to women, and the night after every fair his vehicle with the steamed windows would be sighing on its springs out the bog road until the abashed stars withdrew.

Jude had climbed into the back of the van before he had time to come up with an excuse not to. Inside was a small simulacrum of Moriarty's mind: much was shiny, and nothing in the right place. Thrown-in was the sorting method, and a sublime refutation of the laws of physics meant there was always room for more. It was packed to the roof.

'Everything out,' was the shorthand for the set-up, 'except for that,' when Jude reached for the Foxford blanket and feather pillow that were essential components in the machinery of love, both the worse for wear and smelling like mushrooms and Turkish delight. What Jude brought out he was looking at as he went. Cap-guns, silver or black, those that came with holster and belt with the bullets sewn on, those with the outfit as well, Hop-a-long Cassidy or the Lone Ranger leading the way in a cloth that was a cousin of cardboard but came with a sherriff's badge or plastic eye-mask; for the child of a different persuasion, your tomahawk and scalping knife, your bow-and-arrow set, and here, 'That's a Comanche headdress, boy.'

Tracking the native love for all things western, anything Cowboys and Indians beat Robin Hoods. There were toy soldiers, kits for flying gliders, for unflying model aeroplanes. Games of rings, darts with dartboards, skittles in a net, balls, bats, building blocks with letters on them, magician's boxes, compendium sets, stamps for collecting, puzzles and conundrums, rings that couldn't be separated, playing cards, Dinky cars, dolls of one expression but many dresses, and tea sets for tea parties of people littler than your little finger.

All the wares had suffered some from transit and prior hawking. All had been taken out at fairs elsewhere, and put back in again, Faha being on the way to nowhere and getting first dibs at nothing. But they were still wonderful. It did not matter that the packaging was in some places jaded, that cardboard corners were bent, some clips had come off and rubber bands burst. Everything had the virtue of being new to those who bought it, and Santa had a no-returns policy. To the shoppers, a discovered defect was the first step to getting a bargain. Deals and dealing were respected in both directions, and all the traders operated under a strict policy of *caveat emptor*.

For Jude, carrying everything from the van while Moriarty attended to the first of the female customers, it was as close as he would get to handling any of these things. He had no resentment or bitterness. Rather, from nearness to the marvellous something rubbed off on him, he had the light step and lit eyes of the openhearted and a fantastical flash of being Faha's Saint Nicholas.

The other thing, the one that only occurred to him years later when he would recall what happened that day, was that what he was carrying out of the van that December morning was his childhood.

When all was set up, there was no more call for him. Moriarty gave him the winking eye and a 'Thanks boy' in an accent so rich it felt like payment.

Jude stepped away. The street was thronged now. Mattressbankers, who had made end-of-year withdrawals, tried to suppress the look of children who had hammered the piggy bank. Some, coming by car or tractor into a street invented before parking spaces, drove in as far as they could, abandoning their transport when they were nose-to-tail with the lad in front, one blocking the next, and the next, in a barricading of haphazard design that signalled the shut-down of ordinary life.

The noise of the street rose, many-voiced, in the music of congregation. Acquaintances were mutual and threw a wide ambit; besides neighbours and relations immediate, there were cousins, cousins of cousins, cousins of neighbours, cousins of neighbours' cousins, and their cousins, and their neighbours, all of which proved blood was a river without beginning or end. There was no one not related and on the buying side of the stalls no such thing as a stranger. Women who had seen each other yesterday, or the day before, gave free rein to their genius for story, for the moment they met again they discovered there was something they had forgotten to tell. There were small clusters at every stall, turning from the wares and pausing a possible sale under the oldest compulsion of community, spreading the news. In a world where so many facts had turned out to be false, where yesterday's unthinkable was today's *Didn't I tell you?* where even the unreachable moon had been taken down a peg since the Russians crashed a rocket into her face, the line between the actual and the invented had begun to dissolve.

In Faha, comment and commentary too were close cousins, and because for the bit of news the payment was the bit of news back, it was hard to tell who was doing the telling and who the listening. All of which made for a weave of words and the invisible stitchwork by which the parish was held together.

'Senan McInerney, is he living always?'

'He is, you know.'

Conversations had the effect of throwing a cord around the outlying and drawing it in. As Jude went, he walked through loops of them.

'And you know Timmy Cullen sure.'

'I don't I'd say.'

'You do of course.'

'No. No then, I can't place him.'

'You know him. You know Josie Brennan that was Josie Nealon over in Cranny, the cousin of the Meades who married a Murphy woman in Shanacoole.'

'Georgie Meade?'

'That's him.'

'I do.'

'Well, his cousin, Josie Brennan, her niece was married to a Brian Cullen beyond in the sloblands.'

'Brian? Anything to the Cullens in Kildysart?'

'No then. The Cullens in Drumquin. This Brian, he lived in a right hole now, black as the crow's armpit. Nine of them in it for a finish. One of them, Nellie, the dancer. Mighty dancer altogether. She'd go out over you if you weren't holding on. Well, this Brian, his uncle was Timmy.'

'A bad leg.'

'The same.'

'I have him now. Timmy. And what of him?'

'He's after dying.'

Men, between sucks of smoke, sometimes employed a shorthand.

'Don't Marty Kane take great pleasure in himself?'

'He do.'

'The fair in Kilmihil that time. Patjoe Leary lost the eye.'

'He did. Nobody found it either.'

The newly dead and the taken sick are the headliners in all parishes everywhere, and named in the news that morning was the Canon. Since Sunday when he had gone missing, the state of his mind had been the subject of mostly mute conjecture. People didn't like to say. Not only because illness in priests was a no-go area, but because if you told a lie you might have to confess it to himself later. So, *And poor Father Tom* and an answering nod was the most of it.

Without destination other than following his feet, Jude went down the end of the street and left the village by the most common route, into the cemetery. He went through the stile that was the shortcut for the living and along the stone kerbing of the Browne's plot that was pushed up to the wall, like latecomers who just made it in. The graveyard was as old as the parish and had the look of it. A testament to short-sightedness, it had been built too small and in the wrong place. The whole of it fell away towards the river, which was coming for another bit every day. Not unlike the fair, the layout that began linear had since become labyrinthine as the location proved more popular than first supposed, fitting-in-the-dead a game of reversed loaves and fishes, whereby each day more had to go into less.

There were headstones at all angles, the most ancient un-standing slabs having an uncompromising look of a lid, names and history long since eaten by rain and dressed by a verdant moss so vigorous as to seem a cemetery vegetable. The newest gravestones bore the attitude of monuments, in thrall to the belief they would be standing so until the rising of the faithful on the last day.

The place was empty, the kingdom of the Fahaean dead grey. Beyond, the estuary was moving with effort, the water a burden to be eternally borne. What was spitting from the sky was all the same now, for Jude's clothes and boots were not dry and it would be hours before he was home. He went down the way and along the way and across, quiet in himself and careful not to tread on the buried. In olden days, the first church of Faha was here on the eastern side, two walls standing always, three seabirds on the topmost stones attending. The ruin was roofless and smaller than St Cecelia's, its congregation an imagined crush, but it retained a solemn air, and that sense of spirit-yearning in places where prayers were once said, what had been prayed for, what hopes and mercies, intercessions, indulgences plenary and more, not hard to know. Though the prayers were shot into the rain with poor aim, and those who had prayed them long gone, that December morning something of their candles remained.

Between the rain and the river, the light was abluted. The sky had come down, the spectral air of all graveyards doubled by the remove from the fair and the dying of the year. The living were elsewhere. There were gravel-ways, poorly tended, nettles coming up where they could, from frost fringed or spotted black, on those routes to the dead who were without callers. Jude went past the graves of Melicans, Murphys, Killourys, some with remembrances and flowers, some without, some readied for the Christmas visit, others not yet, past the chemists Arnold Gaffney and his wife Annie, past Davitt's who had the son the lawyer in Chicago, Collins's that had one gone out to Australia, another in Collins Street, Hobart, Tasmania, past the musical Hassetts, the mechanical Finucanes, and the Meaneys who had three daughters nuns, to the grave of his Quinlan grandparents, Packie and Mary, and there, next to it, his brother Patrick's.

Patrick Quinlan had died in Faha the day the electricity came. He was twelve years. The day the power was to be switched on in the parish there was to be a class of ribbon-cutting ceremony on a stage erected outside the church gates. All who could would be there for the moment of history without bloodshed when Faha would become current. Flags and banners were already hanging across Church Street, tin whistlers in last rehearsal. Having delayed beyond the patience of Job, against the forecast coming from the wireless and the farmers' talk that the fine weather couldn't hold, Pat Quinlan had knocked a meadow two days before. He'd get the hay saved before the promised rain, no fear of it, he said, in that same voice that was always daring God to prove himself. There'd be no going to see the electric switching on for any Quinlan, not until the work was done.

The whole family was in the Long Meadow for the most of the two days, turning that hay and turning it again, and again too, Pat with shirtsleeves rolled, Mamie with her hair in a headscarf, the two Talty brothers giving the day, forking and lifting, Patrick doing a man's share, Jude and the small ones picking, until in the end there were twenty-seven trams standing and the air flecked with flying gold. When done, Pat planted the hayfork with a *There now* look, as though this time bad luck was beaten, and God was on his side. The first raindrops were just starting.

'I'm going to the village,' the father said. 'My throat is like the desert.'

'Can I go?' Patrick had asked.

'And the cows will milk themselves,' his father said, walking out the gate and leaving the sourness like a spill after him.

Patrick and Jude Quinlan went for the cows. Jude was eight. He can remember nothing that was said. He can remember no moment when he might have seen what was to come. There was only the ordinary mask of every day, plodding up the overgrown road, pushing away flies, pulling a rib of feathered grass and whipping with it. Under a low cloud of resentment, his brother footballed stones. He did not curse their father, as Jude recalled. But he may have. Patrick called to the cows, and they came to the gate before it was opened. He let them out and hupped them on the way they were already going. The weighted gait of milk cows could not be hurried. In their slow passage from the field to the parlour the clock of a possible escape to the village ran out. By the time the jobs would be done the electric switch-on would have happened, the moment of history missed.

The brothers let the cows into the cabin that passed for a milking parlour. They had done it before. There was nothing marked or notable, the same burdened traffic of six animals with a wake of flies coming past the dunghill and in the doorway into the dark. Both brothers followed from the dazzle of the sunlight into the blind cabin. There was one window, its glass long since surrendering transparency to the workings of weather, toil and time, its sill a store-all for bottles and bits that had escaped recall of purpose. The interior light was less than a gloaming, but the cows showed no heed and went to their habitual places, as if by assignment. Under the tin roof, from the fine day the air inside had no air in it. Particles of mixed origin floated. Secured to the wall were loops of chain. These were to keep the animals in place while being milked. They were old and rusted and had been there since their grandfather was a boy.

Patrick went from one animal to the next, drawing the chains and latching them while his brother brought the buckets. Jude was old enough to carry milk, to tip and fill, but nothing more. So, he was standing by, in the silent awe of watching his older brother's efficiency and practice when it happened.

In the times Jude has thought of it since, he has wanted there to be more. He has wanted lead-up, signposting, clues that the terrible was to visit their family, but there were none. There was, if anything, the contrary. From the fine day in the western window came a floating bar of light, and on it travelled particles, minute and burnished, but travelling, from one world into another, all the time happening and all the time unnoticed, except that Jude noticed. By the glazed intensity, with the golden way and its wayfarers, he was briefly arrested, and if there were signs of doom, he missed them. One moment his brother was on the three-legged stool, his head pressed into the side of a young cow making the hard pulse-music of the milk. The next he was standing with the bucket. And the one after that, which was only a breath, which was only the transit of dust and hay on the angled path of the light, the cow pulled away from the wall in a sudden outrage, in one swift move the chain losing its anchoring and the cow swinging around, her head catching Patrick as she turned so he stumbled backwards and fell. His head hit the concrete pier of the stall behind. It made a *crack* that could never be forgotten, and at once Jude vomited. Wearing the chain, the old cow rushed past him and out the door. She went ten feet and stopped and by the dunghill bellowed.

Jude said his brother's name. But Patrick didn't move. He lay in a twist on the cabin floor, the animals breathing about him.

In his memory, it always takes him too long to get to his brother. He stands frozen in the light. He says Patrick's name again, this time softer, as if the name has already left the world and is being recalled in the way of prayers for the departed. And every time there is the same absence. No story, no meaning. Nothing to which you can hold on and by that explain. *This happened*, the all of it. The stillness of the boy on the ground was beyond that of any living. It was not the lull of rest or the breathing stillness of sleep. It was in every possible way *wrong*. That is what Jude understood. When asked, he could not say how long it took for him to come to Patrick's side. It was not that time stopped; it was that sense had left the world. To move, to walk across the cabin, to continue, had no more meaning than the wayward traffic of worms. He stood. It may have been seconds only, or the time it takes for a soul to reach the afterlife. When he came to his brother's side he knelt. Two of the cows turned their chained heads, one, weighted with milk, moaned. He put his hand on Patrick's bare arm; it was warm but had a stillness unearthly and final. The cabin floor was dark. There was a small wet stain behind his brother's head, not a pooling, not a spilling, not enough to contain a life. The blood was only blood where the light showed it red on the litter.

Then Jude was running. He was in the back door and on the step down into the kitchen, trying to say. His mother was feeding the baby in the cushioned *súgán* by the smoulder fire, and from her first looking his words were not needed. The expression in Jude's eyes was enough, and at once she was standing, putting the baby into the wicker cot, telling his sister Mary to mind her, holding the buttons of her dress closed across herself as she followed Jude out the yard to the cabin.

'O Sweet Jesus,' was what she said. She fell to her knees beside her eldest son and lifted his head into her lap and began a rocking that was like a boat sailing that no one else could board. Then Jude was running to Talty's to tell one of the brothers go fetch Pat home.

In the village the ceremony had ended and those inclined were wetting the head of history, running tabs the future would settle. Pat Quinlan had to be drawn away by the sleeve, because 'Can't it wait?' He was told no, it couldn't, the gravity of the tone like a slap sobering him, and, travelling home, he was a graven figure standing in the box of Tim-Tom's tractor, as though the funeral had already happened.

Patrick was laid out on the table in the kitchen. The other Talty brother had carried him in. The doctor and Father Tom were on their way. Three of the neighbours had already gathered, more coming. The pendulum clock on the wall had been stopped, the curtain drawn, and the prayers started. Pat Quinlan didn't say a word. He walked past where Jude was squat on the floor and stood looking at his oldest son. He didn't reach for him or otherwise respond.

Above the front window was the lamp of the Sacred Heart that had been installed in every house that was to take the electricity. It had come on when the electricity was made live in the parish that afternoon and was burning red now.

Pat Quinlan looked at it. He walked over to the wall switch above Jude, flicked down the pip.

The light in the room came on.

He flicked it off again.

On again.

Off again.

Each time, Pat Quinlan's expression didn't change. There was no wonder or amaze as the room blazed and darked, only a tight-lipped and impenetrable gaze that was the likeness of a distant god, illuming and extinguishing at a whim.

'He took him because He spared you,' he said then, looking down to Jude and recalling the fair day when the infant had hit the pavement. Up he flicked the switch. 'That day. You were the price. I knew I'd have to pay it someday.'

Down he had flicked it. Then he had lifted the poker from the hearth and smashed it across the lit lamp of the Sacred Heart.

***

'Jude, isn't it?'

Avoiding the throng of the fair, Father Coffey had come in the side gate for his daily walk of the avenues of the dead. Hands clasped behind his back, he was in a cassock, coat and the pilgrim's sandals and socks that were his off-duty solution to feet too large for size eleven shoes and toes that refused to touch the ground.

'Yes, Father.'

The curate's eyes went to the headstone, and he nodded slowly. All grief is private, you can only come to the door, and so he said nothing, only 'Patrick'. He looked to the slow transit of the estuary, as though souls trafficked there, then from his coat pocket drew a large-as-a-pillowcase handkerchief and into it let off the head cold that was chronic where the weather runny.

'Rain,' he said.

'Yes, Father.'

'Not heavy though.'

'No, Father.'

The curate nodded at the agreement. 'No,' he said, confirming it, and looked down the slope where the horizontal dead seemed to be heading to the river.

'Do you believe in luck, Father?' Jude asked.

'I believe in providence,' the priest said, too quickly, regretting at once the dry tone of his spiritual director, the Vincentian, Father Aloysius, coming out of his own mouth. 'Which is a kind of luck, I suppose,' he added.

'My father says this is our lucky day,' Jude said.

'Is that right?'

They considered this as the clouds took new positions. 'Well,' Father Coffey began, making the novice mistake of starting without an idea of an ending.

Jude raised his face, his eyes remarkably blue, both arresting and empyrean. Remembering his mother, he pushed to the side the wing of his hair.

'Yes, well,' the curate said. He could not look at the blue eyes, for he knew he could not give them what they wanted. Instead to the mid-heavens, he said, 'Then, that's what I'll pray for.' Father Coffey made a fluent sign of the cross, like it was first nature to him, bowed his head, and for a moment, without sound or movement, prayed for Jude, and the Quinlans, and that today they might be lucky.

When he blessed himself again, time came back on.

'I must carry on,' he said. 'Mikey Corry, God rest him, is to be buried tomorrow.' He looked to Jude, his dark eyebrows lifting, like some lightness was imminent. 'Enjoy the luck,' he said, 'when it comes,' and he lifted a hand a small ways in mild farewell, then stepped away, the three seabirds rising off the top of the church ruin.

***

When Jude Quinlan came back through Faha, the village had emptied its pockets. There was fulsome litter and a low air of afterwards. Performances over, many of the traders were packing up with a heavy hand and an undisguised disappointment. The boom times that were written in the newspapers hadn't reached the parish, money and wallets remaining for the most part inseparable. 'Poor enough Christmas, ye'll have' was the damming verdict of Noone packing up, and Dodd, whose brushes-of-all-sizes fitted into the van like the children in the Fry's chocolate advert, echoed with, 'Dirty one too.' A last-minute offering, Mrs Peggy burst open one of her three-in-a-pack and held out a pair of men's underpants to any passing. At some stalls, for goods unsold, a daredevil bargaining was underway, each side outdoing the other in hiding the truth of their circumstances and making out that sale or no-sale was no skin off their nose.

With the raven head of Sheila Reidy, Moriarty was in grinning discourse, the alibi three packs of cards in a set, scenes of Ireland on the back sides. 'Beauty spots, like.' A court-and-sale in one, the serenade was handicapped by McGreal in the next stall banging two pots in a tuneless music with rasping holler, 'Last-chance-now!' But Moriarty had often overcome worse, and though Sheila shook her head at the brazenness of him, the hand that covered her mouth could not contain her smiling. In human relations ambidextrous, round Sheila's head Moriarty passed Jude the wink and he passing, that boy had brought luck.

After them, the traders left boxes, cartons, papers, wrappings, bags: a drop-it-where-you-stood policy was the norm among buyers and sellers both, and by general consent the condition of the street after a fair was always *pure cat*. It was Faha's lowest grade, was a term without reference to felines, had escaped its origins and survived more than nine lives, its cousin *cat melodeon*, which Sonny Cooney said was cat with its eyes crossed.

In the light rain, the street was darkened, what rubbish wouldn't blow away plastered under the tramp of trade and gawking. In the packing and putting away now, a hopeless melancholy. The promise and possibility of the set-up, the borrowed glamour that came with those from elsewhere, exhausted, in its place the air of a circus tent coming down.

Those parishioners who had come not for purchases but had used the fair as a passport to see the rest of their kind were slow to disperse, and after the traders had decreed the last penny squeezed out of Faha, they stood about in clusters or singly, on windowsills or against walls, in no hurry to go back to yesterday.

If the stall street was bad, Church Street was worse. From a standing sale of hours in a river village with drains at street level, animal waste was everywhere it shouldn't be, and the air properly foul. Along the walls, at the height of a small child, was a dun smear three days of rain couldn't clear.

By the trade of pounds and shillings for living flesh, the cattle had lost their character and become livestock. Most were being readied for a new elsewhere, and the schoolboys and other drovers who would lead them to the station in town had moved in. With invisible whips of top teeth against their lower lips, they separated the sold and got them moving before the animals realised they were in the custody of strangers. To the station was a walk of some miles. The clock ticking was the daylight dying, so all had a pressing urgency in a sanctioned chaos as the fair disassembled before your eyes. Older schoolboys with ash plants and the caps of men played the role of captains, brooked no indecision, and for a short-cut would drive their cattle through you soon as go round. Hours later, the same ones would be walking home again in the absolute dark, a weary look and a half-cigarette, as if they were become old lads whose lives were already behind them. But, for now, the street was theirs and they bossed it without thought of others or that the world would ever be different.

Coming back to where he had left his father, Jude Quinlan was afraid to look for their cattle, in him a bubble of hesitancy and the unearthed aspect of having spent hours in the company of the dead.

Sitting on the kerbstone of his brother's grave, not for the first time had he wondered why it was he was the one saved. Not for the first time wished that he wasn't. Worthiness was a standard that rose while you lived, failing it the experience of every day. Added to this was the unanswerable question of what his life was to become.

If saved, for *what*?

He had joined the prayer for good luck with the priest, and, after, tried to picture where the prayers went. Everything went somewhere was a dictum of the Master's. Everything was made of energy, and energy passed into and out of matter. And in the dreamtime of the cemetery, where no one came or went and the rain defied the laws of falling by remaining a mist suspended, Jude had done just that. He had thought of all the prayers ever said in that graveyard, those in Latin and Irish, and then in English, in form various but intent singular, said with eyes lowered but minds ascending, said over a hundred years of souls departing from that very place, an air-traffic of invisibles accompanied by prayer. And, the way his mind went, soon enough, he had gone beyond the bounds of the cemetery and thought of the prayers of all the parish, the ones said aloud in every house each day, said on knees in kitchens, said beside beds, in beds, with beads and without, said under holy pictures, under crucifixes and Sacred Heart lamps, the ones too not said but issued out of minds, all *upwards*. He had thought of them as a great multitude, rising. In rising they would shed the particular and lose form, be like a cloud maybe, maybe like a host. And what had come to him then was the memory of the insides of the classroom windows blind and running with what the Master said was the brains of the scholars working, their thinking turned to water, and how he had lifted the sash of the window to let the thinking out.

Prayer too went *somewhere*.

Where exactly was where Jude's imagination failed.

Heaven, which had been so far away to begin with, got further away when, in the waiting room of Doctor Troy's surgery, he had seen the pictures of space that were the new must-haves for those who had outgrown comics.

In a *Life* magazine, he saw the Earth from outside it for the first time. It was a vision that had the mixed character of all revelation, for it was both wondrous and bewildering, the heavens vast and empty, and the Earth small enough to be covered by your thumb. His eyes couldn't leave the colour pictures, but his cheeks had flushed, as though in looking he was violating a sanction, as though the photographs annulled Schuster's Bible that began with the creation of the world in seven days. *We are so tiny*, was what the pictures told, *how could any of us matter?*

He had put the magazine back on the table with a sense of the ground giving way beneath his feet. But he had not forgotten. All of which had made perplex the transit of souls to the next life, where out there his brother Patrick might be, whether a prayer could ever reach him, or what he sent back down to his brother ever arrive.

Mick Naughton's cattle came past Jude at a trot, Macnamara's waiting to follow. Deals done, the stalls without walls were come asunder, and in the street a general stir and dissolve. Past the Patriot's Cross, Jude came up along the footpath, and was passing the door of McCarthy's when he saw that his father's animals were gone.

So was his father.

Deftly, between hand and elbow, Delia May was looping rope. Two of her sons were attending her heifers unsold. 'Jude,' she said, without looking at him.

'He sold them?'

She put the rope to the side, took up another.

'He sold our cattle? All of them?' Jude asked, only so that he could hear the answer he already knew. At once, the bubble that was in his chest was bursting, joy lightening his insides the way it does, lending a sensation of lift. It was true after all. This *was* their lucky day. It was. At last, it was. The fact of it was like something tumbling out of the sky and landing at his feet. At once, it changed the air and changed the day and made even bluer his eyes, not just with good fortune, but love of the world, that it could go this way sometimes, that sometimes the good thing happened. Pride in his father was part of it too, and because it had been for so long absent, because for so long it had been thwarted by personality and circumstance, it caught Jude Quinlan by surprise, and the scene in Church Street wavered and blurred until he tilted his head to make sure no tear fell. 'He sold them all,' he said again, this time without the question, this time thinking *Christmas*.

'Lynch,' Delia said, passing the rope to one of her sons before turning to Jude. Her face had in it a sorrow she didn't want to pass on, but knew it fell to her. 'He was owed 'em,' she said.

It took a moment.

Then it took another.

It took long enough for the good fortune that had landed at his feet to put back on its wings and take off.

'From gambles,' Delia said. 'Lynch was owed the sale.'

And it was gone.

Jude stood in the emptiness where their animals had been. He put his hand in his pocket and felt the sixpence.

'Pat was hoping to sell them to someone else for more, pay Lynch some, bring home the remainder,' Delia said.

Her boys were waiting patiently, in her company their manners flawless.

'Lynch gave back some shillings lucky penny. That there'd be something for ye for the Christmas, he said.' She looked away up the street to where Lynch was not. 'The bad shite,' she said. 'Only drinks minerals when he gambles.' She let off some sourness and turned back to Jude with soft eyes and the compassion of a woman who could be mother to all.

'Your father said tell you go home.' Small rain was spitting. 'I have to get these back. Come if you like.'

He shook his head. Delia took the kindness of her eyes away and turned into a drover, nodding to her boys, clicking her tongue and moving her cattle away all in the one.

Outside the door of Mohill's, Jude stood. Over an escaped music of teacups and cutlery, he could hear the rising voices of the barons and the stewarding one of Philo, 'Gentlemen, please!' The call had no effect; in each pub and food-house the action was the same, the parish unloosening its belt. Those who hadn't to go home didn't, abiding in the street and to the fair day granting an air of afters. Whether they would go for the meal or not, or just something to slake the throat, was a debate without words.

Food was offered in three houses, each according to the character of its cook, who had been one time told their meal was *beauty full*, the one word becoming two in an underlining of the indisputable. Mrs O Grady did a gravy that would make cardboard seem meat, Mrs Donnellan's onions sang. Nan Hassett had two convictions, a fish had to be cooked with the tide still in it, and you could never have too much salt. Nan knew that, having come from the sea, people craved nothing else. Her cuisine was salt, with extras, her customers devouring whatever she put on the plate, and after, like the legendary Fionn, licking their fingers. *Just beauty full.*

By silent treaty, the pubs didn't do food. Nor did some of their customers. In an acquired mimic of their animals, these went direct to their drinking spots, stomachs bypassed by lipping cigarettes and an unquenchable urgency for porter. Jude knew his father was one of these. He knew he was already in Craven's.

He stood alongside the wall of Mohill's, engaged none, but lowered his head and let the lock of his hair fall forward.

The poor light of day gave up the ghost. There was no evening to speak of; it was day and then it was night, like that, fallen, the stars attempting a comeback somewhere above darknesses layered.

Cats, from cubbies unknown, appeared in the street, travelling with heads erect like ones who could not be bought and sold, but wouldn't turn up their noses at the fair's leavings. Crusts, crumbs, bits of cold cuts that had fallen out of wedges of brown bread-and-butter too coarse-made to be called sandwiches, were sniffed and considered, all vanishing in a brisk clean-up that left nothing for the mice but the smell. The fires that were burning in all houses in the village sent up a thick turfsmoke the rain sent back down. It was a competition older than matchsticks, and if the wind wasn't playing and the sky lowering, there was only one winner. The street took on the fumy air of Martin Meagher, who lit one cigarette off the other and lived inside a cloud he never came out of, twenty Woodbine in his suit pocket in the coffin.

Traders and farmers departing, there was a closing-down quality to the village. Of Christmas there was no trace. Down the falling twist of Church Street, nothing of the festive, only curtains closing and the world shutting itself in. The exception was Prendergast's, where the television had retired the parlour curtains, and the test card offered a grey illumination towards the church.

Standing by the wall with nowhere to go, Jude waited. He put the sole of one boot against the wall, propping. He replaced it with the other after a time. He squatted on a footpath too mucked for sitting, the rain easing and coming again, easing again, coming again. He moved along from where the haired grass in Mohill's gutter made a spill, stood again, squatted again, stood again. His mind was engaged in colloquy in some other place, and he had to wait until it came back. Those who passed, hurrying for home or shelter, Mrs Sexton in her hat, Doctor Troy in his motor, gave him only the passing glance, for he was a boy, and *Wait there* the common command of all parents.

There, Jude Quinlan waited. But to what end? His mother had asked him to bring his father home. But there would be hours yet before he could even try. Before then he had to make sense of the story – of Lynch and his father and the death of his brother and being the one who was spared. Of the good luck that was always on its way but never arriving, of the prayers new and old, in their thousands, rosaries and litanies and missions and Masses, candles of special intention all burned to nothing. He needed sense of fairies and fairy forts, and whether the day had failed because he had reneged on a deal with the fairies and not gone inside Naughton's fort. Into this he had to add his father's gambling, the knocking on the door of heaven that to Pat Quinlan would not open one inch, he had to add the drinking, and to the accumulated sum of disappointments find a way to forgive. Why did his father not love them enough to stop?

Like all failures of love, it was a question without answer, but, once Jude had thought of it, he could think of nothing else, trapped in the prison of all who have flawed fathers, unable to mend them, yet knowing they are the only ones they will have.

The cold fell down the dark and found the wet in his clothes. He needed to move. He was not a saint; he would wait for his father no more. He went out the way they had come in when the day was young.

He was passing Naughton's Fort Field when he found he was walking slower, then slower still, stopping at last on the raised forehead of the centre of the road alongside the gate he had crossed to get ahead of the cattle.

His eyes had become acquainted with the dark, which was not absolute, but toned in shades without name, as though their maker could make nothing uniform and was each minute creating anew. He could see the line where the land ended and the river began, could see the thorn bushes and the thorn trees, the numerous and varied blacknesses that composed the night country and in which cattle were left out, standing in their own sinking or making small sucking sojourns to ground they had forgotten they had grazed.

He wanted there to be stars, but there were none. He wanted a moon, whole or part, but she was gone. There was only the emptiness of that dark road that was like a yearning that went on and around and on again.

He stood then by the seven-bar gate at Naughton's. He was without intention, had resolved nothing. There continued in his mind the running argument of whether he was right to leave his father and come home without him, whether his mother would want him to wait in the street until the small hours, and whether the failure was his too, being the son who had not died.

Behind his boy's eyes there ran the debate that had no winner, the right thing to do a lifelong quest, and without guidebook.

Then he put his hand on the top bar of the gate.

The iron was cold and wet, and it was cold and wet against his leg as he was climbing over it.

He went across the dark grass and the darker rushes with a sure step, in the panorama of the night the fort of the fairies darkest of all. It was ink until he came closer and could make out the risen shape of the blackthorn tree whose living form was a thousand knots without solution. From a life's argument with the western wind, it grew to the east, and that was the side of the fort he entered, a branch thorning his red jumper as he stooped in over the rim and descended the small earthen slope to the place he had reneged on in the dawn.

Though Jude had passed the field every school-day, though he knew the fort as landmark, same as others in the parish, he had a sense of trespass and knew he should be there moments only.

He reached into his pocket and found the sixpence.

He held it out in his palm, as if showing the silver and the hound on it. Then he bent down and placed it on the ground.

He said no words. It was a place older than language, but he expressed his intention all the same, that in exchange for the sixpence the fairies send the luck. What that would be, the fairies would decide; he would trust them, his silent covenant, because, in the adage of his mother, beggars couldn't be choosers. Jude stepped backwards and was thorned a second time, this time on the side of his face.

He crossed out of there quicker than he entered, and when he had climbed back over the gate, he knew he was walking back to Faha a second time that day.

He came into the village same as before. Same as before, he stood in the vacancy where his father's animals had been, not far from the church gates. The rain had stopped, but otherwise all was unchanged.

He would wait now as long as it took. He would stay until he would bring his father home. He leaned against the wall.

The street showed the genius of its construction, using its twist and fall to run west what had been dropped on it in the day.

Signalling a long night, a small army of bicycles lay along the wall beyond McCarthy's and again by Ryan's. There were a few tractors parked, front tyres turned to the kerb to arrest rolling, and a smaller number of motor cars.

A stranger's car passed, five heads inside the haw of their own making. It pulled over by McCarthy's and unbodied, one by one the figures emerging, each with a lengthening stretch, like ones who had been long-time shelled. Three of the men carried musical instrument cases. One of them was Junior Crehan. Already legendary, that night the first time his magical fiddle would be heard in Faha.

To appear purposed, Jude stepped away from the wall, going past the voices without restraint coming from Mohill's.

In heavy coat and cloth cap, a Tim-Tom came out. He came out to take the air and wait for his brother to finish up a game of Rings that had no final whistle, the two of them travelling home in the one tractor. He had a reserved air but the old-world courtesy of both Talty brothers, even to a boy, and he nodded to Jude by way of acknowledging him. Then he saw the cut on the boy's cheek where the blood had run and dried.

'You all right?'

It was a question with too many answers, none of which were in relation to the thorn-cut Jude had forgotten until Tim-Tom pointed to his own cheek, and the boy brought his fingers to the place and felt and took them from his face and looked at them and said, 'Yes good I'm good thanks,' like that, all in the one.

The man was standing before him, and though they lived in the same parish, he looked into the remarkable eyes of that boy for the first time, and though only briefly, though only for a breath, he was arrested by what he could not have explained but would think of later that night, when the story of the child would at last unfold.

'You going home?' the Tim-Tom said.

'I'm waiting for my father. He's above in Craven's.'

'I see,' he said with deliberation, seeing what was invisible. 'You want to take shelter?'

'I'm good.'

The man nodded. He studied the rain that was only rain where it crossed the compass of the streetlight. A silvered thing it was. Jude was ready to walk on, but, 'I'm waiting too, for my brother,' the man said. His eyebrows were thick and prominent, and his lifting of them was in precis both the coincidence of life and its sometime heaviness. 'Here,' he said. From his coat pocket he took some slab toffee. It wore a thin fur of pocket dust, but he snapped it smartly and handed Jude a piece.

The near-nothing he had eaten that day announced itself the moment Jude saw the toffee. He took it and thanked the man. The fiddle music of Junior escaped from Ryan's windows, in it something of a lay blessing. They listened the while, then Jude said he had to walk for a bit.

He went down Church Street past the pubs, all the time feeling the Tim-Tom eyes were following him as far into the story as he could.

He went up the alley at O Keefe's, maybe to be out of the streetlight or let the dark wash off some of the shame.

He was once more at the rear of the village then, that track without a name that was the unloveliest place in Faha. He moved without haste in an attempt to go nowhere but into the next minute, and the one after that. Barbering done, the O Siochru had long gone and the back door of Mohill's opened with a blaze of light only for the unbuttoning of flies and reliefs of necessity.

How long Jude would wait before he would try and move his father, he did not know. The day had already been so long it had escaped the containment of clocks. He only knew the time from the tolling of the church bell. He went past O Connell's and Clune's and came along the back of the church by the darkness in motion that was the river running. There was a wall as boundary and to hold back the waters that were coming for it, but the church was looking the other way. The wall was rough stone; there was a small gate, but it went unused. In Faha, you came to church in the front gate, out the front gate too. The back gate went nowhere you wanted to go in your Sunday clothes.

But it was here, at the back wall of the church in the village of Faha, on the night of the Christmas Fair 1962, that Jude Quinlan found the child.

3

'Why would anyone *want* to live here?' Charlotte Troy asked.

The question was general, and not to her older sister who, on the afternoon of the Christmas Fair, was crouched below her with a mouthful of pins. Charlotte was standing on the kitchen table in the green silk gown she had bought for the New Year's Ball in Limerick, and speaking between draws of a cigarette she smoked with her head to one side, as if offering her cheek for a kiss.

''tand 'till,' Ronnie said through the hedgehog of pins. She was wearing the browline glasses she needed for close work, but which added fifteen years to her face.

'It's just rain and muck and beasts.'

Though Charlotte Troy was infuriating, often petty, said things without thinking, and could have more wrong opinions than anyone Ronnie knew – though no one living could hurt or upset her more – still, she was her sister and that was the end of it. When she could not undo the knots in her sister's thinking, Ronnie's tactic was to pass no comment and hope life would untangle what she couldn't.

Over in the captain's chair with the leather armrests was slumped a female effigy, composed of dresses, skirts and blouses that were Charlotte's cast-offs and which she had brought out from Limerick because they would be perfectly good for Ronnie in Faha. 'They will cheer up your look, quite a lot actually. And you need to pay attention to these things. I'm only telling you as your sister. And because I know there's not a single good mirror in this house, honestly, not one. But if you don't start paying attention to these things now. I mean I'm already old. Look, look under my arms. Here. This. Look.'

'Stand still.'

'Is this catching here?' Charlotte delivered two smart tugs under the armholes of the gown. 'Or have I got fatter since I came in?'

'Turn.'

For once, Charlotte did as she was told and, on the table, turned.

'Stop.'

'Here.' The cigarette had come to an end. Charlotte passed it down to her sister, who took the butt to the sink and doused it.

'From there, how do I look?'

'The way you always do. Wonderful.'

'Nothing, here.' She laid her right palm on her midriff, and Ronnie took her meaning and looked at her figure. Charlotte pointed for the cigarette case and lighter. 'We have been trying. We are definitely trying. Since Day One really.' She stooped to meet the flame.

Ronnie took back the case and lighter. She laid them on the counter beside the effigy and brought the ball slippers that were a matching green with flesh-coloured undersoles and two miniature bows of black silk. Without looking down, Charlotte lifted each foot and her sister slipped them on.

'Of course, Huge thinks it's his fault. Ever since our first night.' She rolled her eyes. 'He took off his pyjama top, but the matt of his chest is so, it's like being scrubbed by wire wool, honestly, so I told him put it back on, which he did of course, he was so eager. But then he was sort of snortling into my neck.' She made the sounds. 'Like that, so I said, "Don't breathe!" while we made the baby, it was only seconds, then he fell to the side and gasped so. Honestly. So, he thinks if there's no baby it's because he can't do it right.' She waited for Ronnie to say something. She drew on the cigarette.

'I'm sure it just needs time,' Ronnie said, and removed her glasses. She offered her hand, and her sister came from table to chair to floor in regal descent. Her beauty was a thing undeniable, but Ronnie felt no envy. It had always been so; Charlotte was the one who, on entering the world, had been touched by a light that gave her that hair, that skin and those eyes. In her company, her sister felt plain, but never jealous.

'Walk over,' Ronnie said, pushing her hands lower into the pockets of her cardigan.

Charlotte rested the cigarette on a saucer. After being between her lips, it had a sated air, the smoke aspiring softly. 'Turn on the light, would you? Why is it always so dark in this house?'

Ronnie pushed down the pip and the shaded bulb set in amber the long room with the pitch-pine floor and the three weeping windows. Apologetic rain had come in the sashes, gathering in small pools in the corner of the sills. 'Walk over.'

Charlotte went the length of the kitchen as though in traverse of a gallery of the gods. The line of her back was so straight it made the room look crooked.

'How is it?' she asked.

'Back.'

She walked back, her step light, but the floorboards letting out their aches all the same. She stopped and Ronnie knelt below her to make adjustment. They were by the Aga where the chair that had once been their mother's had become Ronnie's favourite. On it, covered in brown paper, was the book that Ronnie was reading when her sister had driven up the avenue.

'You're always reading,' Charlotte said. Idly, she picked up the book while Ronnie took out and put in a pin.

The gasp from her sister was not from the pin. She had opened the book to the flyleaf. 'Where did you get this?'

The book was *The Country Girls* by Edna O Brien.

'I can't believe you're reading this. Where did you get it?'

'Soph sent it from England.'

'I want it. I'm taking it. Is it filthy?'

'Walk.'

Holding the novel, Charlotte walked back across the kitchen. When she got to the other side she stopped, opened the book in the middle, as though to see a picture. In a glance not finding what she sought, she tried another page at random. 'How filthy is it?' Colour rose up her bare neck.

'It's not,' Ronnie said.

Charlotte took the cigarette to her mouth, returned it to the saucer. 'Everyone says it is. Did Soph put this cover on it?'

'I did.'

'Because you know it's filthy. I'm taking it. I'll know if it is. You can have it later.'

'You're not taking it. Walk.'

With the novel playing the part of purse, Charlotte came back across the kitchen. 'Well?'

'It's perfect.' Ronnie closed the sewing box.

Charlotte hunted in the pages of the book. She looked up, said, 'Mr Gentleman?' and then returned to read more.

Her sister made no outward response. Ronnie had long since stopped rising to her sister's provocations. She knew what Charlotte thought of Faha, that, by the caprice of a grandfather who had chosen to doctor in a backwater, the Troys were a family in the wrong novel. She knew that Charlotte found the parish a prison, and that her visits were as though to inmates. She knew too that she could not change this, could not convince her sister of a contrary truth: that although she understood everything Charlotte thought of Faha, though like all small places it was confining, Ronnie had come to the understanding that for her it was also freeing, and she never wanted to leave it. This was *home*. More, with a conviction she knew could not be explained, she felt it was where she was supposed to be.

She carried the sewing box to the press, which was, like every other one in that house, filled with a lifetime's necessities-in-waiting. This made for a crammed look and called for a spatial genius to fit back in what had come out. It was not that father or daughter went shopping. It was the girls' mother who, in an effort to defeat rainy afternoons, had purchased the six sets of matching bed linen, the second sets for when the first was not-drying on the line, the tablecloths, nine, napkins in sets of twelve, times four, then times four more, because by then she had understood that nothing could ever dry in Faha. None of Regina's things could be touched when she was alive, and when she died Time embalmed them. To these had been added gifts made to the doctor, needle-worked or crocheted thanks and kindnesses, some with his initials, some with seabirds flying, many of which could not be used, nor thrown out. The press was the parish in linen and cotton. Under a pressure to always welcome newcomers, the shelves bowed but did not surrender. Here, into a gap that was exactly its own size, Ronnie slid the sewing box.

She crossed and took the novel from her sister's hands.

'I haven't got to anything juicy yet,' Charlotte said.

'It's not that kind of book.'

'You're not going to let your own sister have it?'

'Not until I finish.'

'You're so unkind.'

'I *am* reading it.'

Charlotte turned her back to her sister and Ronnie pressed the three green buttons through so the gown came undone. It would have fallen in a silken flow had she had not held the shoulders. She lowered it and Charlotte stepped out across it like a threshold. She picked up the cigarette and relit it while Ronnie found the hanger. 'Here's what we'll do. You'll give me the book, and I'll find you an actual Mr Gentleman to take you to the ball. In the bank there are several under Huge. He tells me about them. I'll pick you one.'

A small tightening in Ronnie's lips was the only reveal of what she thought of the proposal. Were she to begin to say more, she knew the rest of the afternoon, the evening and the night would not be time enough to get to the end, and nothing would be changed. She took the hangered gown to the sconce, saw the pins were secure and the line true.

'You can't spend the rest of your days' – Charlotte tapped the ash in the general direction of the sink – '*here*.'

'Why not?' Ronnie asked, still looking at the gown, but with a burr of hurt in her voice. She knew it was difficult to change the mind of another, and of a sister impossible, but she could not bear to be thought of with pity, that there was a shelf and she on it.

'I'm sorry but that would be an absolute sin. You think that's what Daddy wants? It's not. You're so clever. Growing up, I always thought *Ronnie will live in London, or Paris*, like in those stories you wrote for us. You remember?'

'They were childish.'

'They were wonderful.'

'I'll go to those places sometime. But I'll come back here,' Ronnie said. 'I actually love it.' There, she had said it.

'And marry *who* exactly?'

Other than a slight creasing at the corners of her mouth, a reflex identical to her father's, Ronnie made no answer, and her sister blew out a theatrical sigh.

'No, I will find you a Mr Gentleman.'

'Please don't.'

'It'll be fun.'

'Not for me.'

That came sharper than Ronnie intended, and she softened it with, 'But thank you.'

Charlotte strode to the effigy and drew up the top layer, considered the choice, selected a fit-and-flare dress of burnt orange, not her colour, quite horrid on her actually, but the cut gave you an hourglass. 'Well, for *when* you do go to those places. Come on. Try this.' She smiled her winning smile. 'Ronnie?'

'After you're gone, I will. Thank you.'

Ronnie moved the kettle onto the hot plate. There were already two presses full of Charlotte's cast-offs, and she was wondering where she could fit these. She opened the lower oven on the Aga and took out the scones that had been warming.

'You can't say I didn't try.'

'I won't.'

'That's the problem with good people. You can't do anything for them, because they're so' – she waited for her sister's eyes to come to her – '*good*.' It was love in translation. She smiled at it, then began to put back on her own clothes.

'Thank you for everything,' Ronnie said.

'I am not a terrible person.'

'No, you are not.'

'I'm actually a good sister.'

'You are,' she said, giving her younger sister what she always wanted from her, approval, and closing a conversation that had no place to go because the positions were both known and unchangeable.

What Ronnie herself wanted was to live in that place she considered beautiful, where she could be of use, and in the paradoxical paradise of a falling-down house be free to live inside her mind. That this was a richness she had come to understand first through reading novels meant that they had a special place in her life, a good one better than the company of ten people. Not that you could say that aloud or explain it to a sister whose thoughts never came in paragraphs.

With a practised hand, Ronnie set three cups and saucers and plates. She cosied the teapot in the one that May Nolan had made for the doctor, then went to get him.

The surgery was quiet. The fair up on its feet now, small sicknesses and complaints would be put on hold for the day. Only heart attacks and fist fights would bring callers. One spring fair, Ronnie could recall opening the door to a man whose nose was a boneless pulp. Above it his eyes swam in sinewy pink and seemed enormous. He stood on the step with his cap in his hands, and said nothing, as though he was Exhibit Number One of Man Still on His Feet, and not a little proud of it. She had brought him in and her father had examined him without comment, neither asking for the story nor admonishing. The man was in there for two hours, and when he came out he had a cartoon-bandaged look that made it seem his head had been sawed in two, the halves only held now by three yards of muslin. Still, when he put the cap on, he was aiming back to the fair.

But for the most part, fair days in Faha were quiet ones in the surgery. The doctor made no rounds and, unless called out, stayed in the confines of his riverside room where he said he would attend to paperwork, but always fell asleep on top of it.

To wake him, and preserve the pretence, Ronnie knocked. She waited the two seconds for him to stretch his eyes and then came in. 'There's tea and scones,' she said.

Her father was in the white shirt that always started the day with an ironed equanimity, until life got its hands on it. From holding up his forehead, at the right elbow the creases were deep and many; from breasting his desk in sleep the front had the line of the textbook where he had been reading of brain plaque. The fire had gone low in the grate, and she went to it.

'Charlotte will be going after,' Ronnie said, when she saw him hesitate.

'Yes,' he said, 'yes,' and stood.

At such moments she saw the age in him, transitions between one settled state and another, literally the joints of the day. She saw the slight pull behind his moustache and the tension in his wrist on the armrest pushing. But she said the nothing that was required of daughters, and once he put on his jacket, she led the way back through the corridor that, between the two fires, was like a sleeve that didn't dry.

'Poor day for the fair,' she said, a comment without a cousin.

'Charlotte,' said Jack Troy, when he came into the kitchen. His middle daughter had escaped the name Charlie on the morning of her marriage. He opened his arms and she stepped into and out of the embrace like it was a thing of silk not skin.

'Daddy,' she said. She was holding the novel down by her side, and as her father sat to table, she put it under her coat in the far chair.

'How is Eugene?' he asked, as though it was a line written for him. The tea came darkly from the spout, the dribble missing the saucer.

'Oh you know. You know how bankers are,' was the script's next line.

Ronnie passed her sister the plated scones.

Charlotte let her face say she wouldn't be touching them. She poured a half-cup of tea, turned the cup on the saucer so the handle was perpendicular. 'I completely forgot about the fair.'

'I told you,' Ronnie said.

'If you told me I would never have come today. Driving through it was like a vision of hell. I won't go back that way.'

The doctor ate the warm scone, the roll of his moustache as he chewed not dropping the crumbs from it.

'They're a bit dry,' said Ronnie, before anyone could praise the scones. She was unsurpassed in finding fault in herself. It was not a ploy. When she voiced a criticism in how she had done something, it was not so that you would tell her otherwise, it was because she had a helpless addiction to truth.

They sat and had the tea and said nothing for a time. The room seemed larger without language and the family small.

'I must fix that rattling window,' said the doctor, although the three of them knew he would not.

'It just needs the wedge,' Ronnie said. 'It fell outside. I didn't get it because of the rain.'

Charlotte turned the teacup around on the saucer. 'We won't be here for Christmas this year,' she announced. They were expected at Hart's and couldn't disappoint, and coming all this way on Christmas Day made no sense anyway and they'd come out Stephen's Day or the day after and bring the presents then and wouldn't it be all the same but without the fuss and she could bring leftovers if they wanted because Hart's would be an absolute feast and Judy would be loading her down with plates of you-name-it and she wouldn't be able to say no without being rude.

'I see,' said the doctor.

'We won't need leftovers,' Ronnie said, with a nibbed sharpness, a parenthesis of smile blotting it.

'No, but just—'

'We'll have plenty.'

About them the house made its noises, small and gapped, like a pulse inconstant. For a time, each of them found a different angle to look at. The doctor's gaze was down the way to the large, tortured, holly tree.

'This is Happy Christmas so,' said Charlotte brightly, standing. She opened her arms to embrace her sister and while she did her father stood and waited his turn. In his eyes was the grief of living but only his older daughter saw it.

'Happy Christmas, Daddy.'

He said it back to her and held her a moment. Ronnie looked then looked away. There was something unbearable in it.

Charlotte put on her long coat with the red velvet collar, and her sister walked her to the front door.

'I'll collect the dress when we come. After Christmas,' Charlotte said. 'You're a star for doing it.' She closed the snap on her bag. 'And you're so good for bringing me all those wonderful clothes, Charlotte.' She craned her ear towards her sister to hear her say it.

'You are.'

'So good?'

'Yes.'

Charlotte gave a little shake of delight. 'I love Christmas,' she said. 'Don't tell Daddy, but we're going to bring you both a television for your present. Huge says we can. Imagine!' She kissed the air near her sister, and then hurried down the steps to the car.

Ronnie stood at the door, watching. Inside her car, Charlotte lit a cigarette, rolled the window two inches to release the smoke, waved, shouted, 'I will keep an eye out for Mr Gentleman. Just in case,' and then was gone.

Ronnie watched the car until it rounded the bend of the avenue, taking her sister back into a marriage that, each time she came, seemed to have boxed up some more the wildest and freest parts of the Charlie she had grown up with. What Charlotte cared about now was conformity, not letting down the side or being a show. Gone now through the doors of marriage was the sister who had once sat smoking on the roof of Avalon, calling invocations to the Greek god of love and asking for a man who could stand naked in the moonlight.

In the village the fair would be packing up, and Ronnie would not walk out this evening. She came in and shut the door, in the kitchen tidied away the things from the tea, replaced her sister's chair in against the table. When all was just so, she had cleared her mind and made time to read *The Country Girls*. But the book was not in the chair where Charlotte had left it. It was not hidden under the cast-offs, and Ronnie did not need to look further.

***

For Ronnie Troy the rest of that early evening was unremarkable. She went upstairs to her room and sat in the Regency armchair that faced south towards the Shannon. She had wanted to read the novel here. In novels and stories, she had found a doorway through which there was first company, and then something more. As she had passed from girlhood, the quiet time for reading had become what she most looked forward to. In *The Country Girls*, she had found something true and compelling, and had wanted to read more. It was not the seductions of Mr Gentleman she cared for, it was Cait and Baba. They were the life of it. She wanted more of them. She wanted to believe that she and her sisters were just like them, but feared they were in fact the haughty Connor girls. She had other books to read or read over. Her eye went to the copy of *The Lake*; she would take it down to look at again, but she did not want to leave the world of *The Country Girls* just yet, and sat for a time with her hands in her lap in the pose that looks like peace.

The room had a dark wood desk with drawer on each side and a wooden chair that matched. It had belonged to her grandfather, and in the general shuffling of furniture that followed his death, when big pieces went up the stairs and down the stairs, into and out of rooms like visitors that had to be newly accommodated, didn't go or didn't fit, lived a week or more in one room before it was decided they just wouldn't do, were brought to another where they wouldn't do either, the desk had ended its journeys here. With a doubled cardboard under the back left leg, it did not move when she leaned forward to write.

Ronnie had always written. She could not remember starting, but the mainspring was likely the rainy day she had read all the books in the house and needed something new. She wrote first for herself, but when her sisters came under her jurisdiction, she would read them the stories that filled her copybooks. Charlie and Soph made no distinction between what was published and what not, a story was a transport, and they gave their endorsement for each by the oldest proof: they didn't want it to end.

Charlie outgrew the stories first, and her younger sister followed. Ronnie didn't mind. By then she was already writing two stories, the one for her sisters and the one for herself. When she was in her mid-teens, she was writing most days, mostly at night, after school-work was done. Never without a book to hand, she confirmed the opinion of Faha: *That girl has brains to burn*. At the time, her stories took place in Paris or London. Back then, even Dublin was too dull for her imagination to walk around in. Real life was elsewhere: there great fortunes and misfortunes were commonplace, and three orphaned sisters could come through all by virtue of wit and intelligence and a bond between them that could not be broken. She finished one story and started the next without rereading the first – she had read that one already. Then one day she was in the library in town and overheard Mrs Hedderman, the librarian, say, '*But it's so poorly written.*' Though she was standing by the shelves and the comment had not been to her, Ronnie's throat blushed and a sour self-consciousness entered her. Even before she got home, she knew that everything she had written was just awful. She didn't need to check, everything of hers was so poorly written. She took all the copybooks from under her bed to the barrel in the yard where Sorley, their sometime yardman, burned all that was too private for the dump.

What had she been thinking? The pages she had written were exactly those you might expect from a schoolgirl who was diligent, proper and competent. They were grammar walking, they had no *life*. And now she despised herself for the vanity. She would write nothing more but read everything. She would give her eyesight to it, reading on windowsills, in the kitchen waiting for the kettle, on the bus home from town, reading in gauzy lamplight, and later in the amber electric that was little better because the tasselled shade was so thick it kept the light contained to up and down orbs that were not near her bed.

But always, across from it, was her grandfather's desk. And one evening, now three years ago, after an exhausting day in the surgery when the sick had outnumbered the seats, Ronnie had collapsed onto her bed with the sense that she had lived through an epic. To still her mind, and to confirm to herself that somehow she had managed it all, she sat to the desk and began to write the day as a story.

It was her first time thinking of Faha as a place where anything happened. The first time her imagination came home, is how she would think of it. Which was terrifying and freeing at the same time. For it meant that she too was home.

Her father had discovered it by accident, when she was in bed bound up with merciless cramps that each month twisted her insides around blades sharpened at both edges. He stood by his own father's desk and saw the foolscap pages, recognised himself at once and stopped reading, not for the first, nor last, time realising daughters were mysteries with no final page.

'You are writing? A story?'

'It's probably no good,' Ronnie had said, and turned into the pillow with pain.

His hand had come out from his side, to reach for her temple, but the gesture faltered, and he stood immobile. He had stood in the tumbled disarray in which she kept her bedroom, the only thing untidy about her and about which he never passed comment. He had waited for the cramp to pass, then asked, 'Why do you say that?'

'Anything I thought good yesterday is terrible the next day.'

'That's how it gets better,' he said.

'By being terrible?'

She knew he did not mean to be dismissive but was only then discovering the thorned truth that there is no response to match the writer's own in the moment of creation. Anything after that, even an *It's wonderful* would not be as wonderful as it was, however briefly, to the writer when the words came through them out of the invisible and onto the page. There was simply nothing that could be said that would not have fallen short. The learning of that would confirm to Ronnie the irredeemable loneliness of all creators, but more, that the only approval she would seek would be her own.

Her father had winced, said, 'That's not what I meant,' but Ronnie had closed her eyes with pain, and he had understood that her writing was an intimacy he should not broach.

When she was well again, she had returned to look at the piece. It was not terrible, or at least not all of it was. To preserve the privacy of a people who considered that the last preserve of dignity, she changed the names and crossed the characteristics. And the day was still there on the page.

Through the doors of the surgery came fresh stories every day.

Haulie Hassett had bested Shakespeare, Sonny Cooney said. Ailing from a heart that wouldn't fill right, Haulie told his three sons he would leave the farm of land to whichever did the most work on it. Delia Connor's cataracts were on the waiting list, along with the thousands of others stepping dimly through their Third Age. Leaving the surgery by the feel of her hand, Delia said she hoped Jesus had enough spit left for her eyes by the time she got to the gates of the next life. Muirean Murphy had a new baby every June, so that when her aunt, the nun, came each August she had the impression it was the same one she saw last year, and that Faha was *Tír na nÓg* for infants.

Day by day, in Ronnie there had dissolved her girlish idea of writing a novel called *The Troy Sisters*, and instead she had fallen into a habit of seeing in Faha the full of humanity, in its ordinary clothes.

The challenges were many, not least because of the inveterate layering of all Irish life, where the most important things were never said, and depth was more valued than surface. But, knowing that that was a description of herself too, she gave herself to it. Each night she wrote before bed, free in the knowledge that no one would ever read her. It was still years before her first book, still years before, after the death of her father, the first stories would finally appear and something of her inner life would be made known, but only through the lives of characters.

***

It was the late evening. The river was gone and the stars were gone and the rain and not-rain alike fell with small voice. December cold came through the slates as if by invitation, and considered the room where the woman was writing the story of Doady and Ganga trying to postpone death. She was wearing the old cable knit cardigan over the thin one, because the motion of her mind did not heat the stillness of her body and her sister had said writing in the cold was giving her rounded shoulders.

The cold was not measured in degrees, it came in a disguise of dampness that was colder than numbers. It was in the room before

Ronnie noticed. Her hands never felt it, but when it landed on the floor and crept along to find her feet, she toed off her shoes and rubbed one foot on the other, sometimes tapping a short tattoo, as if to fright the cold back behind the skirting, but not stopping writing with the blue fountain pen her father had left on the grandfather desk the day after he first read the foolscap.

Still the night came on. *Poor enough one*, crossed her mind, when she paused and pulled the lever to refill the pen from the Quink. But nothing more. Her shoulders rounded, she drew up the high collar of the old cardigan, but did not look at the clock, or consider how long she had been sitting there, for the universal writer's reason: when she wrote, time did not exist.

So, it was in that state that is not-quite-dream and not-quite-woken, her mind beyond her body in a third place, that she was startled by the light.

***

It was small. It was travelling the dark.

Turning to it at the window, Ronnie felt now how cold she was. She stood, folded herself in a cardigan embrace, and looked properly into the night. The light pulsed, passing the old trees. It was coming in from the eastern gate.

Time turned back on. She heard the hard tick of the alarm clock she overwound each night. Quickly she put on her shoes. Already emergency was thrumming her blood. She saw the light stand up the trunks of the sycamores at the bend of the avenue. Then she was out the bedroom door and across the landing and taking the stairs, one hand touching the loose bannister lightly, the other pulling straight the thin cardigan and giving two sharp pushes to where her left fist had flattened her hair.

By the time she was in the hall, the headlamps were in the fanlight over the front door. She could hear the pop-pop of the engine, and if *she* could, her father could, but he had not appeared. She called in the direction of the surgery where she supposed he was brandied asleep, calling not *Dad*, not *Father*, but the name that met all crisis:

'Doctor!'

She turned the large key in the oak door and drew it open to see the three, with the infant cradled in the boy's arms.

***

It was only seconds, but still too long. It was only seconds in which she stood and understood what she was seeing.

The boy was Jude Quinlan.

The two men were the Talty brothers.

One of them was sitting in the cab of the tractor with the engine running, the other was standing slightly behind the boy. All were in tableau in small rain glazed by the porchlight. None spoke. Not the boy, not the man and not Ronnie. Seconds only, but too long, all remained as figures in a setting, attending. It was as though the visitors coming up the avenue and appearing at the front steps of the doctor's house was as far as any of them had been able to imagine. As though the *What happens next?* that leaps to the front of each brain when it meets catastrophe had found only this first answer, and now they let the cradled infant speak for itself.

Ronnie's brow closed. Her eyes went from the baby to the boy to the man and over to his brother, who was facing away to where the eye of the headlamp was glaring. The motor popped.

It was seconds only, but too long. Leaning a little forward, her arms folded across herself, Ronnie put the pieces of the story together.

'I found it,' the boy said. Above the red jumper, his face was paled in the porchlight, a loop of hair flattened against his forehead. He held the infant close, as if expecting someone to take it away.

'That's right. He found it,' said the Talty man behind him. 'He found it and he won't let go of it.' His brother turned in the tractor seat towards them.

Ronnie felt the inquisition of all three. Then she released her arms and with her right hand made a blurred beckon that was three flapped waves towards her own breast, its meaning lost until she stepped in against the door and said, 'Come inside, come in, come in.'

126

But Jude Quinlan did not move. He was looking straight ahead, into the front hallway, but seeing none of it. The cradle of his arms a cross, with one palm holding the infant's head, he stood in the manner of a statue or one who could not go forward into the living story. In silent motion, small rain descended the plains of his face.

'Jude,' Ronnie said. She said it softer than can be whispered.

Whether because he had not realised she would remember his name, or because the saying of it brought him back to the present, the boy's eyes came to her.

'It's dead,' he said.

The word landed its blow, and Ronnie found her hand needed to clutch the breast button of her cardigan. The look in Jude Quinlan's eyes held a sorrow she could not bear and she turned to the Talty man behind him and to the brother beyond and the headlamp blazing away into the darkness. Her chin had a tremor, she tightened her jaw. She clasped the front of her cardigan again, as though to shield her heart. She left her right hand holding on there. In what was only heartbeats, she did not follow the cold of logic, did not say *Why have you come here so?* did not say *Why did you not go to the priest?* but swallowed what thoughts had risen, stepped back out the door and put her hand gently on the boy's wet sleeve.

'Please,' she said. 'Please. Come inside.' She did not take away her hand. She felt the wet cloth that contained the child, and she said again 'Jude' and conveyed with her eyes the only thing that matters in the face of grief, *I am with you.*

Jude stepped across the threshold. He had the baby high up against him and he stood in the front hall and said nothing.

Boy and baby delivered, the Talty man touched his cap to Ronnie and turned to go down the steps.

'Wait!'

Doctor Troy had come from the surgery without notice, his shirt irregular from unscheduled sleep and the grid of his hair awry. 'What's going on?' He stepped in close to the boy and moved aside the cloth that covered the lower half of the infant's face.

'I found it,' Jude said.

'And you'll give it to me now,' said the doctor. He said it so firmly that there was no possibility of anything else.

He took the child in his arms. 'Nobody leaves,' he said. Then he swept down the hall and into the surgery and closed the door.

Gently, Ronnie sat the boy on the bench that was the resting place for all the doctor dropped whenever he came in the door and went out onto the front step. 'The doctor wants nobody to leave,' she called to the two brothers, the one in the tractor and the one now alongside. She came a further step down and called to them again.

One brother looked to the other. The debate between them, positions laid, objections raised and countered, and concluding arguments, all took place inside that look. Ronnie waited.

At last, the brother in the seat turned from the other, did a single up-nod of his head, a gesture mostly chin, that was a translated *Right so*, then he footed the accelerator. The brother whose transport was always in the box at the back stepped away. The tractor jolted forward, the driver pulled the steering wheel about and it took off in a loose arc, eating gravel. When it got to the top of the avenue, Tim-Tom brought her to a stop and killed the motor. He climbed down, righted his cap and walked back towards his brother.

'She'll need the hill to start,' that one explained to Ronnie.

She stepped back inside the front hall, and the two brothers came in and took off their caps in unison and said 'God Bless' in soft echo as they crossed the threshold. Ronnie closed the door behind them.

'Come,' she said to Jude, and touched his arm and then led the three down the hall like a procession of ghosts. When she got to the door of the waiting room she realised this was not a night for protocol and said, 'This way, come into the kitchen.'

The brothers said nothing; they came in trail, holding their caps, the rain in their boots mostly spilled and only the C's of their heels marking the floorboards. Neither had been inside the surgery since infancy and their manner was the same as in church: something larger than themselves happened here. The boy was in some other state. He came, but like one inside a mystery.

Ronnie turned on the light in the kitchen and both brothers blinked at the brightness. The one who had had the few pints more so than the one who had had the minerals, but both lowered their silver heads and sat into the wooden chairs Ronnie indicated.

'You'll have tea,' she said.

'We won't, miss, thank you,' said the brother who was the driver.

'Thank you, miss,' said the other.

'It's no trouble,' she said, lifting the cover from the hotplate of the Aga, drawing the kettle to it. She looked to the boy. He was sitting forward, rocking slightly, his arms down between his legs, palms together like an upside-down praying. 'Maybe you'd like a glass of milk?' she asked in his direction, but she already knew he would not answer. She poured the milk and put it on the table beside him, two biscuits on a plate too. He touched none of it. She brought him a towel from the press beside the Aga. 'Dry yourself,' she said.

She went and sat in her mother's chair.

The western window that had lost the wedge let off its rattle. The small noises of the night's breathing, wind in tree and bush, water of sky and river moving, suddenly seemed to Ronnie things of cold indifference, as though the world had no compassion left. She could not hear the rain against the windowpane and not think of the baby lying in it, and the thought of that filled her not only with grief but with fury. She was aware of it first in the centre of her being, but it came to her hands clasped on her knees and to her jaw and her nostrils. It came and made rigid her spine, it brought heat to her throat and chill to the back of her neck. She was raging, raging without moving, sitting in her mother's chair and looking straight ahead across the kitchen to the wall that was on the list for painting before Christmas. In the surgery, she always felt that what the sick required of her was assurance and calm before they went in to the doctor. And she provided it. It was first nature for her. But here, now, she felt none of this and feared that if she opened her mouth, it would be to scream.

The kettle showed signs of its effort in a series of spasmed protests, grumbles of sound that gathered gradually into song. When the steam was singing, Ronnie rose and scalded the pot, doused it out, spooned three heaps into it, stirred, and then cosied the pot on the side of the range. She took down the teacups and saucers and placed them on the table before the Talty brothers. Neither said anything, but the boy's eyes found her, and a moment after, he reached and took one of the biscuits. Ronnie went to the press where the sponge cake – *too dry* – was in a USA biscuits tin.

'I'll let the tea brew,' she said, sitting again.

There was a vacancy, all sitting in attendance, for what, none could say.

Then, without signal or announce, but same as if, the brother who was the driver placed his cap on the table and got down off the chair onto the floor. He wasn't there two seconds before his brother was kneeling alongside him, by reflex the two old men assuming a position that had been in their bones since they could stand. Neither looked at the other, nor at Ronnie nor the boy. The seats of the chairs they turned into and made as bases for elbows. From a jacket pocket a beads was brought. It came in a leathern pouch of long wear, with a flap cover. The man spilled the beads into the cup of his hand, put the pouch in a side pocket. He let the rosary loose so the anchor of the cross dangled, and before he had blessed himself the boy had slid to the floor and bowed his head too.

The Troys were not a family for the rosary. Of course, all the girls had prayed it in the convent, but when they came home, the beads got lost among the various and sundry that lived in the uncountable drawers. Perhaps because it was the place of medical science, Avalon was not a house for prayer. The girls' mother and father took them to Mass, yes, but that was the extent of it, and none of the sisters questioned it. So, when the two men and the boy blessed themselves and one brother began the Apostles' Creed, Ronnie was a foreigner in her own house. The three were in that head-bowed state that was part-habit part-ritual, a state that, whether through devotion or not, dissolved time and space, and through the rhythm of the spoken words made that kitchen other. Not that they were spoken exactly. From long use, the words of the prayers had lost their edges. Without pauses between them, and the use of that singular intonation that was the one used in every house in the parish, they became a low-voiced chant that was in no language and all languages at once, a tonal music to the Mother of God rising off the cold floor.

To Ronnie it felt as though the fixtures that kept the ordinary world in place had been undone, and instead here was something elemental, open and raw. She could not look at them. All three prayed the rosary every night, she realised. Prayed it on their knees before bed for intentions various as all human hope. But here they were praying for the soul of the infant.

And, though fury and sorrow were still in-thorned in her, she got down onto the floor too.

The brother had flowed into the first of the ten Hail Marys. The prayer was two breaths, the first that took it as far as *Jesus*, the second as far as *Amen*. The Talty man did not raise his eyes to acknowledge her, nor did the other two, but each knew she was with them, and when her voice joined the Hail Mary it was like a moment of chorus.

In Faha, if a caller came in the back door when a family were on their knees, he got onto his, and when that decade ended, the caller would be offered the courtesy of taking the next one. The brother who held the beads let the other lead the second decade. It had a lifetime's practice in it. The two bachelor gentlemen with bowed crowns of the same hair, the same bulbed knuckles, and the same weather-crusted and winged-out ears, were twinned souls with the one voice. Behind them, their boots, toes to the ground, had the look of earthen things. At the end of that decade, the brother let open a small pause, but neither Jude nor Ronnie came in quick enough and the one with the beads closed the seam without raising his head.

And so it was until the end. The brothers shared the rosary, the other two joining in. By the time they were at the *Poor banished children of Eve*, the cold of the floor had come in Ronnie's bones and she felt each of the twenty minutes she had been kneeling. But something else too. She had not the words for it. Perhaps it was the calling of the names for the Virgin in the Litany, *Mirror of justice, Seat of wisdom, House of gold, Health of the sick, Morning star, Star of the Sea*. They were names for a woman, but only a man would think them. And yet, in the calling out was the summoning of a shield against what was to come.

One brother pouched the beads and the other put his right fist on the floor and lifted his left knee, making the small sigh he made every night that was not protest but admission of age in his jointed parts.

Ronnie poured the tea that was stewed now, a black the milk barely clouded. But the brothers thanked her and drank away and ate a cut of cake.

Then Ronnie heard her father open the door of the surgery, heard his footsteps as far as the waiting room where he expected Jude and the brothers, then along the corridor, snapping open the kitchen door to find them with the look of the prayers fresh on their faces.

He was carrying the infant in the crook of his left arm. As he stood he made a minor rocking of it that in those first instants could not be interpreted as instinct or not. The doctor's face showed an immense weariness, eyes small. But then he whispered 'Here' towards his daughter and she came without understanding until she looked at the baby's face. In a softened voice that was the same as when Ronnie was sleeping her first sleep in his arms, her father said, 'She's settled now,' and passed the infant across and into her hold, and they knew then that the girl found in Faha that night of the Christmas Fair had not perished but was living now.

'Tell me exactly where you found her.'

The doctor stood before the boy and gave him the same look he used for patients who had symptoms they wouldn't say. His grey eyes were steady, eyebrows low, and when the boy began speaking, they didn't change. His moustache kept his mouth private. He heard how Jude had come to the fair with his father, how his job was to bring Pat Quinlan home after, how he knew he'd be at the monster gamble, but that he couldn't get him home until late and so had walked about to pass the time, how he had met – he had nodded towards the one of the Talty brothers whose name he was unsure of – how to be away from questions and looks he had gone around the back of the church, and how there, near the back gate, he had seen the bundle.

'She was making no sound?'

'No.'

'No movement?'

'No.'

'She was in the cloth only? No box, no other container?'

'No.'

'There was no note? Nothing pinned or next to the child? Nothing that might have fallen? Nothing you might have missed?'

'No. I looked when I lifted her.'

'You thought she was dead?'

'She *was* dead.'

Ronnie watched the boy answer. It had not occurred to her up to then that he might be hiding anything.

Her father moved a step closer and tented the fingertips of both hands on the tabletop. 'You don't know whose she is?'

Holding the baby high against her and making the rocking motion that was the first language for all of us, Ronnie thought to stop the questions. But her father's eyes had that same look of sorrowful wisdom that came from a lifetime's encounter with the thorns of human story. It was a look that could slip over into despair, she knew, and she pressed her lips and looked at the girl's sleeping face and waited for the moment to pass.

Jude didn't understand the question.

'The baby. You don't know who she belongs to?'

'No.'

'There was no one around? Nobody who could have been standing watching?'

'No.'

The doctor released his fingertips, he looked away from the boy for the first time. His right hand came to his moustache and his forefinger pushed across it once. He looked to the two brothers, the one who was considering the cap in his hands and the one who was rubbing the rosary print off his knees.

'I'll ask one last time,' the doctor said, turning back to the boy. 'Just to be sure. You don't know who the baby belongs to?'

'He has already said it,' Ronnie said, her voice soft so as not to disturb the child in her hold, but with a new inflexion that she had not intended but understood as within the compass of mothers, wanting to be a shield.

Her father looked at her but said nothing. He came back at the boy, waiting.

Jude met his eyes. 'I don't.'

'I believe you,' said the doctor. 'Tell me what happened next.'

Jude told how he carried the child out into Church Street. The child was dead. He had seen his own brother dead and he knew the stillness and the cold, he said, looking to Ronnie. And so he did not run like the time of his brother, he said, but came out under the streetlight not so much for help but because he couldn't leave the child outside the back gate in the rain.

Ronnie looked from him to the infant. By an instinct she didn't know she had, she lowered her head and drew the infant up closer to her, as though to block the girl from hearing her own story.

'Who saw you?' her father said.

'Nobody.'

'You're sure?'

'Maybe Gertie Mohill was at her window, but she turned inside.'

'Nobody in the street?'

'Not until,' Jude nodded towards the Talty.

'I was waiting for my brother, Doctor,' said Tim-Tom. 'He came out before I had to go in to get him. We saw the infant. I couldn't see it breathing, but "Go to the doctor" was what we thought. Go direct and say nothing, and that's what we did.'

'Who saw you?'

'Anyone who saw only the two of us going home, lifting the boy because of the long day he'd put down and the rain.'

Doctor Troy crossed to the window, put his hand on the rattle. The pool in the corner of the sill was considerable.

None spoke. Neither the brothers nor the boy said that the child had come back to life while they were on their knees, but the thought of it was in the room, and staying there.

Ronnie went over and back the few steps the room allowed, the baby in her arms in the deep sleep that is like a linen without stain. She had not held a child so young. Already she was in a state of wonder. The infant was just another, not remarkable except for the countless ways each of us is. But looking into her face Ronnie felt she had never seen one before. The girl's flesh had a flawlessness that took her breath. In sleep the pale, purple eyelids with lashes minute, the closed lips smaller than her little fingertip, yet holding expression. It was the common rapture of all parents, but in those first moments Ronnie Troy felt she was remembering something essential she had forgotten.

The doctor stood with his back to the room. Ronnie could feel his thinking coming out through his shoulders, which flexed forward, as though under a burden of wings. He had a braced quality. He looked into the night in the one direction, not turning his head or otherwise showing he was seeing anything that was out there.

But Ronnie knew he was.

She knew from the time it was taking. She knew from years of seeing him pick not the easiest option, never the common way, but after internal examinations of all possible solutions and a wrestle with conscience that had no final round, choosing a course he believed right. She knew from the very breathing of him, the way he was in the world, and recalled the line of Father Tom who, coming from a meeting with raised voices in the sitting room, putting on his hat, had once said to her, 'When he wants to be, your father can be a right awkward man, right awkward.' So, when the doctor turned from the wet window and announced the conclusion that would affect all of them for the rest of their days, Ronnie was not surprised, but elated.

Jack Troy showed no sign his decision was weighty, but in the same tone in which he delivered all diagnoses, said, 'You must tell no one.'

He looked at the two brothers at the table, their caps held. Their faces were identical, each with cheek patches of purple and red above the shaving line, less flesh than a weathered and exposed mineral brought up from below, making jewels of their soft blue eyes.

'You must go home and you must tell no one,' he said. His eyes did not leave theirs. 'Can you do that?'

There was a pause in which the two brothers' minds met without look or word. Then 'We can, Doctor,' said the brother who was the driver.

'We can,' came the echo.

'Tell no one,' Jack Troy said to Jude Quinlan.

The boy pushed the loop of damp hair from his forehead. 'I won't.'

The two brothers rose, the boy after them. 'Thank you for the tea, miss,' said one, 'Thank you,' said the other. 'Come on so,' he said to the boy.

Jude looked to Ronnie holding the baby. The reluctance that was in his eyes needed no words. But she met them, and with a conviction she only then discovered, said, 'I'll mind her, I promise.'

The word was like a bridgeway, frail but fixed between them. He tested it with his eyes.

'We'll bring you back to get your father,' said the Talty brother, and he put his hand on Jude's shoulder.

The doctor led them out.

With a softly rocking step, Ronnie crossed to the window. She looked down into the flawless sleeping face. 'Now,' she said, and again 'now', the way she did sometimes when she was writing a story and stuck for what happened next. *Now, what?* was what it asked, but this time she knew the answer would not be only hers. To get around the impasse, she bent and kissed the baby's forehead and, without plan or proof, to her whispered the prayer-prediction of all parents, 'It'll be all right.'

When her father came back, he looked more exhausted than when he left. He was in the first moments of consequence, and it showed. Seeing it, Ronnie knew at once that she would not be asking him the question that had been in her since he carried the baby into the kitchen *What did you do to make her live?* and instead turned to the stove and whispered, 'Tea.'

'Not for me, thank you.' He had come alongside, and now lifted the baby from her to examine it once more.

Ronnie felt the removal not as a burden lifted but as a loss. The baby stirred in the transfer, her eyes closed but her head turning, as though for the breast that was not there.

'Warm some milk,' her father said.

Why had she not thought of it? *Sometimes I am just thought-less.* Ronnie poured the milk from the enamel jug into the small pot, centred it on the hot plate. She stood beside the stove and watched the milk, dipping her finger three times before she decided it was the right temperature, if in fact it was. 'Will you test it?' she asked her father.

'It'll be fine.'

'I don't want to burn her.'

'You won't.'

It was a dialogue with precedent in that kitchen. In the plaster of the walls, the oak of the cabinets and the pine of the floor, were the memories of night-feeds of each of the Troy sisters, Sophie who near-slept while she fed, Charlotte, who would not take the bottle, and Ronnie who reached up to try and hold it herself. They were the same scenes that were in every house where children had started life, but not between father and daughter, and not with a found child.

Ronnie dipped her finger once more. 'We have no bottle. Do we have a bottle? Where would one be?'

'Pour the milk into a bowl,' her father said. He said it calmly, but already in his voice, she felt, was the acknowledgement that they were in a confederacy, and that it would require everything of both to make it work. That Ronnie could not imagine how, that she felt that in some way she was certain to fall short of what would be needed, were thoughts postponed under the urgency of new life.

'Go to the surgery. In the third drawer on the left-hand side of the mahogany chest, you'll find a large syringe. Bring that.'

A syringe? Ronnie did not say. She took a blue-banded bowl and poured the milk and was out the door and down the hall in the damp cool before she had time for second guesses. *This house is too cold for a baby*, is what she thought, when she came inside the surgery where her father had let the fire in the grate die. Laid on the air were the coal-fumes that had greased back down the chimney they had gone up. The mahogany chest was the one that had travelled by ship from England. A monster, once it landed in the surgery it was never leaving. In its birthplace it was designed with absolute clarity of purpose: compartments of all sizes, shelves tall, medium and short, drawers with and without dividers, some small as matchboxes, as a conceived replica of the ordered male mind. In Faha, under the exigencies of a country General Practice where the patients had to have enough floorspace to stand, where everything had to go somewhere, and tidying up was a matter of opening the doors and stuffing in, it had been disabused of the notion that order was a requirement for clarity of mind. Ronnie knew what it was like, and as she turned the key, she kept one hand free to catch what would fall out. The third drawer on the left-hand side had first to be uncovered. All surgeries were snowed with pamphlets, brochures, guidelines and documentation from The Department. They came from Dublin in both a mimic of support and unsubtle reminder *We have our eye on you*. Lately they had plastic covers that wouldn't easily burn. The chest was bronchial with them.

Defying the look of holy mess, the large syringe was exactly where her father said. It had a fearsome bulk that would make most patients faint. What was wrong with you to require it defeated imagination, until you remembered that the books on diseases in the five vital organs came with annual supplements that were each as long as the originals. Ronnie hurried back through the hall holding it down by her side. When she came into the kitchen, the baby was awake and her father was bent over it. He was smiling close and sounding a soft 'Yes you are' that was in answer to no question but within a universal language old as the first parents. It was both natural and shocking, maybe shocking because so natural, she couldn't decide. Ronnie put the syringe behind her back.

'Sterilise it,' her father said, without taking his smile from the infant.

She moved the kettle back on the hotplate, put the syringe in the basin and washed it thoroughly. The long window behind the sink held her reflection against the night, and briefly she caught herself in it, the two strands of hair that had escaped clips, the rounded shoulders, the flushed look of her face that while angled down made fleshy her jaw and dissolved her chin. She might have been forty, she thought. An unimaginable age, she could imagine then.

The kettle sang. She brought it to the soaped syringe, for reasons too complicated to unravel now trying not to look at her father as he brought one forefinger in to alight – 'Pop!' – on the baby's nose, all the while studying in the smallest of faces for response.

'It's ready,' she said.

'Bring it and the milk.'

'How hot should the milk be?'

'The temperature of your blood when your mother says your name.'

It was no time to be cryptic. She let a look tell him, and her father read it and in a tone of apology said, 'Let a drop on your wrist. If you feel heat, it's too hot.'

She brought the milk and syringe to the table, took a chair next to him.

'Her eyes are not seeing,' her father said.

Ronnie did not cry the *O God* that was immediate in her, did not shout *No* nor let out a sound neither anguish nor protest but these were present. She looked to her father but he did not turn to her. He was watching the girl, and Ronnie turned her own face upwards, the fist of one hand caught in the ball of the other. She squeezed the hand around the fist tight.

'Now,' her father said. His voice was the same smooth, equable instrument he always used with patients, the one, suffused and constrained, that baffled her, for how did he meet the legion of suffering of every day and night, the knocks on the door that did not know the Hours of Opening, and still retain that calm? It was unearthly. She wished for one minute he could not be a doctor. She wished he would bang his hand on the table and curse and tell God this was not a good enough life.

She would tell Him herself, but not until years later, when her first book would have this moment in it.

Doctor Troy had the baby crooked in his left arm. He angled her higher. 'Milk closer,' he said.

Ronnie drew the wrinkles off with the spoon, put the bowl next to him. Into the milk he dipped his little finger, then brought it to the infant's lips. His touch was barely that. It was a nearness more than a contact, film of milk between his flesh and the child's mouth. The baby's eyes did not follow his hand, and he did not try to show her. Instead, he held the finger where the smell of the milk could reach her, and he waited. Then he took away his hand and dipped once more, repeating exactly what he had done without haste or impatience, with the same result.

'Will I heat it again?' Ronnie whispered.

Her father shook his head once. He rocked the child softly, his eyes not leaving her. 'Try, you,' he said then.

Ronnie looked at her hands.

'Here, take her.'

'I should wash them again.'

'You just washed them. Take her.' He passed her the baby, and she felt the substance of it in the swaddling again and her breath came like a sigh.

'Try,' her father said.

She did exactly what he had done. She used no added pressure, said no coaxing, laid the milk-finger to within the milk's width of the mouth. But this time, the lips moved. They opened, and closed, and opened again, as though testing the world for its taste. Ronnie felt the lips against her skin. The smallest of milk passed on to the baby.

'Again,' the doctor said.

And Ronnie did it again, and again after that, and after that, in a first learning for the three of them that recalled the beginnings of us, that stopped and turned back the clocks and made in that night room with creaking floor and leaking windows a scene in which was present the elemental and invisible force by which human beings were bound.

By the seventh time the lips were seeking, and then sucking. The finger was a poor nipple, and when it went inside the infant's mouth the force of suction was urgent and stronger than Ronnie had imagined.

The doctor stood, took the syringe, pinched up his trousers to kneel at the press under the sink. That press was no different to the others in the house, in character anarchic, but from it he took what he was looking for. It was a bicycle repair kit that had been in there since before the rust had eaten the girls' bicycles. He snapped the catch, found the patch of rubber tubing that was for tyre emergencies, and with quiet diligence, rubber cement and band, made a mouthpiece for the syringe. Once set, he scalded it with the kettle water. There was a smell of hot rubber but he judged it passable and eyed it with a pin.

'Your finger will not be enough for her,' the doctor said. 'In the morning I will go to town and get a bottle. This will keep her tonight.'

The ungainly, improvised air of the thing seemed brutal, but, in the unwritten scene they were in, improvisation was in every moment and Ronnie did not ask if it was safe or would work. She watched her father fill the syringe with milk, squirt some out and lave the tip. Then he came alongside where she was letting the baby pulse-suck her finger in a rhythm regular as a heart.

'Take this,' he said. 'Bring it alongside your finger. Let her sense it. Then slowly withdraw the finger and ease this in its place.'

'You should do it.'

'She knows you now. You'll be fine.'

He was close to her, and she could smell the brandy, smoke and ghost of aftershave that were him even after he was dead.

'Go ahead. Try.'

Ronnie did as instructed. The brute nipple was bigger than her fingertip. When she placed it against the lips, the baby's forehead creased and she turned her head away, and the plan foundered.

'She won't take it,' she said.

'She will.'

There he was again, telling the future what to do, she thought. If only life could be that simple. If only he knew that for her it was not. For her the pieces of the world did not always match up, and there was not a prescription for everything. She tried again. And again after that, and though she shushed, soothed and rocked, and made the sounds that were the ones all mothers made, the baby would not drink. Ronnie knew it was her fault. It was not the rudimentary contraption with the rubber tubing. There was some primal failure and inadequacy in her. The baby knew. She knew that Ronnie was not her mother. She knew the world had betrayed her, that the first covenant had been broken, and she was landed in a displacement in which she could trust no one.

The infant cried.

She cried with her whole being. She cried though Ronnie said *No No No* and *Shush Shush Shush it's all right*, she cried as though in a language older than words, as though in it was the original expression of wound, the first hurt, that was the failure of love. Ronnie stood from the table, went down the room with her, and back up again with her, rocking a little harder now, a little more insistently, saying the sibilant sounds one into the other until they were river and sea in a seashell returning, saying them to the rhythm of her own steps that she slowed now because the room was too small for a long journey and because as she went the baby's crying was first distracted by the rocking and then diminished by the knowledge that it was going somewhere new.

The doctor watched. He watched until the crying stopped but the walking didn't.

Ronnie was afraid if she stopped the baby would cry. She communicated this to her father in eyebrows and lips.

'I can take her,' he said.

Though he spoke, and not in a whisper, she didn't dare, and instead the plan they settled was established through looks, head shakes and the holding up of four fingers. Her father was exhausted, Ronnie would stay with the baby while he slept. At four o'clock he would relieve her and she would sleep, the way the young could, at any hour. If the baby woke, it would be hungry, and she was to try the syringe. A nod said she would. Then the doctor got out of the chair that was as stiff as his bones. He looked at it when he stood, as though the chair was at fault, or he wanted to savour the victory of standing. Then he crossed to his daughter and kissed her forehead, placing one hand against the arm that held the baby. Ronnie said nothing but made an acknowledgement with her eyes.

Then he was gone.

***

The baby was asleep, how profoundly Ronnie couldn't tell. She was rocking it still and moving over and back in that kitchen in a stepping that was a dance before music was invented. The wall clock said it was one o'clock, but it felt like deep night. She had no thought now for what would happen tomorrow, and instead all her concentration went on keeping the child comfortable, and asleep.

Which meant moving.

Ronnie Troy travelled many steps in that room, and hoped wherever the child dreamed she was going was a safe and warm place. Space and time were cousins but not on speaking terms, and neither she nor the baby gave either a second thought, migrating into that other dimension where human beings go when held in each other's arms. And for a duration it was to both as though nothing outside that house existed, no country, church or state, no code, rule or law beyond the one that had no name but was inside you since breath. Nothing mattered but the slow transit of the floorboards that kept the baby sleeping and unaware of the story she had been born into.

Which had Ronnie in it now.

Human nature being what it is, the rocking and sleeping of the child made the rocker sleepy too. As Ronnie's anxiety eased her shoulders softened and her head lowered towards the infant's. Still stepping across the kitchen, her eyes began to close. By a trigonometry not in textbooks, a relation of angle and length, her face now inside the warm unforgettable scent of the child's and she inside this woman's, they were two parts of a triangle in which the third was missing. The rhythmic hum Ronnie was making in her chest, a hum part-song part-nursery rhyme, and which had issued before she knew she was doing it, was for herself too. It soothed her as it did the child, and after a time that was no-time and all-time, the way that near-breaths can mix and match, they were two who were one.

When her foot bumped the chair leg, Ronnie understood you could walk yourself into unconsciousness. She needed to lie down. The baby was deeply asleep, but the cold air of the front hall would surely wake it. The stairs, that were the exposed bones of the house, ache-creaks in most steps; the upstairs landing with its mouse-run skirting and threadbare Persian runner that no longer hid tooth-gaps; the obsequious humidity that fogged the glass of the barometer, buckled all the tongues in the grooves of the wainscot and in winter made those parts of the house that were far from a fireplace a formless creature of dampness; these were bracing for any visitor, never mind a baby. Her own bedroom, even if she made it that far, by this hour would have been occupied by the gelid air that slid nightly through the slates, guaranteeing that when she woke each December morning under eiderdown and blankets the tip of her nose was polar. No, she would not take the baby there. Instead, in a measured action that all mothers only realise they know how to do when they do it, she came over to the chair by the Aga, and, with arms enfolding the baby, placed her left leg forward and began to lower her body, her right knee descending as though in genuflexion until she made contact with the edge of the seat, easing herself back and down into it in a hands-free sitting whose goal was singular and simple: *Don't wake the baby.*

The child didn't stir, and not for the last time did Ronnie Troy think what a whole, enfolded, innocent and peaceful thing was an infant in sleep. She let her back meet the support of the cushion. With her right hand she pulled gently at the woollen throw, drawing it up and settling it over both of them until they were a picture of ones in a Pullman seat, travelling into unmapped country.

That country was first the night. It was first only that horizonless agglomeration of dark that is half our lifetimes, but for which the verb is fallen, and for good reason, and which, without book or company, and with the infant asleep on her breast, to Ronnie Troy felt like a curtained desolation. What stars had been minted the clouds had stolen. The black of the near view was not as black as the further, but blackest were the bare sycamores whose branches reached in all direction, like a demented basketry abandoned mid-weave. Ronnie turned from the window and the spat rain and looked into the distance of the room where she saw not the buttermilk wall nor the crowded press, but the story.

The story was the other feature of that night. Already Faha had stepped, stumbled or fallen out the doors of public houses and wound home from the Christmas Fair. Already whoever had left the baby by the back gates of the church was in an elsewhere, and for the first time since the birth, its mother was without her. That mother, Ronnie thought of now. She thought of her who was without face or body, but a flesh same as the one on her breast, thought of her not with judgement, or recrimination, with no avidity to know her circumstance, but with only the wellspring of human pity, for surely that mother was in pain, and she looked down at the sleeping infant, and in a voice that reason would say would not carry beyond the end of the table, towards the window Ronnie Troy whispered, 'She's all right. I have her.'

She would not fall asleep tonight, not with the baby in her arms. She could stir and wake and fall out of her hold. *Yes, with me, she could certainly fall.*

'Stay awake, Ronnie,' she said softly. 'Stay awake.'

The clock was on the wall behind her, and she could not easily turn to it. So, the night went clockless and the minutes dissolved in an unmarked time whose only measures were the tolerance of the human frame to stay in a chair and the breaths of the baby. By the simple fact that it was the warmest spot in the house, Ronnie was sitting in the seat that had become her mother's in her last year. And by an unproven logic whereby we leave some of ourselves in the furniture, she thought of her now.

A finely made, soft-spoken gentlewoman, Regina Troy was not a natural fit for Faha. The thing she put you in mind of was a paper kite, with thin light struts and a flutter ribbon of nerves that spun wild in the smallest breeze. She was not built for big wind, and soon enough the buffeting of life on the western edge of a wet nowhere loosened the struts and undid the glue that kept all in place. Rapidly her eyelids blinked at what came her way each day. In fraught moments, she cupped her hands together in front of her and shook them, the way you might before you throw the dice. That the difficult births of each of her daughters didn't kill her was a mercy of God, there was no other explanation, the other side of the bargain that each birth seemed to take a little more of Regina away. That is how it seemed to Ronnie when she was old enough to notice. Her mother's nerves were a sixth entity living in the house. There was no remedy for your own nature, Jack Troy said. Any bottle or pill would only act as disguises, and so, instead, like all families, in order to keep living together the Troys instituted a custom of their own invention. When Mommy was bad, when the nerves were at her, Regina took to her room where she fought them on her own, the three sisters becoming a smaller family whose Daddy was away at work while Ronnie played Mommy, only this time with living dolls. It was not something she resented. She took to the role with the same seriousness she brought to everything, and her sisters seemed none the worse for a childhood without parents in daylight hours. When their mother came downstairs, or was well again, her absences were not mentioned, and the house took on the holiday air of a visiting aunt.

Only she was their mother.

There were in fact all kinds, was Ronnie's deduction. It was a reasoning in testament to the breadth of creation, but also the inevitable conclusion of one who had lived outside the definition of herself since she was six.

When her mother's cancer came, it came swiftly, travelling from her pancreas into her other organs quicker than she could say *I have had this pain.* Without discussion of something that she considered natural, Ronnie took on Regina's care. Neither of her sisters were candidates. And so, in one of those knots the world makes out of the human enterprise, the child who had been the mother became the mother to the mother who became a child. Ronnie had never lived outside the house or with another human being, but she had a nurse's knowledge by proximity and a temperament that could remain calm in the face of calamity.

What Ronnie did not admit, even to her diary, was her own loss. There were times when what she most wanted was to be held by her mother, to lay her head in against her breast and have her arms come around her. Just that. Not to share thoughts, not to talk or tell stories or dreams, but only to close her eyes and rest her head inside that Tide and talcum, rose and jasmine that were her mother when she breathed her. But even before Ronnie felt it, it was already too late for that. Regina was sticks and paper, she was a near-transparency, evanescing into a memory that she herself was witness to, her eyes growing larger as her frame diminished, and in them a child's look of fear of the dark that was to come. In the end it was Regina who wanted Ronnie to put her arms around her. '*Would you mind?*' she had asked in a bird's voice that could be denied nothing, and Ronnie did, bending over her when her mother sat in this same chair with this same blanket over her, hugging on to her from above and feeling her mother's head come in against her breast like one seeking home.

This she thought of now.

In the long night she missed the mother she didn't have, and the one she did. She was away in the memory of her when her head rolled.

'Stay awake,' she said, as though to a reader tired.

Her body announced its reality through aches in her neck and shoulders. She eased her head to the right, to the left, and at once the baby stirred and opened eyes that were seeing or not-seeing, it made no difference, because already her face was tightening into the first cry of hunger.

'Shush, shush shush.' Ronnie stood with her and resumed the rocking that this time was no remedy, and she lifted the cover of the hotplate and brought the milk pot to it. Then, with a one-handed dexterity you don't know you have until you need it, she drew the milk up into the syringe, all the while rocking the infant whose cries rent the night in an alarm that had no off-button. It was three in the morning. Ronnie wanted her father to sleep until four. She did not want to fail him or the baby and carried her down the far end of the kitchen in a living proof of Sonny Cooney's adage that saints are not only the ones whose cards live inside missals.

'Shush,' she said, 'it's OK. You're OK,' to no effect at all, spouting some of the milk against the only part of her flesh the baby wasn't covering, adjudging it safe, then bringing the amateur nipple to the lips that were too engaged in outcry to feel it.

Until they did.

The instants between the first sensory apprehension of the warm milk bud, and the opening of the lips to receive and then suck on it, were a history of the world in miniature. Seeing it, Ronnie let out a sigh. She wanted to shout out, she wanted to let back her head and cry the single *Yes!* that is the testimony of all when endeavour meets engagement and one of the cogs of the universe turns. But because she was Ronnie Troy she did not. All of her was quietened, composed, like some clasp closed. She came back to her mother's chair and settled them into it. Eyes shut, the infant sucked on the syringe. Ronnie kept her thumb ready to apply pressure, but there was no call. The force of the suction was beyond equation and defied the size of a baby no bigger than two hands. Wonder was a word thinned from use, but it was what she felt watching the girl feed in that night kitchen with the single bulb burning and all Faha asleep.

'That's a good girl,' she said, 'good good girl.'

They were words without response, but natural to Ronnie saying them.

'You are. You are a very good girl. Now let's see if we can do this. Up you go.' She stood and let the baby on to her left shoulder, patting its back as she walked once more down the kitchen. 'There, or like this? Is that better? I think yes that's better, isn't it? You have to teach me. All right? You teach me what you need. Good girl. Yes. You like that, don't you? OK. OK now. We are OK. We are OK.'

Again, Ronnie Troy walked the floorboards, but this time with a budded confidence that came from the nestle into her neck and the fact that the child was fed and did not cry. They went like some on a winter's journey, towards a door they were not sure would open. But they were bound to their course, and to each other now, and across the boards in a mesmeric rocking went Ronnie's sensible shoes, past the clock showing four and the place where the baby was asleep once more.

What was left of that night passed in the unregulated term that occurs when the thing that is supposed to happen doesn't. Either the doctor did not set his alarm, or his exhaustion made him deaf to it, for he did not relieve his daughter at four, nor at five, and she did not go to wake him. Between the jolt-naps that marked the jumps in time from then to morning, it made no odds. For, settled once more in her mother's chair by the stove, in time that was unbounded and tranced, Ronnie floated into a doubled peace, in which she was both the one holding the baby, and the one being held.

***

She woke when her father's footsteps crossed the ceiling. The floorboards announced his consternation when he saw the clock, and soon the stairs were suffering the slap of his leather soles. He came into the kitchen with a creased look, as though it were his daughter's fault he had overslept.

Ronnie was feeding the baby for the second time. She had cleaned and changed her, a face-towel as emergency nappy, three skirt-pins keeping the triangle in place.

Her father came close. He touched the infant's forehead for her temperature, and she paused mid-suck in query then resumed.

'She's fine, isn't she?'

'You should have called me,' he said.

'There was no need.' She bent lower to the baby as though for corroboration, and then nodded to the syringe. 'It worked. This is her second feed.'

'I'll get a bottle in town this morning.'

In the long windows a begrudging dawn was hauling thin light once more out of the dark.

'Can she see us?' Ronnie asked.

'Too early to say.'

'I think she can. Look at how she responds.' She made a pantomime face over the baby. But the child's expression did not change.

'If she can see, she can't see that far yet,' her father said. He had brought an ointment and applied it to the baby's eyes. 'Have you had breakfast?' he asked.

'I'm fine.'

He moved the kettle and cut the loaf and to the table brought butter and one of the ten pots of blackberry jam by which Mona Ryan paid for the paring of her corns. He laid the two cups and saucers, the two plates, two of the unpressed napkins with the Admiralty insignia in the corners. While Ronnie walked, winding the baby, he made a pot of tea. All the while he said not one thing. When he sat and said 'Tea is drawn' he did not say it in her direction but generally, as though it was a fact he had no hand in.

Ronnie sat; the baby asleep on her once more.

Her father poured the tea.

There fell an interlude of sorts. What curtain came down did so without notice, and though neither spoke both knew it and knew that they were only at a pause in the action, and that those consequences that were waiting in the wings were the same ones that all could imagine and seemed inevitable in that time and place. In the pause, they did not leave their seats nor pass comment on what had happened so far. They did not speculate on how things would go, but both remained in silence, knowing the story had deepened as it went, and everything up to that point might have been fable.

Ronnie drank her tea. She felt her father's weariness coming across the table. It was as though he was the one who hadn't slept, she thought, and by a human equation for which there is no science, in his company Ronnie felt she had. Despite the weight of circumstance and uncertainty, she was aware now of a glowing not quite euphoria but near enough, a lightening that was happening inside her by the minute and to which she was more witness than maker, as though it were a thing bestowed. It was the lack of sleep, Ronnie told herself. It was human chemistry – or was it algebra? – what happened when X was subtracted from Y and – she couldn't think of the rest, her brain was addled, but her spirit wasn't. Maybe it was only what happened when you escaped the routine of day-night-day, when you found yourself outside the bounds of what you knew; maybe it was normal, to feel this, this – she couldn't think of the word for it, unless it was, no, hardly, well maybe – *blessed*.

She was sitting with the child on her left arm in a position that both had learned without lesson. They fitted in such a way, and in such a way were inside each other's living and breathing. Ronnie could not stop looking at the baby. *It's ridiculous*, she thought, lifting her face but with the breaking of a smile. *Stop looking at her.* It was a command that counted for nothing, because, though she kept her head upright for some instants, she was defeated by a stronger force still, the smell of the baby. It overwhelmed all. It was a smell unmatched in the world, and she surrendered to it again now, lowering her face to the sleeping child and closing her eyes so the smell came about her and held her in it, and was, though all else might fall, the fundament of goodness.

Ronnie kept looking at the baby, while her father looked at the way ahead.

What daylight was delivered now showed the trees outside darkly. Spectral, the limbs of the old sycamores were raised, outward and skyward both, like nature's fresco of the heavens beseeched. A salt wind had come up the estuary into the wounds of the dying year. Through the unmet joins of the sash windows, the branches sounded a glottal Old Irish none could understand. Seabirds' cries were the rest of it.

When the interlude was over, the doctor signalled it by standing. 'You can manage until I get back?'

'Of course.'

'We must let no one know, not yet,' he said. His eyes met his daughter's, and she read there all that he was not saying.

'I understand.'

The doctor went to his surgery and shortly returned with an emptied drawer for the baby's cot. The right-angles of the carpentry had a crude look when Ronnie thought of the eggshell skull, but she softened the interior with a dressing of teatowels and a cushion that had been sat on so often it was an envelope of feathers. The doctor took the wireless from the kitchen and installed it in the waiting room. Though the signal there meant the broadcast seemed to be coming from under the sea, he left it up loud and let the sponsored programme fill the front hall.

'If she cries, the patients won't hear her,' he said, when he came back into the kitchen.

'If it doesn't wake her.'

His eyes considered the sleeping girl, went from there to the weeping window. Directly he crossed to the clothes press and took out two towels long and short and brought them to the sill and sash, for soaking and stuffing both, making temporary dam against what leaked in from the outside world. It was an uncarpentered solution, but Ronnie could see it solaced him, did not say she could have done better, knowing there was always mystery in how the things on the long finger at last got done.

'We could call off the surgery for today?' she said.

'And tomorrow? And the day after?'

Father and daughter shared the look of ones whose plan has no second page. Then the doctor, who had a lifetime of emergencies behind him, said, 'We do not get to live only the best parts of life. We will work out something. When I come back with the bottle, I will light all the fires. You will be able to bring her upstairs.'

He paused then, the full weight of the story on the white-shirted shoulders, on the grey eyes, and the eyebrows that lowered towards each other like a roof whose eaves could not meet. It lasted only seconds, only the time it took for Doctor Troy to agree with himself that this was the right thing to do. He nodded a soft nod, and to his eldest daughter said, 'OK?'

It was a threshold moment. Neither could have said what exactly was being asked or what lay ahead. Like all roads in Faha, you could only see the next bit. *Contra mundum*, the doctor did not say, but Ronnie saw it in her father's eyes and in the set of his jaw. *He is ready to meet all that is asked of him*, she thought. *As am I*. She looked down into the baby. 'Yes,' she said.

Then the doctor was gone. She watched the Morris pass through the front circle and as far as the bend in the avenue. In the front hall and through the entirety of Avalon House, the wireless was playing the Andrews Sisters' 'Sleigh Ride'. Ronnie lowered her head into the smell of the sleeping baby.

'We are all right, so we are,' she whispered, in a voice that was her mother's. 'Aren't we?'

She waited a half-second and then, like her own mother to herself, answered, 'Yes, we are. Yes, we are.'

4

The doctor arrived in town before the shops were open. The day was dull, the sky clearing out one shower after another, between them a disgruntled light. He parked in the grounds of the hotel and sat for tea and toast in the breakfast room. Higgins snapped the menu closed, but otherwise made no comment on the doctor's choice to pass over the rashers, sausages, eggs, tomatoes and Clonakilty pudding, both white and black, that escaped the kitchen on the fried smell of a spitting fat.

Through the hotel, in red and green tissue, Christmas was everywhere. Gold tinsel, which was this year's step above the silver, was twisted around lamps and fringed shades. Smoke- and sun-paled paintings of eighteenth-century landscapes had collars of gold and silver about their frames and, tucked overhead, the sprig of holly.

It was early. There were residents at three tables only, commercial travellers with tan shoes and newspapers they read from the back to the front, all having appetisers of tobacco. One, who lifted his head to suck smoke, passed a quiff nod to the doctor, and Jack Troy returned it but otherwise had no engagement. He lowered his face and drew his right palm from forehead to chin, as if to erase what was written there. He had no newspaper, so he turned to the window that gave on to the cathedral, from which first Mass had emptied, leaving the doors open, in yawn or invite. He kept his gaze there, aware that he was in one of the moments of his life. What had happened during the night he could not fully accommodate inside himself yet: that the boy had brought the infant to his door, that they had thought her dead, that she had seemed so when Jack first held her, when he carried her down the hall and into his room – she was not breathing, he would stake his career on it, he had found no pulse – and was lifeless still when he tried to warm her against himself, when he took off the wet blanket and swaddled her, and still so when he breathed into her, and paused, and again a second time; but not the third. The third time, life rose up through her, vivid and palpable and startling. It came into her eyes and her mouth and her chest, and he had let out a cry that not age, reserve, nor years of doctoring could stop. For, in his arms, she was alive who had been dead. In the instants of it, reason was elsewhere. At first there was only the rushing white elation in his spirit: she was breathing. It overtook all. *She is breathing.* What cases he had seen before, what injured or ill, grave or dying, mattered not at all at that moment. There was only this girl, small as his two hands, and the air coming and going now through her in the rhythm that joins humankind. Involuntarily, he had tilted his head upwards. He had found his own breath where he only now realised he had left it, and by degrees came back from the height to his measured self. *Be a doctor*, was the dry counsel of his father. *What the patient wants is for you to be a doctor, not wringing your hands, not weeping, not anything in fact like a human being. A doctor.* Like all advice from all fathers, it was useless until it wasn't. And shortly Jack Troy had restored himself to his professional equanimity, though his eyes were polished.

It was mechanics, not miracle. He took no personal credit. On this he was clear. It had nothing to do with him, he had done nothing any mildly knowledgeable medical person wouldn't have done. The heart is an engine, it had started again, was the all of it. This much he could settle now in the cold light of the morning, though when he had washed his hands in the basin, he had had to still their tremor.

He had told the Talty brothers and the Quinlan boy to tell no one. The command had come out of his mouth with a certainty he didn't have. Nor did he have a plan. He had carried the infant out of the surgery with a winged joy he had forgotten existed.

In its simplicity was a perfection that made argument redundant. The child was breathing, the fact of that like a linen folded inside him. But in the ten steps he took through the cool damp hall, the world returned, and before he reached for the crackled porcelain of the doorknob, he knew that it fell to him to shield her. From what he did not elucidate, but in that country the story was familiar; he did not need to. Like any reader who does not want the book to go the way they imagine, he wished for an ingenious plot, but had no idea what that could be. Until he knew, Jack Troy wanted the clocks to stop. He wanted the impossible, for a hand to stay the tide of sequence and consequence, for what was inside him to remain as it was, luminous and clean and good, and for the infant to retain the innocence she had at that moment.

The Talty brothers had the lips of crypts, and the Quinlan boy the steadfastness of a captain, but the doctor was not born yesterday, and knew that in Faha the lid never stayed on a story. It blew off through pressure and confluence, the need of things to be told and the porous nature of a people living every day inside the same rain. So, soon someone would know. And ten breaths after that, ten more would. They would know the way the people know everything first, through hearsay, which travelled quicker than fact and without the baggage of truth, and then they would want to see for themselves.

So, what to do?

The doctor had no idea. They could not keep the child hidden in Avalon, and they could not bring her outside.

Faced with a crux, he was one who, since boyhood, was unable to be still. A problem unsolved was against nature, and from those evenings when he twisted in his desk applying formulae in search of mathematical solutions that were convoluted until they were obvious, to his days in the Royal College when he learned that the human body contained the answers to its own questions, he could not abide not knowing what, how and why. But this morning, sitting by the window of the breakfast room, he was aware of a calm uncommon in him. It was more than that, too. He turned his examination on himself to try and ascertain just what it was.

The word he came to was *inspired*, finding within it both *in* and *spirit*, and, remembering his Latin, the *inspirare*, breathing-into, that contained the exact action of the night surgery and the otherness he had felt when the child's heart started beating, as though a third party was present.

It was not the case, of course. But strange was the commonest word for our experience, and here was the strangest: in the breakfast room of the Old Ground Hotel, eyes on the cathedral across the way, Jack Troy felt that the girl had breathed something *into him*.

'Tea, and … toast, Doctor.' Higgins brought them himself and placed each with a performed propriety. He stood back and erect, face of waxed floor and eyelashes mopping. 'Will there be anything else today?'

'Thank you.'

'Very good. Enjoy your … breakfast, Doctor.'

***

Doctor Troy chose the least-frequented of the town's three chemist shops. It was through the alley off Parnell Street where the Fergus flooded each year, and in retreat left its memory under the linoleum. The shop was narrow and dark, had an air of apothecary and smelled of river. Christmas was lettered in a strung cardboard whose *Merry* had perished. From too long an acquaintance with physical complaints and pharmaceutical remedies, the chemist, Griffin, had withdrawn to a backroom where he measured his day in thimbles of Power's whiskey. Mrs Griffin was front of shop. When the doctor came in, she was under the counter, plugging in the bar heater that saved her feet becoming stones and hoping this time there wasn't too much river in the socket. She rose up with the jingle and had her hair pushed in place before he came to the counter. She was a woman in her fifties who had put on a decade in marriage. For what was wrong with her, the shop had the righting, and she had gone through most medicines by an amateur diagnosis that found when she read the back of any package she could say, 'I have that too.'

To the doctor, her greatest virtue was that she did not know him.

Mrs Griffin's smile was like neuralgia, but it was offered genuinely to a stranger who didn't know there were better chemists on O Connell Street. Under the brim of his hat, the doctor mumbled 'baby's bottle' and went to the shelves with the air of one seeking the illicit. But, in an exact replica of Georgie Griffin's mind, the shop had abandoned the vanity of organisation, and nothing could be found except by his missus.

'A baby's bottle?' she said, coming from behind the counter, taking a good look at the man and his moustache, and smiling some more at a handsomeness that had defeated the years and produced a newborn. That was men for you. She had socks over her stockings and legs without blood in them. With a stompy gait, she brought a folding-step to the wall shelving, climbed to the height where the doctor's face was at her skirt and the conversation backsided. 'Is it her first?' she asked.

'It is.'

'Isn't that niiiiice.' She lengthened the adjective to give her time to look at him. 'Boy or girl?'

'Girl.'

'Niiiiice.'

She turned, took out packages and passed them to her left hand for holding while she rummaged some more. 'Yours?'

In the pause without answer, she clarified, 'Your first too?'

'Yes.'

'Nice.' She stayed looking, and the doctor discovered that for women the allure of a man with a baby did not grow old. 'Here we are.' She brought down an eight-ounce bottle without packaging and blew the dust free. Tonguing her forefinger, she ran it round the rim for what remained. 'Scald it first,' she told the novice with the grey hair, before adding, 'This one comes with two teats.' She let that information bridge the look between them, and the flush that was almost girlish, then burst it with, 'If only I could find them.'

'I need them more than the bottle.'

'He's a pure terror for putting things where they shouldn't go,' she said. History and intimacy in it, neither of which the doctor wanted.

'I need them.'

'Well, they're here somewhere.' From behind the counter, she got the horn-rimmed glasses that were only for when she needed to see. She stomped across to a glass cabinet that had the key hanging by a string and had turned what was inside upside down before she called, 'Bingo.' At the counter, she removed the glasses and restored her look of appraisal of the handsome man with the young wife. His eye, she saw, was on the packaged bottles of scent behind her. He looked away as soon as she caught him, but the catch was clear, and she turned to the shelf and took down the priciest.

'For the little lady, for Christmas?' she said. She didn't have the energy for a wink but put it into her voice.

On the counter, Guerlain's Vol de Nuit.

'Katherine Hepburn's favourite, so it is,' said Mrs Griffin.

The doctor let the brim of his hat shield his eyes, the only visible signs that his heart had been pierced a jump in his chin and a rise in his gorge.

The hat dipped once by way of yes, and with a 'Nice' that was both congratulation on the sale and wonderment at the soft hearts of men, Mrs Griffin had the perfume in the bag before the customer could ask the price.

Without his asking, she produced baby powder and oil and ointment and cotton buds and muslin and plastic pants and a glass disc that would bang when the milk in the pot was coming to boiling. She jabbed the prices down on to the keys of the old register with an accountant's glee and told the sum.

The doctor paid without comment and was at the door with the paper bag when she called after him, 'Happy Christmas. I hope she thrives.'

It was said in goodwill, customary and blessing both, but it had a pointed end, and by the time the doctor was hurrying across the flooded footpath to the car it was stuck in his head and all he could think of was the burden of responsibility to make the child thrive. Life is not a given, even when granted, and he had a flash memory of first fatherhood he had forgotten, when, despite seven years of medical studies and the hundred and three textbooks whose bindings came unglued as they entered his brain page by page, every hour he had feared some harm alighting on the head of his first-born daughter.

He had been gone two hours. Anything could have happened to the baby in the interim. He thought to stand into the telephone box near the cathedral, call to assuage an anxiety that was as acrid as it was uncharacteristic, but he knew that Mrs Prendergast would recognise his voice, and, with a helpless addiction to be first to know, stay on the line until she had the meat and bones of it. So, he passed the green cubicle with the flittered phonebook that was an emergency toilet-paper, and made do with a telephony older than Graham Bell, nodding a single nod towards the cathedral and letting his look be a prayer without words.

The doctor drove home with the same *That she might thrive* embedded in him and was none the better of it when he was coming up the ruts of the avenue. Through the rainscreen he looked at the exterior of the house, as though for clues to what was inside. The perfume he took from the bag and installed beneath the passenger seat, pausing only the heartbeat that was Annie Mooney in that seat when he was taken by that scent for the first time.

He came in the front hall to the choral sublimity of a Mendelssohn motet coming from the wireless he had forgotten he left on. There were three patients in the waiting room. The doctor had long since dispensed with the need to explain lateness and all who sat in the strange cameraderie of illness were happy with the nod he passed through the open door as he took off his coat and hooked the hat in the hall.

He went directly to the kitchen with the package. Ronnie held up a finger and then stood sidelong to show the baby asleep in the drawer. He came over to look in at her and was eased to see that in the ten hours the infant had been in Avalon she had in truth thrived. Acknowledging that sleep is the prime goal every parent wishes for a newborn, he stepped back the way you might before a bomb, then saw the splayed copy of *The Lake* face-down on the counter.

He looked to his daughter and, without warning, was greatly moved. To mask it, he asked the only question he could think of, 'Trouble?'

'None.'

He pressed his lips and let the moustache do the rest.

'Did you get breakfast?'

'I did.'

She opened the paper bag. He had got everything they needed, except cloth nappies. But she had already commandeered a cotton sheet that would make a dozen and she took up the dressmaker's shears to begin without comment.

How was she still awake, still standing, he wondered, and not for the first time considered that God's first mistake was starting with a man. 'You need to rest,' he said.

'I rested while she was sleeping. I'm grand.'

***

For the remainder of that day, Doctor Troy saw his patients, those that were waiting and those that came with a shipwrecked look and left puddles where they sat. At one point, he thought he heard the child cry inside the pronounced punctuation gaps of the Radio Éireann news, and raised his voice in a declarative tone that was so sudden Una Cooney thought he was telling her that what she had also came with deafness. At another, in the ceiling boards above he heard the tell-tale footsteps of his daughter and knew from the beat that she was rocking the child. It went over and back, and over and back in a hypnotic that he didn't realise he was nodding to until he saw Rory Collins's eyes rising and drew him back to earth with the word haemorrhoid.

Work was a habit invented to stop the mind from going else-where, but what the doctor diagnosed and what prescribed that day he could not have told, for he skipped his notations after hours and had to trust they were dispensed to a cloud in his head that would burst when he saw the patient in front of him. When he saw the last one out, it was with the relief of one who knew the bomb hadn't gone off, and he came into the kitchen with a lightness as unexpected as it was certain. They had made it through that day.

Ronnie was nursing the infant in her mother's seat by the stove. 'Did I make too much noise?' she asked.

It had to be his fault that she always found fault in herself, he thought. Her first instinct was always failure. How he had given her that, he did not know, but it hurt him standing there and he wanted to say so. He wanted to tell her that she was fine and good and that he was sorry for failures of fatherhood too many to count over too many years.

'No,' he said.

'She cried once, but only for a moment.'

'It was fine.'

'Tomorrow, I'll take her into Charlie's room. It's the biggest and gets the morning sun, if there ever is any.' Ronnie's smile was wise and forgiving and she turned it to her father.

He had the fingers of both hands under the tabletop and was holding with his thumbs. He took them away now and for no reason he could name rapped the knuckles of his right hand three times on the timber. 'If there is any.'

From the baby, sucks came, clean as clockwork, one after the other in an urgency that said: *For life we know what to do without being told*. Father and daughter had the same compulsion as everyone else, to sit and watch, but the doctor broke his by announcing he would make the tea this evening. Ronnie said she could do it in a minute, but he was already going to the larder to see what the makings would be. As he cut the loaf on the board, he found solace in the screened sense, the house once more its own quiet kingdom of man, woman and child, and a stay on the world that, for this evening, might not be turning.

Normal is a term that has no normality: the peculiarity of every individual guarantees it. So, the meal the doctor served, bread-and-butter and cheese, half a tomato and half a boiled egg each, and a chicken whose breast meat had gone but whose drumsticks did honour as centrepieces on the plate, had a look of normal, if it was summertime. It made no odds. Ronnie thanked him when she sat from winding the child on her shoulder, the cloth for catching spit-ups still in place and the bottle with the tide gone out in her hand. She lowered the baby into the nest between elbow and body, put the bottle next to the teacup, and served herself in the manner of everyday.

Again, her father was struck by how natural Ronnie was with the child. It was not second nature to her, it was first. She had no hesitation, no questioning. How she carried and cared for the baby were revelations to him, and like most revelations they could only be observed until their meaning was clear. They had the tea in customary quiet, the baby asleep in the nook of Ronnie's arm. 'Will I pour you a second cup?' he whispered at one point, 'We can manage,' Ronnie's answer, pouring and milking and stirring the tea with not a geek out of the infant, then one-handedly drawing up the copy of *The Lake*.

***

Recognising that crises adhered to no schedule, it had long been the practice in Faha that if the doctor hadn't called to the post office by noon to collect his paper, then Timmy the postman would drop it in on his way home. The *Irish Independent* was on the table, back in its creases after a standing reading Ronnie had done earlier, where the rocking blurred all but the headlines of the killer smog in London and His Holiness's grave illness. As though in a play scene of the kitchen set of the Faha Players, where reality had to be established by a mannered casualness, the doctor shook out the newspaper and held it at the distance his eyes had to go before seeing clearly. The pages were filled with advertisements, small columns of news in between. The space age for toys was announced, alongside Tred, the self-shining floor polish. Thinking, as always too late, of what he should get Ronnie for Christmas he was looking at Guiney's advertisement for what looked like female Russians in beaver lamb coats at sixteen guineas, when the knock came to the door.

Father and daughter exchanged a look of thieves. He had not seen the headlamps of a car and, standing, tried to remember if he had put the latch on the door. In waking hours, the house had the same open-door policy as every other one in the parish. Callers knocked and let themselves in at the same time, announcing themselves as they came down the hall by a heavy tread or a *Hello!* that ran ahead of them, like a herald. Patients, each after their own fashion, knocked or didn't, but either way came in and sat in the waiting room, head bent and hands clasped between knees in an unearthly patience that understood life was a waiting room.

Doctor Troy was at the kitchen door before it could open and the baby be discovered. His look to Ronnie was easily translated, and she replied the same. Then he opened the door and was relieved to hear the knock on the brass ring a second time. The latch was down. In one part of his brain, he was inventing a reason to say why the door was locked, in the other he was finding the calm to face someone else's crisis.

When he opened the old door, Father Coffey was on the top step, his bicycle below with the timid light on. He was among the last people in the parish that Jack Troy wanted to see then, and in the rush of thoughts that came through him while he held the door, prime was *How did he find out?*

From long acquaintance with calamity, the doctor's face had mastered impassivity. He could be told of any disaster or tragedy and in the lineaments and planes of flesh and bone there would appear no register. *Hold fire* was his father's precis for a profession that required you to be human and not, and a manner that did not flinch when the enemy was right in front of you. So, he did not immediately greet the priest, nor ask why he was there, and instead did what he had found expedient in the first instance of all fresh catastrophes: nothing. He waited for the priest to fire first.

'I won't come in,' Father Coffey said.

The doctor's hand was still on the door, and he kept it there while he took in the priest's predicament. Father Coffey's glasses were pimpled with rain, but the alarm of his eyes was unmistakable. From a pumping cycle from the Parochial House his cheeks were empurpled and his nose red. For some instants the muscles of his lips fought a battle between urgency and decorum, the former winning when he at last announced, 'He has locked himself into the toilet.'

The Canon, it transpired, had been in there since he said a first Mass that broke the record for brevity because he took a short-cut through the Confiteor after *mea maxima culpa* and got to the Agnus Dei without passing Go. Whether it was a proper sacrament or not was a debate for another day, but of the twelve disciples who took daily Mass at eight o'clock in all the seasons of the rain, none asked for their money back. The old priest had returned home with the low hum that was now so constitutional that it caused no comment, but when Father Coffey greeted him going up the stairs, he had answered 'Ducks and geese, ducks and geese' in a code that was a head-scratcher worse than Kelly's nits.

Father Tom had gone to his room and shut the door. The curate had never seen inside it, and when he heard the noises above, he wondered if the Canon hadn't a cannon up there. There was rolling and dragging, something wheeled and metallic, and a weightiness that made sigh the ceiling. In the event, it was Father Tom's steamer trunk, the one he had come with, and which had burst two discs of Martin Daly's back getting it up the stairs, and whose contents remained a mystery until three days after Tom died. By a strength none would have granted him, the old priest had pulled the trunk over the door saddle, into the upstairs landing, and across it into the toilet, where his voyage was ready to sail. When enough time had lapsed for privacies, the curate came upstairs and rapped on the door with a muted knuckling that he hoped had a question mark in it. No answer came back, except for the mewling of the sibby who, whether prisoner or passenger, was bound for the same Hy-Brasil as the Canon.

Father Coffey had gone down the stairs to find a solution, but after two hours the only one he could come up with was to go back up the stairs. Among the various tactics he tried was an urging tone, then a pleading one, sitting on the floor with his back to the door and saying he would not be leaving until the Canon came out, asking if he could bring a plate of the fried sausages that to the old priest were a better draw than ice cream and jelly, coming to an end of offers after he confessed that he had five Quality Street secreted in his room and if the Canon came out they could share them over tea, at last trying to force his way in with a shoulder that had never seen work and bounced off the door with a surprise of backwards.

None of this did the curate tell the doctor on the doorstep. Instead, he relayed the critical fact that the parish priest had passed the day in the toilet, without food or water, and was astray in the head by reason of a senility that had him thinking he had sailed to an elsewhere. He did not add the *I told you so* that makes the devil smile, but he did something with his mouth that was it in another language.

'I will come,' was all the doctor said. He shut the door on the priest and had his coat and hat on when he came back to the kitchen to tell his daughter the emergency was not theirs. The baby was asleep in the drawer and Ronnie washing their ware. It was a domestic painting, *Mother & Child in a Tableau of Contentment*, but he darkened the corners by saying, 'Answer no knock, only the phone.'

Then he was gone, the car overtaking the curate, and arriving in the gates of the Parochial House with the headlamps turned off. He let himself in and passed through the pressing damp of the hall and up the stairs whose newel post had said goodbye to the perpendicular, drawing the same conclusion as always, that the house was falling down because the priests could not afford to keep it up.

'Tom, it's Jack Troy,' he said to the toilet door.

The Canon was asleep in steerage, his head on the trunk, but he lifted it now to see if they weren't at last come into the harbour of the next life. The cat came under his hand for a rub that had to compensate for food. She called to the doctor in a high pitch that was easily understood, and he said, 'Let her out to me, Tom.'

On the old priest, the pungency of the toilet bowl and the ammonia of the cleaner acted as smelling salts. Waking now, he was surprised to find himself barricaded in the smallest room and first wondered why the curate had done it. 'Jack?' he called.

'I'm here, Tom. Open the door.'

Father Coffey had landed alongside him and was using the lining of his jacket to unblind his glasses.

'Coffey's locked me in,' said the Canon.

The curate made a fish-protest, opened his mouth, closed it again, but did not take the hook.

In the end, it took them the most of another hour to get the old priest out. He came sidelong through the opening after the cat when at last the trunk had budged, but did so with the blithe expression of one who had been to an amusing matinee. He had taken out his teeth and when he smiled, he proved the formula of Felix Pilkington, who had reduced Shakespeare's seven ages to three, 'Once a man, and twice a child.' The greatest perplex was that the incident was erased from his mind once it was over and left him in the becalmed and holy state of those whose minds are a blank slate. For a moment all he did was blink. His big white hands he brought together in front of his midriff and acted as though the gathering outside the toilet was a parish meeting, which required nothing of him but to nod when the Master spoke.

It was the doctor of course who took charge. Noting the shuffle in his step, he took the old priest's elbow and led him down the stairs while Father Coffey, his body without curves, slipped in the opening to take his turn at last in the toilet. The cat, in testament to a nature that could not be legislated, went back in with him.

In the smaller of the two parlours, Doctor Troy sat the Canon. There was no fire in the grate, the room colder than outside and only partially drier. He turned on the standing lamp that, with its red tasselled shade, cast an air of bordello, opened his Gladstone bag and found the ophthalmoscope. 'Look here,' he directed, holding out his left hand as target while he leaned in to see into the depths of what otherwise was hidden. 'Now here.' He was close enough to smell yesterday's cauliflower in the priest's breath but continued his examination with a command that knocked down the remnants of dignity, 'Stick out your tongue.' That it was the same action the priest faced when all the parish stuck out their tongues at the Communion rails was not lost on either of them, but forgoing the depressor that might have continued the imagery as host, the doctor took the priest's tongue between thumb and forefinger and moved it in a perfunctory manner as if it were the clapper of a cracked bell. Whether satisfied or not, he passed no comment. Without the basin that was always at arm's length in the surgery, and too lazy to go as far as the kitchen, he took out his white flag of a handkerchief and dried his fingers in it. While he was folding it back into his jacket pocket, he gave his last instruction, 'Touch your nose.' The Canon did it with each hand and grinned a boyish grin of top marks. Finally, with appraiser's eyes, the doctor did an audit of Father Tom's face. To test its elasticity, he touched the priest's crêpe flesh with his warm fingers. The contact lasted an instant only but startled something in Father Tom. He made a slight shudder, neither pleasure nor pain, but a registering that opened his eyes, and Jack Troy understood at once: since Tom had reached adulthood, nobody had ever touched his face.

'What is your name?' he asked.

'Tom,' said Tom.

'And mine?'

'Jack Christmas.' The priest's mouth was closed, but the muscles of it jumped with the joke that he knew was in circulation in Faha. That it was one against himself made his telling of it funnier to him, and the humour widened and brightened his eyes while he waited to see if the doctor was going to declare him bananas.

After a single beat of alarm, Jack Troy saw the knowingness in the Canon's expression, issued a blow-down in his nostrils that passed for comment, and closed the Gladstone bag. 'Stay here,' he said. His manner was so decisive that when he opened the door brusquely, he found the curate, who was certainly not listening in but studying closely a flaked-off patch of wall plaster in the shape of Wales.

'He'll be all right,' the doctor said without stopping, going into the other parlour that had the locked liquor cabinet with the key behind the feet of Saint Francis. The cabinet was a store-all for the Christmas and sacramental gifts pressed on the priests, most of which came in bottles. He had the whiskey and two cut-glass tumblers in his hand when, behind him, Father Coffey said, 'But he's not.'

He was the junior, and his hot cheeks showed he was aware of it, but he was also young enough to believe that, in many situations, he knew best. 'Clearly, he's not.' It was the opening gambit in a debate he had prepared for since the first Sunday of Advent. 'The Christian thing to do is admit it. It is unfair on him,' he said, adding, 'And on me,' with an editor's wince, because he hadn't been able to decide if that made his case stronger or weaker. 'There is a plan in place for situations like this. There is procedure, to preserve dignity. We have to do what's best for him, *Jack*.' He had never said the doctor's name before, and it came out of his mouth like a lump of turnip.

It was a debate of only one round. Jack Troy did not take his turn but stood with the whiskey and glasses.

'He's clearly…' Father Coffey fished for a kindness, '… ill.'

'Well, one of us is his doctor,' the doctor said, with a coldness not intended, but which came from the knowledge that he had taken his eye off his patient and indulged in the vain hope that things wouldn't get worse. He made a curt nod that was his signal for *Discussion over* and was in the hall when he heard the priest call after him, 'Who will be responsible if he jumps out the window? Or, or throws himself into the river?'

When he came back into the room, the Canon was where he had left him, but was looking into the fireplace the same way you do when the flames are in it. It was a philosopher's pose, and bestowed on the older man a cloak of serenity the doctor did not want to disturb. He poured two whiskeys, sat with them in his two fists. He knew the Canon's drink from years of late evening summits and secret summonses, when parochial crises were laid out without dressing, and his opinion was first among those the priest sought, 'Because,' the Canon had said, both bigging and littling the doctor in the one phrase, 'you are the most intelligent man … in Faha.' Those meetings had ended in a glass. The two men were not, in the normal definition, friends, but time, proximity and communal care had wed them.

The doctor waited for the old priest to come back to him. The signal was an 'Ah' from Father Tom, and a crinkling around his eyes in recognition of the whiskey. They drank it unpolluted with water in sips that smarted until savoured, and when he had adjudged the alcohol had entered the Canon's bloodstream, the doctor said, 'You have moved from the middle to the final stage of dementia, Tom.'

Father Tom smiled a buckled smile, hapless the expression in his eyes.

In an even tone Doctor Troy spoke through the stages of the illness without taking his eyes off the priest. The time-shifting, difficulties with language, eating and dressing, the depression, apathy, delusion, hallucinations, falls and incontinence, he told them all and spared nothing in a bedside manner more suited to corpses. He wanted the older man to see the thing clearly before he responded, but his tactic was for nought when the Canon replied, 'You won't let them take me, will you?' Before he got a reply, with a pathos found in children, the old priest added, 'I wouldn't be allowed say Mass.'

Doctor Troy returned no answer. In the rubescent light that was a lesser version of the red light bulbs that had come to Faha that year for Christmas, the two men sat without saying more, nursing the whiskeys in a time-honoured defence against the cold coming into their bones. In the high-backed chairs that were like leather overcoats unbuttoned, they looked off at different angles.

Putting down his glass, the Canon cupped his knees, rocked softly. It was the smallest motion, but in the stillness that had gathered, gave the impression he was going somewhere. The low engine-noise of his hum confirmed it.

As always, it was impossible to tell what the doctor was thinking. Life had given him a mask for a face, planate cheeks with rivering blood vessels, deeply recessed eyes and sheltering eyebrows that, lowered, seemed to want to join up with the moustache and show no expression at all. But, after a time that could not be told, because in that parlour the clock on the mantel was only a decorative gesture and all the watches the doctor had been given lay unwound in the drawer next to his bed, he lifted his leg off the other one and leaned towards the priest to ask, 'Do you remember a girl, Tom?'

The lean was not enough to stop the Canon rocking, but the tone in Jack Troy's voice paused the humming.

'A girl who had a child,' he said. He linked his fingers in a loose basketry, looked down into them, then again across at the priest. 'This was twenty years ago. We were almost young, and full of certainties, though that is no excuse.'

The older man met his gaze and then looked away, rocking still but slower now, as though the engine that was taking him away was failing.

'Mary, her name was. She had a newborn, and she came to me. She was afraid and she trusted in me. I brought her to you.' In the empty basket, the doctor studied the memory that had become fresh when he rushed into the front hall and saw the Quinlan boy holding the child.

The rain caught the wind and implored the windows to let it in. It made bursts of thrashing, answered in the chest of the chimney by a hollow moan.

When the doctor spoke, his voice was lower still. 'They came for her and the baby in a Ford car. Three of them, two men one woman, all business. The mother and child crying. We stood back.' He was telling it to himself, saying it aloud for the first time in twenty years, and by saying bringing it back to a doubled reality where he was both the younger doctor and the older one looking at him. *The hardest person to live with is yourself*, was a saying of his father's. *Regret is the salt in the wounds of life, it keeps them stinging. And stops us making the same mistakes.* Jack touched his tongue on his lower lip, leaned forward towards the priest. 'Do you remember, Tom?'

It was a moment intimate as in any confessional, but this time was without reconciliation, because Father Tom showed he had gone nowhere by an answer that attested to the selfishness that comes to us all when our self is vanishing. 'You won't let them take me, will you?'

Jack Troy sat back into the armchair. The basket came asunder. He made a fist of his right hand and softly twice punched it into the palm of his other, as though it were a gavel and the verdict coming. He lifted his eyes to the ceiling, where the red lampshade let escape above it a circle of unblemished light, and he wondered not for the first time if forgiveness existed.

'Well, I do,' he said. 'I remember.'

***

There was a time, the following morning, when in Avalon House it was possible to believe the world could come right.

At midnight, when her father had not returned, Ronnie had taken the baby upstairs to her room, where a second drawer turned into a second crib, for which the infant showed her approval by sleeping four hours straight, feeding, and then returning to her dream of swimming in a white river, warm as milk. The rain spent itself in the night, and the day, when it came, had a shy, washed light.

When Ronnie left the bedroom with the baby, she knew her father was up. The wireless was on and, from the fires he had lit in every grate, an escaped smoke was loitering in the stairwell.

To date, the doctor's score on domestic duties was low. At the time, it was understood to be the inevitable result of brains in boys, and mothers who, in wonderment at an intelligence that had travelled through their wombs, kept forgetting to tell them to pick their clothes up off the floor. Added to this was the natural male blindness to bins that needed emptying, to the order of the linen closet and the cutlery drawer, the sheets with the sheets and the pillowcases with the pillowcases, knives with knives and forks with forks, to the dust of the floor and the film on the windows, along with a fathomless tolerance for living in rooms that, left to their own devices, would soon recall the cave of the caveman. From time to time, like a seasonal flu, the doctor could take a fit of tidying, dragging furniture about to clean what was under it, or pulling everything out of his wardrobe onto the floor with the intention of a ruthless audit and the bagging for the poor of things he no longer needed. It could last an hour, rarely longer. For soon, the nostalgia of old clothes would seep into him, or the drive would be diluted by the evidence that he had thrown out nothing, and the frustration of folding cardigans with the sleeves to the front, or back, he couldn't tell. Then it was either throw out everything, or throw them back into the closet. At different times he had chosen each solution, but, most often, the flu went off him before the task was completed, and, when he came home from house calls, found nothing on the floor of his bedroom and four pairs of socks darned, he had the guilty blessing of having an angel for a daughter, and resolved that next time he would spare them both the humiliation by locking his door. He never did, of course. And Ronnie never spoke of it. His suits were always stabled in perfect order next to his shirts, and the buttons that had gone missing re-joined the cuffs so quickly that he wondered if they had fallen off at all, and if it wasn't him who had put everything back on hangers. Aware that even angels must tire, he would go through periods of attempting small reciprocal gestures, watching out for assistances he could do, tidying what was already tidy, putting a chicken in the Aga that he promptly forgot, but in the end finding that the thing that brought the smile to his daughter's eyes was when he brought her home books.

Like all household arrangements, it was made up as they went along, and like all such escaped the judgement of right and wrong by the oldest alibi, family.

But, that morning, carrying the baby into the bathroom so she could do a right-handed facewash, the child on the natural shelf of her left hip, Ronnie realised at once that her father was not himself. She had it from an obvious clue: the toilet-roll was on the holder. It was not on the floor alongside the toilet bowl where, from his seating position, and not wanting to twist to take the sheet from the holder on the wall, the doctor customarily left it, and she customarily put it back. Briefly then, Ronnie had shared the dilemma of her father and wondered if she wasn't the one who had done it, but when she felt his shaving brush was still warm and saw that the basin had been left without the high-tide tracery of minute hairs he always left after he pulled out the plug, she had all the evidence she needed.

When she arrived in the kitchen, the doctor was in his shirt-sleeves at a table set for breakfast for two. He looked like he had lain all night on conundrums, but he rose when his daughter came in and examined the infant. 'She slept?'

'She did!' Ronnie said it with the imagined pride of a mother, and flushed a little at the side of her throat in the knowledge that she was not one. Still, it came through her, and her father witnessed it, and knew the plot was twisting into a knot he hadn't intended. It had only been a day and a half. He studied the baby's eyes. Already the erythromycin had begun to work on the infection.

'Getting better, isn't she?' Ronnie asked.

'She will be fine.'

'Really?'

'Yes.'

Ronnie's exhale of relief was another signal impossible to ignore, and her father turned away towards the stove. 'You sit, I'll serve,' he said.

It came out more command than invitation but had the virtue of novelty and Ronnie did as she was told, talking to the baby and telling her, 'We are going to sit and have our breakfast, so we are. Aren't we? Yes, we are.'

The doctor passed her the warm bottle. The infant had no hesitation, and neither did Ronnie, the two of them closing a circle. Her father pulled up his sleeve-garters to preserve the cuffs and cracked eggs into the pan. Neither what missed the edge and slid down the side, nor what fragments of shell got into the pan, were any of his concern. His back to his daughter, he flicked fat on to the yolks with the silver spatula, seeing more clearly than ever that love could not be foreseen or contained, and all the while trying to keep the eggs from exploding.

'Here we are,' he said, with small triumph. He slid an egg Ronnie hadn't asked for onto her plate. It was collared with a burnt frill, but the yolk was intact. From the wire toaster under the lid of the second hotplate of the Aga he brought two slices.

'Will you hold her, and I'll eat quickly?'

Her face had a glowing. You could see it right there, something coming through her. Her forehead was different, he thought. *She is more substantially herself*, it occurred to him, and he was moved, and resorted to the knitting of his brows and the uplift of his chin that he used to stave off any emotion that caught him unawares.

The bottle finished, Ronnie had passed him the baby at the same time as the question, and the doctor took her at an arm's distance, the way he did all handed-off infant patients, angling back his upper body and making between his and the child's head the V of formal waltzers. He went down the kitchen with her like that, but soon enough must have read the clue in the stance, for, to his daughter's amazement, without music or prompt, with the baby Doctor Troy began to dance.

It was first just a sideways sway.

First, it was only a lean to the left, and back, and again, a flexion in the line of his trousers, an angle off the perpendicular so slight that if you walked in you would not have been able to tell. Until you saw the sway back. Because now it was already something. It was a man dancing in a kitchen with a baby, a step, and another, an over and back that repeated and made a pattern that declared its otherness from the ordinary by the fact that human beings move towards purpose. And this had none that was obvious. A sway and a step, and another back. A linearity that was tentative until it was discovered introductory, for, his eyes not leaving the baby's, this time when the doctor drew his shoe over, he drew the other one back too, and now was dancing a step-slide-step in 3/4 time of such smoothness that the years fell off him and the dawn kitchen might as well have been the Queen's Hotel, where Jack Hanley & His Showband hit the beat so true the dancers took the wax off the floor home with them.

With the baby, the doctor danced. A scene licensed by the infant's smile, which had the effect of dispelling breakfast decorum, letting the second egg spit and explode, while man and child crossed the floor in a series of moving boxes and a hum so low that it was made for an audience of one, and could not be ascertained until the next time around that, yes, some beats behind the wireless, the doctor was singing Sinatra. In keeping with his character, in dancing Doctor Troy's face did not alter, nor did he lose or exaggerate the tempo. He revealed nothing but had the rise-and-fall surety of a ballroomer and the floating grace of those of his generation whose mothers had taught them how to make posture, line and hold, eloquent.

With the mesmerism that happens when your parent shows you a home movie from before you were born, Ronnie looked. But she looked away when she thought what she was seeing was a moment from her own babyhood. She could not remember her father dancing with her, but he must have, she thought. *He must have.* The knowledge had such bittersweetness, like apples in Faha, for it recalled an Eden she felt the loss of, without any memory of being there. She looked back, and this time let out a 'ha!' that was shorthand for amazement.

The couple went down the kitchen to the low humming, past the long windows where the morning was looking in, and where the sight of the doctor dancing on his own in a waltz of one could only confirm the general opinion in the parish that intelligence was no bulwark against idiocy. Doctor Troy did not care. What had come over him was old as life on earth, a pulsed response to another, outside of and even before the existence of reason, a prime and primal engagement that took its continuance from the expression in the baby's features. She liked it! And that was everything. And if it took away the persona through which he met the world, if it rendered him in the general soft-mouthed and eye-watery category of doting grandfathers, what of it?

With the baby, he danced.

He danced without losing form, and only a few times closing his eyes. There may have been a smile inside the moustache, but from its long service as shield, it was impossible to say. Still, the joy in the room was as unmistakable as it was rare, and because it had come unbidden, had the feel of blessing.

Sinatra finished singing before the doctor's hum. But before the next request for Mary from Cork was played, Ronnie brought her plate to the sink, and the moment was broken.

'Now,' said the doctor, with a soft heel-stop and almost-bow, handing off the baby the way you might a partner too beautiful. Ronnie took the baby with the rhetorical question, 'Did you like dancing?' and reclaimed her with a nuzzle into her neck and an inhale of that smell that defied language.

It moved Jack Troy to see it. But he took his jacket from the back of the chair and regained himself with two small tugs on the hems of each sleeve.

'Thank you for breakfast,' Ronnie said. 'It was lovely.'

It was hard to look at her, she was so happy.

The baby is not ours, he wanted to say. *This is only for now.* But he could not hurt her that way, and instead back-tossed his head at the compliment and let his eyebrows say it was nothing. 'Keep her quiet,' came out too bluntly, but he was at the door and did not trust himself to turn back.

***

It was an undeclared phenomenon, but known to many in General Practice, that with the approach of Christmas came ailments of anxiety in all forms. From their seats, in constitutions conditioned to the everyday, at Christmas there arose sicknesses that, like Good King Wenceslas, sought seasonal attention and *Just something to get me through, Doctor.* In Faha, the colds that were called flus, the pulsing, throbbing, splitting, chilblains, catarrh, general weaknesses, *the same old problem that always flames up this time of year*, the burning, aching, itching you couldn't put a finger on, and the chests that became welcoming harbours to a visiting bronchial phlegm, greenish, brownish or *Is it yellow-greyish Doctor?* filled the seats in the waiting room with a sniffling hacking population who studied their shoes or smoked cigarettes while the wireless played carols in the hall. Doctors were scored not by their bedside manner, but by whether or not they gave you 'the bottle'. Prescriptions were the same as passports, and if you had one in hand going up the village, chances were that for Christmas you'd be, in a phrase that must have been coined elsewhere, *right as rain*. What size vat Ciaran the chemist had in order to fill so many cough bottles was unimaginable, but he never ran out; the shop cleared your sinuses just by standing inside the door, and in January the empty brown bottles of four fluid ounces could be found inside every stone wall and ditch in the parish. Christmas was its own exigency, shared the character of a timebomb ticking, only with red ribbons, and exerted a daily pressure that found expression in bodies whose vulnerabilities were exposed in the annual run-up to find the presents that Santa Claus wasn't bringing. Still, there was no resentment, the mood of the parish best summarised in the saying of Thomas Carr, who conflated the two great events of the Christian calendar, declaring we all had to carry the cross for the birthday of baby Jesus.

Like decorations taken out of the box, patients the doctor hadn't seen since the previous year came into the surgery with the same worn look and the same bemusement that another twelvemonth had gone by and still they had not been thrown out. He dealt with them all the same way: succinctly, confirming his otherness by telling and listening to no stories, asking only the most pertinent questions and, for the most part, cutting off the patient whenever

they took the long run-up, or went so far back into the beginnings of their complaint that the history would have taken till Saint
Patrick's Day. The doctor had lived long enough to understand
that, in an island country, sideways was the way all stories wanted
to go, roundabouts the native way of getting anywhere, and that
there was a good reason there was no straight road in the parish. By
instinct, he knew too that, in a thesis that could not yet be proven,
the telling of symptoms was the first part of the cure. In some
cases, the most important part. So, on occasion, when he knew
the patient had a dire need, he let the recounting unroll while he
went to his desk and performed a pretend consultation of his notes,
a filing system of index cards that lived in a series of shoeboxes
without lids, which no one was allowed to see, not because the
cards were both yellowed and greyed, or because the handwriting
was that of a drunken spider, but because many of them referred
not to the patient but to his father or mother or grandparents. As
a system, it had its own unique strength, for there were often times
when Doctor Troy drew out a card and found that he had treated
the same ailment in the ancestor and prescribed the same remedy, a
validation that his judgement had not declined, or improved, with
age, and of the theory that in Faha time did not go straight but
round and round.

That day he saw four patients an hour for seven hours, with two
breaks for the toilet and one for the plate of food that Ronnie had
left on the kitchen table under a teacloth. He ate standing, then
went upstairs with a cat-burglar's step to find where she and the
baby were hiding. They were in Charlotte's room. The window gave
on to the breadth of the river. Its chest puffed by rain, the Shannon
flowed with imperious indifference. He looked out at it rather than
at his daughter, while he asked if she had eaten, already knowing
the answer – 'I'll eat when they're gone' – and that this hiding
was not a viable way forward. They could not sustain it, but when
he saw how Ronnie and the baby were already one, he could not
imagine an alternative.

For the rest of that afternoon, while patient after patient sat in
front of him, his mind sought one. Diagnosis required little of
him; his mind wrote the prescriptions long before his hand did,

and instead, in that company of coughs, discharges into handkerchiefs that were never full, and nasal drips backhanded or let drop into the valley between knees, Doctor Troy considered what to do about the child.

At the time, the most notable feature of the country's education system was that it was problem-based. Everything was a problem, and everything had a solution. It was a philosophy with a foundation in mathematics, had the beauty of simplicity, and the virtue of reducing the complexities of the world to twin choices, the right one and the wrong. In all subjects, for every question, an answer. And one answer only. Any answer not in the book fell under the general category of cheek and was dealt with accordingly. For some students, there was an appeal in knowing there was one true and absolute solution, and finding it was a further step into understanding the mystery of the world. As a schoolboy, Jack Troy had been one of these. He had loved problems, preferred mathematics and the sciences for their factual purity, peerless logic and virtue of being indisputable. That six decades of living had undone all certainty did not mean that the processes trained into his brain had been dismantled, and so, with no change in his expression that a patient could discern, he went down the roads of all options. By five o'clock, when the dark had made golden the lamplight and the last of the patients had to go home to their tea, the doctor had arrived at the edict of Brother Xavier, whose nickname was X, and who, quoting the philosopher Sherlock Holmes, said that when all other solutions had been tried and failed, the one that remained, *No matter how improbable, boys*, had to be the correct answer. So, following a formula not found in Euclid, but in keeping with the textbook theory that any proposition not self-evident but proven by a chain of reasoning was the truth, the doctor let the Given be the positions of both the Church and the State, the Variable whether the mother of the child might come forward – and if not what Ronnie would allow, and on what evidence – before mentally drawing the line, writing the QED and the conclusion that had the mixed virtue of being obvious and fantastical, but either way was the only one he could think of.

Noel Crowe is what his mind said, after he had closed the door on the last patient.

Noel Crowe was the answer.

The moment Jack Troy thought it, he knew it was right. It was, if not self-evident, certainly *Right there.* And he recalled again the last time he had seen the boy, on the front steps, the ardent look of him, the way he held out that book that even now Ronnie was rereading for the umpteenth time.

Noel Crowe is the answer, he thought again, and he had a flash of X's gleamy smile, hands behind his back while he peered down at a copybook where, step by step, the solution was emerging. Added to this was the maddening feeling, common among those who have reached the end of racking their brains, that the world had been trying to tell him the answer all along.

And, in fairness, he told himself, to be fair now, he had sensed it. That must be why he had written the letter.

The doctor came into the kitchen with unknotted step and the *ah-ha* playing in his eyes. To camouflage it, he picked up the baby, made an elongated 'Yeeeesss' and shook his head back and forth in a gesture only understood by infants. This time he did not dance, but his manner was the same as, allowing his daughter not for the last time to think there was no end piece to the puzzle of fathers. 'I have to go out,' he said.

'There was no call-out.' Her brow closed. 'At least, I didn't hear one. Was there?'

'No.'

'You'll have your tea?'

'I won't. I have to go.'

'If there's a caller, will I say where you've gone?'

'No. I'll be back after.' He handed her back the baby. Even more than that morning, he was struck by her ease and naturalness, and could not understand how, with so little sleep, and having spent all day in hiding with an infant that was in fact a stranger to her, she could be so. There was no doctor who did not witness marvels daily, if only how people were able to carry on with bodies that failed them in all the ways the body was supposed to work. The marvellous was what flooded him then, in the gifted belief that what had happened, what had come to their very door, and what was happening here in front of him in a daughter more extraordinary than he had granted, was not random, but had a purpose, which was, he dared to think, love.

Surprised to find he was not too old for rapture, he pursed the moustache. Sentiment is a privilege of age, but the doctor was not ready to reveal it lest he experience the humiliation of a daughter more hard-headed than he. He turned on his heel with his commandant's step, but at the door could not resist testing his theory.

'Crowe's,' he said. 'I'm going to Crowe's.'

He watched Ronnie's face for the tell-tales of a subterranean desire, and thought he spotted some when she replied, 'Crowe's?' Although she did not say the boy's name, there was an inflexion where some feeling escaped. 'Have you heard something?'

'No.' *Have you?* he wanted to ask. 'I meant to check on them.'

'Say hello for me.'

He looked away from her as soon as she said it, but in his mind, he was clicking his fingers. That was it, she was waiting for Noel Crowe to come back. By the time he was down the front steps and into the car, he had the conviction of a conspirator, and the singular focus of a father who would knock down the world to make the path for his child.

In the village, Clohessy was hanging a string of Christmas lights inside the front window of the shop. He was ahead of Bourke by a week. He had them plugged in to catch any bulb blown or blowing, and against the reflections of the plate glass was a figure in a tangle of bloodied thorns. He paused to salute the doctor passing and took his glance back as verification that he was right, electric lights *bate* tinsel every time. In Prendergast's, the television was rolling its picture of *Dragnet*, but the heads of all the Prendergasts stayed watching. On the wall behind the television, in the oval mirror that acted as a second screen, Mrs Prendergast watched what passed on the street.

Inside the church gates, the first stages of the construction of a crib were underway. It was Father Coffey's innovation. It had come to him when he was visiting the High Babies with a picture-book of the story of Bethlehem, and one of the Meades said Santy could have been born in their cowshed but they had no wise men, or sheep, or shepherds, or straw, or reindeers, 'only cows and rushes, Father.' To bring the message back home, the curate had a vision of a nativity play not in the school but in the churchyard, with real animals – he would ask the Talty brothers, who kept the cleanest yard in the parish – out under the night sky as the parish came to Midnight Mass. He had leaned on the authority of the collar to convince some adults whose sins he had absolved to play the mute parts. The nuns would elect a Virgin Mary. Already, a framework of the crib was built in rough timber. It was the second draft, after a man from Boola saw the first and said, 'Is it how ye're planning on hanging Jesus?'

In the crib, as the doctor passed, was Harry the sheepdog.

The doctor drove out the end of the village. The wipers, that he turned on by habit, rubbered the window and he realised it was not raining. The night in fact was clear and still. For any used to living inside a perpetual rain, it had a parcelled air of novelty, and as the headlamps picked up and put back the countryside, the doctor had a sense of the parish waiting, quietly, in expectation of what was known to be coming. He knew it should not be the case, knew that any day or night was the same but for our making them not, and yet what he could not deny was something other, something that was in the houses he passed, and came out from them, was in the air itself, in the dark and the dying of the year, in this end time, not only the calendar measure of more of our physical life gone, but the thing that followed, which was to do with the spirit.

As a medical man, Doctor Troy had no professional opinion on what could not be proven to exist. If it could not be ascertained through the five senses it was not within our reach, and yet. *And yet.* There were times when, even in that sinking parish on the furthermost edge of nowhere, he had encountered patients of such fortitude in the face of suffering that he was forced to agree with the poet who said that, if seen, the human soul would cover the earth.

Driving from the village, through the two crossroads, round the blind bends at Considine's and Cotter's, he passed no one. The grey bone of the road glistened. In the newspaper, he had read of the frozen air that had descended on Russia; the reporters, who were guilty from having not been in the war, described it like an army that would march slowly now across Europe. Nothing would stop it. Germany was feeling it. France would be next. In Faha, such reports only underlined that the world was elsewhere, extremes unknown, the news disarmed by distance and remoteness, only surviving in the universal dream of children, that there could be snow for Christmas.

But, that night, it was colder than any yet. Was it more still too? So much of reality we make up to match the one in our minds, the doctor could not be sure. But he thought it was. The thought turned into a chill, and he gave a small tug to the tasselled scarf just below his neck.

He drove on, travelling in that inner country where the body is stationary, but the mind moves faster than the wheels. What he had was an apprehension of some confluence, that he was a cog in something larger than himself, and, though it went against his nature, a cog the last thing he ever wanted to be, it was the truth. He could not have explained why but he knew that what happened next mattered enormously; he could not have reasoned it out in front of judge and jury, but it was a fact to him, same as his own blood and the light in which it lived. *What happens here, what I choose to do, matters.* He was not an innocent, nor did he fool himself. He knew that grace and redemption could not be traded, and we had to live with our life's failings the same as with our own face. But still, he could not escape a burdened sense of consequence and importance, for the child, for his daughter, and for himself.

Beyond the Fort Field, he stopped the car in the middle of the road. He turned off the engine, and after moments got out. He was not far from Quinlan's place, their turfsmoke trapped from travelling by a cold press of air. He walked a few paces from the heat of the bonnet and stood. The cold found him straight away. The air was clean as a knife and came for his cheekbones and the tops of his ears. His breath evanesced like something freed. The tip of his nose produced a startled droplet and he took it into his handkerchief. The sky arrested him. Through the haw on the windscreen he had not been sure of the fact of it, but when he pocketed the handkerchief and looked up there was such a hood of stars, so many and so polished that they brought the effect of all such nights: you feel you have never seen one like it. Beyond two fields, the wound of the estuary was a blackness pin-holed and immobile. You could not see the water moving, only that the land ended, and where it ended was bedded with fallen light. About all was the stillness that seems composed, seems to speak in a language not ours. Standing there, under a masterpiece sky, the doctor let the cold come on to him.

In a life that had few moments of pause, this was one, and he knew that it was called for, knew that here and now, not far from Crowe's, might be the last moment in the story he would only see what was directly in front of him. He raised his head and looked up beyond the horizon of his hat. It was the character of all life that the more you looked the more you saw, and with night skies of absolute stillness and clarity the stars behind the stars were a theatre of revelation and had the placed-ness of that supreme geometry that gave the Greeks their stories.

For some years, Jack Troy had not been able to say aloud the first Latin line of the Apostles' Creed, could not bring himself to pray what he did not know to be fact. He could not say he believed in God, but neither could he say that he did not. In his reasoning, he was of a mind too peculiar to adhere to any doctrine, and he could not allow himself the comfort of a divine mercy, for he was too suspicious of anything that pardoned humanity. But still. Beyond that reasoning, there was this something that had no name, that in six decades of living was both occasional and familiar, a prompted moment of clouded complexity he could not parse except to say that when he felt it, he felt less alone.

The cold fell from the stars. He stood long enough for it to get inside his clothes and for the landscape to assume the strangeness of other places that have their own life without us. In a strategy not in textbook or theology, but, with the practical experience of a medical man, taking account of an Almighty, who, at great age, must have been badly near-sighted at this stage, Doctor Troy stood there long enough to be seen.

Whether he was or wasn't was the same unknown as for us all, but he said an 'All right' to the stars and himself and returned to the car. Nothing had come or gone on the road. In the mirror his grey eyes were his father's and he let them look at him as he turned the ignition. Both knew that, for the solution Jack Troy had formed in his imagination, he needed the patient he was going to visit to die.

If Mrs Crowe died, then a telegram could be sent to her grandson, and Noel Crowe would return to Faha. The steps that had to follow, the doctor knocked together for the convenience of a plot that had to move quickly before the secret was out and the rap came on the door. It was predicated not so much on love but on Noel Crowe's intrinsic innocence and goodness that anyone could see and that he hoped America had not yet undone, on his daughter's bond with the baby, her affection, yes certainly at the very least that, for the boy, and the fact that without a husband she would have to let the girl go. In that first rush when it came to him, it had been with the *Of course* that seems to make perfect sense of all improbabilities, seems to have been not only staring us in the face but patiently waiting for us to figure it out, and with the *This is why this happened* that sometime seduces even the most sceptical.

Being irrefutable, perfect sense is the last refuge of a plotter, and the doctor had succumbed to a logic he forgot he was inventing. Noel – even the name had the prompt of a Christmas visit – was the solution. Once he had conceived, or perceived it, the rest was only helping it along. Ronnie had spent considerable time walking and talking with the boy. Had they not gone to the pictures once too, or was that with Charlie? Was there something about the tennis net and the two of them? In any case, just the other week she had been speaking with the grandfather about Noel, which certainly prompted her to take out that novel he gave her, and even this evening when the doctor said where he was going, there was that '*Say hello for me*' that was love in a see-through mask of politeness. With the lopsided bias of a Cupidian analysis that concluded the only reason the boy and his daughter were not already together was because of Ronnie's reluctance to abandon her father, and went as far as *Who am I to keep them apart?* the doctor made peace with an emergency plan whose upshot was that, unbeknownst to himself, when Noel Crowe returned for his grandmother's funeral he would also be coming to his own wedding.

The christening the doctor left until later.

In parishes everywhere, stratagems around babies were old as the codes that tried to contain them. That infants were sent to be raised by aunts, that there was some whose sister was their mother, whose mother was their grandmother, and every other twist that desperation could think of, was not new, and in this Faha was no different to anywhere else. There were surprise engagements of short duration and others of many years that both ended with hasty trips to Irwin's jewellers in Roches Street or McDowell's the Happy Ring House in Dublin, the date for the wedding set. *Babies come early in that family* was a saying that needed no translation, for men were men and women women, and, in Sonny Cooney's summation, the dish always runs away with the spoon. (It would be another ten years before Sonny would have to concede a dish sometimes ran away with a dish, a spoon with a spoon, not to speak of forks.) From this, the doctor took some comfort, convincing himself that his scheme was not as outrageous as it seemed, and would in fact be the natural conclusion to a story that he had disturbed by a forbidding manner and a bristle moustache that lent him a perpetual look of disapproval.

When he came into Crowe's front street, he had the sixth sense of doctors on call-outs who know how the patient is before they see them. In most cases, the doctor could tell the gravity of a sickness as he knocked on a door, and that evening, he knew before he had stepped down into the kitchen that Mrs Crowe was living still.

'God bless,' he said softly. He tilted the rim of his hat but did not take it off and kept the bag in his hand.

'Doctor,' said Mossie Crowe, looking up from the fire with his beautiful eyes and ruined smile.

'Doctor,' said Bat Considine, not taking his face from the Sunday newspaper he had brought with him for reading by Crowe's lamp. A fiercely intelligent man, never out of the cap and greatcoat he wore over an imperishable suit that was brown once but aged claret, and '*supposed to look like that*' his answer when Devitt asked was it oxblood or what was in the dye. Bat called in on his neighbour many evenings and, after a one-sided dialogue so habitual the dog could have written it, read his paper by fire- and lamplight, passing oblique comments on the state of the world that were none the less pithy for the fact that his neighbour could hear none of them.

Mossie rose. From keeping his boots to the fire for a drying they never fully achieved, the soles were hot, and he did a shifting step in place while, from his throne on the crocheted pillow, Joe the dog watched with one eye, and now the other, to see if this time they were actually going somewhere.

'O now,' Mossie said. He was in his workday suit with the wine slipover. His shirt was collarless and open, the pink cords of his neck showing. He turned down the dial of the wireless.

'I'm done up in the bones, Doctor,' said Bat Considine, without looking up, and with that suddenness and shyness that were the badge of his kind in the parish. He had never been inside the door of the surgery, preserving the condition of his body inside an inviolable privacy that would only cease when McCarthy put the fresh underpants on his corpse.

His comment was a fishing that caught nothing, because the doctor had the learned deafness required in his profession, for everyone he met had something wrong with them. Already he was scanning the room, his conclusion as swift as it was disappointing: since he had last been there, not a thing had changed.

'How are you, Ganga?'

A question without answer, but the asking was a way to look at the old man's face. The light in the house was dim: only when you stood in it did you realise how bright was the electricity the rest of the parish was now living in. The lamp turned the room tawny, amber in pockets, but nowhere bright. The smells the walls contained were turfsmoke, tea, wax, milk, bacon, cabbage, leather, rope and paraffin. They were the same smells that had been there since the first Crowe carpentered the crooked door on to the stacked stones and called it home. The only sign of the season was the Christmas cards that were ranged on the dresser, in colour and depiction tokens of another world.

'She's the same, Doctor,' said Ganga. 'Just the very same.' He blinked rapidly. His round face had a gleaming it never lost, cheeks high and shone, eyes of Clare blue that was the sea of a good June. That his wife's condition had not changed was the best news, and by the way he told it you could tell he admired her for it.

'Some fighter,' said Bat into the paper. 'Napoleon would have been glad of her.'

The doctor went down into the room, crossing through the parlour with the two good armchairs facing the grate with no fire in it, a brass set of tongs, poker, shovel and brush awaiting their day. In the middle of the house the air was colder. But when he came into the bedroom the smoke of the far chimney met him, a pall coming out and climbing up past the outside of the breast, where an embrowned tongue on the wall showed it was chronic.

The patient was as Doctor Troy had last seen her. She was lying in the tucked bed that had the neatness of an envelope ready for posting. Only her hands were outside the fold of the blankets, about them the same beads that acted her participation in the rosary said each night over her. Her eyes were closed, sleeping or resting a distinction unnecessary at the end of life, but her breath when he leaned down to her was even.

'Hello Aine, Doady, it's Doctor Troy.' He said it without expectation of response and was holding her birdlike wrist.

How could she still be living? was what he thought. She was beyond eating or drinking, on the ledge between this life and the next, but day after day remaining so. It was a condition he had seen before, this remaining. He had sat at bedsides where the last breath was each one that came, and then, just as he was about to stand and make the solemn pronouncement, another breath followed, and he had to pretend he was only adjusting himself before the death watch resumed. The space between breaths could be so elongated that it stretched the limits of credulity, at the last possible moment the dying declaring themselves not dead in a macabre game too cruel to have been invented, but on which none could call time for the simple reason that it was the soul's business.

He sat in the visitor's chair that had the two good cushions. More prayer cards, miniature crosses, beads, saints' statues, and other tokens had come since he had last been. The deep sill of the window was a thronged grotto of them. For a moment he had the nonsense idea that they were looking on, and by instinct angled his back around and his head a little lower. He watched for the rise and fall of Doady's breath. What came was barely that. It was the thinnest of actions, so slight as to make it seem impossible that in such a thing was life, and without it, none. And again, it came. And again, he watched. The third time, he got up from the chair and poked at the sods in the grate to see if he could enkindle a flame. The turf was a smouldering mass and though he jabbed at it he could not eradicate last summer's rain that lived in it, and more curling clouds came out and rose up into the rafters and the thatch.

'Christ.'

Doady's face remained unchanged. She was wearing the glasses her husband put on her in the daytime, took off to signal bedtime. Though his thumbprints were in them, they gave her a serenity she never had, but also the rumoured omniscience of the dying who, whether their eyes are open or not, are already looking back at us from the doorway of the next place. Which may have been what caused the doctor to resume his seat, lean down to her tiny figure in the nest of blankets and through the smoked air say, 'There is a child.'

It was a behaviour unlike himself, but had the alibi of a baby and an eldest daughter who was attached to it in a bond that he would rather die than break. So, in a whisper that was as unnecessary as it was guilty, Doctor Troy told Mrs Crowe the story he had invented as solution to the triangular problem of a love with the one side missing. He told it in a soft voice but reasonable tone, and used the storyteller's trick of balancing each outlandish step of the improbable with something that could not be disputed. So, a child needed love. Love had to be taken where it could be found. Not for the first time, an accident of chance, pure chance, had separated true love just when it was taking wings. In his young and courting days, the doctor had read enough bad poetry to have recourse to all the metaphors and imagery that sprang from heated loins, roses, feathers, flames, which were available to him now in telling of the relation between Doady's grandson and his daughter. He told it with the straight face that was his since he first grew the moustache at thirty, and he carried on right up to the axle detail on which the entire story rested.

'Because,' he said, 'he will be home for your funeral.'

Carried by the exuberance of the telling, he almost expected Doady to nod.

Conclusion delivered with a rogue's candied plausibility, he leaned back in the chair. By a crook's instinct, he took a guilty glance behind him at the ranks of saints' cards. They were the same impassive faces prayed to for intercession, but their reputation for unreliability discounted them in a crisis that had to be resolved before the baby was discovered, and neither did they stir now to admonish a doctor prescribing death.

Because his was a proposal without possibility of approval, and because, in the poet's words, between the emotion and the response lies the shadow, the doctor took Doady's hand in his. 'It's a three-part solution,' he said. 'Your grandson will be happy, as will my daughter. As will the child.'

The patient's eyes were closed, lids the violet of a September evening after rain. The flesh of her face was slack and in repose had the translucency of last skin, when it is easy to imagine the substance of the body thinned by what is leaving through it. He held her hand. It was small as a child's, but ancient too, and, laid in his, frail as a nest. In it was her lifetime and its lines. Looking down, what moved him was the thought of all the days and nights it had handled, the purses of the fingertips polished.

The dying defy all clocks. But somewhere in that no-time, in the dimness of the light, and before the ache in his lower back told him to stand, Doady's left hand shuddered. A pulse, that in paucity of language we call electric, passed through her, and now the fingers of her hand tightened around the doctor's and she was grasping them in a clasp as astonishing as it was tenacious. Her eyes had not opened, her face had not changed.

A licensed tourist of deathbeds, Doctor Troy was long familiar with end-of-life rallies, spasms, terminal lucidity, when patients had suddenly opened their eyes and spoken, sometimes with perfect sense, sometimes in torn streamers of language that came with the urgency of last messages but left a bitter aftertaste because what they told could not be deciphered. He knew that the living longed for a word, any word, sign, to come back from the bourn of the next life, and that those on the frontier of death were endowed with a perspicacity they never had when alive. In a parish in which there were stories of every kind of human behaviour, those of the dying were the ones that bent towards the miraculous, and in the graveyard by the river were any number of Lazaruses.

So, he was not alarmed when Mrs Crowe's hand gripped his. But what pulsed through her pulsed into him, a currency that travelled up his arm and out through the rest of him until it reached the short hairs that stood on the back of his neck. Each squeeze of his hand registered, with the importunity of the taps of the telegraph machine, but without the codebook to turn them into words.

After the first startled moments, Jack Troy could resume his professional stance and act the doctor to himself, saying: *These things happen*. But because she did not let go, and because the plot he had outlined depended on her complicity by death, the hold had the character of a naked moment between them. He looked at Doady's face, saw nothing but the serenity, then looked at the fingers that were holding on so tightly the bulbs of the knuckles were white as onions.

***

When Doctor Troy came back into the kitchen, he carried the down-blows of the smoke in his clothes and in his person, and his eyes had a caustic look even more sorrowful than usual. The return of the doctor from the patient's room has the same feeling everywhere, and in Faha the tension was doubled by a General Practitioner who was more taciturn than a timber soldier. He came in with bag in hand and took a position by the dresser, above-side the fire, which was the place in that house for speeches.

But he made none. He moved his mouth some, looked down towards the hearth while considering what to say. Aware that he was trying to legislate for the two most ungovernable parts of life, love and death, Jack Troy had the weary look of it, and the knotted gut of all of us who must live with thoughts unconscionable.

Intelligence was its own licence, and though Mossie Crowe did not take his eyes off the doctor, he did not disturb the thinking. He held his big hands on the ball of his belly. He blinked. Bat Considine turned the page of the newspaper to read again what he had read three times already. With a dog's instinct for a thing that is about to happen, Joe stood, and, one back leg after the other, elongated himself for extra importance.

The pause was instants only, but time was invented to make measured what is not, and there was no gauge for the duration before the doctor spoke. In it swam the soul of Aine Crowe, in this world or another, undeclared.

In case he missed what came next, Ganga watched closely what he could see of the doctor's lower lip. At last, from a nature blind to despair, and because the doctor had not stepped forward to shake his hand and say he was sorry for his troubles, he smacked his palms together. 'The same? Am I right, Doctor?'

'Just the same.'

Ganga caught the nod not the words, formed two fists and did a single short punch of both to signal she was a fighter. 'She'll make Christmas?' To which he made his own answer. 'She will! By God she will!'

It was his best news and released a clasp in him. He might have danced a step if Doady was alongside, but he made do with another little punch of nothing and a turnip smile of one tooth. 'Mairtin is coming for the Christmas, Doctor. Home from England. I told her. Hold on, I said. Hold on.'

But for what? Jack Troy did not say. The happiness in the old grandfather was too present. It was all that was left to him of fifty-two years of married life, but he savoured the remnant same as it was the first night he gave his girl an orange squash in Longworth's heaving hall.

Knowing he was unable to hold up his side of any dialogue, but bursting with undanced feeling, Mossie resorted to a speech fitful as any unscripted, bubbles of giggles where the fullstops were. The canals of his ears dammed, he spoke at a volume fit for a hall. 'Her people were Kerry. They weren't having me at all. They were not. No, they were not. Her father'd deaden the air of any room he walked into. Mine had stolen a hundred yards of stone wall in Cappa. Stole it stone by stone over three months. 'T'wasn't noticed till gone. I had to carry the bicycle on my back across the fields so I wouldn't be seen courting by her Aunt Nancy, God rest her.'

'Harridan. Swept to eternity,' said Bat, not taking his head out of the paper.

'Fierce girl for prayers and fierce for dancing, my Aine. Think nothing of ten miles for a dance, and ten miles back. Wear you to a flitter dancing. You'd be breathless for a slow one. "No lurching! No lurching!" Father Conway roaring.'

'Paralytic stroke, same man,' said Bat, licking the finger to turn the page.

'It would be breaking for day you'd be coming home. She had one sister went out to mind a millionaire lady's child, Fifth Avenue, New York. The other went for the nuns after Micho Clancy showed her the print of the horseshoe on his backside. Fierce prayers they were, all of them. Her mother'd make a *builin* didn't need any butter. You'd eat it seven days and be happy out. God you would. "Good black earth here," she said first time she walked out in the haggard. Heel of her boot digging. "Good black earth. Fierce for dancing. Just fierce."'

The memory came sweetly aground, and after a trinity of blinks, Ganga closed his hands on his belly and said the soft 'O now!' that was his cue for someone else to speak. When none that he heard did, he remembered he had to be the woman of the house too and said a loud, 'You'll have the tea, Doctor?'

'I won't, thank you.' The doctor's eyes went to the telephone on the wall. By the close relation of spoken and written words, there the grandfather stuck letters. There were several wedged in behind the instrument, giving it a one-winged look, one with an American stamp to the front.

'I will so,' said Bat, same as every night. 'Two broken biscuits.' He folded the paper with magisterial authority, finding folds he alone knew, and by which he was able to fit the whole of the world's news back inside the pocket of his greatcoat. 'I went out over the handle-bars of a bicycle one time, Doctor, got pelted down in the road. I'm done up in the bones,' he fished again, with the same no-luck.

'You have a letter from America?' the doctor asked Ganga. He pointed at it.

The old man plucked it out of the nest. Inside was a photograph of a family standing beside a concrete shamrock in Albany.

'Johnsie and family, Doctor.'

The doctor looked at it, and while looking let out a casual, 'Nothing from your grandson? Noel?'

The question had come out from under his hat. The grandfather knew there was something asked, but had not seen the lips, and looked to Joe for an explanation. The dog wagged its tail, came for a hand, and got it, while to the doctor the old man turned his baffled smile.

'That turf hears more than him,' said Bat, finishing the folds.

Ganga offered the child's blackboard, but the doctor shook his head. With the dropped shoulder of one who needs to get away from what he has just revealed, he turned to the door, standing on the back step to say, 'I will call again tomorrow.' That last word he made clearly, and for Ganga underlined it by a curved movement of his forefinger into the air to the right, where the future was. 'I will try and call every day,' he added, but in a lower voice.

'She'll make Christmas!' Spare of gestures, the grandfather made the same small fisted punch, and the good news, which had come from nothing the doctor had said or done, bowled him across to the back step to take Jack Troy's hand in both of his, and shake it vigorously now. It was the same handshake of the old people in the parish, a pumping, as if from the well, and not stopping until every drop of gratitude was brought up. 'Thank you, Doctor, thank you!' he said, brimming and pumping some more, in an acknowledgement that left no room for doubt: Doady Crowe would stay alive until Christmas because of the good Doctor Troy.

***

What possessed you? was a question common in Faha. Asked of children by mothers, and of husbands by wives, it occurred with enough frequency to attest to two things: in the chronicle of human endeavour there was no end to unaccountable behaviour, but also, you were not entirely the captain of your own fate, something could come over you. The best answer to the question was a lift of the shoulders and two palms opened, to indicate what had dropped from the sky. This had the virtues of suggestiveness and silence, because what had possessed one could possess another, and because you couldn't argue with a mime. That, in the heat of the moment, it was the answer hardest to find, that instead any number of the possessed had set out on carefully stepped explanations of how and why they had done what they had done, was proven by the amount of broken crockery that ended up in the ditches, and the perpetual scarlet of the clipped ears of schoolboys.

In the days that followed, what possessed Jack Troy could have been condensed into a single word, *child*. In it was both his own eldest, and the infant. That the two were inextricable was made plainer each day. Outside and inside of surgery hours, there were no times when Ronnie was not carrying, feeding or watching over the baby, and when, in that house where nothing was ever thrown out, after a rummage that roused the spiders from their ancestral homes, Ronnie found the baby clothes that had been hers, the picture was complete. By a similarity he only saw when the infant was in the miniature Victorian dress his great-aunt Flo had made for Ronnie, the doctor found his clock wound back. It was uncanny. All day he preserved the mandatory reserve of his profession. But at early breakfasts and late teas, that were the only time the three of them were together, and the only time nobody else saw him, the doctor found himself succumbing to the gaiety of grandfathers who know they did so much wrong as a father the first time, and who, from an appreciation not too late of the shortness of life, let the rules fall away, coming instead under the governance of the tiny hand clutching their forefinger.

This, he would say, is what possessed him.

This was the reason he went to Mannion's travel agency in town, to enquire the price of an aeroplane ticket to the United States, but not buy one. The reason he went to the bank after and placed an order for dollars at foreign exchange. The same, two days later, when he brought home the brown envelope with the currency of a country he had no intention of visiting, placing the greenbacks on his midnight desk where the brandy bottle contained more light than liquid, where on unheaded paper he wrote a one-sentence, anonymous second letter, to Noel Crowe, *Come back to Faha*, enclosing the banknotes for the ticket, and letting the fourth glass wash away the sour taste of selfishness in the guise of seasonal charity.

It was the same reason that when, first thing the following morning, Doctor Troy stood on the buckled linoleum of the post office collecting his letters, he told Mrs Prendergast that if anything came for Crowes, she could put them with his, for he would be visiting the house every day. That it was outside of his character he hoped was disguised by the unbound ambit of a doctor's duties and the good will of the season. In the parish it was a given that Christmas was the alibi for all from drunkards to housebreakers, and, in the annual lead-up to the birthday of Jesus, white lies were not only told to children.

But when, with the sibilant sigh of one flat-out, Mrs Prendergast took out her pencil to make the note, calling to Timmy sorting in back, 'Crowes with Troys,' the doctor had the sense the edges of his plan were not glued down.

'Mrs Crowe only has a short time,' he added, needlessly.

Mrs Prendergast's neat face had turned up to the doctor with a look that could open envelopes, it was in the purse of her lips and the points of her eyes. Behind her, Mr P sang in his cage. Being the first to spread the word was still a station of standing, fell under the rubric of communications attached to her office, and Mrs Prendergast liked to be ahead of all funerals in Faha. 'She'll make Christmas?'

'I couldn't say.'

The postmistress didn't look away. The tweed suit she was wearing had a tensioned button below the amplitude of her bosom. Like all her clothes, it had a lady's scent of mothballs and perfume, but when she turned herself around to face you, angling back her head just a bit, the button looked like a bullet ready for firing.

The post office was in its busiest weeks. With lists that were kept from one year to the next, only the occasional line through the name of a deceased, the parishioners were under an unwritten imperative to get their cards in the post before Christmas. Addresses, jotted in the book in the inks of five different pens, or on envelopes that outlived the letter they contained, had to be deciphered and scrupulously copied, often in the hand of a scholar son or daughter who already had the welt on their finger, had the best writing, and on the cleared space of the kitchen table under the one burning bulb could keep the lines from the shameful tendency to slope down the envelope. In a parish where neither were needed, house numbers and area codes put an official stamp on all letters going foreign, and underscored the vastness of geography and the miracle of a postal service that could put a pin in it. Because to receive a Christmas card from someone you hadn't sent one to was a mortification without remedy until next year, through the post office in Faha came an annual deluge of them. The letterbox in the wall was a mouth that could take no more, and only men tried stuffing more into it. Instead, by ten o'clock most days there formed an arterial line of women in as far as the counter, with more cards than could be contained in handbags, but also with the wrapped parcels that came in every shape and size, the ones with the cakes and puddings weighing more than a small child and smelling of spices that lived in the press all year until Our Lord had to be born again.

Mrs Prendergast had more questions for the doctor, but before the dialogue could continue the doorbell jingled and the first of the day's customers came in. Mrs Mac and Bridey Eyres both had the small triumph of beating the queue, both said 'Doctor' and lowered their look in case they were disturbing something important, or he saw what was wrong with them.

'I'll let McCarthy know,' Mrs Prendergast said, in the swallowed voice of a conspirator. She took an envelope to make a note of it. Winter sunlight angled into the shop, now a playground for dust, trafficking motes of gold twisting. Into that same illumination, some surplus of Mrs Prendergast's face powder fell, flesh-coloured, as she bent to write the name of the undertaker as a reminder, underlining it twice with an air of fatality. When she came back up, she gave a straightening tug to the jacket that put the Safety back on the button.

She's not dead yet, Doctor Troy had not said. But when he got into his car outside the church, it was the same as she was, and he the one who had killed her. Both of which were nonsense but were inside the compass of what it was that was possessing him.

**

With Father Coffey's direction that work only start when first Mass was over, hammer blows were raining down on the nails of the crib. There was a man and a boy at it, Harry to the side making a good attempt, but unable to quite cover his ears. For moments, the doctor had watched the village stirring. There had been frost. The day was bright, the light hard and true. There was blue in the sky, what clouds there were like hung washing, cleaner and whiter than you thought you'd seen them before. With a juddering loose steer that made the right and left sides of the street the one, came Sheehan's tractor; on the large ticking frame of a bicycle that was kept in the same condition as it was when new, and off which now he swung the leg with the dismounting ease of a Western cowboy, Michael Dooley; at the door of Bourke's Daddy Bourke, looking down at who had just gone into Clohessy's. All the unremarkable ordinariness of the December day the doctor had remarked with a sense of immutability, that the comings and goings of the parishioners, getting their bits, were in a continuum, but he felt removed from it by trying to live a life without cracks and a plot that depended on too many uncertainties. The engines of an aeroplane overhead recalled him to the transit of souls, from here to there and there to here, and he turned on the engine.

Putting to one side the patients who would already be waiting for him, and with the compulsion of those who must turn the page for what happens next, he drove out to Crowe's.

When he got there, the door to the cow cabin was open, from inside a man's voice commanding, 'Easy now, easy.' Briefly, the doctor suffered the delusion his letter with the dollars in it had travelled three thousand miles at the speed of thought, that Noel Crowe had received it, climbed the steps onto the first aeroplane back, and was now here in his grandfather's cowshed. That it was a conclusion without logic was not as important as what Jack Troy was to say to the boy, and he came to the door and stooped in, peering into the dark with small eyes.

'Doctor,' came from the far side of an old cow, and from there rose the white head of one of the Talty brothers.

'Tim.'

They exchanged a look without expansion. The night scene they had shared was in it, but neither of the brothers would ever mention it, and the doctor's inscrutable character went before him. With Doady in her last days, neighbours called to Crowe's to do their bit. None were asked, and nothing was planned; they appeared in their own time and with their own agenda, the women bringing the baked goods or foodstuffs that fed the ones who would come next, the men attending to the jobs in the yard and with the animals. It was an arrangement old as the parish and with the unsaid mutuality that comes from close living in a place that had the air of last stop before eternity.

As comment, the doctor declined the brim of his hat a touch, turned back out into the light. He was not two steps beyond the sops on the threshold when he stopped and came back. He stooped in a second time, and a second time the Talty brother raised his head from offside the cow.

'She's thriving,' the doctor said and, though he did not need to, added, 'the baby.'

The other nodded, but said the nothing he had promised, and Jack Troy stepped away again. That was when he saw Mamie Quinlan at the door of Crowe's henhouse, collecting eggs. Realising that she could have heard him, and facing the crisis of the red-handed, to stop and invent an explanation or keep going, he chose the latter, letting his stride speak for him and shaking an inside head at what it was that had possessed him to speak. That Mamie Quinlan would cross directly to the milking parlour and ask Tim-Tom *What baby is that?* he left to fate and the character of two brothers silent as stone walls, the same fate tested a second time, when, at her kitchen table that evening, Mamie would say *The Doctor was talking about a new baby* and Jude Quinlan would be betrayed by a blush so deep and sudden that any looking would have thought him the father.

'She's improving, Doctor,' was what Ganga said to Doctor Troy when he stepped down inside the back door. The wireless playing loud, he said it again, in case deafness was general. 'Improving, I'd say.'

This good news had rubbed the old man's face like a chamois and it fairly shone now. Gladness was pumping through his skin. His eyes had the glazed look of answered prayers, or someone struck by lightning, and he passed on a little of it to Joe who came under his hand, one ear and now the other. 'She took some water from me, she did,' Mossie said, stepping back to let the doctor go see for himself.

Doctor Troy showed no sign that for him the good news was bad. He carried the Gladstone bag down to the room. On first glance, Mrs Crowe was as he had left her. She had been washed and changed and turned but was laid out with the same inertia as last repose, the glasses on her closed eyes, the beads entwined through her knuckles. With the understanding that she had rallied some, the curtains had been pulled back and the window opened. The cold clear air of the December day had come inside; it declared itself, sharp at your nostrils and the base of your throat, and made life seem more present. With the contrariness of many houses in the parish, once the window was opened, the draw on the fire was perfect. The sods sent up the smoke in an innocent good behaviour, even granting a small heat to the vicinity.

'Doady, it's Doctor Troy,' he said, without looking. He put down the bag and opened the snap. He brought up the stethoscope and leaned over the patient, listening and looking at the same time in an examination that was no less professional for the fact that he did not want the news to be good. In that room of saints' cards, with her soul waiting for transport, Doady Crowe made no response whatsoever. She was not improved in any way that he could see. But neither was she worse. He sat and took her hand. This time it did not squeeze his. He leaned in until he was inside the smallness of her breath.

'Doady,' he whispered. But there was no response.

Unable to administer anything medical, Doctor Troy put away his instruments and closed the bag. He cupped his hands on the balls of his knees. *At every moment in the world a person dies*, was something his father liked to say. He said it both to leaven the weight of death and to vivify those still in the now. But even he had acknowledged that life was bordered by two mysteries. Mrs Crowe's breaths continued their numbered climb, but where the summit was remained unknown.

When the doctor came back into the kitchen, Ganga raised his round expression from the *súgán* chair. 'Am I right, Doctor? Improving?' His deafness had made all questions rhetorical, the answer he was looking for only a nod, which the doctor gave, then gave a second one, because lies loved nothing more than their own company, and the good news made the old man happy as Christmas. The old man was so flooded with elation that a drop stood on the end of his nose. It fell when he bent down to pass the good news to Joe.

The doctor drove home with no sense that the plot was moving. He was burdened with the twin convictions that time was short and he should be doing more. Both were furthered by his return to a kitchen that on first sight had been commandeered by an army of angels. Like wings, across the air before the Aga were numerous cloths of white cotton. Unable to risk the nappies being seen on the outside clothesline, Ronnie had rigged one at a rising angle from the hook that held the tea towel to the bracket of the Sacred Heart lamp. That the doctor had not wondered where the dirty nappies were going, and that there were far more of them than he would have supposed, only served to underline that the obvious can evade your nose as well as your eyes, and there was more to babies than grasping your finger. That their kitchen was turned into a laundry did not escape him either. His eyes took in the sight of it, and his gorge rose. Other laundries were in his mind, and when he spoke his voice was throttled. 'I would have done them,' he said. It was almost a whisper.

'What?' Ronnie had the baby on her hip and was reading to her from *The Lake*.

'The nappies. I would have.' He came closer to examine the child's eyes. They were a blue we make lesser by comparing it to other things.

'Better, right?'

'She will be fine.'

'You will be fine! Did you hear the doctor? Fine! You will be fine, so you will!' Ronnie brought her face close to the infant's and shook it over and back, with closed lips making a vibrating *mmm* that was the same message to babies in all languages.

Watching, the doctor found his heart could ache some more. He had to get out into the hall. He shut the door on the room of white cloths but carried the scent of the Omo with him. Down the corridor, the waiting room was open, coughs and sniffles punctuating the broadcast of 'The Ballad Tree'. He needed a moment before beginning.

What was in the kitchen, he knew, was love. But he knew too that love is dangerous, because it brings us to our best selves, and because purity is a commodity the world can only tolerate in thimbles. *Where are you, Noel Crowe?* was the only thing he could think of, until Bid Healy toddled out from the waiting room pulling Sean Patrick by the hand, a crusted impetigo under his nose, and asked, 'Is it us now, Doctor?'

***

Living in a parish that had the character of the bottom of a pocket, with only one way out, meant that everyone knew who was where and doing what without being told, or, when told, came back with a dismissive, *Sure I knew that.* In this way there was no news that was new, because someone had it before you, and someone before him, and her too, anything that happened getting picked up by the wind and travelling on, and, a snap of the fingers later, at the back door of every other house, drawn in on boots and set steaming before the fire, to take on the cooked nature of story.

So, before anyone said it, it was noted that Miss Troy was not seen on her bicycle, pumping her legs on those windy, hilly cycles that were constitutional for her, eased the burden of every day answering the door to illness, and went some way towards covering the melancholic truth that she had no friends in the parish. The nods and head-lifts that were salutes in local idiom when she passed field, ditch or front door were not delivered, and, as if by an inner accountancy, were discovered by the vague awareness of a surplus. *Do you know who hasn't passed in a while?* For a time, everyone supposed someone else must have seen her, and her disappearance was not actual until it came up in conversation. It was not until something got into the talk that it grew arms and legs, where it went then, literally anybody's business. Both because of the fenced pale around those in the medical profession, and because, living in Avalon House – *The Troys are not the same as us* – no one asked the doctor if his daughter was taken ill, or why she had not been seen in the parish since the Christmas Fair.

Ever since the fair, on Sundays, the doctor had taken to coming to first Mass alone, which, at nineteen minutes, was the exact time it took to say the Latin, with a consecration so swift that it shared the attribute of Flaherty's three-card trick by being over before you could see how it was done. Father Tom had not been seen on the altar since the word went out that the chest was at him, and through the remainder of Advent, Father Coffey said all Masses. That Miss Troy was not with the doctor was first put down to his reputation for aloofness and a vocation whose responsibilities had no off-button. He was a man who always had to be elsewhere. Sickness knocked at your door, even when you were sitting on the toilet, Sonny Cooney said; that was why doctors were always washing their hands. So, when Doctor Troy swept in and out of the church alone in the dark of Advent dawns, he did so without question, and his daughter was assumed at Second Mass, until it was mentioned *She wasn't, you know.* On the Feast of the Immaculate Conception, there was no sign of her. That she could have cycled over to Boola was not beyond possibility. There were always some who, by virtue of a nature that found everything near to them worse than what was far, went to the next parish for absolution. But the general verdict was that the doctor's daughter was too sensible for that, and there had to be another reason for a disappearance that left the true story hanging on the three dots of an ellipsis.

Did you see her when you were in with your stomach? was a question that stumped any answer, because only saints can see beyond their own suffering, and the need to get into the waiting room ahead of the next one overrode the courtesies. Besides, Ronnie Troy had been showing in patients for so long, and had a manner so self-effacing, that even on a good day it was hard to remember if she herself had been there or not.

No, mind you. I don't believe so. No, I'd say.

None of which constituted more than a thread in the fabric of Faha in the lead-up to Christmas. But it was a thread, and, because hanging, provoked an itch for pulling. For two weeks, Ronnie had not appeared with her two books at the library counter in town, and overdue fines of thruppence per book per week were pencilled into her record for the first time. When Mrs Prendergast came in for the murder mysteries that Mr P had mocked her for reading, the librarian, who was a set-dancing Looney from town, asked her about the doctor's daughter. 'She's well, is she?'

Mrs Prendergast kept the letterbox of her lips closed but made an assonant 'ah-ha' that she could not be held to, either way. She came back to Faha with the vexation of finding out from a townie something in her own parish and pulled on the thread that evening during the break in *Radharc* by asking Father Coffey what was wrong with Ronnie Troy.

The curate was unaware there was anything the matter, but, like her, did not want to say. He felt the shepherd's burden of a pastoral care for a flock that jumped the walls. The question provoked his fear that, from a life focused on the invisible, he would miss what was in front of him. His saying nothing was as good as a story though, and by the time Mrs Prendergast was in her bed with the Colonel, the Butler, the Maid and the Mistress, the mystery had a disappeared daughter added into it, and Featherstone was Faha, only in better shoes.

The following morning, her 'And tell me, how is Veronica?' was the doctor's first inkling that his daughter had entered the parochial conversation, and at the counter he answered a blunt 'Good' and not the *Why do you ask?* that was his first response. Instantly he knew that if the question was in the post office, it had been delivered out around the parish too. He knew that, once walking, it would go everywhere, and he drew in his shoulders like one defending a blow.

'She hasn't been seen for a bit,' said Mrs Prendergast, the tip of her tongue following the question out onto the crimson of her tiny lower lip and holding there, as though to see what it licked.

'I've seen her,' the doctor said, and pulled up the muscles of his smile.

Whether his answer was sufficient, he did not wait to see. He touched the brim of his hat with a gloved hand and withdrew from a scene that would require more lies the longer it went on. When he sat into the car, his heart had taken off in the un-reined race of the guilty when discovery is imminent. He had a sense of the story itself as particles in the air, viral, transiting and thickening by the moment.

***

By a happy marriage of nature and profession, the doctor had for a long time achieved his ambition to live a private life. He wanted no personal attention from anyone living, and for the most part got none. That no one ever asked him how he was, that none knew what was going on inside him, was the way he liked it; it kept the world at arm's length and preserved the secrecies of a personality too complex for explanation. On the periphery of the medical profession because he had no affinity for the dimples of the golfball, he had one doctor friend, McMahon, a classmate at the Royal College, who was now in General Practice in Crosshaven, and was the only person he played chess with. They played by post, one move at a time, so that a game took months. The doctor played mercurially, for it was the only time he didn't have to take care. Although each move came on a headed paper with nothing but the algebraic notation and the spider Arabic of a signature initial, the games acted as a diary of the inner dynamics, the trials, raptures and convulsions of his soul. When he was in hopeless love with Annie Mooney, he lost two years of games in a row, but he offered no explanation for his loss of form, and by his friend was asked for none, for between them it was understood that in all chess games life was the third player. Those games were as close as Doctor Troy got to sharing anything about himself, and so he had arrived at the cusp of his sixtieth year with the quiet satisfaction of achieving his goal of being the last private person in the world.

To the doctor then, this talk about his daughter was triply upsetting, not only because it announced the amateur detectives on the trail, because it made the Troys a topic, but also because, in Faha, the human tongue was a propagating tool without parallel; it got into every nook. It was a certainty that, if not ablated, by noon the following day the story would bring a knock to the door. He leaned forward in the car, pulled the choke and turned the key with a roughness that was his curse in another language.

In the black beret and long coat of a clean revolutionary, Father Coffey was coming down the churchyard with a question. But the doctor drove away with a suddenness that left the curate standing, and the story with nothing to do but spread.

When he got to Crowe's, McCarthy's hearse was parked in the gate.

The moment the doctor saw it, he thought the story had got ahead of him. She was dead then? But in the post office he had not been told. If the hearse was here, it was impossible Mrs Prendergast did not know. Was that what Father Coffey had been coming to tell him? The pieces didn't meet, and he moved his neck inside a shirt-collar tightened by a distending guilt that the grandmother's passing was the next step to his daughter's wedding. His heart was still racing. He could feel the thump into the left side of his neck and angled down the rear-view mirror to let the doctor in him take a look.

Mrs Crowe was deceased. He took off his gloves, got from the car without his bag, his features set in that graven compose that was the universal passport for those entering the house of the dead. Along by the hearse he passed, the engine still warm. From beneath it, feathered rush of life, a hen darted, and reset his heart. By an instinct he didn't acknowledge, he looked to the bare branches of the sycamores, as though expecting crows, or other signs of a life expired. The sky had the bruised grandeur of fallen majesty, the dawn's pinks and oranges and purples trammelled under banks of cloud, but no other portent. He came down the back step and into the kitchen with a 'God bless' so soft it would not reach the ears even of the Almighty.

In front of the fire was not McCarthy, but Young McCarthy, a two-dimensional youth who had not said goodbye to pimples before he said hello to cigarettes. He was thin and tall, with a topping of flop hair that had so far escaped the Christmas cut. In a black suit that was made for someone with shoulders, and chest, he was an apprentice undertaker who felt like a gangster driving the hearse, but grew smaller when the doctor walked in. Ganga was by the window, scratching his head in case that helped. The doctor went to him with the handshake of condolence, but before he could say anything, Young McCarthy betrayed his callowness by sucking on his ciggy and lipping, 'He won't give me the photograph.'

The doctor did not look back at him. He was shaking Mossie's hand and having his own shaken vigorously. The grandfather had the same light as always in his eyes, showed no sign that the other half of his life had left the world, and kept shaking the visitor's hand, as though he believed that was what the doctor wanted. That the shaking and pumping may have continued until one or the other conceded was a possibility not tested because Young McCarthy, whose relationship with time was that there was not enough of it, tossed his butt and said, 'I can't be waiting around.'

Doctor Troy turned on him a look in which was the young, the country, and the road to Hell. But the youth saw none of that.

Ganga had bent to shake the paw of Joe, who had been waiting his turn.

'I've to get the photograph or there'll be nothing top of the coffin.' Young McCarthy's face had a scorning aspect; it was in the curl of his lip and the flare of his pimples, and was aimed generally at a world stupid and slow. 'I've tried telling him. He says I have the wrong house. He says she's not dead.'

The truth is always understood before your senses prove it. Doctor Troy knew the moment he heard those words that, on his indication, the message had gone from the post office to the undertakers, and, from the inveterate chaos of a builder-undertaker who always had five jobs on the go, finished none until the next five were underway, and had given promises for the five after them, this was a case of what Sonny Cooney called premature death.

'Wait here,' he said, and went down to the room where he found Mrs Crowe living as before. As before, he took her hand and said who he was. As before, they sat like antique figures betrothed, in a relation beyond words. And as once before, after an interim that may have been the time it took for her spirit to travel back the distance it was from her body, she squeezed his fingers.

He came back into the kitchen and with an undisguised impatience told the youth, 'Mrs Crowe's still living. Go.'

That the doctor felt some relief that Doady Crowe was still amongst them was a perplex he couldn't solve. He drove home through country dulled under ponderous cloud, on every road a pale litter of ribs of hay from morning feeds fallen, in the fields wintering-out cattle in their standing posed, the beards of the rushes brown. There was no trace of the sky-drama of the dawn, but upon the scene it was easy to lend an interpretation of attendance, of a stoic December waiting for an event as invisible as it was certain to be coming. In all, this paused sense, and within it expectation. Passing, the car rose up the small birds that homed in thorn bushes, but these were only visible in the mirror.

He came up the gravel of the avenue at a crunching speed and sent the same signal twice by taking the front steps with the nimbleness of a fifty-year-old, not remembering his heart until the drumbeat accompanied him in the hall. When he entered the kitchen, it was to tell his daughter there was talk in the post office, but he was diverted when, the baby asleep under criss-crossed banners, Ronnie greeted him with, 'Why is Crowe's post with ours?'

Briefly, he faced the dilemma of the liar who has to remember what he has told to whom. But he saved face by looking away, taking up the letters and cards on the table, saw there were none from America, before responding with a non-sequitur that deflected explanation, 'You need to show you're alive.'

Once opened, the surgery door was not locked until the evening, but those whose illness always occurred in the middle of the day were accustomed to sitting out the hour in the waiting room, because of the Christian concession that even doctors needed to eat sometime. So, at one o'clock that day, with three bronchial patients in the three corners, Ronnie Troy appeared at the door and told them the doctor would be with them after his dinner. She cycled down the avenue and into the village with the purpose of showing that she was still living, while the doctor took the infant into the top floor of the house.

With each day, the baby's character was establishing. She had a steadiness in her gaze and a general serenity that refuted the reputation of infants, and each day seemed to show some knowledge of the world she had landed into. It could not be so, except in the way that it seemed to be. She had a deep calm, or gave you one when you held her. The gift of it was in her nature and when the doctor walked the floorboards with her held against him, he was restored to his earlier self, when fatherhood was that thing of hope and prayer, and when to shield your child from harm was the sole propose of your breathing. Her eyes watched him as he went, the thin light of the midday coming on his face as they came to the window, leaving it when he turned. The light that crossed him, by which he was illumed and shadowed, was the sum of the baby's gaze. Time and again, he watched her expression change as he crossed the room with her. Light was a magic he performed, and was all she required of him. It was as though each time the window might not be there, each time the journey might not end in light. But it did, and when it did, her eyes, her whole face, transformed, and Doctor Jack Troy forgot that his heart laboured and that he had thought it a thing too old for exaltation.

'Good girl,' he said. He said it first to the room general, his face not inclined, then again, looking directly into her remarkable eyes. 'Good girl.' He saw his breath on the air, and only then realised how cold it was in that room. He touched her nose and chastised himself for forgetting the first rule of doctors. He brought her closer inside the wing of his jacket and carried her like a living contraband down the hall to a south-facing room. 'She will be home soon,' he said. 'We will stay up here just a little longer, all right?'

His tone and manner were unlike himself. That he had not used that voice since he had held his daughters, he did not acknowledge, for we are all young when no one can see us. He nodded to the infant, as though reaffirming a pact. He gave her his finger, which by the fierceness of her grip, she seemed to want. Then, by a prompt too deep inside him to explain, he lowered his head to the child and whispered, 'I loved Annie Mooney.'

There was instant relief in it, and pleasure too, and though the baby's expression did not change he found he wanted to say the name again, and he did, a summons and confession both, this time changing the tense of the verb from past to present, which changed nothing but brought his contained smile, and joined him and the infant in a further conspiracy of the heart.

He raised her against his breast, and they crossed and recrossed the high room like that, finger-bound, across floorboards that made the wooden notes of a travelling music.

(The doctor did not consider then that the noises of that room might be heard below. What possessed him was love. He did not suppose that the rhythm of their to and fro would travel through the joists, that it would announce itself in a general rise and fall not consistent with a doctor at his dinner, and in a house whose bits were fused together, with joints arthritic since the river had said its first hello, the pacing would lift the eyes of the waiting room with a Pentecostal look that would not be spoken of, but would be backfilled into the story later, when, after much palaver, the teller would deliver what he had found out, only to have his cough softened by a *Sure I knew that*, or worse, *We all knew that*.)

The doctor bore the baby across the room while Ronnie showed Faha she was living. That this was a stay only on a story whose character was that it could only go the one way, he well knew. But a summary of every doctor's life was transforming one thing into another, and when at the window he saw his eldest daughter in her long green overcoat, cycling up the avenue with the shone eyes of an appointment with love, he knew he could not surrender to the State what was breathing in his arms.

When Ronnie found him, it was with whispers, and they left that room with the same housebreaker's walk that had become theirs when there was company. Passing the bathroom, the doctor pulled the chain on the lavatory, the doleful clatter, flush and suck ball-cocking down through the house in an alibi none could question.

He returned to his patients with a look of having pulled up his trousers, and by each the noising in the floorboards was forgotten under the imperative of what was sitting on their chest.

***

That afternoon Doctor Troy attended to his patients in a perfunctory manner, but none could tell because they only had ears for what he said about what was ailing them. When the last one had left, he put the latch on the front door, killed the wireless, and found that, instead of his habitual withdrawal to the leather divan for an interlude that was a necessity for those who have all day dealt with sickness, he wanted to see the baby. It was a thirst he didn't know he had until he registered the absence in the crook of his arm where he had held her. He came into the kitchen with the prime yearning, to hold her again, but Ronnie, who was more rigorous in routine than even he, put a dent in it by asking, 'Are you not going to take your rest?'

He lifted the baby from the makeshift cot.

'The tea's not ready,' Ronnie said.

'That's all right.'

He held the baby out from him, as though at that arm's length the measure of human life might be seen better, as though looking at the infant from that distance he could see what it was he was supposed to do next. The girl crinkled her nose. In infants, it passed for a smile. She hung there in that mid-air, legs dangling, and the doctor looked at her, and his daughter looked at him.

Then, whether because Ronnie Troy was the eldest, because she had already adopted a philosophy that life was a thing of disappointments, small and large, and it was best to face them head on, she folded her arms across the breast that missed the child and with brutal directness asked the question she didn't want answered, 'What are we going to do?'

She did not add *We cannot go on like this*; she did not need to, it was there.

Her father held the child an instant longer. With his cryptic character, he did not show that the question had pierced him. His moustache moved some, but his grey eyes did not change and for a moment he leaned on the still current convention that parents did not have to answer their children.

He drew the baby to his face.

Ronnie waited.

The morning after the infant arrived at the door, Ronnie had asked her father about the child's mother. After a discussion of short duration and studied silences, both agreed it was most likely that the mother had come with the fair and gone with it too, had left the baby at the church gate in her best hope and would not be back, except in the happenstance of future trading where her eye might look for what she had left there, and hope to see a grown girl. '*If she comes looking, we will hear,*' the doctor had said. '*And we will bring her here, and we will have kept her baby well.*' A summary that drew the line under any other possibilities, it established the confederacy in which they went forward. It was founded on a concept of guardianship, and the learned wisdom of parents that your children do not belong to you. But it did not account for how such a thing would be possible in a country where the concept of family was defined along one line, and a baby in the street belonged to the State, who, with haste to be unsoiled, would hand it off to the Church.

The doctor had a plan, and it was not outrageous, he told himself, but he could not reveal it until every t was crossed and i dotted, which, in this case, meant until Noel Crowe landed for his grand-mother's funeral and was told that Ronnie Troy loved him. Then, because the youth had a pure nature that any could see, when the doctor confessed to him that he regretted standing in the way of the courting the first time round, the inevitable would follow, and Noel Crowe would not make the mistake that Jack Troy had with Annie Mooney and miss the love of a lifetime.

That secret plots were also in the character of the season did not escape the doctor. In the run-up to Christmas every household in the parish ran a sanctioned subterfuge. There were wooden farm-sets hidden in cowsheds, open-eyed dolls in the back of presses, and Matchbox cars in sewing boxes on top shelves, all licensed by a Saint Nicholas addicted to charity without fingerprints.

So, as he handed the baby back to Ronnie, the doctor was able to answer with the circumspection of other parents in December, 'We have to wait and see.'

'See what?'

That one he did not answer. And, because the girl giggled when she was placed into her arms, Ronnie was diverted by the immediacy of babies, for whom there is only now.

The doctor said he would make the tea, and again there settled over that kitchen the semblance of a hushed normality, a scene domestic and serene that, if you were standing outside, say, by the holly tree, had come under the cover of darkness, say, and – what harm? – had sawn off enough berried branches to set up a small Christmas commerce, to make the few shillings in the square in town, and when you looked up to the long windows saw captured the doctor and his daughter, say, saw them pass a child between them, well that would be the very picture of family itself.

Until you thought about it later.

Then, studying where the picks of the holly leaves had scored crosses on the backs of your hands, it would come back to you and, for no reason other than the emptiness of time and the standing that the telling of news bestowed, you'd tell the room, *The one of the Troys has a child.*

***

The following morning, Saturday, the doctor saw the ravaged tree as he drove out. He had to stop on the avenue. It was his own fault; he had had the idea for the fence, but not the wife to remind him to do it. On the offside of the house, the limbs of the holly had been hacked. From work in darkness and haste, it had an even more butchered look than last year. It saddened him to see, not for the theft, for who after all *owned* a tree, but for the wounded dignity of such a venerable thing. Which was absurd, of course.

And yet.

Jack Troy had told himself that he was not going to become one of those old men who succumbed to sudden depths of emotion. In his last months, his father could cry in mid-sentence, his eyes becoming strangely, unspeakably beautiful, his voice a tenor's, and the whole of him softly convulsing at a memory he could not even get as far as saying. At that stage, the old doctor had an Apostle's beard, and to accommodate it, sat with his head angled back. In his chair, his words would break off and he would wave a hand at the rest of the sentence, as though it could depart upwards without being spoken. To say that what seized him was the sentimentality common in old men who have spent a lifetime ignoring their heart was a diagnosis his son refused to give. Instead, because of the nakedness of it, he had adopted the view that in the doorway of death his father had become a living version of his own soul. He showed what he felt without shield, and what he felt was enormous. But to his son it was also unbearable, and when at last he had walked from the graveyard, he had vowed that with him it would not be like that.

And yet here he was, paused in the avenue with the engine running, six house calls to make, feeling sorrow for a wounded holly tree. It disturbed him. But that it portended something was a thought he would not pursue. He rolled up the window, went down the avenue and attempted, in that fatuous phrase, to put it out of his mind. That there is no such place for putting things was proven by the number of times the image of the tree returned to Doctor Troy that morning and afternoon. While sitting by bedsides, taking temperatures, turning patients, evaluating sores, throats, chests and pulses, and afterwards standing by hearths, *Warm yourself, Doctor*, it would come to him, the sundered holly, and with it a gathering sense that catastrophe was on its way.

Which was another nonsense. And something the medical scientist in him mocked him for letting across his brain. He would not hurry home, if only to prove that he was not some softening old man. Faha was full of figaries. If you wanted to find them, there were *pishogues* under every stone, people who would translate every mood of the weather, every expression of the natural world, and tell you what was going to happen to you tomorrow on the third bell of the Angelus. They were vestiges of a culture departing, not yet gone. But Doctor Jack Troy was a disciple only of the empirical, was what he told himself. He stayed out longer than he needed, and when he returned home in the swift dark of late afternoon, he purposely did not look towards the tree.

'Did you see the holly?' was what greeted him.

'I did.'

'Next year you should put up the fence.'

The baby was sleeping. The doctor went to the window and realised at once that whoever had been at the tree had had a view into the kitchen. A small 'ha' escaped him. But even as that piece was falling into place, he saw Father Coffey cycling up the drive. In his long black coat and beret, with a black umbrella held over him, he appeared like a figure out of Keeley & Patterson's Circus, in a funereal version.

'Curate,' the doctor said. He did not look at his daughter, for he did not want to risk her seeing his fear that they had been found out.

'When he knocks, I will answer it,' Ronnie said.

She checked the infant was soundly asleep, and when the double hammer sounded, she pushed her hands into the pockets of her cardigan and went with the greeting face she offered all patients. She had used it so often she did not need to check it in the hall mirror and drew open the door with a welcome that none could have guessed false.

Father Coffey had come for two purposes. The first was to see Ronnie Troy for himself. Having not yet established a network through which to learn everything that happened in Faha, he had not been told that the doctor's daughter had cycled through the village. With the virginal earnestness God must love in young priests, he had come under his shepherd's licence to find out what had happened to one of his flock. Into the delicate matter of enquiring about Ronnie's whereabouts he had prepared three routes, but found the map redundant by her standing in front of him in the flesh, without the tell-tale signs of injury, illness or malfeasance that were the earmarks of cheap storytelling.

'Father Coffey,' said Ronnie. When no reply was returned, when all he did was stand facing her, she added, 'Are you coming in?'

At the time, the curate had fallen under the spell of the revivalists of the Irish language. It was a movement that had about it a revolutionary aura, to reclaim a heritage, speak in our own tongue, *an teanga beo*, and had a sense of standing up after being long put down. That his own school Irish was the same stiff, laborious un-fluency as everyone else's in the parish did not deter him. Neither that he got caught in *tuiseals*, couldn't keep track of *seimhius*, and was by *gramadach* so tongue-tied that before he said anything he seemed to be visited by an exigent *cigire* in a grey suit, fanatical for correction. Such things were only sent to test us, was the gospel of his mother, and besides, before the end of the year help was coming. The national broadcaster had announced it was going to air the first episode of *Daithi Lacha*, the cartoon David Duck, no relation to Donald, but who, wearing only striped underpants, was going to make learning Irish fun for all. And so, with his Cuban zeal at the time, Father Coffey persisted, and maintained a vision of a future Faha in which no word of English would be spoken.

'*Dia dhuit*,' he said. He wanted to add her name but could not think of the Irish for Veronica. Despite the umbrella, the rain was in his roundrims, and in the doorway he had a blind look.

'Are you coming in, Father?' Ronnie asked again, with no more welcome than the first time, no less either.

Because the Irish required him to add a verb in the affirmative, and because to do this, crossing from one language into another, with the *cigire* standing watching, was beyond him at that moment, Father Coffey replied with a readymade sentence, '*Cupan tae, le do thoil.*'

'Tea?' said Ronnie.

The curate walked past her with a nod of raindrops and was on his way down the hall before Ronnie realised he was going to the kitchen. 'Father!'

The tone was like a hand on the back of his collar. He had never heard her use it before and he turned. He was still wearing the rain on face and glasses, and under the domed light in the hall had the appearance of a pantomime seer.

'I've a good fire down, Father,' Ronnie opened the door into the front parlour, 'in here.' The smell of the smoke came out. Since she could not take the baby outdoors, the whole interior of Avalon House had been commandeered for their walks, upstairs and down, in and out of each room several times, the child falling asleep now only when in motion, and tending to open her eyes the moment Ronnie stopped. So, even as she held open the door to the priest, Ronnie knew that she had been in the parlour with the infant in the afternoon and, because all children leave a trail, was trying to remember if she had covered it up afterwards.

The curate could tell the kitchen was out of bounds. Probably because it was untidy, not fitting for the unannounced visit of a priest, which was how people in the parish were, but not what he wanted. Not at all. He was not the Bishop, he was not even the Canon, for goodness' sake.

'No need for fuss on my account. The kitchen is fine for me,' he said, and reached for the porcelain doorknob.

'No.'

It was a command. That it was so unlike her required explanation, and she took three steps down the hall to the priest, beckoning him to her at the same time, before dropping her voice into the whisper of conspirators and delivering the merciless sentence that is the Rubicon for innocence, 'My father is Santa Claus.'

Only the black eyebrows showed Father Coffey's expression. They rose above the blind glasses, then lowered in a joint presentation of puzzlement.

'He's in there,' Ronnie whispered. 'Wrapping my present.'

Only her left eyelid twitched twice; the rest of her, through a composure so complete, hands by her sides, lips at ease and eyes steady, made plausible an excuse plucked out of the legitimised convention of the season. And while the curate tried to accommodate this intimacy into the phlegmatic character of the doctor, Ronnie led him into the front parlour.

'He's like a child. I have to be surprised,' she said.

The cloth, she plucked off the arm of the chair before the priest could smell it. She saw no other trace of the baby and completed the performance by a forbearing shrug and indulgent smile.

'Through the door I'll tell Santa you are here, Father.'

'Don't disturb him, I can wait.' Father Coffey had taken off his glasses, and his eyes had that peculiar vulnerability of ones used to being shielded. They looked exposed somehow, but when he turned them to her, she had a contrary sense of being seen more clearly.

'And yourself,' he asked. 'You're well?'

The priest was about the same age as her. In a different country and time, they might have been colleagues.

'Me, Father?'

His long frame was stretched out and he was feeling in his trouser pocket for the handkerchief to dry the lenses. He found the cloth, between thumb and forefinger taking off the rain, but looking at her again now with the directness used to supplying the prompt for confessions. 'Yourself. You're quite well?'

The room was lit by two standing lamps and the low glow of turf in the grate. Together they made the amber atmosphere that was the measure of every evening-time in winter. That no one could quite see across a room or make out exactly the features of someone in the chair on the far side of the fire were both given, for night was night and darkness not yet gone from the world. But even in that low light, the question struck something guilty in Ronnie, and she wondered if something about her was showing that she was all day and night now with a baby.

She knew she was already changed by the experience of having the child in the house. She had not given birth to it, but from round-the-clock company and care, she knew she was different. How exactly escaped definition, it was inside her, but in the moment the priest asked, she feared it was on the outside too. She met his look with not a little of a defiance that was new to her, but she knew she would need in the days ahead.

'Never better, Father, thank you.'

'Good. That's good,' he said, but without conviction, not taking his look away just yet, because in his experience revelations commonly came on the heels of denials.

To break the look, Ronnie threw him, 'And you, Father?'

It was the priest's turn for the unexpected. 'Oh,' he said, briefly angling his face to the ceiling, as though it was a question going over his head. Then, as signal that that part of the dialogue was done, he knocked his wet sandals together to let off the rain and put his glasses back on.

Ronnie went to get her father, exhaling when she closed the door.

In the dusky light, the curate considered how easily stories were invented in that parish. It was the fault of the estuary, of a tide always coming and going, always saying, and saying so, just at the shore of comprehension. Or of the low ground that was part water. Or of the rain that was part earth. Or the mist that could not make up its mind if it was sea fog or river breath, whether coming in or going out, tasted of smoke or salt, and made not a soup of the air but a brumous ghost that went everywhere. It was a condition of place, story. And with only one road to the outside world, invention had nowhere else to turn. Out of a hidden bicycle, or a man's underpants, Faha could make an epic. Veronica Troy was perfectly fine, perfectly.

By an indulgent shake of his head, Father Coffey ticked her off his list, and was reviewing his tactics for the more difficult item on his agenda when the doctor came in with an air of reduced time and impatience thinly disguised. It banished at once the incongruous image of him as Santa Claus, and so completely that the very idea of it seemed beyond even a child's imagining.

'Michael.'

'Doctor.' Father Coffey had stood up before he realised it. He made it seem an exercise in straightening his trouser creases, gave a little tug to his waistband, and sat again.

Providing no encouragement for niceties, the doctor did not sit. On the hearthstone, he backsided the fire and waited.

'All well?' asked the curate. 'Set for Christmas? We have all year, and yet always the rush, isn't it?' He let that out to see if it would catch anything. When it didn't, he added the axiom of Martin Meagher, whose wisdom came in the capsule of a single phrase, *The world is the world.* Martin often said it a second time for those whose dosage was two, but in the doctor's case the curate left it at just the one.

'There's something on your mind, Michael?'

'There is,' said Father Coffey. With the diligence of a student actor, he had rehearsed the scene several times that afternoon, playing both parts, allowing the doctor an unforthcoming character of chronic recalcitrance who could not be argued into any position, while taking the voice-of-reason role for himself. The thing was to step it out. To not be rushed. 'There is, in fact.'

The doctor had the next line. Only he did not say it. He held his hands clasped where the fire made warm the small of his back and tried to ascertain if the priest had been told about the child.

Father Coffey tapped both hands on the low table in front of him. It lent weight to the unsaid, or did in rehearsal. 'Yes,' he said, as though concurring with a point made. Finding that the nap on the left knee of his trouser was in a circle raised, in three smart strokes he brushed it smooth. It was the last part of a prelude whose aim was to control his breathing, and when done he reached inside his jacket and from the breast pocket took a white envelope. This he placed on the table in front of him. He did so with a stagey emphasis just short of the histrionic code in the silent pictures, without the organ accompaniment or the title card *Envelope!* but with similar intent. Having played his principal prop, the curate sat back from it, and waited to be asked what the envelope contained.

That he had underestimated the gap between rehearsal and life was made clear when the doctor did not deliver the question, and the silence that thickened – not deafening, for it made loud his own heartbeat and the pulse of the pendulum clock in the hall – threatened to overwhelm all.

For one illogical moment, in a brain-leap that had been his since boyhood, the curate considered that the scene had already happened, that the doctor was not only omniscient, and knew what the envelope contained, but like Martin de Porres could be in two places at once, had already written his signature above the line Father Coffey had tapped out on Mrs Queally's typewriter, and there was no need for anything further. He could stand and take his coat and leave without any unpleasantness at all. None at all. He had put both hands on the balls of his knees in preparation for push-off when he realised he was failing the fortitude required of priests, and reached out and picked up the envelope, and held it towards the doctor. He met Jack Troy's eyes for the first time, and, with the same even delivery he had mastered in the bathroom mirror, said the scripted line, 'We need to do the Christian thing.'

In the script, he used the doctor's first name. In reality, he did not.

Briefly, the doctor bulbed his cheek with his tongue. The moustache lop-sided, then righted, without any other part of him moving. The white envelope was held towards him. Now he did know what was in it, and as he stepped down off the hearth and took it, as he opened and read the single page addressed to Bishop Rodgers, the curate's signature on the bottom, the vacant space next to it awaiting his own, he had to fight the temptation to turn about and post the thing into the fire.

In a further departure from rehearsal, Father Coffey did not wait for the doctor to finish reading. He launched into a speech of persuasion that would have been no more effective on Jack Troy if he had been listening to it. In it was 'Poor Father Tom', and 'For his own good', and 'Deserving of dignity', 'Danger to himself' and 'His final reward'; in it were the same arguments that everywhere sought to separate ailing elders from their own beds and make neat the derange of dying by housing it elsewhere.

'Medical certification,' was what Doctor Troy heard. He finished reading and lowered the page.

Father Coffey's speech had coloured him. He had come almost to the end of what he had written, and the ardour burned in his cheeks. Rimmed, his eyes were rounder than in life, and wore the firelight flickering.

'As his doctor, you are the authority. Once you sign, I will send it to His Excellency and we can rest easy knowing we will have done the right thing.'

This last the curate delivered in an indisputable matter-of-factness that allowed him to take out the fountain pen from the other breast pocket, unscrew the cap, and present it, handle-first, like a mercy pistol.

'Thank you,' he said, adding at last a soft, 'Jack.'

And then, nothing.

The doctor did not take the pen, he did not drop the page, did not turn and ball the Bishop's letter for the fire. He did not make a speech, engage in any argument for or against, did not say a single word that might have betrayed what he was thinking.

Instead, it was as though the preceding had not in fact happened, as though it had been negated not by discourse, not by debate and counter-debate, but by a denial so absolute that it was possible to change reality, to make the moment not-happen, and continue to not-happen, as though *as though* itself was the real thing, in parallel and true, and in that reality there was no need to answer, no need to take or refuse the pen, because in that one it was simply inconceivable that Jack Troy would ever sign an old priest, addled or not, to be committed against his will. In that same nothing that was happening, in that colder of the two parlours of Avalon House, smoke coming from the fire when his backside left the plinth, some in scent ascending, where the married lamp- and fire-light made of that room a twilight in which both men looked like waxen versions of themselves, what was conceivable was that the doctor would walk from the room, that he would exit like a figure in a play, leaving the priest in an unwritten scene, with nothing to do but cycle home.

But he did not.

Then he did not some more.

Jack Troy stood, employing his genius for detachment.

In Faha, it went without saying that doctors had minds that went to the bottom of things, a journey not inconsiderable, and as consequence were slow to say. It was not only allowed but expected that a doctor wouldn't answer a question directly. There was so much to consider. So, in the beats that followed there was as yet no alarm for Father Coffey. Briefly, he thought of repeating his speech entire, but rejected this as weakness, and instead, in an attempt at lightness, drew back the fountain pen and mocked himself with, 'You probably have your own pen.'

He was diligently screwing the cap back on when there came the baby's cry.

It came through two doors and down the hallway, its pierce softened, but still enough to be nothing other than itself, and it brought up the curate's eyes instantly, as though with them he was listening. He had the *Is that a…?* in his expression without moving his lips, and by instinct had inclined his head in the direction of the distress.

The baby cried a second time. It was a cry shaken or rocked or otherwise stifled, had a reverb pulsated into it as the cry came against a cotton breast, but was still undeniably itself. There was a baby in the house. Were there visitors? Had somebody called? Had he missed something? The curate looked to the doctor, as if he had already asked these questions, but he got no answers. Instead, the doctor looked once more at the letter. He had decided to read it again, it seemed, and though not in the lamplight did so intently now while the third cry sounded, quieter still, so both men knew the baby was being carried away from them to the far end of the kitchen.

In the doctor's hand, the page did not waver. His grey eyes did not come up from it.

Father Coffey thought to again take out the fountain pen, reached for it, but instead straightened the line of his jacket. He leaned forward in the chair, pressed down the soles of his sandals and saw a small leakage stain the parquet. He looked towards the room door, as if to see beyond it. *Whose baby was it was in the house?* It was not yet a question of urgency, more of interest and surprise, but it took on an added pique when the curate realised that for the first time in that house Veronica Troy had failed the standard of her flawless hosting: she had not brought him his *cupán tae*.

Because the letter was awaiting signature, because the doctor was so concentrated on the page, and because any disturbance might divert from the main business, Father Coffey did not ask about the child. Both men had heard it, and it existed in the space, but as a ghost. *Later*, the curate thought. He would ask later. For now, the crux was the certification. That it mattered so was not callousness. Of everyone in the parish, the curate was the one most burdened by an excess of conscience. A hundred times he had turned the question of the Canon over and back. On his knees at his night-prayers he had asked for strength. Because he knew that he did not have it. Taking the elder priest from the bathroom after he had pulled up the flaggy underpants at the old man's ankles, helping him back when once more Tom fell out of the low side of the lopsided bed that was customary for priests, wiping the detritus off his chest because midway to his mouth the Canon forgot the food was on its way, or because he drank his tea now only from the saucer, tipping a fair amount onto his cross, all of it revulsed the young priest, made a ticking bomb of every moment, and unseated the contemplative calm needed for the Spiritual Exercises. *O give me strength* had been his prayer for months, until, without his deciding, it changed to *O give me guidance.* And what he had been guided to was the letter now in the doctor's hand. This was the way forward, and was, he absolutely believed, the right thing to do for the good of the Canon. Sat forward, he placed the upright fingers and thumbs of each hand against each other, like an air church. He pressed them, pliable to a point, and let them resume form. He tapped the whole twice against his lips. And still the doctor was staring at the page. The letter was not so long. He had already read it once, and now had taken almost as much time as the composition.

'I'll hold on to this,' the doctor said at last, when he realised the baby was not going to cry again and the crisis had passed. He was already folding the letter back into the envelope, and before the priest could ask why, added, 'It won't go in the post until Monday anyway. I will call on Tom.'

He walked to the door and had already opened it before Father Coffey realised the scene was over.

'I'll just look in on Veronica,' the curate said, when he came out into the hall. 'Tell her not to bother with my tea.'

'I'll do that. Goodbye now, Michael.' The doctor extended his arm towards the front door.

The two men looked at each other for the first time. That there was something awry in the space between them was apparent. That in that front hall there was something untold, the priest knew, but the eyes of the doctor were steady and with the letter still to be signed Father Coffey would not draw any trouble.

'All right so.'

The curate put on his beret. He came out into the porchlight, the door clunked behind him. Before he was on his bicycle, he heard the slide of the bolts. He had forgotten his umbrella, but he no longer had the letter for the bishop he needed to keep dry. And now, there came to him the transparent ploy of coming back tomorrow unannounced to collect the umbrella. Because *Whose baby was that?*

'I'm sorry. She just … out of nowhere. One minute she was asleep and then… Did he hear?'

'Yes.'

'What did he say?'

'He said nothing.'

The doctor poured himself the tea that Ronnie had made for the visitor but had left aside when the baby started crying. Like most ceramic teapots in the parish, it dribbled down the spout, but he ignored the spill and sat. Suddenly the entire plot, the story that they were in, that he was partly making up, scheming for it to twist now this way and now that, was an intolerable burden. It was absurd, the idea that his eldest and most sensible daughter had fallen in love with an infant, that in order for her to have any possibility of a relationship with that child she needed to be with a man, that that man could be Noel Crowe, who might be home for his grandmother's funeral, and, by natural proximity and the deep sentiment of all returned immigrants, would resume not only walking out with Ronnie but walking up too, in this case the sloped aisle of St Cecelia's. All of it was now so outlandish, so beyond the reach of the everyday that the doctor's head spun at the contrivance – how had he even considered it? What had possessed him? Yes, his daughter had cared for the boy, he was sure of it. Yes, the boy had cared for her too, and, men being made the way they were, most likely had cared the more fervently. He had given her that novel – the doctor had not read it, but when Ronnie had taken the baby on one of their walking tours of the house, he had skimmed the pages and understood the gist of it was ardent letters between a priest and a woman – and after the visit to the boy's grandparents it was rarely out of Ronnie's reach. Yes, there had been a reasoning to the whole scheme. But all of it had profoundly exhausted Jack Troy and he resolved that it would end there and now.

They could not go on like this.

In the morning, he would tell the curate and take the child where it had to go.

'I want to give her a name,' Ronnie said. The infant was on her lap in her mother's chair. 'You should have a name, shouldn't you?' She touched the tip of the baby's nose. 'Yes, you should.' Touched it again. 'Yes.'

When she turned to her father he saw yet more joy in her eyes, and it saddened him more than could be told.

'I want us to baptise her,' Ronnie said. 'Can we?'

The doctor found his heart was at the base of his throat. His 'Yes' was too quiet to be an answer, and so he coughed softly and asked, 'What do you want to call her?'

His daughter looked at him, and then at the girl. 'Noelle.'

***

On Sunday, when he knew Father Coffey was saying second Mass, the doctor visited the Parochial House. He came in past the fresh holly sprigs above every picture and found the old priest in the kitchen with the sibby on his lap. In striped pyjamas that were the costume of jailbirds in the silent pictures, the Canon paused the mumbled Latin of an outlaw Mass-for-one and looked up at his visitor with a smile so warm it seemed he had forgotten human beings existed. The twin tufts of white hair over his ears were unbarbered and upright, he was unshaven for three days, but otherwise himself, in gentlest version.

'It's Jack Troy,' said the doctor.

'I know who it is.' The glee on the old man's face, part-innocence and part-devilment, not only recalled himself as a boy, but made it seem that he was returned to a benign childhood.

By a grace not in the textbooks, the doctor knew such was possible. It was not always the way, but in the parish, there had been several examples. Murt Casey, a man who'd give a saint a pain in the face, who life had turned into a walking knuckle, he was that closed, in the three days on the dais of his deathbed opened the fingers of himself like petals and became a lucent gentleness with only the kind word or extended hand for those who came down into the room. When he died, he went with the benevolent smile in the official portrait of Pope John. It was a thing to be witnessed, redrew the definition of character, and lent credence to Sonny Cooney's theory that God made only good people.

With an apprentice's diligence, the Canon rubbed a rub between the sibby's ears. She pushed the back of her neck into it, twisted her head for more, got more, and both remained so in a scratching-itched contentment that asked for nothing else.

Between cats and their keepers was a closed orb, and the doctor knew that he was extraneous. He asked no questions, and instead drew his conclusions from the unspoken answers of a behaviour that was the picture of placid. He was long enough in General Practice, and in a parish where the old twice outnumbered the young, to know that this was temporary. Father Coffey had neither the guile for lies nor the flair for exaggeration. The doctor did not doubt that the curate's account was accurate, and that with the Canon there were many fraught times. But storytellers skip the everyday, mistaking the ordinary for the dull, seizing on the sensational and leaving out the habitual that is in fact the fabric of life. The condition of Father Tom was not only one characterised by domestic catastrophe and distress. This too, this calm, smiling, benignity, this recalled boy in a wrinkled flesh, was how he was. The truth was less dramatic but told a fuller story. The doctor sat awhile, saying nothing.

The particular stillness of Mass-time on a Sunday morning, when it was not fanciful to sense something of the prayers of congregations invisibly rising, was always a setting for contemplation, and in this the doctor was the same as you or me. He looked out the kitchen window at the estuary, the river on its back, imitating quietude. He drew his right hand down over his moustache, and did it again, in a settling gesture that for him was a prelude. Then, each sentence a step, he said, 'There's a baby. It was found. It is in my house. My daughter wants to care for it.'

Whether the doctor expected the confession to provoke a memory-response in the Canon, that Father Tom would return to a solemn, sacramental behaviour and call for his violet stole, or he had spoken knowing that there would be none of these, it was impossible to say. He was not looking at the priest, he was looking at the river. The day was cold, but no rain was falling. It was one of those days in the run-up to Christmas when you expect nothing from it, knowing all energy and light must be going towards what is to come.

'I heard that,' said Father Tom.

'You heard?'

'I did.'

The old priest made again the dimples of his imp's smile, but turned them down to the cat, who cared less until the rubbing returned.

'Who did you hear it from?' It was an instinctual question, but Jack Troy regretted it the moment it came out of his mouth. The answer did not matter, and already he was past it, already he was considering the implications of a plot that had got ahead of him and doing what all fraught fathers do when trying to make smooth the way for their children, going into the near future. It was not difficult. Those factors that governed the present would still apply, and human nature hadn't changed since first walking upright. There, he could see what he had always known but through love denied: that the child would never be allowed to stay in Avalon, that those forces that were the designated custodians of what was deemed right would be coming, and soon. He could see it as clear as though it had already happened, and he had already stood in the front hall with Ronnie while they carried the child out the door past them. He could see his daughter's face and hear her wail, and the perturb was such that it filmed his flesh with chill and made hammer his heart.

He would not let that scene happen.

The doctor's gorge rose, and he tried hard to swallow the stone of reality. Although Christmas was painted a fairy-tale time, and although since the first it had married women with miracles, he felt nothing of that, but only an overwhelming sense of defeat. He looked away to the brown river. He felt the world and he had grown incompatible, and the relation had expended him beyond enduring.

But through all of this, his face remained the same. The same grey eyes in their sunken pods held the same steadfast gaze, the lips the same pressed line. None could have told what devastation he felt, nor that in that kitchen, with the Canon across from him, he was already drawing up a battle plan of the desperate.

To the question asked there came no answer, and in truth the subject of the child seemed to have sailed away into a depthless oblivion where so much that passed through the mind of the Canon now went. It was uncertain whether the old priest had been serious or not in stating he had heard about the child, and now the doorway to that was gone. Father Tom, it was apparent, was in one of those grace periods of calm that could last minutes or hours and then vanish without trace. He rubbed between the cat's ears. He said nothing more about the infant, nor the doctor's daughter, nor did Jack Troy ask.

Like a married couple, without their saying so, the two priests had devolved a division of territory in the house. In the kitchen, one end of the table was the Canon's, the other the curate's. They never sat at each other's places. So, Jack Troy did not need to ask, he took the letter to the Bishop from his breast pocket and placed it on Father Coffey's plate. 'I must go,' he said.

'*Pax vobiscum*,' Father Tom gave him, along with one of those looks the elderly have, earned from surviving this long, who knows how.

Avoiding the holy bottleneck of the village at Mass-time, the doctor drove round the back way and out the far side of Faha. He wanted to meet and see no one, for it was easy to suppose the knowledge of the child was in the breeze, was in the furze bushes and the rushes whispering, was in and out of every farm and house in the parish. He knew the custom of the country, knew what talk was, and how a poverty of event bigged what elsewhere might be small. Out by McCarroll's, he passed Dan Sheehan, whose starter for home was the jingle of the Communion bell. Dan stood with one foot in the ditch at the noise of the motor and looked, not raising his hand for the seat, but ready to accept one too. The doctor slowed but did not stop. He had the hallucinatory impression he had an exposed heart and was trying to figure where he would find the shield. He went east through three crosses without looking, went past Quinlan's cattle on the long acre, into and out of blind dips and bends shouldered by thorn bushes, until the car brought him where he had forgotten he was aimed.

The Master's house was the same one he had grown up in. A bachelor, he lived there with his widowed mother, Mary. A farmer-schoolmaster, he had been up before the day, been to a brisk first Mass, and in his suit trousers and wine slipover came out from a second breakfast at the ruckus of the engine arriving in the front street.

'Trouble, Doctor?' was his greeting.

By the time Jack Troy had driven away fifteen minutes later, he had ascertained two things. First, that the Master would organise an immediate rota of care for the Canon. These would be hand-picked; they would be informed of the nature of the illness, share a badge of discretion, and have the advantage over any chosen by Mrs Prendergast in reporting any worsening first to the Master, and then the doctor. They could be men or women, would be in the Parochial House on shifts, attend to the needs of the old priest when they arose, but aim for the character of the mystics by being most of the time invisible.

The second thing that he ascertained required no asking. He deduced it the same way everyone in Faha did with anything important, from what was not said. For a people whose actual history was hidden even from the historians, all knew that in that country the spoken word was the last place to find the truth. So, it was in the nods, looks away, hunches of shoulders, jaw clenches, in the gaps between sentences more than what was in them, that the doctor knew that the Master had heard about the child, but was not going to ask. There was only this tenuous presence, and Jack Troy neither sought to draw it down nor explain his part in a story that had come knocking on his door.

He refused kind Mary's offer of tea and boiled cake with a curtness unnecessary, but within the circumference of his reputation. That it would only add to interpretations of what was going on with him, he knew as he drove away, but let it be so. Trickier would be his other house calls, for it vexed him that the story would get out of the Morris before him, not because it would be brought up, but because it would be a hundred times larger by not.

As he went, with a contrary aptness to the season, the sense the doctor had was that, in that parish, the invisible child was everywhere.

As usual now, he drove out to Crowe's, brought in the cards that had come, none from America.

One of the few dispensations of deafness was a licence to forgo words without weight, and Ganga skipped all greeting for an announcement of, 'He's coming, Doctor!'

For an instant, Jack Troy forgot that the grandfather was not in collusion with him, thought that the dots had joined, and this was the news he had been waiting for.

'He's coming too, for the Christmas!' Ganga said, after three blinks adding, 'Her favourite, Mehaul,' and beaming the look of fathers whose children one by one were returning.

The doctor went down to the room, where still Aine Crowe was not dead. He held her wrist and felt for the pulse. It was small as a sparrow's, but distinct. He laid her hand back on the other where it completed the picture of a supreme repose, a kind not known on earth, he thought. Being proximate to it was its own salve, and he allowed himself stay the while. The spirit of him sat down, and in the stillness of that room he was in a waystation, off the main track, knowing that what was to come would be coming soon, and maybe here, in this room of transition, was his last chance for peace.

Because it is the instinct of all living to act as though death does not exist, the neighbours had decided that just because Aine Crowe was lying on the edge of life, there was no reason she shouldn't have the bit of Christmas. In a decorative scheme without design or coordination, from their own boxes some had brought those rejects and leftovers that lived on year after year in every house, because to throw out something with Christ in the name was a passport to doom. Once the first folding paper bell arrived – only the clasp busted and repaired with two hairclips – the second one was not far behind, of different size and look, but what of it. There was a child's colouring of the manger with crayoned star, another with sticklike Mary and Joseph and enormous baby, a wooden snowman with bite marks and an obese Santa hanging from the end of the curtain rod. Yoking one end of the year to the other, tucked into the Brigid's Cross that in that dampness never dried out, was a twist of berried holly. The effect was not so much festive as funereal, as if here Christmas came to die, and in the sadness he could not stay.

When the doctor left, he had no destination or aim other than to avoid the human race. For three weeks now he had missed Sunday lunch in the hotel in town. He drove west, and west again, losing and gaining the estuary and following the first route out of that country, to the sea. When he came to Kilrush, the town was in a brown, companiable gather of newspapers and shops after Mass, the postponed rain putting off the disperse for a bit, and there were *There's the doctor* looks as the car noised past. Briefly, he had a flash that even here the news of the child had travelled, but dismissed it as the referential thinking of the paranoid. Clarity and composure had always been the notes of his nature, and these must not be abandoned now.

He drove out of the town, came to the westernmost cliffs at Kilkee. Here was an edge, an end of country, an open sea, and a sky so enormous that into it you could send your soul. The doctor parked and got out. The wind came at him hungrily. He had to hand his hat and hold the coat at his chest. There were swift buffets, gusts without announce or duration, pushing at him, seabirds air-dancing in a rising falling above the laved pavements of the pollock-holes. In the sanctioned hectic of the season, when all sought a lit indoors, he was alone in that place of bare beauty. His trousers flagged off his shins. Assiduously, the Atlantic salted his moustache, stung in any place the skin was sored, in the cracks at the corners of his lips and in the lower lids of his eyes. In minutes his cheeks were raw. There were not clouds, there was cloud, seamless, complete. It was not raining, but water was in the wind, in the spray, in the turbulence of a white tide that since forever was throwing itself against the country.

There was a track, tacky mud, and he went some ways along it before stepping up onto the sponge grass alongside, and with the composed steps of the older, making his way towards the cliff edge.

The sea below had its own mesmerism. To look down from the ledge of black rock provoked an immediate vertigo, and hand on hat, he swayed, but remained where he was, gazing down to where the waves crashed and died in skeins of foam. He stood on that boundary, a single figure on the blown edge of the country, where, by an unprovable thinking, from above he might be seen.

'Help me, Annie,' he said then. 'Help me.'

***

At last, the doctor came carefully back from cliff to car. He drove home to tell Ronnie that the word was out, that the news of the child was abroad in the parish and that they were about to enter their most difficult days.

When he came into the front circle, he saw the curate's bicycle against the wall.

When he opened the front door, he realised that he had forgotten to lock it after him. He looked in the front parlour for the priest, and then in the second parlour, and then in his surgery. When the curate was in none of these, the doctor knew that the story had gone three pages ahead of him. He came down the hall to the kitchen door with the knowledge that he didn't want already entering him, and when he opened it, it was only to confirm that the inevitable can only be diverted not denied.

Sitting below the crossed banners of nappies was Father Coffey.

'Father forgot his umbrella,' said Ronnie.

It was a line out of another story. In this one, it had the air of a mannered comedy, was so beside the point that for a moment all might have been in *The Forgotten Umbrella* and none speak of what was lying against Veronica Troy's breast.

'The front door was open,' said the priest. As alibi, he looked at the umbrella at his feet.

Well, that explains it, the doctor did not say. He was looking not where he most wanted, to his daughter's eyes, to read there how much she had already told, and what he might say next.

'Just a push, and it ... opened,' said the curate. 'I called out, but...' With the unease of one muddying further his white lie, and the social awkwardness that would be his until he was fifty,

Father Coffey studied his hands. He stretched out his sandalled feet and, when he remembered his mother, drew them back under him at once. If he smoked, it would have given him something to do with these huge white hands, and briefly, between fore and index fingers he made the gap for an air cigarette. Whether he would have attempted to smoke it went undiscovered, because, in the prescribed behaviour for those who are caught not in one corner but all four, the doctor delivered a performance of perfect normality, crossed the kitchen, and in the guise of doting grandfather bent to kiss the baby's head.

'And how is little Noelle?' he asked. 'Good?'

It was his first mistake, a line with no sequitur, but even without looking back the doctor could feel it register in the curate.

'She's good,' said Ronnie.

'Of course she is.' And now he looked at his daughter. Ronnie's eyes had the same steadfastness as always, they held the same melancholy, the same forbearance and knowledge, and met his in one of those bridge moments between parent and child too profound for language. He did not look away, and still did not, and then, from the many lies he could tell, chose the one that he thought lesser, would divert the crisis, and buy the time that is never available when the story is one of love.

'Your fiancé has his ticket,' he said. He saw the sentence enter Ronnie. He kept his face in front of hers, blocking the priest, and in quick succession saw the pulses of the puzzle cross her forehead. Ronnie opened her mouth to speak, but was her father's daughter and said nothing, finding that the baby required shaking and moving, and she turned to carry her down the room.

'He will be here before Christmas,' said her father with a gaiety so unlike him that it risked undoing what had just been knotted. But he went further still by turning to the priest and saying, 'Noel Crowe.'

'Noel Crowe?' said Father Coffey.

'The grandson. I was up at Crowe's. He's coming home. From America.' The doctor did not look down the room for his daughter's reaction, but he listened for it, in the delusion that in gasp, breath or shuffle he might detect approval.

The announcement was rash, and the thought that went into it – none – created as many problems as it sought to solve, and only served as proof that when the doors are locked the windows are tried. What the doctor was counting on was his place in the community, his profession, the years he had on the curate, and the fact that he had seen him in the surgery in only socks and under-pants. These, he hoped, would give him a little leeway, and in a tactic out of the chess books, he showed no weakness but pressed on with: 'It's a secret, Father.'

The discomfort that was one of the priest's principal traits at the time was not only for his own skin, but for the times he frequently found himself feet-first in the stickiness of his parishioners' private lives. In the seminary there had been no preparation for this, first, because none of the teachers were married, none knew first-hand of the numberless ways human relations could go wrong, or acknowl-edged that one plus one did not always equal two, and second, because once that book was opened, once you started a chapter of *What to do if*, no one would ever get to ordination.

So, in the ticking moments while Father Coffey pressed his hands together, then found that what he wanted to do was make two fists and knock them softly, tap-tap, against each other, what was flying through the curate's mind were unjointed bits of infor-mation that did not cohere into a story. There was, in fact, a baby. That was correct. But *whose baby was it now?* was a piece not yet in place, although now there was this Noel Crowe, and an engagement, secret or perhaps not, who knew; in the Big House things were different, but because they were not in the right order, because this bit was outside of wedlock, which was its own catastrophe, and that bit was outside of the country, which was inconceivable, and because nine months was as far as he knew still the measure of female gestation, and he could not recall Ronnie Troy going to the States nor Noel Crowe coming home from the States, it was as though he had a bit of each of them in his two hands but could not find the wherewithal to stick them together. Tap-tap went the two fists against each other. Father Coffey looked down at them, and for once adopted the character of the doctor and said nothing.

Ever since boyhood, the curate had found a secret thrill in the labyrinthine contrivances of mystery novels: that these were set exclusively in a seaside England, where murder was more plentiful, that they were populated by a circular cast of changing names but set character mattered not at all, for the appeal was the same since curiosity first met construction, and was the same one that occupied him now in Troy's kitchen: *How was it done?*

'Noel Crowe?' he said at last.

'That's right.'

Having tested the uneven ground where his lie had brought him, the doctor too was aware that the important thing to do next was nothing. He was already too far gone to come back. All of his life he had feared his face betraying him. At his age, he had almost vanquished it, but in this moment could not be certain. He found angles to look at. Ronnie was still turned away, holding the baby, and he tried in vain to read her shoulders.

'I see,' said Father Coffey, blindly. It was a known fact among priests that in every confession box lies were told. That there were lies told about the lies told was a given, but to get to the bottom of falsehood would be a journey as far as Eden, and instead, as a stop-gap, absolution was aimed at only what had risen to the surface. So, in fairness, the curate knew there was more to be told, but took the way of least embarrassment because it would come out eventually.

'The wedding?' he chanced.

'Just after Christmas,' said the doctor, with an equanimity that surprised even him. He sensed that Ronnie closed her eyes on that, but he could not be sure.

'I see. Well...' said the young priest, standing and taking the umbrella. His head brushed a nappy, and he ducked lower than he needed. Because he was caught between not wanting to play the caricature, appearing open-minded and modern, and what he knew was the Church's ruling for this child outside marriage, the curate forgot to finish his sentence and moved out from under the line. He put both hands atop the umbrella and stood, as if at any moment a train might pass through that kitchen and he'd jump aboard.

Neither of the Troys said a thing.

No train coming, Father Coffey looked to the doctor and said, 'We might have a word.'

They went down into the surgery, where the fire had died. The doctor switched on a single lamp.

'You did not sign the letter.'

'I did not.'

'You won't sign it?'

'I will not.'

The curate was vexed. He could find no way to offer it up or come around it. The stubbornness of the older man was too wilful.

'When I came from Prendergast's after Mass Tom Joyce was in the front parlour.'

'He was.'

'He says there's a list being drawn up.'

'There is.'

'Is the Parochial House to become a train station?'

'It is to become a parochial house,' said the doctor. 'That is, one the parish will come to, to take care of an elderly priest who has served them, until medically his needs are greater.' He looked directly at the curate then. He was too tired for defiance. He had come to the end of the heart, was what he felt. The compassion that had flowed out of him every day for decades in that house and district, the love he had given and the suffering he had felt, had a limit, and he had arrived at it now, and did not have the energy to argue or explain. In the poor light from the single lamp, his complexion was waxen. The chastisement that was in his tone, he had not meant. But when tolerance is grown thin, acid comes through.

The curate sat, forked the fingers of both hands, slid the prongs against each other. He said nothing for some time, and both men waited at the impasse.

'And if I say no?'

'You won't.' The doctor was standing in his traditional place in front of the fire. That it was unlit mattered not; it was the place for delivering verdicts.

'Why won't I?'

'Because one day you or I may be in the same place that Tom is now, and at that time what we will be hoping, what we will be praying for is that there is still enough decency in the world to allow us every last chance to sleep in our own bed, until that is impossible and we need professional care. But until then, we will be hoping, we will be praying, there will be someone who still sees us as people not patients. That's why.'

Father Coffey pushed back in the chair; his legs went out in front of him in the minor confusion of which one of them was the priest. 'I am not a villain,' he said.

'I know that.' The doctor looked up into the shadows, pulled thumb and forefinger down his moustache. 'If it is unworkable, if he worsens, if his needs cannot be met, I will see it and be the first to help you.'

The golden lamplight benefited the scene; it made the exchange seem to take place in a twilight where definitions and roles were not so drawn. Conversely, it allowed both to be more themselves.

Father Coffey drew his legs back under him, but the scent of his socks rose. They smelled of stale rain or wrung river, and it seemed to him then that the smell was going everywhere in the room. By a prime instinct he looked across at the doctor's feet, to see if it might be him. But the black shoes with their broken backs were on the hearthstone, and he knew the smell was his alone. Once caught, it could not be unsmelled. He moved to let the sandals out in front of him, drew them back at once, and leaned forward. In the valley between his knees, he tapped his hands against each other in a discreet fanning.

Through all of this, the doctor did not move or speak further.

In his black clothes, the long figure of the priest dissolved into the dimness until he raised his face. 'We can try until Christmas.'

Then the doctor made his third mistake of the evening. Because he thought the matter dealt with, because half of him was still thinking of Ronnie in the kitchen digesting the news of her betrothal, and because he was not ready to confront that without reinforcement, he went to the press and took out the brandy. He brought two cut brandy bowls that were his translation for truce and poured a measure in each.

The novelty of the gesture caught the curate off-guard, and before he could say that actually he only ever took a little wine, he had the bowl in hand.

The doctor made no toast, but raised the glass as if, then carried it to the beaten leather armchair and sat. He drank with the same deep privacy of those who have too much on their mind, looking into the liquid and away into the shadows, seeking no conversation from his company, only the silence and refuge that the drinking bestowed. If he had his way, he would sit there sipping until the world went away. From the bottomless well of his own memories, the glass would refill of its own accord, and he would stay with it in hand without movement or words, the priest would reverentially leave, Ronnie and the baby go up to sleep, and the night fall around him.

Sorrow is the longest thing in life, and going back the preferred way of an old mind. What thorns of regret or seeps of nostalgia had already come into Doctor Troy's brain could not be told, for under the aegis of men-at-drink, there was no protocol to enquire. Instead, he remained in a paused comma, head forward and back curved with the golden glass held just in front of him.

It took a little time for the curate to realise that he himself was not there. For he was only learning as he went, understanding in slow sips of a scorching brandy that was in fact better, deeper, more bodied, and could he say *souled*? than wine, that this was how two equals, two men of a certain standing, who had come to a certain understanding, certain, absolutely certain, and standing on understanding – *souled* was certainly right – behaved, in the, whatever the rest of that sentence was. No but, you sit and you sip. That's what you do. You sit, and, you know, the other thing, sip. And when the doctor pours himself a second, and sees you, as though you have appeared down the unlit chimney, and he raises the bottle in an offering without language you reply without language and see that by a lay miracle you are back where you started with a full glass once more, and you, you know, sip.

And so, for a time, the priest gave in to his deepest longing and mistook the scene for one of camaraderie. He had never experienced such with his father, who only drank alone, and he drew a deep satisfaction from sitting in the half-dark with a man who was known to shun company. That there was no dialogue didn't matter. That was how it was done, this men's business. It was a step forward for him, and in secret he couldn't help but feel a little guilty gladness that the softening of the Canon's brain had brought it about. He took a sip. Across from him, his father was taking a sip too. Both of them smelled like socks, and had always done, and there was nothing wrong with that at all.

It was only sometime later, a period not measured except in liquid, when the doctor reached and filled his own glass for the third time, and ignored the curate, that Father Coffey understood with certainty that if he stood and left, the doctor would not notice. Which was galling. And more so because now he was a brandy drinker, like him, and liked a sip, a sit and a sip, and was doing both perfectly actually, first class in fact, the sitting and the sipping, and he would just finish this last drop, sip in fact, and stand, *seas suas*, definitely *suas* and not *sios*, not sit, because no sipping left, and how big your fingers were through the goblet, enormous fingers in fact, and there was a last drop, sip, and *an rud is annamh is iontach*, rare is beautiful, which, in a potent combination of gall, disregard and Napoleon brandy, misguided in comradeship and succumbing to the crow's temptation to always have the last word, brought him to put down the goblet with a sharp clink and shatter the doctor's aloofness with a statement that in every other version of himself he would not say. 'That baby is not Noel Crowe's.'

For a moment the declaration hung, strung across the air. And in that moment several scenarios could have unfolded. Any number of storytellers could have set off in their own versions of what happened next, putting in denials, heated arguments and counter-arguments, from the leather seats and on the floor, some pacing, pointing, shouting, as two men contended the fate of a woman and a child.

All of which fell short of the actual, because, in an unpremeditated move that found him for the first time in his life playing the announcing part of the Angel Gabriel, what the doctor replied was, 'It will be.'

That took the wind out of the priest. His body sat back in the chair before he told it to, while his brandied brain tried to come about the news of a baby that preceded not only marriage but intercourse. He looked across at the chess set where the pieces were in endgame and white losing. 'It will be?'

'It will be,' said the doctor again, as though submitting to the rule of spells, where the same thing said three times became true. Realising now that the evening was to become longer, he brought the bottle to the priest and poured a new measure.

The curate made no objection. He would take no sips, for already his judgement was swimming, but the gesture was one of inclusion and that was his weak point.

'The child was left at the fair,' said the doctor, when he had resumed his chair. His voice was even and unchanged by sipping his fourth measure. 'She was thought dead. She was brought here, she revived. My daughter cared for her, then fell in love with her.' He paused on the steps of his story, but the curate let only his white face respond. 'Some years back, when he was home and called at the house here, I believe my daughter cared for Noel Crowe. But I, without saying as much, may have indicated that I disapproved. That he was not of her ... that he was not a suitable match. And because she holds me in a certain regard, because she wants too much to please her father, I believe the relationship foundered, and he went away. It was my doing.'

Now he took a sip of the brandy, and this time closed his eyes on it, keeping them closed while holding the liquid inside himself. It was a child's tactic to make the world look away and worked as well now as then.

Father Coffey knew something was being asked of him here. He was moved the same way he always was by the truth, which had an intimacy that was privileged and tender, and in its company something essential and profound was occurring. He took a sip of the brandy. *Souled.* Then leaned forward towards the doctor who still had his eyes closed and asked, 'What is it you are trying to do, Jack?'

The doctor's eyes opened on the peculiarity of his name in the priest's mouth. 'That's easy, I'm trying to be a Christian,' he said. 'Only the Church and the State are in my way.'

Father Coffey felt the barb but knew enough not to show it. He took a sip.

'My father left the Church, or it left him, I can't be sure which. He could not stay in an institution that had Father Kelly in it. But one evening after dinner he set me a question. "What if," he said, "what if it's the people that have a higher sense of what's right and wrong than those conscripted to enforce it?"' The doctor paused. He drew his forefinger across the spittle on his moustache, then asked: 'To love the stranger, isn't that what God wanted?'

'You can't put yourself on God's level.'

'That would be easy. God knows all the answers. I'm trying something more difficult, the human level.'

Jack Troy's manner had changed in an instant. It was as though up to now the brandy had achieved an equilibrium inside him, and then, on a single sip, tipped it over. In a sip, he discarded the reserve of his character, escaped his natural reticence, and pointed his forefinger in the wake of his own words to prod them on. 'The human level,' he repeated, louder this time, as though for ears further away. He leaned forward, the lamplight blading his left cheek and leaving the other side in darkness. In that light his eyes were those of a long-distance sea-swimmer, pursed and bulbous both, and his tongue crossed his lips with circumspection, as though testing if all the world was salt.

'My understanding,' he said, 'my understanding, and you can correct me if I am wrong, is that for the accomplishment of what was intended, God is required to have a patience not otherwise imaginable by human beings, except vaguely by the word unearthly. My understanding is He sees and knows, and foresaw and foreknew, all our errors, all our wrong turns and catastrophes, and still loved us. *And still loved us.* Not because but despite. He has already seen that child and seen to it that she was brought to this house, and seen to it that my daughter would love her. He has already read this story, and knows how it goes, because he knows there are humans in it. And that's where His patience has to come in. Because. Because in some part of Him, in some part of Him He remembers that He made us with the intention of love. And that no matter how many times, no matter how many ways we find to defeat that intention, it is still there. Still there. And beats any regulation, ruling, decree or code, is beyond all jurisdiction or legislation made by man, because it pre-dates all, didn't even need to be commanded. Love. That's my understanding. And that's what's in that kitchen. That's what came to this house the day of the fair. And that's what I am going to try and keep alive. You can go ahead now and tell me where I've gone wrong. Father.'

The doctor sat back out of the lamplight and lowered his forefinger. He found his mouth dry and his heart racing, and in some part of him realised that what he was hoping for was to be struck down. It was as though, empowered by brandy and passion both, he imagined he might have talked the Almighty down into that room.

'You go ahead, tell me,' he said again, but he was not looking at the curate. Then, after only two breaths, he plunged back in again. 'What I am doing may be wrong. But' – the finger was pointing again – 'what I am going to choose to believe is something I heard in church once. Forgiveness. Forgiveness for mistakes made down here, because we are down here, and can only see what we can see and think *This seems the right thing to do*. Forgiveness, which I'm going to say seems to me an essential component of, an outright necessity of,' – he wet his lower lip – 'love. And so that's what I'm going to choose to believe in, and in patience and forgiveness that pass our understanding, except where we get glimpses of them, like I have, in that kitchen. *Father*.'

A speech like that still retained the nobility the Romans had granted it, applause or silence the only appropriate responses. Father Coffey chose the latter, and both men sat for some time in a quiet the priest considered companiable.

The word *love*, said aloud, had the character of a swung thurible, the frankincense of it everywhere.

The west wind, that could not leave that parish alone, moved about outside with chronic restlessness, came to doors for draughts and windows for whistles, turned over what was not tied down, and though invisible made its presence known through a low but constant agitation. In Faha, the wind was too common for comment, and most gave it no more than a nodding notice. But in the pause after the speech, when in the surgery was the rawness that follows things only said in darkness, the wind was like an army outside, general and restive.

The moan-music of boards, both dry- and wet-rotted, inside the house was too familiar to the doctor for him to give it attention, but what he did hear was the kitchen door open and close, footsteps come to the surgery, pause, and then proceed up the stairs with the studied step of one bearing a child. It was a relief he didn't realise he was hoping for until he felt it. Looking into his daughter's eyes, he would want only to see what all fathers do, but even with the brandy now tip-to-toe he had enough discernment to know that none wanted their engagement announced to them.

And yet, maybe it would still work out. Arranged marriages were not unknown in the parish. Fahy in McCarthy's Hardware got his wife in the post, and though she shrieked when she saw him, it was not a complete catastrophe.

In the hall, the pendulum of the clock pulled time obediently along. Most of an hour of the world fell away without either man speaking, the night absolutely fallen.

The cold that the brandy had held at bay came at last into the doctor's bones. When he stamped a foot, the curate's head jerked.

'You were asleep?'

'I don't think so. No. No. I'm sure I wasn't. No,' Father Coffey said, with the widened eyes of Saint Peter.

The meeting had ended, and yet they were still in it, like a reader who has closed the book but does not leave the story. Each in a manner of their own acknowledged to their body that it had been neglected and moved moderately the joined bits of themselves. The doctor sighed, because he was not in his bed, and because once again nothing had been solved. He was aware that he had not spoken as much in a long time, aware too that in the slumped reverie that followed his speech he had found himself thinking of Annie Mooney and Regina. It was inevitable; love said aloud was always a summons, and as he stretched his neck his eyes gazed upwards to where the two women were near or not. To close the session, he rubbed his face in both hands in a wash without water then stood.

Father Coffey stood too, his hand going to the headrest because the house had lost its stability. What he had prepared to say was less important than staying upright, and he waited without opening his mouth in case it was not words that came out.

'Are you all right?'

'O yes.' Perpendicularity pulled the stopper in him, and a large belch announced. He put his hand across his mouth. It saved spewing but set the room aswim. The doctor, likewise swimming, but more accustomed to the stroke, took the crook of the curate's arm. 'Oh I'm sorry,' said Father Coffey.

'Here now.'

The long and the short linked, they turned together to aim towards the door. They got it in their sights, but the room had got longer and the floor less flat and what a distance it was, what a distance, and if you blinked and held your blink and then opened your eyes to check, it had got further away still, which was impossible, nonsense, *seafoideach*, but blink again and look again and the door was floating just up the wall, and if you kept your eyes on it you could track it and then lower your head and bring it back again almost to where a door should be, if it wouldn't keep moving, and 'I'll just…' said the curate and without finishing that sentence gingerly lowered his long frame back into the chair. He put his head back and made a groan and closed his eyes, and even before the doctor brought him the tartan blanket, Father Coffey was in the dreamless sleep of brandied angels.

***

The morning after intimacy is its own country. You go softly there. That country has its own code, its own custom and language, which is more tender, shyer and kinder than the one that applies when people are in ordinary daylight. All of which was a prospect Doctor Troy could not stomach, but he was saved by the ringing of the phone in the front hall and the voice of

Tim Talty telling him that when he came to help Mossie with the cows, Mrs Crowe was dead.

Jack Troy hung up the receiver and looked to the closed kitchen door where the smells of breakfast were escaping. He had slept in his suit. He needed to wash and shave, but he had the alacrity of one who feels a hand has alighted on their shoulder and he took his hat and his commandant's coat. Instead of entering the kitchen to see his daughter, he resorted to a brusque behaviour not unknown to him and shouted from the hall, 'On a call,' then went out the door with a captain's stride to see if maybe God was on his side after all.

***

When Father Coffey woke, there were shards inside the jelly of his brain. When he moved his head to the left, they floated across to that side and pierced, *O Merciful God*, the same if to the right. Only if he kept his head perfectly level did he avoid pain. And so, as if balancing a crown weighty but invisible, he came from the surgery with head erect, hands out and studied steps, like a tightroper in training. From the surgery to the front door was a journey of twelve paces only, but to get there without being heard was another story. He slid one sandal after the other in an attempted noiselessness familiar to the guilty, but was defeated not so much by the give of the boards as the sharpened instinct of mothers, whose ears are as alert as birds' eyes, always on the lookout.

'Father?'

The curate stopped where he was. According to Sonny Cooney, the brandied brain could sometime access the genius of a Napoleonic strategy, and there may have been a moment when Father Coffey considered pretending that he was coming in not going out, that he was the first patient of the day, suffering from an ailment of walking backwards.

He did not move.

'Father? Are you all right?' Ronnie was standing in the kitchen doorway, but modulating her voice so that it carried outward but didn't rouse the baby inside. A whisper-shout.

But it went through the priest's ears like a skewer. He clenched his eyes, and then his nose, as the fried fat travelled the hallway and was in his stomach before he thought to close his mouth. He felt his insides lurch, and with a hand on his midriff made the groan that either precedes or pauses vomit.

'Are you coming in, Father?'

He gave the only answer he was capable of without voiding himself and shook his head, gingerly, and once only, for when his head went to the left his eyes didn't remember to follow. What he was trying to accommodate was his guilt in leaving the Canon alone in the house all night, how he had let that happen, how many brandies he had drunk, the tabulation of what he would have to confess, and a mortification that he had not the Irish for, but came in gaseous waves, all while under the distinct impression that a merciless axeman had split his head from crown to apple. That under these circumstances, as the memory of the doctor's parochial scheme of care seemed to come back to him, he retained the training of his mother and her gospel of the primacy of good manners above all else, was heroic, and though he stepped his way onward to the front door without further dialogue, when he reached the threshold and the fresh air he turned back to Ronnie and with timid voice offered the only thing he could think appropriate for an engagement-and-baby combination that had skipped both sex and marriage: '*Comhghairdeas* ... Congratulations.'

***

When the doctor came through the village, he had a sense of imminence that was characteristic of the season. In the churchyard, the carpentry on the crib was complete. From a lifelong experience of storms that never made the national news but lifted roofs just the same, the best of stuff had gone into it, and it had an undeniable substance. To any passing, it said *Christ is coming here*, and none could have said otherwise. In secular counterpoint, for the Christmas programmes that were a novelty not yet unwrapped, in the same street five more televisions were going in, and Cowboy, proving that people can defy their own reputations, was delivering on his promise to have them humming before Santy landed. In a pair of high-topped black runners that had come in an American parcel, he was on one roof or another, cigarette lipped, securing the aerials on to chimney stacks that up to then had been the highest thrones of crows. The skyline of the village was changing, and from now on above the houses on Church Street would be an indecent look of iron skeleton, confirming the general understanding that the future of mankind was upwards.

From the few he passed at that hour, the doctor translated looks, nods, both down and up, into final confirmations that his story was everywhere.

But not the part that was coming next. Not the genius part, that had Noel Crowe in it.

He drove with the same loose steering as always, taking for himself a generous portion of the centre of the road, but faster now, because of his conviction that things were come to a head. That he did not suffer the agonies of the curate he attributed to the mercy of a liver that looked the other way, and the bad habit of a lifetime. But, without a breakfast, he had a vacant feeling inside that he would only later understand was not about food.

In the front street of Crowe's there were already two tractors, and against the cows' cabin four women's bicycles. When the doctor got out of the car, he knew that this time it was true: Aine Crowe was dead. Even her hens knew it and hunkered under the hedges where the funeral eggs would be found.

This time the doctor did not bring his bag. Too often he had been called to the house of the dead, and all that was customary in such was so familiar to him that he could have directed one blind-fold. There would be neighbours in the kitchen even at that early hour, and there would be food coming, and more food after that, the relation between death and sustenance the same the world over, and the engine of prayers would already have started. In the same way, his arrival had an air of finality. All eyes came up to him when he stepped down into the kitchen, and in chorus the murmurs of 'Doctor' were not so much greeting as acknowledgement that he had the next bit. He did what was expected and went directly to

Mossie in the chair by the fire. Joe was in his lap. Because, when it came to bereavement, people in Faha were helpless with generosity, there was a large tumbler of whiskey at the grandfather's feet on the floor, but he had not touched it.

Doctor Troy took his large hand. 'I'm sorry Mossie,' he said.

The old man's eyes were beautiful in grief. They were a blue that could not be matched, both pale and deep, and in their tenderness of after-tears held the testimony of true love and could not be long looked at lest they break your heart.

'O now,' Mossie said, shaking the doctor's hand, like he was the one consoling him.

Across from him, in the seat that was his by right of way, sat Bat, eating a ham sandwich. 'Gone to her reward,' he said, chewing toothlessly with a round motion, 'Gone to her reward.'

'We called the curate, Doctor,' said Tim-Tom, 'but he wasn't there. There was no first Mass said this morning.'

'He'll be here before long,' said the doctor, without elucidating, taking off his hat and carrying it down to the room.

At the doorway he paused while the Hail Holy Queen finished. There were four women around the bed, and when they saw him, they rose and withdrew with nods or a whispered 'Doctor', as though death was only sleeping.

Jack Troy sat in his same place by the bed. The top sash on the window was lowered and in the room the damp weather that was neither rain nor not-rain but a cloud-lining that was Ireland in December. He did not need to feel for a pulse. Aine Crowe was as before, lying with the same linear repose, but had gotten smaller since her life left. This too the doctor had witnessed so many times that he no longer started when he looked down into open caskets and saw the diminished figures. This was not what moved him then. What did was the memory of one of Doady's visits to him in the surgery. She came rarely, but like many of the older people, once she did it was with a gathered ball of complaints. Whether she waited to have enough to get value out of the call, or thought each thing too insignificant to bother the likes of the doctor, once she was in the upholstered leather of the patient's chair she unwound the ball, one suffering at a time, so that in the end the marvel was that she had walked in through the door and would march back out of it. Once, well down in the list of her setbacks, she told the doctor that she could not get to sleep. Whatever way she was made, she said, the moment she laid her head on the pillow her mind woke up. In vivid support of her point, inside her glasses her eyes had opened wide, and she shook her head at the condition of the brain inside it. To his own embarrassment, the doctor had asked the nonsense question, if there was anything bothering her, and heard the answer of all mothers, her children. *But the way it is, Doctor,* she had said, *I don't like to be lying awake and him snoring beside me. He'd fall asleep same as you'd click your fingers. And I'd be lying there half the night in the dark.* Confidences were commonplace in the surgery and at the time he'd passed no comment, relying on the unproven adage that patients could cure themselves some, just by talking. *It is not chance,* his father had said, waving the stethoscope, *that a doctor's first instrument is one of listening.* But then, Doady had deepened the intimacy by telling him that she had asked Mossie not to fall asleep before her.

'*Is that wrong of me, Doctor? Only I get desperate lonely, lying there in the night.*'

She wanted no pill, and he had offered none, understanding that in her question was encapsulated the dilemma of all long marriages, which one would go into the dark first. That she wanted it to be her, and that now here she was on the bed, made his gorge rise. He looked up to the ceiling and swallowed the emotion.

Doady was no longer where she had always been, on her side of the bed. Now, no doubt by her husband's hands, she was moved into its centre. The two valleys either side of the ancient mattress were apparent under the covers, but she was in a third place, in a ceremonial middle, and made no indent, so light was she now.

The doctor held his hat between his knees. Slowly he ran the rim through thumbs and forefingers.

The recent dead contain their own contradiction; they are gone, but perhaps not yet so far that they can't hear us. To this, in the circumstances he found himself, the doctor added a further one: if the dead are nearer the mercy of God, perhaps they can plead for us? What of the afterlife he believed he could not have said.

Actual belief escaped language. The moment you tried to express it in words, you traversed into the realm of reason and soon found that there was nothing there that could be proved. And yet, you believed there was. In this conundrum, the doctor sat, caught between asking Doady Crowe to explain him to the Almighty, and the knowledge that she was beyond all words now.

He wanted to say he was sorry for wishing her dead. But she was dead now, and only what is said in life counts. He stood and looked at her a last time. 'God rest you,' was what passed from his lips.

When he came back into the kitchen, the women filed back to resume the prayers. Extra cups and glasses and plates had arrived and festooned the dresser. On the floor inside the step, a small platoon of stout bottles was standing. As though to make room for the doctor, the men had withdrawn outside and were ranged along the windowsills and front wall, smoking, and saying the things they said every day about the weather that was here, the weather that was gone, and the weather that was coming. Only Bat and Mossie were where he had left them, leaned forward, facing the fire and the black kettle hanging from the crane.

Condolences are an expression best in brevity, and the doctor signalled his intention to stay a moment only by putting on his hat. But when he stood in against the fire, he saw the child's blackboard at Mossie's feet, and on it, a slanted listing of chalked names in the grandfather's hand. He took it up without asking and recognised what it was before Bat said, 'The family, to be notified.'

'Forthwith,' Bat added, with lieutenant's emphasis. From under the cushion, he drew out what passed as Aine Crowe's address book, and the doctor took it. The book had alphabetised tabs protruding from the pages, but family, friends and acquaintances had quickly outgrown the alphabet, and the spur-of-the-moment nature of living, when the book, or the pen and the book, were never at hand at the same time, meant that its pages had quickly become interleaved with scraps and notations of all kinds, addresses torn from envelopes, brown ones, blue ones and white ones, bits of grey cardboard, brown too, numbers and names of now unknowns, crossings out and re-address corrections for cousins and cousins' cousins who had moved not once but twice, into places more eminent than Faha because they came with codes that were printed in block capitals, and gone over twice.

The doctor looked at the blackboard. His eye went down the names of the Crowe children but stopped when he read the last one listed. *Noel, in New York* was what Mossie had written. Jack Troy raised his head and looked up into the rafters. His moustache pulled to the right, and he breathed down through his nose the sigh that was just ahead of what he was about to do. He put the blackboard back on the ground and opened the address book.

From there to where he was standing beside the telephone hanging upside-down on the wall, the fragment of paper with Noel Crowe's address and a phone number in his hand, was a matter of seconds. He could not have said that he made a decision as much as a decision was made and he was following it. He had turned the crank with an urgency that can wait no longer to find out what fate has in store, and when Mrs Prendergast came on the other end, he offered no explanation but gave her the number in New York. With her postmistress's professionalism, she passed no comment, but repeated it back to him importantly.

'That's correct.'

'Hang up, Doctor. I'll call you back when I'm through.'

The doctor did not turn back to see if anyone was looking at him. He stood by the window. Pat Quinlan on the windowsill outside moved off it.

The mind can cross the ocean quicker than a pulse in a cable, and Jack Troy was in the apartment building in New York before the telephone there had started ringing. It was still night there, and like all calls outside of waking hours would be an alarm that foretold only bad news. He could imagine it ringing now, imagine the first and second bells and the stirring that wanted it to be a dream only.

(What he could not imagine was that the phone was a communal one on the ground floor of a building where none of the residents knew or spoke with each other. That when the call was answered by the busboy who had the misfortune to live in 1A, he would say he had never heard of a Noel Row, be on the point of returning to his bed until Sheila Prendergast stopped him with the same voice that had marshalled her children into a troop, pulling on a common chord by saying this was about a beloved grandmother who had just died.)

All of which happened before the phone throttled once more in the house of the dead and the doctor snapped it up and Mrs Prendergast said, 'You're through now, Doctor.'

'Hello?' said the voice of sleep in the faraway.

'Is this Noel?' asked the doctor.

'Who is this?'

'Noel Crowe?'

'Yes, it's me.'

'This is Doctor Troy, in Faha.'

At the ringing of the phone, Pat Quinlan had come back to the front window and looked in, and Jack Troy turned on the half and held the receiver lower, so from outside it seemed he might be speaking to his heart. He waited for his name to register, heard it said back to him with a question mark, which he answered with 'Yes' and then he waited. He supposed that Mrs Prendergast, and so the whole parish, was listening, and for three heartbeats he hoped he would have to say nothing, that Noel Crowe would know without being told what had happened, that he would say he was coming home immediately. But the crackle and hiss that passed for silence on transatlantic calls showed only that it was his turn to speak, and at last the doctor said, 'Your grandmother is dead.'

'Doady?'

'Yes.'

Again, the crackle and hiss, before Noel Crowe said, 'Is Ganga, my grandfather, is he there?'

'He is.'

'Is he all right? Can I speak to him?'

'He is all right. He has company and good neighbours. But he cannot hear.'

The doctor had turned in the direction of the grandfather, but Ganga had caught nothing of the call. From the bedroom, the prayers had switched back on.

'They sent me money for a ticket home,' said Noel. 'They didn't say it was them, but I know it was. It was posted in Clare. How they got the money I...'

The voice on the other end breaking, the doctor turned his face once more to the rafters. He did not correct the story, but waited longer than he thought bearable before he heard:

'I can't come.'

Jack Troy closed his eyes, taking the blow.

'I just can't.'

The doctor's heart was racing now. He felt it in the whole of his chest and up into the left side of his throat. He felt it like a torrent trying to pass through an opening too narrow, and for a moment was not sure if it was his ears that were ringing or the undersea line.

'Will you tell Ganga, will you let him know, that I...'

'I will,' said the doctor.

But he said it so low in his chest that it was not heard, and Noel Crowe asked again, 'Will you tell him?'

'Yes. Yes, I will.'

There was still a remnant of chance in him, and grasping for it, he thought to say *My daughter was asking for you*, but before he could steady himself enough to say it, he heard the voice on the other end say the thing that was the signal of the ending of every phonecall: 'This will cost him a fortune.'

To which the doctor was unable to make reply.

'I better go,' said Noel Crowe. 'Thank you for telling me, Doctor.' And then, with a metallic click like a lock closing, he was gone.

***

A heart cannot break; it is made of muscle and chambers and electricity, it is tissue and arteries, and is nothing but an elaborate pump inside the walls of your chest, was what Doctor Troy was telling himself when he hung up the phone. His heart was not broken, though for a moment he had the phantasmagorical sense there was a spear hanging from his chest.

'You'll have the cup, Doctor,' said Delia May, who had arrived without his notice and commandeered the tea-making.

'I have to go,' he said. He did not realise his right hand was against his chest, as though to keep the spear from going deeper, or falling out. Like all walking around with heartache, he was surprised that it could not be seen. 'These,' he picked up the blackboard, 'someone needs to call the rest.' And then, because the mechanical part of him was still working, he touched his forefinger to his tongue, and with a contained grief rubbed to ghost the chalked name of his daughter's fiancé.

To get out into the air was an imperative, and the doctor forwent the niceties with a low tilt of his hat and purposed stride, just as McCarthy's son was sheeping in to make the arrangements. When he got to the car, he still had his hand inside the coat at his chest, same as the picture of Napoleon, only Napoleon didn't have the spear. Drops of the day sounded on the brim of his hat and made the case for reality. In crises, the world is reduced to only what must happen next. He remembered he should breathe, but breath brought pain, and *Just get inside the car and go* became the new command. To get inside onto the seat without drawing attention to what was sticking out of his chest, required all his concentration and will, but he managed it the same way he had all the torn moments of his life, by understanding that what suffering was his was his and not another's, and so that must mean he could bear it.

Only when he turned on the engine did he see that the car was boxed in. As though, with death, order was dispensed with, those tractors and cars that had come after him had driven to a stop and were now at all angles between the cabins and the dungheap and the public road. Doctor Troy closed his eyes. Then, because he could not possibly get out of the car, because he knew that everything he had tried to do had met failure, and because the last straw is always small and seems insignificant, with his fist he thumped the horn of the car. The sound blared out. And again, he hit it. And a third time. Because it was out of character, because it ripped the air and tore up the conventional quiet that falls around the house of the newly dead, the men came to their motors swiftly, only one of the Tim-Toms looking in the car window to see if maybe the doctor was having a touch of a heart attack.

The doctor backed out without a glance right or left and put another brick in his reputation for conceit. When, beyond the Fort Field, he passed Clohessy driving the head-wrecked curate out to Crowe's, he gave no wave. He drove the way we all drive when what we are seeing is not the road. That within less than half a day after announcing to his daughter that she was engaged, he now had to tell her it was called off, was a predicament without precedent. That in that country, without a husband, there would be no chance of Ronnie adopting the baby, was at the point of the spear, and he had withdrawn his chest and was leaned forward like a question mark over the steering wheel as he came through the village.

He did not see Cowboy give him Cowboy's salute of a crooked finger, nor Mrs Prendergast at the post office window translating his demeanour and adding it to the emotion in his voice on the phonecall to America. The doctor saw nothing of the village now, not the increased custom in the shops, not those who had come for the reckoning of what they had put on the long finger, nor those who needed it extended, not the huddle of Christmas trees that Bourke had put standing at the gate of his yard, nor the new ones that came in boxes, had a mixed character of pricey but everlasting, one of which was set up in Clohessy's window. He saw none of it. He was in the elsewhere of the heart and had the same feeling as all readers who are approaching the narrow end of a book: *How is this going to end?*

But now, for the first time since he could remember, Jack Troy had the realisation that he was no longer the agent of that. That this was the plight of all parents who cannot plot their children's path to happiness was no comfort. For he was a doctor, making good what had gone wrong had been his life for half a century.

When he came up the avenue into the front circle, rain thickened. A western front that closed the sky was coming in over Faha. Behind the house, the river, neither grey nor brown, but that colour it borrowed from bruised cloud, flowed with the same indifference as always, but through the windscreen it appeared to him imprisoning. He turned off the engine, but for a moment could not get out of the car for the feeling that the world was forsaken.

Not for the first nor last time, he wished Annie Mooney was alive. He wished he could go to her door and climb the stairs to her room. He wished he could place his hat on her table and lay his head in her lap and say nothing and have nothing said, but be in the stillness and repose of profound love, by which all failures are absolved.

What fortitude it took to open the car door, to put on his hat and take the front steps, was the same as for all who despair, but with the added salt of knowing he was about to break his daughter's heart. When he came in the front hall, he knew there were patients waiting, even before he heard the hacking and sniffles that were the heralds of Christmas. But only as he was passing the wireless, did he realise that it was not on, and because he knew that Ronnie never overlooked a detail, it was as clear a signal as any that they were in a final phase of the story.

He turned the handle of the kitchen door without a speech ready. But as it happened, he need not have worried. The dish that flew at his head did all the talking.

It was the first time in her life that Ronnie had ever thrown a dish. Her plan had been for argument, for berating, yes, for letting him know, and in no uncertain terms, just what she thought of him and his fiancé announcement, which contained not only the embarrassment of being a hopeless case, but the shame that now the whole parish would know it. The volume of things she needed to say had become greater throughout the morning. Half of them she told to baby Noelle as they went up and down the floors, and to that rhythmic step that was her preferred way of being in the world, the infant's head nodded in mimed agreement.

But then her father had not returned home, and she had had to let in the patients. And although none of them said a word about baby or engagement, Ronnie felt that they did. In a small place the stopper on a story doesn't stay in for long, and, just like her father, she translated all looks to be knowing ones.

Well, if they knew, they knew. Ronnie left off the wireless, and for the first time when the baby cried, she did not carry her to the far end of the room.

It was the same sense of abandon that made her forgo all speeches and grasp the soap dish when she saw her father enter the kitchen. She did not fire it to hit him exactly, and when it sailed past and shattered on the wall the clack was so loud it was clear she could have brained him.

'*Noel Crowe!*' was what she said.

With his lifelong weakness for privacy, the doctor patted the air towards her with both hands. It was only a whist in another form, but in the circumstances came across as a putting-down gesture that backfired badly, because Ronnie went louder. 'Noel Crowe! I am to be married to Noel Crowe!'

The doctor knew that to those in the waiting room, it was an announcement as clear as a reading of the banns, and his moustache pulled in a grimace, because the logical thing was to turn towards the hall and shout a pantomime *No, she's not!*

Instead, he patted the air some more and said the one word that could make things worse. 'Sshh.'

'I will not shush.' Ronnie turned to the baby, who knew to stay quiet in the cot-drawer. 'I haven't even seen him in four years.' Her back was to him, but he could see the colour come in her profile. 'Why not just go out and pick someone off the street? You, here, please marry my daughter.'

'I was mistaken. I thought—'

'You did not think to ask me?' She turned on the sharpness of the question, and he could see the hurt he had put in her eyes. 'Did it not occur to you that I might have an opinion? I am not a child.'

'You are my child.'

He looked away to the window where the rain streaked and the daylight was soiled. He put his tongue in the purse of his cheek lest he say another wrong thing. But it seemed that that was what Ronnie was waiting for. She stayed facing him, her arms crossed and her breath pinched through her nostrils. What hurt was in her unsalved by his apologetic manner, the doctor realised that she was caught in that place between striking out and falling to her knees. Another might have said sorry then. But the word seemed puny for the thing he was feeling, which was not only guilt and regret, but the loss of grace in the world.

He looked down at his hands. On the forefinger that had erased the boy's name from the blackboard was a white smudge. With his thumb he rubbed it away.

'Anyway, he's not coming,' he said. 'Noel Crowe.'

'How do you know?'

'I spoke with him on the telephone. I told him his grandmother was dead.'

'"Oh and by the way, would you marry my daughter?"'

There was only the one soap dish, or another might have flown.

'I did not mention you.'

Ronnie remained immobile, transfixed by a hurt so profound that she thought the rest of her life would not repair it. Her brow was furrowed with three uneven lines and her eyes at that moment seemed to have the look of sixty years.

'I thought he would come home for the funeral. I thought he would see you, and the baby. And...'

Even as he was saying it, the doctor felt again it was a fiction whose premise was preposterous. Like all dreams, in the light of day it came asunder. Had he really thought it possible that Noel Crowe would come and marry his daughter? Had he invented it, the summer love between them, four years ago, and was it because that was when he himself was in a hopeless autumnal love with Annie Mooney?

'And what, take pity?'

He could not answer, because every time she spoke, the hurt in her went through him. The rain came at the windows. Along the windowsill, a paused parade of Christmas cards. On the low plate of the stove, the kettle's sigh.

In sleep, the baby stirred and moaned, and with a natural ease Ronnie leaned over and laid her hand on her. The hand covered the most of the child's torso, like a human dressing, the weight and warmth of it alone resolving what ailed her, and the baby slept on.

'To keep Noelle, you will need to marry,' said the doctor. He said it with the same even delivery he used to all patients facing difficult diagnosis. 'To have any hope of keeping her. Even then, those who, the authorities, they may not let you. But if you were married...'

He was talking to Ronnie's back again, her right hand still on the child's chest. With the pragmatism required of all mothers, she had taken to putting her hair in a bun. A brown barrette gripped it. He could see her thinking, but not know what she was going to say next.

When she turned to him, it was without the fury, but with a cool that matched his, and so, was more unsettling. She pushed her hands into the pockets of her cardigan and did the last thing he expected. She smiled. It was the smile that we use for sorrow, the draw of the muscles of the mouth that signals surrender and defeat and admits that these were both not only always possible but inevitable. 'Father,' she said.

And that was a further signal. He knew something was coming, but not what was.

'I won't be marrying anyone.'

Ronnie said it simply, without the slightest trace of dramatics, stated it as a matter of fact that she alone knew, and that was as indisputable as if she had gone ahead through the pages of her life, seen what it was and how it went, and had then come back to tell the future to her father. She said it without sadness or self-pity, the same as she might the colour of her hair, and in such a way that at once it seemed a truth that was there in that kitchen with the rain meeting the windows and the kettle gathering to whistle.

'You can't say...' her father began. 'You can't know what—'

'Listen to me, please.'

That *please* stopped him.

'Not every woman wants to marry. I won't be marrying Noel Crowe, not next week or the week after, or any time in the future.'

Again, her voice was perfectly calm, her brow clear and her eyes steady as she delivered the coda. 'And I won't be marrying anyone else either.'

When she said it, it felt like the truth. And like all truths had the character of a blade clean and cold as it entered him. Not just because the way she said it made it seem inarguable, but because it recalled the exact words of Annie Mooney, who one evening had told him that in the aftermath of her husband's death the whole parish had seemed bent on her marrying again, various gents' names dropped in conversation at the chemist counter to see if they stirred, or took.

'*Imagine*,' Annie had laughed, telling him. '*Well, I won't be marrying again, not any Tim, Tom, or anyone else either*,' she had said, and then looked to him, whether as a test or to concur that the notion was nonsense he could never decide.

'*No, of course not.*'

Now, standing in the kitchen, the doctor swallowed his words. He looked to the floorboards in the far corner, then to the banner of white nappies. He drew his hand down his moustache. He nodded the nod that says 'I see' even when we don't, but he did not reply to his daughter.

It fell to Ronnie to close the scene.

'Your patients are waiting,' she said.

'Yes.' He could not meet her gaze, for he thought she was more courageous than any woman he had ever known, and he feared if he looked at her his eyes would betray him. He tilted his head back to mask the possibility of tears, then turned this into a nod, 'Yes. Of course.' And he turned on his heel and left the room with the same purposed stride he always used, with his chin forward and his chest out, and no indication that he knew he was in a plot with no resolution but grief.

***

Those patients Doctor Troy saw that day had all heard the dialogue in the kitchen, same as it was written on a page. With heads craned and the good ear cocked, they had added this latest instalment to what was already abroad in the parish generally, and, in the silence after, enjoyed some of the superiority of those who are a chapter ahead of the rest. But when the doctor called them into the surgery, none drew down the subject nor let on that they had been the fly on the wall. As always, they spoke only of what was happening inside the perimeter of their flesh, and waited to hear if it could be fixed before Santy. If the doctor was gruff, he was always gruff. If his manner was cool, it was the same as yesterday's and pardoned by his penning the prescription.

One by one, Jack Troy saw them off. Where his mind was could not be read, but the decades of curing the same complaints meant that he misdiagnosed nothing. His own hearing had the susurrus of living inside a perpetual rain, and though he strained he could not hear Ronnie or the child in the kitchen. At one o'clock she had not come between patients to tell him his dinner was ready, and he had not taken any. He had stayed inside his leather and mahogany prison, looking only for the sustenance of a brandy that he remembered too late had been emptied into the curate. When he called 'Next!' and no one came, the day was gone, and the darkness that shrouded those western places at the death of the year seemed to be inside him as well as out.

On extended fingertips he leaned on his desk, trying to find a way forward. There was none. He knew the clock was ticking fast now to the knock on the door and the man who would come to take the child. And it would be a man, plausible and perfunctory, in sober suit and tie, faceless but for the set jaw and deadened eyes that were the inevitability of one trapped in the routines of officialdom. He would come without malice, without the slightest personal interest in the child, who already would have become a case, have a cardboard file with a file number blackly inked on the top right corner. He had come to resolve the case, he would say, pinching the creases of his trousers to sit, and then, because human desire was too lawless for governance, taking out the forms with the boxes that would try and contain it. Date of birth, actual or estimated, weight at birth, actual or estimated, distinguishing markings: he would ask each question with a robotic detachment, fill the boxes with perfect equanimity, and achieve the tepid satis-faction of form-fillers who love leaving no box blank and getting to the bottom of the page. Nothing of the girl herself would he ask. The name that Ronnie had given her, Noelle, would slide off into oblivion, and she would become *Female Child, Found at Fair*. At last, the man would present the form to the doctor for signature and say something about taking her off his hands.

And because Jack Troy knew that there was nothing that he could do now to stop this, because he would have no option but to sign, he was forced to the acid conclusion: *I am just as bad as all of them.*

Without the brandy to antidote this, and with no remedy he could offer his daughter, he swept into the hall, took his hat and coat from the stand, and was in the car before he knew where he was going. He followed the headlamps into Faha, but pressed the brake when he came to the graveyard.

In a custom undiminished by time, in the parish the places of the dead were always freshened for Christmas. With a ferocity for growth and a defiance of disfavour, the weeds whose seeds travelled on all winds found both gravel and pebble accommodations, and if not pulled would bury the deceased a second time. So, on hands and knees, with trowels, buckets, plastic bags or margarine containers, a small army of men women and children went at their family graves, picked the moss out of the chiselled names, washed the green out of the jamjars and stood upright the stalks. Some, in a bow to both weather and season, placed snaps of imperishable holly, but, bettering that this year, was a new cemetery fashion of plastic flowers. They had been offered at the fair in single stems and bunches, came in colours more luminous than nature, and sold out on the remembrance slogan, *They will never wither*. These, even in the starlight, the doctor noted, as he came in through the graves. That they made the dead more dead was his own judgement, but in them he found too something moving, the eternal yearning to bridge the darkness, to be seen, heard or felt across the other side of life.

Though the place was a maze, the doctor went without needing to check the way. When he stood at his wife's grave, he did not pray, but he took off his hat.

'Regina,' he said.

In a small mercy commonly granted the bereaved, since she had died, the doctor's wife had got younger. She was no longer the frail pale figure of her last days, but instead, in death was returned to her healthy self of twenty years earlier. This was the woman he saw when he thought of her, and the one in whose company he stood now. Added to her vitality was the best attribute we wish for the dead, omniscience. From her vantage she could see how things were, also perhaps, how they would be.

Hat in hand, the doctor stood. The rhythm of his heart was out of joint, and he tried to right it by holding his breath. It was then as though an invisible halt was on him, and he was waiting to see if the light would turn green and there was more life to live. There at the graveside he expected no sign. Clay was clay, flesh was flesh. But Regina had been Ronnie's mother, and though he could not have explained it, that seemed to him the reason to stand there. In all children's lives, there were some moments only mothers could negotiate, and as he exhaled, he wished she were the one living.

Across from McCarroll's, he could see the dark mound next to where Mrs Crowe's plot was already opened. Beyond it was Annie Mooney's grave. He let his thoughts but not his feet go there, acknowledged to himself that that love was still not dead, then he put on his hat and left, wishing all could forgive him, help him, and show the way.

When he got in the car, he realised how cold he was. He drove up Church Street, stopped at Ryan's to get a bottle of brandy from Seamus, then saw the boy squatted down against the wall outside. He did not know it was Jude Quinlan until he was standing alongside, and the boy looked up at him.

'What are you doing here?'

'I'm to bring my father home. He won't come yet.'

'Get in the car,' the doctor said.

He went into the smoke and shadows of the bar. At the counter he asked Seamus for a bottle of brandy that had no licence to leave the premises, except for the one all doctors have. Then he went and took Pat Quinlan by the arm and, by force of will, brought him out and into the car, driving father and son home with no word passing except for the father's sodden 'Happy Christmas now Doctor, happy Christmas to you,' when he let them off at Quinlan's front street. When the father went ahead, the doctor called back the boy and at the lowered window gave him a five-pound note. 'Your father won this at cards,' he said, 'Give it to your mother.'

That it was as unbelievable as Christmas, Jude didn't say. He took the banknote, looked to the house and then back to the doctor to ask: 'Is she all right, the baby?'

'Yes.'

'I told no one. But they know.'

'I know. It's all right. She'll be all right,' the doctor said, but felt the ashes of empty language in his mouth.

He drove home with the brandy in the passenger seat. He came in the house with a soft step, and when he closed the door inside the surgery, he was aware of his relief and cowardice both. All the things he wanted to say to his daughter were still inside him, but what the first words were, he had no idea.

***

From that moment to the one when he opened his eyes in the middle of the night was a measureless gap crossed only with ribbons of dreams, but when the doctor tried to lift his head from the divan the muscles in his neck told him he had been prone for hours. Something had woken him. In that house, it could have been any of those whose winter quarters were under the skirting boards, could have been the wind or the rain taking some more of the house for toll, and he turned over and tried to deny it had happened. A triangle of arm for pillow, he closed his eyes, but in vain, because his ears remained open. Had he heard something, or what was it? He opened his eyes, as though to help him hear. The room was in the double dark of night and curtains, and looking into it had an abject pointlessness, but none of us are all reason and he rose his head and studied what he could not see, only feel. *Something has happened,* was as far as he got. Which was a nonsense, he knew, and most likely the fault of Napoleon, who had invaded his right temple. He pressed his fingers against him and lay back again and closed his eyes and took the way of all flesh: *Whatever it is, it can wait until morning.*

Which was why he did not see Ronnie in her green gaberdine and headscarf, paused on the stairs. She had her tan suitcase, and the baby was wrapped against her breast. She feared each footstep would betray her and had stopped when a midway tread protested. She had waited for her father to come out and was ready to tell him why she and the baby could not stay. She was ready to say again that she knew that for her there would be no marriage, but that for her no other love could be as real, as tactile, as all-consuming as this one, no moment in all the years to come like this, for, with a ferocity she had not known she possessed, she loved this child, Noelle, and would rage against any hand raised against her. She was ready to say that for this child she could not stay in this house or this country, and that she knew the grief and loss of that and what suffering it would cause, but that there was no other choice that she could live with.

But her father's door had not opened, and she had carried on down the stairs and along the hall. In the kitchen she left the note she had written three times that evening, tearing the pages from the latest of her notebooks before putting it carefully back atop her folded clothes. Then she and the baby slipped out the back door and into the night.

***

When the doctor woke for the second time, it was because his arm was dead. He lumbered his body around and looked into the dark and remembered the something that was happening and the need to go and check it, then he turned onto his other side and fell back asleep.

***

The night was clear, the teeth of the frost already in the gravel of the avenue. There were such stars. It had been a long time since Ronnie Troy had walked at this hour, and it seemed to her new country. The baby slept. The cold that at first had shocked had a kind of cleanliness to it. The air was pared. Everything was stripped away, and she felt as clear of her intention as she had about anything in her life. They went out the gateposts and Ronnie paused and took the last breath of home. There were no cars, bicycles, tractors or trampers. Faha seemed in a spelled suspension, or like one looking the other way, and she hoisted the bundle of Noelle up and in against her. 'You are not mine,' she said to the sleeping infant, 'but I am yours for as long as you will need me.' Then she stepped out to take the middle of the road that led to the outside world.

That she was in a story familiar to all, that there had been many others before her and would be many after, with child and without, departing in darkness and with no goodbye, was no comfort, for the suffering of each is incomparable and no two stories are the same.

How quickly you grow accustomed to the dark, she thought. The ditches were plain now, silvered with frost and more beautiful than in daytime, even the road glittered. Her heels clacked along it, the suitcase with the milk bottles in it knocking. When Noelle wrinkled her nose at the cold and appeared on the point of waking, she told her, 'It's OK it's OK it's OK,' in a rocking rhythm like that, not stopping, not even slowing, the warmth of her breath reassuring the baby back into a travelling sleep and making them once more the original, conjoined shape of mother and child.

And suddenly Ronnie Troy was a mile from home, and then another and another, and, like the ones guided by a star, she bore on, journeying with stealth and resolve, but no certainty other than the knowledge that this was how this story had to go.

***

Absence is its own presence; it occupies the same space. This was the doctor's conclusion when he woke the third time. Something was gone; it was absent, and could not be recovered, and what that was, was hope.

It was still dark, and he lay staring up at it, reassembling the events of the day and night, and looking at them, the way one does at a wound. The room was cold and the aches in his back and neck a torment in measure to his sense of failure. He turned this way, worse, that way, worse again, then threw off the tartan blanket and gingered his socked feet onto the floor. The dark was spinning some and he waited to see if it would stop, blood pounding in protest and his stomach turning over the nothing that was in it. He pushed a swallow back into his sandpapered throat, went to the window and drew back the curtain for the universal remedy of daylight, but the dark was still on the land and in the bare trees and on the river beyond, and dawn a mercy unavailable. In his slept-in shirt and suit trousers, his iron hair pushed up on one side and down on the other, a face pale and drawn with swollen purses for eyes, he had the look of all of his years and the peculiar vulnerability of every man in his socks.

For a time, he did not move away. For a time, his own face was the thing in the window looking back at him. It was the time it takes all of us to figure out how to go on living when in the company of despair, and it could not be abbreviated. In the end, only the next moment could be discovered, and this was to turn on the lamp and find his shoes. He pushed his feet in past the laces that were only undone on Saturday evenings when he took out the polish, and he opened the door of the surgery. At once, he sensed the same something that had happened. His eyes went up the stairs, as though they could see what had come down them. He listened for his daughter's step, but the house held only that ghost silence that is particular to places where people have once lived and left some of their laughter and their living. The doctor looked at the seven-day pendulum clock, but in the crises of everyday the winding had fallen off the list of priorities, and it was stopped with joined hands at half six the previous evening.

He went into the kitchen, and when he turned on the light his heart smarted to see how tidy it was. In drawer and dresser everything was in place. This was typical of his eldest daughter, and he could easily picture her turning her upset into a neatening of every corner, but it was not until he ducked instinctively, putting the kettle on the stove, that he realised he had ducked from nothing, because the white flag they had lived under since the fair was taken down. There were no nappies hanging.

Nor was there the strung line.

As with all things gone, he looked some more while his brain tried to understand, and then he saw the letter.

It was stood upright against the blue-banded milk jug, *Father* written across it.

Like the missives of all children to parents, he had read it before he opened it. He knew what was in it the moment he saw it. When he took out the page, his hand was shaking and he used the second one to small improvement, then put the letter on the table and pressed his weight down either side of it. 'O God,' is what came out of him, but it was neither prayer nor appeal, only the involuntary response to the irreconcilable truth that things could get worse than you had imagined, that there was more pain than the one you were already suffering, and that all that was left to you was to fall to your knees.

The letter was short. It was written with a steady hand and in the erect and proportioned measure of the nuns' teaching, its purpose only to deliver two facts: Ronnie was gone; she was taking the child to England. There was no anger, nor recrimination, no justification, no whys or wherefores, all of which were by the by now, just *Goodbye Father*, and below where she had signed with her Christian name only, the post-scriptum, *Your Christmas present is in the press in my room.*

The doctor raised his face to the ceiling. He did not say the *O God* this time, but it was there, and there a third time when he tried to breathe, because sorrow and love had taken all the space in his chest, and he realised his prayer to die was going to be answered now. Now, of all times.

And he brought his hand up over his head, as though it might be taken from above, and then *crash!* smacked it palm down on to the table.

It was *No!* in any language, it was *Get Back, Go away*. And even as he took up the letter and put it back in the envelope, he was already giving out to himself for delaying so long; as he was rushing down the hall, he was telling himself he was the worst father; when the car keys were not where they always were, because Ronnie always found where he dropped them and put them back in the dish, he swore he would never touch the brandy again if only God could tell him where they were. When he put on the greatcoat and found them in the pocket, he said *Right so* in a verbal contract that was not binding, but intentional, and then he came down the front steps and was sobered by the dark cold in which now all he could picture was his daughter and the child. Before he opened the door of the car he was arrested by the sky, clear as far as the stars. Upon such skies there is a bestowed character of vision, and the doctor took longer looking than the urgency asked, whether to let God see him, or the other way around.

It is not too late. I am not too late was in the turning of the key in the ignition. From a chronic moisture that could not be sealed out of anything in the parish in winter, the inside of the windscreen was blinded. He sleeved an arc and leaned forward to peer through the smear. There was only one road out of Faha to the world. Past Clancy's and Corrigan's places, it wound through two townlands up to the mail road where, even at this hour, there would be occasional cars. If she made it as far as there, someone would surely give her the seat, and then she would be lost to him. This was the doctor's calculation; it was made in less time than it takes to say, made in the breath in which a parent thinks of their child and in spirit moves towards them, and as the car raced down the avenue it was with that twinned sense of severance and seeking that makes up most of existence.

The Morris came down and around the bend, shooting gravel to the side. Whether from motor, incline or desperation when time is short, she picked up speed on the downhill, and when the doctor sailed out the front gates with his characteristic disregard for looking right or left, the wheels met the ice and the back of the car tried to come around to the front in a clockwork the doctor could neither stop nor slow. There was an instant of wild careen, an instant in which he was aware he was going around and not forward, in which he was braking and then remembering he was not supposed to brake, in which his head seemed to be spinning and the moorings of his neck muscles wildly pulling, and then the crash that was coming was inside his understanding, was there faster than it happened because, even as he was wrestling with the steering wheel and remembering he wasn't supposed to, he knew there was no other way for this to go, and the stone wall that was coming was coming out of the nowhere where all disasters hide, and his head bounced back off the windscreen before he knew he was being thrown towards it. His eyes went wide, and then closed, and then, on the side of the road not twenty yards from the house where he had served the sick of the parish for nearly half a century, four days before the Christmas of 1962, Doctor Jack Troy fell into darkness.

There is nothing else I can do, Ronnie told herself, going into the cul-de-sac of the situation once more, and coming out the same way. She had walked all the way out past Corrigan's and Clancy's places. In both farmhouses, no light burning. When the headlamps of the first car came up, she had turned into the ditch, and it had passed. She had come a good ways with the dawn still far off. *There is nothing I can do but this.* It was a fact. There was no pity in it, no despondency, only the acceptance of a fate that began the moment the Quinlan boy had placed the baby in her arms. At that moment, this road was laid, and it was only to her to realise that all others were closed. She knew now how this would go. She knew the weeks at home with the baby were a fairy-tale time that could not have lasted, knew that no mother was coming for the child, and that running away to England was the only reality left. Running away to England was what England was for. If it did not exist, Ireland would have invented it. But it was a reality Ronnie did not consider rosy. In her mind she had already sat in the doleful bedsit that could not be warmed, cooked on the twin hot plates, their clothes in a press whose doors would not close from being painted so often. On her checklist was coins for the meter. What lay ahead was the massed and anonymous world and the way of the exile, whose idea of home was always near and unattainable at the same time. She knew what she was losing, knew the kind of work she would have to take, and how her life would go from the moment she stepped onto the bus to Dublin, and then onto the ferry.

Ronnie Troy knew how that life would go, the same as you or I do. For that version of the story was already well-worn. It was so familiar that it no longer needed telling; *Gone to England* was enough. That version would transpire with the inevitability of all human heartbreak when choice is constricted, but contain too a valiance and courage, a lifetime's determination of a single woman making a way and raising a child. It was the version of the story that would seem most credible.

But in Faha, the credible was a term long since exploded. What definition it had had to be expanded every day, because men and women kept finding new ways to confound it, and every true story in the parish was concluded by the phrase *You just couldn't make it up.*

***

Just so, not ten minutes after the doctor had crashed his car into the wall, Father Coffey came upon him. With the security of Master Quinn keeping night-watch over the Canon, the curate had stepped out before the dawn to walk his Prayer to St Francis around the village. Since the seminary, he had adhered to the Aquinian schedule of abbreviated sleep, and the dark before day was the only time he was sure not to encounter penitents. In his black beret, black gloves and new wool coat that his mother had sent, he had the look of one of God's spies. His breath vapouring, he had gone up the vacancy of Church Street, where only Harry watched him, then, with the studied vigilance the ice demanded, down with the fall of ground that led to the cemetery. In the crystalline dark he had toured the dead, and at the opened grave for Mrs Crowe that was covered with a green felt, prayed perpetual light for her before crossing back out over the stile and up the rise towards Avalon.

He saw the car the same way we all see disaster, without first understanding it. The engine was still running, the headlamps blazing, but they were aiming upwards, as though that were the destination. There was no other vehicle, and that it was the doctor's car and only yards from his own house were pieces of a puzzle flying through the mind, but Father Coffey had no time to catch and assemble them. He was hurrying and slipping and slowing, only to hurry some more. He was praying the prayer of only two words that was without denomination but was on his lips even as he was pulling open the door and seeing the body.

'Doctor!' he said, pointlessly, for the doctor's eyes were closed and his head back over the seat. There was no blood. No wound was apparent, and as Father Coffey leaned in over him to feel for his pulse, he was praying the same *Please God* over and over, without saying it aloud, without thinking of it. Then, by an instinct old as sky, he paused and looked upwards, just for the same time it took for those two words, then leaned in again and felt again, and this time found the pulse.

How it went from there could be condensed into three sentences. Tim the postman in his post-van stopped. They carried the doctor from the car with the day breaking violet in the east. The doctor opened his eyes and blinked the three blinks of one coming back from knockout blows, the first face he saw in his next life the curate's, who asked, 'Do you know where you are?' and Jack Troy resumed himself by the look he kept for idiots and effed out, 'Faha.'

But that was not the bit you could not make up.

That bit began later that morning, when the doctor, lying on the Persian rug with the pathway worn in it, heard the front door open. Though the bulletin *No Patients Today* had gone out via priest and post office, though the Morris was still halfway up the wall across the road, though the doctor had prescribed a flat-on-his-back remedy for a neck that seemed unable to hold his head when standing, he knew that there would still be some patients whose every day was an emergency and prone consultation better than none. He heard the door open, cursed himself for not locking it, and from his place on the floor called out a 'Not Today!' that shot pain up both sides of his neck.

The front door closed.

And a baby made a cry, and was softly shushed.

Then Jack Troy heard the footsteps he would have known in dreams, and his eyes went to the door of the surgery that was only slightly ajar, and now there was Ronnie in her running-away coat and headscarf, Noelle bound to her, and with a statement that both explained why she had come back and confirmed she was her father's daughter, with steady voice but scheming look, she said, 'I know what we will do.'

***

Of all the traditions associated with the season, in Faha, one remained inviolable. Its origins lost in the indexes of history books and the earliest chronicles where Christian and pagan ways were married, in modern times it borrowed the character of Santa Claus, but without the red suit. After another bumper year of trading, the shopkeepers would give a little something back to their loyal customers. This comprised flour, sugar, tea, general foodstuffs, fancies and sundries, drawn from all corners of the shop, and handed over gratis in what was called the Christmas Box. From the second week of December, both Bourke and Clohessy would start laying aside the cardboard boxes, small, medium and large, in their back rooms. In a decision that showed the bluntness of his nature, Daddy Bourke left his boxes uncovered, Batchelors Beans or Chivers Jelly, while Clohessy, who had a touch of breeding, had a girl, Sheila, who papered his in seasonal wrapping, sometimes adding a sprig of holly if there was some to hand. She it was who was tasked with writing the *Happy Christmas from the Clohessy Family*, originally on cards from the shop, until it was discovered that Bourke made a tidy saving by writing it on the cardboard itself, and that became the way. While the boxes were gathering, a general audit of the customers was taking place. This was done by eye not account book, by Daddy Bourke himself at his place inside the front door, where he watched the sales leaving, or by Mrs Clohessy, inside the nets of her front window. That those who shopped at each establishment were blood relations, neighbours of blood relations, or ones who had fallen out with the other place, made no difference to the size of the Christmas Box. It was calculated on the purest scales, custom and coin. That there was not, and had never been, a summit, no get-together of the shopkeepers to establish the convention or how large were you making your boxes this year, meant that the first ones going out the door of either shop set the Christmas standard of So-and-so, which was Sonny Cooney's shorthand for *Did you see what that So-and-so got?* Bourke made a point of giving his largest customers their boxes at the start of December, so that Clohessy might be pressured into going larger, a rumour that circulated annually but could not be proven because goodness of heart was credible at Christmas and the benefit of the doubt came free of charge.

For the customers, the custom, while unshakeable, came with an unwritten etiquette: when the box was handed over, often with a by-the-by look and a *Just something small for the family*, it had to come as a complete surprise and be rewarded with a thanks-very-much that both acknowledged generosity and sealed the contract of custom for the year to come. In the parish, people were expert at this, and in performed gratitude could give the Faha Players a run for their money even if, once outside the door, they looked inside the box and saw the salad cream that was six months past salad days, and the lime jelly or tinned grapefruit you couldn't pay people to take.

This year, when the country was at last getting on its feet, and the new electric cash registers made taking money effortless, both shopkeepers had independently decided that the curation of the Christmas Boxes could be stepped up a gear, and more than food-stuffs could go into them. *Know your customer* was the gospel according to Bourke, and there could be no better demonstration of this than the tailored individuality of each box. In the evenings, when he ceased sentry duty at the door, he came back into the storeroom where the boxes were lined up, like the parish in card-board. He looked at the name on the box, summoned the person or family, and then went out about the shop in the all-season runners he wore for his bad feet, taking from the shelves with a gener-al's aplomb and the benevolent infallibility of Santa Claus. Razor blades, soaps and creams were this year added, but with careful adjudication not to those customers who needed a wash, Andrews Liver Salts only for those who would not need them. The few fuses a safe bet for all, that would be blown in the novelty of an electric Christmas.

Boxes had to be given out by midnight on Christmas Eve, so that in the run-up both shops took on the character of bedlam. Pushing and shoving was too blatant for decency, and instead, lists-in-hand, a general shuffling, subtle elbowing and sidling was the nature of the shopfloor, licensed by the lit fuse of Our Lord's birth and the broad understanding that queueing at the counter was only for Protestants. Those coming in had to get past those coming out. There were some, tobacco'd desperados in boat-like wellingtons, who called for cigarettes over the heads of the ones in front, which meant that when the doctor came into Bourke's three days after the crash, he was at first lost in a sea of shoppers and would have gone back out if it wasn't as far as going in.

That he was upright at all was confirmation that doctors didn't get sick. Only the burgundy silk scarf around his neck told the story of his pains, but those whose heads hadn't bounced off a windscreen took it for a seasonal fashion and supposed the story had been exaggerated.

At all other times of the year, a customer might have stood aside for the doctor. But the day before Jesus was its own emergency. This was a throng, fresh from confession, and instead he got apologies in nods, and turned backs, and had to bide his time. It was his first time out of doors since he had what Faha called *a bit of a tip*, and he concentrated on the prime essential, staying upright.

It was not as easy as it sounded. Since he had met the wall, he had a vertiginous sense of falling forward, and in the closeness of the crowd this worsened. To save himself, he put his hand out and met the back of Delia May, who turned at once.

'Oh Doctor,' she said, while her kind eyes took him in. They stayed on him just long enough for him to know that the story of the child was in them, then with a back-siding that was hands-free and blindly done, she reversed back Devitt who was beside her, and said, 'Step ahead of me, Doctor.'

'I won't.'

'No, do. Do.'

The doctor stepped into the space that was not there a moment earlier, and when Tim Talty turned to see him, said, 'Doctor,' and stood aside, and Matty Riordan did the same, he understood that it was not merely the name of his profession that was clearing the way, but something other, and that was the child. For now, there was no one in the parish that did not know that the infant had been found outside the church wall, that she had been brought dead to the doctor, who had saved her, whose daughter had taken to her like a mother, and then run away with her, and then come back with her, even before she knew that her father had taken off in an intrepid pursuit on ice and brandy. No one who did not know that, against all odds, Ronnie Troy had chosen Faha over England, and that was the answered prayer of her father, who, against an equal number of odds, was standing by her, because of what none would say but all knew was the always inconvenient actuality of love.

That this was true was confirmed when Doctor Troy found himself at the counter. The hubbub dropped a register and Daddy Bourke himself stepped forward to serve him. Again, the doctor had the sensation of falling or being pushed forward, and he tented the fingertips of both hands on the counter and in a throttled voice said, 'A present for my daughter.'

'Of course, Doctor.'

To the side, Bourke called out 'Lady's Giftset!' and one of the schoolgirls playing elf went off and brought it back quickly. With fat index finger, Bourke pointed out the various items behind the plastic, as though doing a tot, and surprising himself at the good value. 'Wrap!' he called then, and the same girl took the set to an operating table where scissors and red ribbon flourished. Looking at the horde waiting to get to the counter, Bourke called 'Hurry up now!' before any time had passed, and stooped to tap the price into the new electric register that had the numbers smaller than his fingertips, and the difference between seven-and-six and seventy-six a feather's touch. He entered the numbers as though performing a grave operation of the highest intricacy, and when the drawer flew open it was a victory. The doctor paid, and the girl returned with the wrapped giftset.

'And something small for the family,' Bourke said then, drawing up on to the counter the box marked *Troy*.

In it was the tin of biscuits and box of sweets that had become traditional through the triumph of advertising, a package of crackers, a slab of cheese, two jars of preserves, a handful of oranges, a boxed Oxford Lunch, a man's aftershave. These things Jack Troy saw without needing to look. He saw them when he lowered his head by way of thank you, then, even as he lifted the Christmas box to turn, he saw the baby powder, the baby bath oil, the set of three dribbler's bibs, the cream for nappy rash, the bottle of gripe water, and the plastic rattle with the three silver balls inside.

'Happy Christmas now, Doctor,' Bourke said, putting the giftset on top.

'Happy Christmas,' the doctor said, and he looked at the shop-keeper directly, sending the message that he knew all was known and that the knowledge was neither shameful nor wrong, but was the nature of human beings from time's beginnings and would be to its end. He carried the box ahead of him out of the shop, finding that it gave him balance.

It was Doctor Troy's first time being naked in the parish. Contrary to his character, the privacy he had guarded for a lifetime was that morning laid bare and now of no concern to him. He felt the lightness the confessed feel at Christmastime, and carried the box to the car with an understanding of the poet's line of what enterprise there is in walking naked.

After three days in Fitzpatrick's garage, the Morris too had come back from the dead. With a nearly matched headlight, two beaten dints, and a front panel in almost the same colour, it had a bandaged look but the valorous air of having survived catastrophe. When the doctor sat in, he did not turn on the engine right away. He sat and watched the village the way one might if new to the world. He was familiar with clinical studies of a bestowed euphoria after near-death, and knew that these were short-lived, that the heightened awareness of the sensual substance of life and our being in it was a gift whose battery was worn out by the repetition of days, but that morning, in the living flux of Christmas Eve in Church Street in Faha, that did not matter. Through the windscreen he watched the people coming from last-minute shopping, watched the salutes and greetings in which the only subject was *I can't believe it's Christmas*, and the only wish that it be a good one. He watched them with a tender heart, watched them coming from Ryan's butchers with wrapped hams, sausages and slabs of bacon, watched them coming in and out of the chemist's and McCarthy's Hardware, which this week would not close for the half-day, and he succumbed to the seasonal sentiment that was chronic but harmless: it was possible to believe in human goodness.

'You're becoming a child again,' he said, by way of redress when the emotion brimmed, and he turned on the engine and drove back to Avalon.

When Ronnie saw the things for Noelle, she suffered the same pangs as her father, but with a practicality that saw her realise that for the first time since the fair she could take the baby outdoors in the daylight.

'Is the pram still in the attic?' she asked.

When eventually they got the thing down into the front hall, Ronnie with a magnificent crown of attic cobwebs and her father with the bemused look of one who remembered pushing each of his daughters in it, it was testament to the desire of all to live in ordinary continuance.

That Christmas Eve the day was dry and for a time the river wore the clear sky like a silk. The gulls escaped the dullness of their metallic colouring and took the shape of white figures of three, drawn against the blue. A three here, another high one there, as though they knew three was the number of Christmas. Aware of the doctor's circumstances, and under home pressures that had no valve until St Stephen's Day, no patients called to the surgery. Noelle was set in the big navy pram with the white tyres, asked how she liked it, then Ronnie pushed her down the bumps of the avenue and back up, a shortcut to one of those fathomless sleeps by which infants remind us of innocence.

Gradually, there fell the introspective suspension particular to that afternoon.

At the front and back doors of the house, tokens of thanks had been left. All of these were the same as last year, bags of turf or wood blocks, potatoes, cabbages, onions and, with an apologetic air, some fine berried holly too, but when the doctor brought them in this year, he had the same sense he had when sitting in the car, and he had to swallow and steady his head. For what it was, was a thing absurd to say aloud, for at every minute and in every place on the planet it was a given. And yet, there it was, constricting his throat and drying his lips, the understanding that he was part of humanity.

To settle himself, he went into the surgery and took up the paper. Ronnie had lit the fire, though he could not remember when. He read the headline that His Holiness was back to his normal health, his personal doctor, Professore Gasparrini, declaring it was untrue that the Pope was suffering from cancer and announcing that the Holy Father would be delivering his annual message, retelling the story of Christmas to one thousand pilgrims. The doctor turned through the pages without attention, ads for Beechams Powders, Wash-and-Wear Courtelle Cardigans, the Turkey-into-the-Oven instructions by Monica Nevin. Though they had no television, he had the curiosity of everyone without one, and looked at the listings: *Father Knows Best* and *The Day of the Census: Conversations in Bethlehem*. In the *Champion*, two pages of advertisements attested to the arranged marriage of saints and dancing on St Stephen's Day: in Saint Patrick's Hall, Corofin, Jack Hanley & his Showband; in Saint Michael's Hall, Kilmihil, Billy Cummins & his Orchestra; Saint Senan's Hall, Knockerra, the Golden Star Ceili Band. There was no parish that didn't have a saint and a dance. On the following page the doctor's eye caught the short report, *Doctor Not Injured After Crash*, and he had a novel moment of reading about himself as a character in a story with a happy ending.

He put aside the papers and sat then.

When Ronnie knocked and told him the ham was ready, dark had fallen. He came in to the rich aromas of the kitchen, and they continued the tradition of Ronnie's mother, who always served the ham and the first pudding on Christmas Eve. The baby was awake, and on her back on a terrace of towels. Ronnie took a plate and sat on the floor beside her.

It was Christmas, no Department man would be coming now.

Beneath the banner of white nappies that were hanging once more, she let Noelle smell a spoonful of the pudding, and when the baby opened her eyes wider in response, Ronnie said 'She likes it!'

'Likes the brandy in it,' Jack Troy said, with a grandfather's grin. 'O now!'

***

That the doctor and his daughter were going to Midnight Mass was a decision neither would remember making. But when they were both taking turns getting ready, it seemed inevitable. In his bedroom, the doctor had the same gratitude he always had that his shirts were pressed and hanging, and he made the same mental note as always to tell Ronnie that she didn't need to do that.

When he was dressed, Christmas-groomed to the best he could manage, without the awareness of making a decision, Jack Troy went to the bedside locker. He moved aside the journals and papers that were a camouflage for a contraband he could not risk Ronnie seeing and took out the Vol de Nuit.

When he had opened his eyes after the car crash, after the roundrims of the curate the perfume was the second thing he saw. With the velocity of all destinies, it had flown from its hiding place under the passenger seat, hit the dashboard and landed next to his hand. That the bottle had not broken, that the priest did not find him laved in a lady's scent of Paris, were mercies he forgot under the astonishment of still being alive. The bottle had travelled home with him, and he had hidden it without further intention other than by knowing it was there to revisit in memory the reality of love.

Now he undid the packaging with a tremble in his hand. The glass bottle was cool to the touch, the substance of it strangely comforting. He aimed it high into the emptiness of the bedroom and, with a firm finger, pressed.

The scent showed itself briefly, and into it, with closed eyes, Jack Troy stepped.

***

'You look young,' Ronnie said, when he came downstairs, then caught the scent and let her eyes hold her father for just a moment, just long enough to see the edges of his mystery, then look away lest she see more. She was wearing the one of Charlie's dresses that was not too bright or too short or too Charlie. Her hair was in the bun that would remain her style for the rest of her days. It said a final goodbye to her girlhood, and in the front hall when she was putting on her good coat, and Jack Troy was holding Noelle, he thought *She is herself now*, and that seemed a victory of immense courage, and when he handed back the baby he had to stop himself from one of those spontaneous embraces that rise in the aged. He stood and looked instead. But when Ronnie tenderly kissed the baby's head, his reserve was flattened, and he stepped forward and pressed the two of them in his arms. He held them long enough for what he could not begin to say to be translated, and when he stepped back again neither father nor daughter could face each other.

They went in the Morris at twenty to midnight. Ronnie sat in the back seat with the baby in her arms. They went the roundabout route, for it was one of the sights of the year to see the candles lit in the windows of every house in the parish. Curtains drawn aside, the flames stood inside the glass, sentries to a faith for another year not yet defeated, showing one house to another by a pinprick of light that in the dark rise and fall of the ground looked like landed stars. Ronnie showed them to Noelle by a 'Look! There's another!' that the baby did not acknowledge, though neither did she protest.

Even before the Morris turned into Church Street, the throng was apparent, cars and tractors in the angled abandon down both sides of the street, bicycles against bicycles along walls, and in the two shopkeepers' yards no space left for those who still travelled by horse and car.

Santa Claus had already arrived in the parish. Whether from nearness to the North Pole, or because he couldn't trust the weather in the morning, he generally passed in the middle of the evening, sometimes with a knock on the door and a disappearance when a child answered it, saw the sack and looked skywards, sometimes when bath time was happening, and the soap still burning the eyes of the pyjama'd when they came out, one and two and three, and saw the stockings had been filled. So, by midnight the air was already tinselled with the excitement of children and the relief of parents. As a charity to those who lived a life of the last minute, both shops were open, but would close their doors five minutes before Mass in a herding accord that had been reached with Father Coffey, who hated an altar entrance diluted by dribs and drabs. The same accord had been reached with the publicans, but getting some clients upright would be an Olympian challenge, and these stayed slumped where they were and got Mass only by ricochet.

With room for only one car, the doctor drove slowly up what was now a one-way both ways. He was not going to park at the edge of the village and walk up with Ronnie and the baby, and instead proceeded in the imperious manner of Peggy Moloney, who was new to driving and supposed all other cars would get out of her way. Not a practising Christian, Harry lay in the middle of the street and, with his chronic dog's bronchitis, rose in his own time when the nose of the Morris was breathing down on him.

In the gates of the church, drove the doctor. The sloping yard was short; it was for the priest's car or the hearse, and one side of it was taken up with the living nativity that had two of Talty's cows, O Malley's goat and Breen's ass, under the nervy steward-ship of a schoolboy shepherd, at the straw-strewn edge of where Mary and Joseph were attending the birth of a baby doll. Alongside the crib was Mrs Queally and the nine heads of the choir, sing-ing the last 'Silent Night' of their repertoire before taking their places in the organ loft.

When Doctor Troy got out of the car next to them, his shoul-ders had gone up in his habitual defence. But almost at once he recalled that everyone knew the story, and he raised his chin and nodded to the choir, whose key changed slightly, but only Maureen O Moore, the almost soprano, would have deducted points. He opened the back door for his daughter, and when she emerged with the baby in her arms, the eyes of all went to her to see for them-selves that the story was fact.

It is the custom maybe in all country places that women fill the pews of church first. Without the need of a stand-off with God, they come in ahead of the men and begin the prayers of private intention before the communal moment is announced by the jingling of the silver bells. So, when Doctor Troy and Ronnie came in the back door and up the Long Aisle, the Women's Aisle was already full, a rhythmic rosary knitting the air. The main pews were filling by procession, families coming in at the pace at which people look at each other when they're in their best clothes. Hats that only came out for Christmas, the red felt one, the blue one with nominal ostrich feather, the green with seven plastic cherries, and the brimless pillbox or what passed for that in Faha, sat atop women's heads in milliner's homage to the saviour of the world, the half-can of hairspray securing the foundations. Those scrubbed children who, by age or convenience, had the dispensation to stay up, moved up the aisle with a nun's reverence and mimicked the manners of adults in the theatre of a midnight birth.

Catching the optimism that was the talk of the country, the sacristan and his wife had outdone themselves this year and set twice as many of the long white candles as last year. You could butter bread with the scent, Sonny Cooney's review, it was that thick. He, for once out of his council worker's dungarees, marching in with the hair-oiled propriety of pure gent, and only betraying it by the salute of one of his huge mitts.

The Troys took their customary place, and the doctor opened his coat and put his hat alongside him. Noelle was sleeping in the crocheted white wrap Ronnie had chosen as her Christmas wear, and when Delia May was posting the Morrisseys, one after the other, into the pew in front of them, she looked in and drew down the edge of it to see the baby's face. She nodded to Ronnie and whispered 'Beauty-full,' and in that moment the doctor understood something of the solidarity of women, nodded to Delia taking her seat, and thought being naked in church not the worst of things.

Sitting there in the suspended time before the bell rang, his head turning to look in on the baby, came the answer to the question Jack Troy had had on the First Sunday of Advent: *How to continue living?*

Only through the birth of a child, he thought, *is the lure of death conquered.*

It was a statement worthy of his father. And he recalled then the fantastical notion of the old man, who, in his last year, claimed that the purpose of ageing was to grow into your soul, the one you have been carrying all along.

Yes, Jack Troy thought. *The one you had as a child.* He lifted his head to tilt the emotion back into his eyes, saw that each Station of the Cross was dressed in richly berried branches of holly, and smiled.

As if by a magic learned over generations, an instant before Mass commenced, the church was filled. The pews that were already full expanded some more. In the loft the choir began, and the congregation rose, as onto the altar, with an elongated retinue of altar boys, came Father Coffey and Father Tom.

The Canon was beaming, as if to the imminent birth he was a close relation. There was a satin seat set for him on the right-hand side of the altar, and to the relief of the Master, on watch from the door of the vestry, he took it before the *Spiritus Sancti* was out of Father Coffey's mouth.

The curate was saying Midnight Mass for the first time. With his back turned, he intoned the Latin with a solemnity that could not be faulted, but almost at once, Noelle cried.

Her cry was first only a small sound of protest, and Ronnie rocked her gently and said the sounds that returned us all to sleep once.

But the child cried some more then.

And louder after that.

And soon there was no one in the church that could not hear her and know that this was the child that had been found on the day of the fair.

Gertie Mohill it was who turned around first. With a universal mime, she offered to cradle the child, and Ronnie passed Noelle to her.

Gertie bent over the baby while, with his back to the congregation, Father Coffey continued the Latin. She held the baby in close to her, whispered as if secrets in its ear, but to no result, pressing the baby against her breast, a little furrow coming on her brow when Delia May offered to try. Gertie kissed Noelle's forehead goodbye, then passed her over.

And when Delia May failed to stop the crying, though three of her children tried pulling faces, she passed the baby into the offered arms of Mamie Quinlan.

Alongside her, her Jude was shy to look at the child, but when he did his eyes were shining, like one given a gift.

In six years, Jude Quinlan would be gone to an uncle in Queens and his furniture removal business. In nine, he would be in Vietnam, and before the Christmas of that year word would come to the parish that he was missing in action.

Once more he would be named in prayers.

And once more they would be answered.

Jude Quinlan's eyes would have the same shining when at last he would return, undead, to Faha, to acknowledge that maybe the sixpence had bought more luck than he had supposed, and to see again the place where one Christmas fair he had bargained with the fairies and found the child.

Now, Jude looked away up to the long candles.

And then his mother passed the baby to him. It was her acknowledgment of his part in the story, which she knew now. His father Pat knew too, glancing across at his son, and would glance again too when, later, Father Coffey would begin the sermon that had come to him in the graveyard that day. 'Today,' the priest would announce in his tenor's voice, a round-rimmed glance seeking Jude, 'is a lucky day for the world.'

Jude Quinlan held Noelle Troy in his arms.

It was a moment only, only the pause between one cry and the next, between passing her on to the next mother opening her arms to take her, but in the gaspy silence of that moment, into the infant's eyes he tried to send his own prayer to and for her.

Nora Eyres took a turn, to no avail, Mina Corry wanted a try, and was passed the infant, with the same result, and so on around the church, until even into the tweed arms of Mrs Prendergast, all with varying degrees of not quite success, and not quite quietness, while all the time Father Coffey was continuing his inaugural Midnight Mass to an unscripted accompaniment of the first sound of humanity.

It would become a famous moment in the parish. The time of the child. Not because of the inconvenience of the crying or the intrusion of nature into the enactment of a sacrament, not because of a petty disapproval nor censure, but because of what happened next.

Noelle had travelled five pews up and across the church. She had cried and stopped some and cried some more, and Ronnie had debated the debate of all mothers in church, whether to pick her up and take her outside or would she stop at any moment. The doctor had showed no concern. He had arrived at the serenity that knows the world is larger than himself and was sitting with the same attention as one being told a story. The Christmas Mass continuing, the baby had arrived in the arms of the postmistress, where, instead of reading the solemn instruction in Mrs Prendergast's face, she had cried louder still.

Which was when Father Tom stood up.

He stood up from the red satin seat, and with the open smile he had come in with, he walked towards the altar-rails. Then he waved down at the baby.

Although rare are the moments when life resembles fairy tale, on Christmas morning there was precedent.

More exaggeratedly than before, the Canon waved. He did it with both hands now, twinkling his fingers, and making the sounds that were goo-goo in all languages. And to all in that packed church, what was soon apparent was that before their own eyes their parish priest was become once more a child.

Although his cheeks were burning and his voice quivering, Father Coffey had enough diplomacy in him not to stop the Mass.

At last now, with punctuated sobs that seemed like a slowing engine, Noelle hushed.

Ronnie rose in her pew and walked up the aisle to take her in her arms once more. Father Tom waved his goodbye to the baby with the same piano fingers, and Ronnie acknowledged him with one of her father's nods.

And as it continued, in the same unbelievable way as all of ordinary life, Doctor Troy had the sense that in that small and crowded church in Faha was a spirit of generosity that in this world had not yet been vanquished. He did not know if he believed in the Holy Spirit, but if asked he would have said that night was the closest he came, that there was an otherness, a largeness apparent and invisible there at the same time, something that did not exist in the textbooks but was the same thing that had been since the beginning, which was that there was something more than the perimeter of flesh, something else and beyond explanation, and which was felt in that part of us that, for lack of any better, was given the word soul.

In the growing warmth of the congregation at Communion, the doctor sat back in the pew. While Ronnie went to the rails, and he held the sleeping Noelle, he was thinking of his daughter's genius for joining up the bits of every day, and the scheme that had come to her in an epiphany the night she had headed for England.

Tomorrow, on the day of the first martyr, Saint Stephen, when Charlotte and her husband, Eugene, came to Avalon, they would be introduced to baby Noelle for the first time. They, because they had the conventional shape of a family, could be the ones to apply to adopt her. In name, Ronnie would be her aunt, but soon enough Noelle could return and carry on living with her.

The doctor did not know yet if it was possible. He knew that Father Coffey would be essential, knew that the first step was to invite him for brandy on Christmas night, but not that the curate would tell him he too played chess, and they would begin the first of those Gordian games that would continue until the doctor's last days. He knew time would be against the scheme, but not that the coldest winter in a century was coming, that all through January the road into Faha would be a polished ice no Department man would travel. He knew that in that country there were more ways of resolving the crises of life than were written in the history books, but he knew too that any outcome other than the one where the baby was taken out the door would be a small miracle.

But, isn't it funny, at that moment, eyes lifted and a smile breaking the line of his lips, there, at Midnight Mass in the sloping, slowly sinking church of Faha, the congregation filing up and down the channel of the Long Aisle like a tide, and he in secret communion with the scent of Annie Mooney, that was exactly what Doctor Jack Troy felt would happen. A miracle.

THE END

Acknowledgements

My thanks to all those readers who came to Faha in the pages of 'This is Happiness' and said they didn't want to leave. To all who told or sent me stories from their parents' or grandparents' worlds and attested to the enduring power of story to bring back what has perished. As always, each book is born of others, too many to list here. But local histories continue to provide me with an invaluable richness and a glimpse into lives less celebrated, and I am particularly grateful to Jackie Elgar and Patricia Sheehan for their 'Three Men from Clare.'

To Grace McNamee, champion of Faha, and all the extraordinary team at Bloomsbury USA. To Paul Baggaley, Allegra le Fanu and the equally committed team at Bloomsbury. I am deeply grateful to you all.

To Charlotte Norman for her forensic attention to the manuscript, and to Martin Keane for giving it the west Clare eye.

As always, my heartfelt thanks to the incomparable Caroline Michel, and all the team at Peters, Fraser & Dunlop.

And last, the first. To Christine Breen, my children Deirdre and Joseph. And Esme Willow, born during the writing of these pages.

A Note on the Author

Niall Williams was born in Dublin. He is the author of nine novels, including *History of the Rain*, which was longlisted for the Booker Prize, and *Four Letters of Love*, which will soon be a major motion picture starring Pierce Brosnan, Helena Bonham Carter, and Gabriel Byrne. His most recent novel, *This Is Happiness*, was nominated for the Irish Books Award and the Walter Scott Prize, and was one of the *Washington Post*'s Books of the Year. He lives in Kiltumper in County Clare, Ireland.

A Note on the Type

The text of this book is set Adobe Garamond. It is one of several versions of Garamond based on the designs of Claude Garamond. It is thought that Garamond based his font on Bembo, cut in 1495 by Francesco Griffo in collaboration with the Italian printer Aldus Manutius. Garamond types were first used in books printed in Paris around 1532. Many of the present-day versions of this type are based on the *Typi Academiae* of Jean Jannon cut in Sedan in 1615.

Claude Garamond was born in Paris in 1480. He learned how to cut type from his father and by the age of fifteen he was able to fashion steel punches the size of a pica with great precision. At the age of sixty he was commissioned by King Francis I to design a Greek alphabet, and for this he was given the honourable title of royal type founder. He died in 1561.